To Jason,
Beware
of....

HELL HOLLOW!

Ronald Kelly

Sinister Grin Press

Austin, TX

www.sinistergrinpress.com

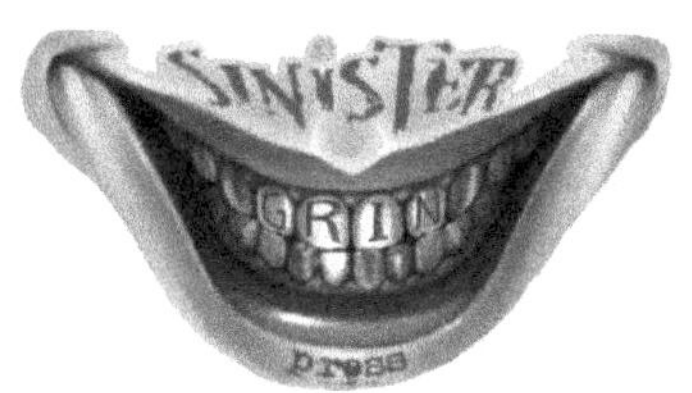

March 2016

This is a work of Fiction. All characters depicted in this book are fictitious, and any resemblance to actual events or persons, living or dead, is purely coincidental.

Cover Art by Keith Minnion

Book Design/Additional Art by Zach McCain

Test Design by Travis Tarpley

ISBN: 978-1-944044-23-7

Hell Hollow was originally published by Cemetery Dance Publications in 2010.

To Mark, Carletta, & Holly Hickerson.

McCAIN 2016

PROLOGUE

"Well, come on!" urged the older boy, who looked to be around eight years of age. "Stop dragging your heels if you want him to help you."

The other boy, who was barely five, struggled to keep up. "I'm a-coming!" he called.

He cradled something small and still inside the front of his buttoned coat. "You just hang on, Lady. We'll see if this here gentleman can fix you up."

The bundle simply twitched and whimpered softly, but not nearly as much as it had an hour before.

Together, the two boys made their way down the kudzu-covered slope of a deep, wooded hollow. The autumn of 1917 was in full swing. Maple and oak grew around them in abundance, their golden leaves just waiting to shed from their branches and fall earthward after the next hard frost. Further down, in the bottom of the hollow, stood a thick stand of pines. The grove was choked with dark shadows, even though it was only a little past one in the afternoon.

"You think it's safe to go down there?" asked the younger boy. He had never ventured past the edge of the South Woods, let alone into its deepest hollow.

"Why, of course," said the other, straightening his wire-framed spectacles. "Anyway, if you don't get some help soon, we're gonna end up digging a grave out behind your pappy's barn."

"Don't say that!" moaned the 5-year-old. He felt close to tears, but did his best to fight them off. It wouldn't help poor lady one bit if he went to squalling all of a sudden.

It wasn't long before they reached the bottom of the hollow. The moment they got there, the silence of the autumn woods gave way to the sound of music: A 5-string banjo picking "Beautiful Dreamer".

"That must be him up ahead," said the bespectacled boy.

"I reckon so," replied the other, continuing to cradle the shivering bundle beneath his woolen coat.

They reached the edge of the pine grove and found what they had come looking for.

A cabin wagon—similar to what a traveling circus might use—was parked in the middle of a grassy clearing. Its wheels were bright candy apple red and its sides were painted in bold letters of green, red and yellow. The words said it all: DOCTOR AUGUSTUS LEECH'S TRAVELING MEDICINE SHOW—MAGIC, MUSIC & MUSE—FEATURING THE GOOD DOCTOR'S PATENTED CURE-ALL ELIXIR.

The younger boy marveled at the medicine show wagon. Even though he wasn't yet able to read, he knew about the man who had showed up out of the blue. His friend had told him what he had heard in town. How the mysterious Doctor Leech proclaimed that his wondrous elixir had the ability to cure everything from a toothache to tuberculosis.

In fact, that was the reason why they had decided to trek into the wilderness of the South Woods shortly after dinnertime.

Tied to a tree next to the wagon were two coal black horses. The two boys stayed away from them, though. They looked moody and downright mean, as though they right take a bite out of you if you wandered too close.

As they stepped around to the far side of the wagon, the banjo picking ceased and a voice called out to them. "Welcome to my humble campsite, gentlemen," it invited, its tone silky and alluring, like the sideshow barker at the county fair. "Come and join me by the fire."

They turned and, for the first time, laid eyes on the man that the whole town of Harmony was talking about. He sat on a mossy log before a crackling campfire; a tall, lanky fellow with raven black hair, a waxed mustache and goatee beard, and the darkest eyes either had ever seen before. But it was his attire that interested them most. In addition to woolen britches and a starched white shirt, he wore a black frock coat with dangling tails. And atop his head was perched a tall, stovepipe hat of the same dark hue.

It looked similar to the hat Abe Lincoln wore in their history books at school, except this one was a little dented and dusty in places.

The older boy cleared his throat nervously. "Uh, are you Doctor Leech?" he asked.

"That I am, lad," he said with a thin smile of pearly white teeth.

"And what they say is true? That you can conjure magic and such?"

The man's narrow smile rose at the edges, linking with the curled ends of his mustache. "Undoubtedly," he said. "Observe!"

The two boys watched in amazement as the medicine show man cupped his lean hands together, then opened them. A slimy green toad sat within the cradle of his palms. He closed his hands again. The next time he opened them, they revealed that the frog had been replaced by a gray mouse. The long-fingered hands closed and opened a third and final time. The rodent had changed into a bird that looked to be a dove, though it was pitch black in color. The black dove flew toward their startled faces with a fluttering of wings, then soared upward and disappeared into the treetops.

"Did you see that?" said the older boy excitedly. "He's surely a sorcerer, if ever there was one!"

"A minor feat," said Leech, waving a bony hand in dismissal. He eyed the two boys curiously. "But you didn't come here to witness a few silly magic tricks. Your journey has a much graver purpose, or am I mistaken?"

"No, sir, you're not," said the older boy. He nodded toward his companion. "His pup is sick. Bad-off sick."

The 5-year-old unbuttoned his coat and revealed a spotted puppy. The dog breathed shallowly and yellow mucus rimmed her half-closed eyes. "She's feeling right poorly, mister."

"Yes, I can see," said Leech, his grin twitching at the corners a bit. "But what could I possibly do to help this ailing creature?"

The older boy pointed to the flamboyant words that were painted on the side of the wagon. "Well, we kinda thought maybe you could heal her...you know, with that miracle elixir of yours."

A strange look came into the dark eyes of Augustus Leech; a humorous sparkle, as well as something else. Something that was vague, but not at all nice. "Yes, of course," he said. "Please, let me see the poor animal."

The younger boy stepped forward and handed the pup to the tall man. Leech cradled the dog in his hands, stroking its speckled fur tenderly. "Yes," he said softly. "I can feel your hurt, your pain. Deep down, festering. But not to worry. I have just the thing for you."

The boys watched as Doctor Leech took a bottle from an inner pocket of his frock coat. It was a long, narrow glass bottle with a paper label affixed to its front. Leech uncorked the bottle with his fine, white teeth. He then wedged a thumb between the whimpering pup's jaws and, prying them apart, poured several drops of the dark elixir down the animal's throat.

"There we go," said Leech, placing the dog upon the ground. He grinned at his audience of two. "Now... *watch!*"

The boys did as they were told. At first, the puppy simply laid there, whining. Then its eyes opened widely. They watched in utter fascination as the dog suddenly jumped to its feet and began to leap around playfully.

"Lady!" cried the 5-year-old. "You're okay!"

"Why, of course," boasted Leech. He corked the bottle and returned it to his coat pocket. "My elixir cures all."

The younger boy knelt and called to the dog. Lady ran to him and nearly knocked him down. She licked at the boy's face. The 5-year-old caught a peculiar scent on the animal's breath; a smell like cotton candy and castor oil combined.

"How much do we owe you?" asked the one with the glasses.

"Absolutely nothing!" Augustus Leech. His grin grew broader, until it seemed as though it might split his face in half. "Let us just say that this is my...umm...good deed for today."

"Gee, thanks, mister," said the 5-year-old.

"But you may do one thing in return for my services," said the lanky man in the stovepipe hat. He stepped over to his wagon and reached under the seat, bringing out a stack of brightly colored handbills. "You can pass these out for me. To let folks know when I'll be coming to town."

"Sure thing!" said the older boy. "I'll even put one up in the window of my daddy's store."

"Excellent!" said Leech. "Oh, and one more thing." He extended his right hand, splaying his fingers like a fan. Magically, two cards appeared out of thin air. He handed one to each boy. "A little something for the both of you."

They took the cards that were offered to them. They were larger than normal playing cards and bore separate illustrations. One depicted the image of a confederate soldier holding a musket in one hand and a cap-and-ball revolver in the other. The second card showed a spaceman and his rocket ship on the crater-pocked surface of the moon, like something out of an H.G. Wells book.

"What're these for?" asked one of the boys.

"They are very special," the medicine show man told them. "Just place them beneath your pillows tonight and see what happens."

"Thanks a lot, mister!"

The two bid the mysterious Doctor Leech farewell, then headed back up the steep slope of the backwoods hollow. Surprisingly, Lady beat them to the top, jumping and yelping happily all the way.

"He sure fixed up my pup, didn't he?" said the younger boy with a big smile on his freckled face.

"Didn't I tell you?" replied his friend.

The boy with the spectacles reached the lip of the hollow before his companion. When he got there, he froze in his tracks and stood perfectly still. "Don't move," he warned as the other boy reached level ground.

"Huh?" the child asked, puzzled. "What's the matter?"

His pal simply pointed at the speckled dog that stood a few feet away. At first, the 5-year-old noticed nothing out of the ordinary. Then he saw it. The dog stood almost *too* still, his body and legs trembling, his tail curved upward like the blade of a scythe. But it was the puppy's eyes that frightened him most. They were *red.* Not bloodshot red, like those of a drunken man, but *glowing* red, like the hot coals of a potbelly stove.

"What's wrong with her?" he asked in a whisper.

A thick, foamy string of saliva dripped from the corner of the pup's mouth as its jaws parted in a toothy snarl.

"It's done gone rabid, that's what," said the elder boy. "Plumb stark raving mad!"

Suddenly, the dog charged toward them, snapping and growling. The two boys dodged Lady's attack and high-tailed it for a tall oak nearby. They pulled themselves onto its lower limb as quickly as they could. The younger boy barely made it, however. He felt the pup's tiny, sharp teeth nip at the heel of one of his new winter shoes as he scurried up.

They sat there, out of reach, for the better part of 10 minutes, watching the dog snap and snarl and foam at the mouth. One moment it would circle the tree like a bobcat on the prowl, then the next it was spring up at them, much higher than a normal puppy should be able to. It turned its viciousness on itself as well, biting at its own haunches until it drew blood.

Then, without warning, it stopped. It stood rigid and still for a long second, then threw back its spotted head. It opened its slavering jaws and, with a tormented howl of agony and loss, pitched over and fell into a motionless heap at the foot of the tree. From where they sat on the limb, they could tell that it would menace them no more.

Cautiously, they hopped down. The older boy walked over, squatted, and stared into the dog's open eyes. The red glow that had blazed there so brightly slowly faded and winked out completely. "She's passed on," he said. "That elixir...it must've been too strong for her."

The 5-year-old stood there, but he didn't cry. Instead, he looked toward the dark hollow that dipped several yards away. "No," he said grimly. "He knew what it'd do to her, but he didn't care."

At that moment, a sound drifted from up out of the hollow. A peal of sinister laughter full of cruelty and dark amusement. And both boys knew who it came from.

"Let's get on home," suggested the 10-year-old.

The younger boy didn't argue. Together, they ran through the woods as fast as their feet could carry them, leaving the evil laughter and the lifeless body of the speckled puppy behind.

PART ONE

HARMONY & DISCONTENT

CHAPTER ONE

"No!" said Keith Bishop. He sat at the breakfast nook table with his arms crossed, letting his cheese omelet and wheat toast grow cold.

"Ah, darling, it'll be so much fun!" said his mother. Felicia Bishop took a small bite of egg, making sure none of it fell off her fork onto her jacket of burgundy suede. "You will simply love it."

"No, I won't," Keith said defiantly. "I'm not going and that's final!"

Robert Bishop took a sip of his coffee and let his eyes rove along the columns of the stock market page of the newspaper, picking out abbreviations he and his stockbroker knew by heart. "I'm afraid you'll just have to get used to the idea," he told his son.

"The arrangements have already been made."

Keith shook his head in disgust. "I can't believe this!" He looked at his mother. "You can't be serious. The whole rest of the summer?"

"It will only be four weeks at the very most," she assured him. "And it will be a good change of pace for you, sweetie. You know, sunshine and fresh air and all that jazz."

The boy looked over at his father. "Dad, can't you...?"

"I'm afraid not, Keith." Robert looked up from his paper. His face wore that ironclad, no-compromise expression that he sported in the courtroom when he was representing a corporate client. "Our plans have already been made. This is the only chance this year that your mother and I are both free to take a vacation. After September, our schedules are completely tied up."

"Don't you think we deserve to have some time to ourselves, Keith?" his mother asked.

Keith bristled at her use of psychology. She was trying to make him feel guilty now. But then, that was her bread and butter, wasn't it? Playing games with people's heads and charging them an obscene amount of money to do it.

"I didn't say that, Mom," he told her. "It's just, well, why can't I stay with Uncle Richard and Aunt Sophia like I did when you went on that Caribbean cruise a few years ago?"

"You were 9 then," said his father. "You're 12 now and, to tell the truth, they're just not accustomed to dealing with a boy your age. Particularly one with, shall we say, behavioral problems like yours?" Robert took another sip of decaf. "Besides, they're going to Cancun the second week of August and they certainly can't take you with them, now can they?"

Keith sat there and stewed in his own juices for a few minutes. It wasn't that he begrudged his mother and father for spending a month in Europe. They worked hard at their careers; Robert was the best corporate attorney in Atlanta and Felicia was a respected psychiatrist that catered to the city's affluent. They certainly deserved to take a hiatus every now and then. And it wasn't that he was upset because they weren't taking him with them. He remembered his last trip to Great Britain and Europe when he was 8 years old and, in his opinion, it had really sucked. Just a bunch of drafty old castles and people jabbering in languages he didn't understand. He would take Six Flags or Disney World over Italy and France any old day.

And he certainly didn't mind enduring a few weeks away from his parents, either. Keith was very independent and didn't need anyone hovering over him every moment of the day and night. He had been a certified latch-key-kid since third grade and pretty much knew how to take care of himself. In fact, he really only saw his parents three or four hours out of the entire day; two in the morning before they left for work and maybe a couple at night, even if that much. Robert and Felicia Bishop were terminal workaholics. Keith had eaten microwave dinners more nights than he could remember, due to the overtime his parents put in after their regular working hours.

No, the thing that angered him most of all about this "arrangement" his mother and father had made behind his back was *where* they intended to send him for the long summer month August.

And that was to his Grandfather McLeod's farm in a little town located in the hills and hollows of central Tennessee.

"But I don't even know the old guy," he complained. "I think I've only seen him once or twice in my entire life."

His mother took a sip of her orange juice. "Oh, you've seen him more times than that," she said. "I know we haven't kept in touch with Papa as much as we should have, especially after your grandmother died, but who can these days? Especially if they have a career?"

"It'll be weird," continued the boy. "I won't know anybody there. I'll be miserable!"

"You're being too melodramatic, Keith," she said. "You'll end up having a fabulous time. There are all sorts of things to do on your grandpa's farm and you'll have your cousin Rusty to pal around with."

Keith had to strain his brain to even remember Rusty McLeod. All he could recall of his cousin was that he was red-headed, skinny as a beanpole, and meaner than a snake with a belly rash.

"But this place you're sending me to," he protested. "What's it called?"

"Harmony," said his father with a trace of disdain in his voice.

"Yeah, Harmony," said Keith. "I know what that's going to be like. Hicksville, USA, that's what. Just a bunch of tobacco-chewing rednecks and hayseeds with double-digit IQs."

"Well, it's not all that bad," said Felicia.

"Says who?" asked Robert, arching his brows over the top of his paper.

"You're not helping matters, dear," she said sweetly. "I'm trying to be encouraging to Keith. Sarcasm will only make him more resistant."

"Sorry," he replied, then turned his eyes back to the stock report. He saw that Microsoft was down a point and groaned softly.

"Really, Keith, don't be such a whiny baby," his mother told him. "You knew that we've had this trip planned since the first of the year."

"Yeah, but I didn't know I was going to be shipped off to Mayberry R.F.D.," grumbled Keith.

"Please, darling," she said, iron replacing the honey in her voice. "No more complaints. Just accept the fact and learn to live with it."

"But, Mom—!"

"You heard your mother, young man," said his father sternly, using his intimidating lawyer voice.

Keith clammed up. He knew that he had lost whenever Robert Bishop used the term "young man" in his presence.

He frowned and sat there quietly, picking at his omelet with the tines of his fork.

Harmony, he thought to himself. *What did I ever do to deserve this?*

After his parents had left for work, Keith left the Bishops' townhouse condominium near Woodruff Park. It was an elegant structure of tan brick and light gray trim that had cost his mother and father a good $500,000, and that had been eight years ago. Keith figured it was probably worth twice that much now.

He locked the door behind him and started toward the Peachtree Center Mall. Keith arrived at the shopping complex a few minutes after it opened at 10:00. Even at that early hour the place was crowded. Most were kids his age or older, out on summer break with nothing to do but hang around the mall. There were also a few tourists who had journeyed to Atlanta to visit Six Flags, Stone Mountain, or to see the Braves play in the stadium that coming weekend.

Keith's first stop was the video arcade, his favorite spot in the entire mall. The place was packed with kids similar to himself, as far as adolescent fashion and attitude was concerned. Keith's dark brown hair was styled into a spiky flattop with the sides and back of his head clipped close. He wore an oversized Atlanta Braves t-shirt, black shorts and Air Nikes with the laces loosened and the tongue protruding. In all, he looked like any other urban kid who lived within the limits of a big city like Atlanta.

He headed straight for the Lethal Enforcer game and was glad to see that no one had hogged it before he got his chance. Keith was a great fan of police and private-eye shows and even hard-boiled detective novels when he found one that didn't bore him out of his skull. So this game, more than any other in the arcade, appealed to that particular interest of his.

Keith quickly changed a $20 at the counter, then ran to the game and began depositing quarters in the slot. He withdrew the blue plastic magnum revolver from its holder then chose the bank robbery scene, his favorite. Soon, he was blasting away at ski-masked terrorists toting Uzis and thugs decked out in trench coats and sunglasses, carrying sawed-off shotguns.

He played the game for an hour before he finally grew tired of it. Besides, his right hand had begun to cramp from pulling the trigger so much. He took the escalator upstairs to the food court. He bought himself a hamburger and a chocolate milkshake, and ate it at one of the dining tables.

While he sat there, Keith had time to reflect on the discussion he had endured with his parents that morning. Not that it had really been much of a discussion at all. They had laid down the law to him and mapped out their plans for the remainder of his summer seemingly with no consideration for his wants or feelings. They were like that; more concerned about themselves—their careers, their social standing, their vacations—than they were about him. He couldn't even remember the last time his father had congratulated him on a good grade or his mother had told him that she loved him.

Not that he really needed all that emotional crap. Keith was a loner of sorts. He was fiercely independent and unaccustomed to being told what he could and couldn't do. And that was one thing that bothered him the most about where he would be staying during his parents' trip to Europe. They were packing him off to the boonies and he had absolutely no say in the matter. And, frankly, that pissed him off.

Well, if that's the way they want to play hardball, then fine, he thought to himself as he finished his burger and got up, leaving his trash on the table. *I'll just be a colossal pain in the ass for Grandpa McLeod and everybody in that hick town. They won't know what him them after I rattle their cage!*

Keith walked along the rows of shops and boutiques, his anger slowly giving way to boredom, and then boredom to mischief. He spotted a Champs sporting goods store and his lips curled into a wicked grin.

Through the open front, he could see the only sales person on duty waiting on a couple of customers at the counter. He ducked into the store without drawing the man's attention and made his way down one of the back aisles.

He reached the clothing section and began to browse absently through nylon warm-up jackets and running apparel. When he was certain that no one was watching—and that there were no security cameras in the place—he took a black and red Braves cap from a rack on the wall. Keith studied it for a moment, then stuck the tag up under the crown and tugged it over his head.

Slowly, he made his way back down the aisle, toward the open corridor of the mall. He peeked around a display of golf clubs and nine irons. The cashier was waiting on another batch of customers.

Quickly, Keith walked toward the entranceway, eager to make his exit. There were no electronic theft-detection panels to walk through, like at other stores. If he could only get outside without being noticed, he would be in the clear.

Suddenly, just as he was almost out the doorway, a man's voice called out.

"Hey!"

Keith froze in his tracks. He swallowed dryly and slowly turned around.

Fortunately, it wasn't the cashier who had spoken. Instead, it was a man calling to his son, wanting to show him a selection of aluminum baseball bats. The tension drained from Keith's body and, with a sigh of relief, he left the shop. Swiftly, he dodged out of sight, heading toward the escalator and the lower level of the mall.

The stunt he had just pulled reminded him of the remark his father had made earlier that morning.

Behavioral problems. Keith really couldn't deny that he had been in more trouble than most of the kids he knew. He had been caught skipping school several times as well as participating in other forms of mischief that would have once branded him as a juvenile delinquent. The shoplifting was another matter. He had never been caught and his parents had no earthly idea that he had ever done such a thing, although Keith had gotten away with the act a couple of dozen times. Sometimes he felt a little guilty about the lifting, but, hey, a lot of kids did it these days, mostly for the thrill. Keith was just a little better and a little more prolific at it than most.

He turned the cap around on his head until the bill was pointed backwards. He smiled when he hopped off the escalator and saw a Ray-Ban sunglasses store directly across from him.

"Such a boss hat deserves some cool shades to go with it," he said to himself. Keith carefully cased the joint and, satisfied that it was a piece of cake and entered the shop, determined to exercise his secret skill once again.

CHAPTER TWO

Jasper McLeod climbed out of his old Chevy pickup truck and shut the door. The hinges squealed like fingernails on a blackboard. The elderly man made a mental note to spray a little WD-40 on them. Of course, he had already reminded himself a hundred times before in the past two years, but had yet to remember it when he was back at his workshop.

It was late evening, nearly 7:30. The sky was streaked with broad splashes of purple and pink. Jasper knew the sunset wouldn't last much longer, however. The colors were already darkening. Soon, twilight would engulf the little town of Harmony. But, more than likely, that wouldn't do a thing for the temperature. It had been in the mid-90s all day long and, even though the sun had set, the air was still uncomfortably hot and muggy.

He made his way past a bank of old gasoline pumps—not digital, but the kind with revolving numbers—and crossed the crushed gravel to the weathered structure of Hill's General Store. The old building looked the same as it had back when Jasper was a child, when the business had been owned and operated by Wilbur Hill. It was run by Wilbur's son, Edwin, now. It had been since the late 1940's.

The outer walls of the store were covered with bare wooden slats and rusty metal signs advertising Orange Crush and Beechnut Chewing Tobacco. The roof was constructed of sheet tin, corroded a dark orange in places and sporting new patches of gleaming metal in others. The porch was high and the steps leading up to it were 2-by-4s that had withstood the ravages of time—as well as the weight of countless customers—for nearly a century.

No, they just didn't make places like this anymore. Everything now days had to be constructed of concrete, glass and compressed particleboard. This was hand-hewn lumber and hammered tin; materials of a bygone age. That's why Jasper felt most at home there—even more so than his own farm, or at least during the past couple of years.

Spryly, Jasper made his way up the steps to the porch. It was cluttered with bags of chicken feed and peat moss for planting begonias, empty whiskey barrels bought from the Jack Daniel's distillery over in Lynchburg, and all manner of garden implements; hoes, rakes, and long-handled scythes for harvesting hay and alfalfa, just in case someone had the notion to go back to the ways before tractor and combine had been invented. The merchandise sat on the porch of Hill's store from mid-March to early-October and he never brought it in at night. Not that anyone would steal the stuff. Harmony had a few bad apples but, all in all, it was a good, Christian town with more than its fair share of honest folks. In big cities like Nashville or Chattanooga, storeowners invested in iron bars and fancy burglar alarm systems. In Harmony, people invested in the trust of neighbors who had lived there since birth. It might seem a little naïve, but there in the heart of Hawkshaw County it was pretty much the way things were.

He opened the screen door and stepped inside. Jasper's entrance was heralded by a copper cowbell that hung above the sill of the door. It jangled loudly in his ears, causing him to nearly jump out of his skin. He had been coming in and out of that store for most of his 95 years, and he had never quite gotten used to the bell in all that time.

"Edwin?" he called out.

"I'm back here in the stockroom," answered his best friend from beyond an open door at the rear of the store. "I'll be out directly."

"Take your time," he replied. Jasper walked over to an ancient Coca Cola box—the kind where the bottles stood up in the bottom—and rummaged around until he found what he was looking for. He pulled out a frosty bottle of Sun Drop and shucked off the cap with the chest's built-in opener. He held the bottle against his forehead for a second, savoring its coolness. Then he upended it and took a long swallow. The soda pops they sold in aluminum cans in those new-fangled vending machines just weren't as cold and didn't taste as good as the glass-bottled drinks that Edwin Hill kept in the old-fashioned refrigerated chest.

Jasper stood there and looked around the store. Like the exterior, the interior didn't look much different than it had since Jasper was a tadpole. Wooden shelves held canned goods, boxed cereal, and cake mixes, and stacks of chambray work shirts and denim overalls in the dry goods section. On the long counter stood gallon jars of five-cent bubble gum and sticks of brown horehound candy, as well as cardboard displays of Tic-Tacs and Slim Jims. Jasper breathed in deeply. The smell had never changed either. The store was still rich with the scents of chewing tobacco, cider vinegar, and peppermint. Jasper relished the aroma. He thought about the new Wal-Mart over in Manchester. You couldn't smell a dadblamed thing in there, just purified air and that was all.

The old man ambled toward the back of the store, where an ancient potbelly stove of cast iron stood, along with a couple of high-backed chairs. Between the chairs was a flimsy TV table with a checkerboard and checkers laid out on its top. Edwin had already set up their game, which they had indulged in every Friday night for the past 50-odd years.

Jasper took his place on the right side of the board and stacked his black checkers in a single column. He took another swallow of Sun Drop and then cracked his knuckles loudly. He was primed and ready to go.

A moment later, Edwin Hill emerged from the stockroom. He was a short, chubby man who wore black horn-rimmed glasses. Physically, Jasper McLeod was the complete opposite of his friend: tall and gangly, with a thick shock of silvery hair. The two had been best friends for most of their lives; Edwin was 97 years old, while Jasper was 95.

"You ready to get your skinny butt whupped again?" asked Edwin, taking the chair opposite Jasper.

"That ain't likely to happen tonight," said Jasper with a grin. "To tell the truth, I'm feeling right lucky."

Edwin eyed his friend curiously. "Now, I ain't seen you smile like that since before Gladys died. You haven't been nipping at the bottle, have you?"

Jasper laughed. "No, that ain't it. I reckon I'm just looking forward to having my grandson stay with me for a while."

The storekeeper nodded. "That's right. You're picking up at the airport this weekend."

"Saturday noon," replied the elderly farmer.

"What's his name again?"

"Keith," said Jasper.

"Yeah, right." Edwin nodded as he moved one of his checkers forward. "Can't say that I'd know the young'un if he came up and looked me square in the face, though."

"Actually, I feel about the same way, I haven't seen him in so long," admitted Jasper.

"Been pert near two years now, the way I figure it."

"A shame how Felicia's treated you since she went off to Atlanta and married that big-shot lawyer. Just up and forgot about you and Gladys, and snubbed the folks of Harmony to boot. Why, she hardly said two words to me when they were down for her mama's funeral. Then, as soon as the casket was lowered, they were in that fancy Mercedes of theirs, squealing tires and heading back for home."

"Aw, they weren't that bad," said Jasper, sliding one of his black checkers toward the center of the board.

"Well, just about." Edwin worked a chaw of Redman in the pouch of one cheek, then spat a stream of tobacco juice into an empty Maxwell House can that sat next to the stove. Years of misplaced shots had left a gummy puddle of dark brown spittle around the base of the coffee can, permanently affixing the makeshift cuspidor to the floorboards.

"They've got their reasons, I reckon," said Jasper, although his voice held a trace of doubtfulness. "They live way off in Georgia and Felicia and her husband both have careers that keep them busy. I don't expect them to run up here on a whim and visit me every month or two."

"Every year or two is more like it," said Edwin. "I don't mean to hurt your feelings, Jasper, but your daughter's turned her back on you. She's gotten caught up in all the glitz and glamour and high society, and forgotten her roots. She thinks she's too damned sophisticated to associate with the folks she grew up with. Why, I remember when she weren't nothing but a skinny tomboy of a girl roaming around Harmony in her bare feet and her hair up in pigtails."

Jasper smiled fondly. "Yeah, but that was a long time ago."

"Not all that long," protested Edwin. "Fact of the matter is, she just don't have no cause to treat you the way she does. She's more concerned about her life in Atlanta than she is about her own family."

"Aw, quit your fussing," said Jasper.

Edwin shrugged. "It just gripes the hell outta me to see you treated that way. Frank sure wouldn't turn his back on you like that."

Jasper knew Edwin was right. His only son, Frank, was a cross-country trucker and he didn't get to see him as much as he would have liked, but they still had a firm and close relationship. Felicia was another story and it was her indifferent behavior that irked Edwin the most. Felicia had swept her family and her hometown beneath the rug, and there was no denying it.

That was what made it particularly painful to swallow; the fact that every word of what Edwin said was true. Felicia had once been a happy and affectionate girl who enjoyed climbing trees, swimming in creeks, and roaming the Tennessee backwoods. Then she had grown up and gone off to college on a scholarship. After that, she had opened her psychiatry practice in downtown Atlanta and met Robert Bishop. In a span of only a few years, Felicia had changed. The further she climbed the ladder of success, the more alienated she became toward those who had raised her, as well as the town that had nurtured her since birth. Jasper like to think that the old Felicia was still there, hidden somewhere beneath the surface. But, if the last few visits were an indication, he was afraid that she was gone for good. It seemed as if her rare visits to Harmony were purely out of daughterly duty and nothing more.

Edwin jumped a couple of Jasper's checkers and gathered them up with a chuckle.

"Better concentrate on your game, buddy," he said.

"Then you'd best keep your trap shut about my daughter," grumbled Jasper. "You know she's a pretty touchy subject with me."

"Sorry," said Edwin. "Didn't mean to ruin your sunny disposition."

Jasper nodded and took a drink of his Sun Drop. The soda pop nearly slipped through his hand, the bottle was so sweaty. In the darkness past the store's screen door came the singing of crickets and the winking lights of fireflies.

"So, are you anxious to see the boy again?" asked Edwin.

"Sure I am," said Jasper. "I've been waiting for a chance like this for a long time." The elderly man studied the checkerboard and then made another move. "But, to tell the truth, it sort of scares me a bit."

"How come?"

"I reckon 'cause we're more like total strangers than grandfather and grandson," said Jasper grimly. "I've never been around him more'n a couple hours at a time and, even then, he wouldn't have much to do with me. It's different with Rusty. He lives less than a mile from the farm and he's grown up knowing me—staying all night at the house and helping out with the chores when his grandma was ailing. We're closer than two peas in a pod."

"Well, maybe you'll be the same way with Keith after this visit," suggested Edwin. "I mean, he'll be staying with you for an entire month and that's enough time to do almost anything."

"Except maybe the impossible," said Jasper. "What if he resents being sent down here for the summer? From the way Felicia talked, the boy didn't have a clue about what they had in mind. What if he ends up hating me for ruining his summer vacation?"

Edwin shrugged. "That could happen, especially if he's as much of a spoiled brat as I figure Felicia and that gold-plated husband of hers has raised him to be. Just do what you can and hope for the best. If it doesn't work out, then at least you tried."

"I am to do just that," Jasper told him. "Give it my best shot."

The elderly storekeeper made a move that took three of his opponent's checkers at one time. "Well, I'll be honest, if you don't try any harder than you have on this here checker game, then ain't gonna do no good a'tall. Now set your mind back on your playing and crown my checker there."

Jasper picked up the Sun Drop bottle. "I'll crown *you,*" he told his friend. "If you don't stop sidetracking me with talk of my family problems, I'll wallop a goose egg on your noggin with this cold drink bottle."

Edwin mustered his most wounded frown. "Last time I try to give you any friendly advice, Jasper McLeod," he said. "From now on, I'll just keep my mouth shut."

"Lordy Mercy, that'll be the day!" said Jasper. Both men laughed and resumed their checker-playing.

By the time they finished up at 10:00 that night, they had played four games; all of them won by Edwin Hill. But Jasper didn't mind much. His thoughts were occupied with more important things.

Jasper's wife, Gladys, had died of cancer more than two years ago, and he still grieved for her as strongly as he had the day she had passed away. He knew that wasn't normal. A man had to face up to the reality of death and go on with life, but he'd had trouble doing that. He reckoned it had to do with the fact that had been married to Gladys for nearly 60 years, which was no small piece of time in his opinion. He had grown accustomed to the sound of her voice, the way she had smelled of cinnamon and Ivory soap, and how the mattress of their bed felt with her weight on it. All those things were gone now and it was like she had taken a big slice of him away with her.

He dreaded going home to that empty farmhouse, the same as he had since the evening he had returned home after Gladys' funeral. The house was too empty. It lacked the happiness and love that his wife had blessed it with over the years. Now, it was just a dismal shell of wood and tar shingles, completely devoid of soul.

Jasper hoped that Keith's visit might alter that, if only in some small way. The elderly farmer had been alone since his wife had died. If his hopes panned out and he and his grandson forged some sort of bond, even one of mere friendship, then maybe he would feel as if he had gotten back some of the family he had lost during the past few years.

CHAPTER THREE

That night, Jasper McLeod had a strange dream. A dream that echoed of another time; a time similar to that of his own youth, yet one that was beyond his childhood recollections.

The darkness of night pressed against the windowpanes of a rural farmhouse. An autumn wind blustered outside, howling like a mourner in torment. Then, abruptly, the front door opened and a rawboned man stepped inside. His face was long and grim, and his work-hardened hands were balled into angry fists.

"How is she?" asked the farmer, removing his hat.

His wife simply sat there next to a wooden cradle, quietly shaking her head.

"I think she's dead, Pa," said a young boy beside her.

The farmer closed the door behind him then crossed the room slowly. When he reached the cradle, he stared at the three-month-old child. The baby was dead, that was for certain. Her face was swollen and blue, as if her windpipe had closed shut and she had been unable to draw breath. Her eyes—sky blue, like his own—stared blindly up at him.

"Lord have mercy on this child," he whispered. With a trembling hand, he reached down and closed her tiny eyelids with the tips of his fingers.

Silence filled the room. Death had come, through treachery and ignorance, and there was nothing anyone could really say or do.

"Damn him!" cursed the farmer. His hands clutched the wooden side of the cradle until the muscles bunched beneath the skin and the knuckles grew bone-white from the strain. "Damn him with his jokes and his conjuring and his nigger-faced banjo-picking!" He stared at his daughter, lying still and cold beneath hand-sewn

blankets, but he did not cry. He would cry later, at the burial.

"Was it him, Pa?" asked the boy. "That fella in the black coat and the stovepipe hat?"

"It was him," said the farmer. "He suckered us. Suckered us all with his lies and fancy talking."

The boy thought of the bearded man and his medicine show. It had seemed like innocent fun at first. He'd reeled off some sidesplitting jokes, pulled rabbits and doves from his top hat, and played "My Old Kentucky Home" and "Camptown Races" on the catgut banjo, his face painted coal black with big white lips. Even the selling part had seemed interesting, holding up his wares and preaching on their miraculous virtues. But, in hindsight, the boy also remembered the one time he had seen the man before he had come to town. When a mission of mercy into the dark forest of the South Woods had turned into something evil and deadly.

"Are you sure he was responsible?" asked the woman, speaking for the first time in an hour.

"Damn sure," said her husband. "The sheriff checked it out. He was the same one who killed five young'uns over in Bedloe County year before last."

"How many have died?" she asked softly.

"Here in Harmony?" Anger blazed in the farmer's eyes. "Twelve so far, counting our own. Seven young'uns and five adults."

"Lord Jesus help us!" cried the woman. She buried her face in her hands and began to sob.

The farmer stared at his daughter for a long moment then covered her with the blanket. "The Lord will take 'em unto heaven, but it's up to us to set things straight here on earth."

His wife looked up, her eyes brimming with tears. "What're you gonna do?"

The farmer said nothing at first. Then he walked to the hearth and took down a rifle from over the mantle. It was an old Winchester lever-action. "I'm going after him, that's what," he said. "Gonna make sure he doesn't have the chance to do the devil's dealings again."

"The Bible tells us that only God has the right to judge a man," she reminded him.

"It also says thou shalt not kill," he replied, jacking a .44-40 cartridge into the breech. "And this son of a bitch has done his fair share of it in the last few years. It's only fitting that we put and end to it."

"I suppose so," said the woman, though her voice held uncertainty.

As his parents discussed the matter, the boy walked to the table and stared at the bottle that stood there, uncorked. It was tall and skinny, made of cloudy glass and sporting a colorful label with elegant lettering. It wasn't the sight of it that drew him, but the smell that drifted from the bottle's open mouth. It was intoxicatingly sweet, like a combination of molasses, peppermint, and soda pop. But there was something else there as well. A mixture of dark, forbidden scents. The earthy odor of graveyard earth and the sharp muskiness of snake hide.

"Stay away from that, son," said his father. "It's poison."

The boy stepped away from the table and looked the man in the eyes. "Can I come with you, Pa?" he asked. His heart ached over the death of his baby sister, but his mind boiled with rage.

The farmer stared at him for a long moment, then nodded.

"No!" cried his mother. "He's too young. He's only five!"

"Old enough to see evil stricken down," declared the farmer. "Fetch your coat, son."

The boy did as he was told. He pulled on his woolen coat, as his father kissed his mother and then walked toward the door. Soon, they were outside, standing in the moonlight. The boy was surprised to find a dozen other men on horses, waiting for them. They held torches and guns in their hands, and their faces were tight with fury.

The farmer mounted his own dapple gray mare, then held his hand down. "Come along, boy. Time's a-wasting."

The 5-year-old took his father's strong hand and was lifted onto the rump of the mare, just behind the saddle. He held onto his papa's coattail as the horse was spurred forward. It wasn't long before they were traveling at a gallop. The others followed closely.

The boy turned his head and peered behind him. In the darkness, he could see the lighted window of the farmhouse. The silhouette of his grieving mother stood against the pale glow of lamplight. He recalled how she had wailed at the moment of his sister's dying gasp, how she had fallen to her knees and torn at her hair. He kept the image fresh in his young mind as he hung on tightly to his father and let the horse carry him swiftly into the black forest.

CHAPTER FOUR

Allison Walsh set the pump nozzle back in its cradle, then turned to her Ford Taurus and screwed the gas cap back into place. She shut the little door on the left rear fender, then walked toward the bright green and yellow structure of the BP station.

It was 2:30 a.m. and the place was empty, except for the clerk on duty. She was sitting on a stool behind the counter, drinking a cherry Icee and thumbing through a copy of *Soap Opera Digest.*

Allison took a short walk through the narrow aisles of the convenience store, picking up a bag of pretzels and a soft drink. When she reached the counter, the woman set her magazine aside. "That gonna be all for you?"

"I got $25 worth on pump number four," she said, yawning and running a hand through her thick brown hair. "Oh, and a pack of Merit 100's."

"Menthol?"

"No, regular."

The cashier nodded, shucked a pack of cigarettes from a rack overhead, and laid them on the counter. She rang up the purchase and took Allison's money. "Which way are you heading?" she asked, handing the woman her change.

"Back to St. Louis," replied Allison. She uncapped the drink and took a long swallow. "Just spent a glorious week in Fort Lauderdale. Nothing but sun, surf and studmuffins in skimpy bikini trunks. Pure paradise."

The cashier looked a little envious. "Should've known by the tan," she said, then went back to her reading.

Allison picked up her pretzels and smokes and started for the door. She felt 100 percent better than she had a week ago that was for sure. She had been totally stressed out, having taken over the position of feature editor at the newspaper she had been employed at for the past 15 years. His climb to the top had been a long and tedious one, but it had been worth it. Sure, it was full of headaches, too much overtime, and little chance for a social life, but she was making nearly twice the money she had been making this time last year. And the stress wasn't anything that a week in sunny Florida couldn't alleviate...at least temporarily.

She was walking back to her car, when a voice came from behind her. "Ma'am?"

It startled her. She stopped dead in her tracks and stood there, clutching the little canister of pepper spray she kept on her keychain. She snaked a manicured nail beneath the plastic guard and disengaged it. Then she slowly turned around.

A man stood against the wall of the station, next to the ice machine. He was tall and dark-haired, wearing jeans, a flannel shirt, and a black Grateful Dead t-shirt. Next to his feet was a plastic trash bag, apparently stuffed with his belongings.

"Yes?" she asked cautiously.

"Well, I know you'll probably say no," said the man, stepping away from the wall. "But you wouldn't consider giving me a ride, would you?"

"No," said Allison firmly. "I'm sorry, but I don't pick up hitchhikers."

"And that's smart, too," said the man. "A pretty lady like you can't be too careful out on the road by yourself. But I wouldn't ask if it wasn't an absolute emergency."

As he stepped out into the bright glow of the florescent lights, Allison saw something gleam above the breast pocket of his flannel shirt. It was gold pin in the shape of a cross. Allison had seen them before in religious bookstores in some of the malls back in St. Louis.

She was on the verge of saying "I'm sorry" and walking off. But something about the cross pin stopped her. It took some of the threat away from the lanky, long-haired fellow with the scrubby mustache and goatee. She relaxed her grip on the pepper spray a little.

"Emergency?" she asked.

"Uh, yeah," said the man. "I've been working a construction job here in Marietta and my folks up in Chattanooga called and told me that my father's in real bad shape. He's had a stroke and they ain't sure he's gonna make it. That's why I'm out here in the dead of night, trying to get a ride up there."

"Why don't you drive yourself?" she asked.

The man looked a little embarrassed. "Ain't got no car, ma'am."

Allison shook her head. "I wish I could help you, but—"

"Please," he said, his eyes pleading. "You're the third person I've tried this morning. I really do need to get to Chattanooga. My daddy, he's a good man, a Baptist preacher. I haven't been the son I should've and I'd really like to get there and make my peace with him before he gets much worse. I'd sure hate to lose that last chance, if you know what I mean."

Allison thought about it for a second. Yes, she did know how it felt to be estranged from a parent and miss the opportunity to reconcile with them. Her own father had died unexpectedly eight years ago and she regretted never having the chance to tell him that she loved him and was sorry for all the bad feelings they had held toward each other for so many pointless years.

She stood there for a long moment, debating on what she should do.

"I'll be glad to pay for the gas up there," he offered.

The gesture seemed to make her decision for her. “Okay, but only to Chattanooga. No further.”

Relief flooded the man’s face and he smiled. “God bless you, ma’am.”

A few minutes later, she was pulling off the exit and back onto the long, dark stretch of Interstate 75 again. Allison had chosen to drive at night, intending to breeze through Atlanta when there was no traffic to contend with. She had driven the city during the rush hour before and it wasn’t an experience she wished to endure twice in a lifetime.

“What’s your name?” she asked. They had been on the road 10 minutes and her passenger had done nothing but sit silently next to her, staring absently through the windshield.

He turned his head and grinned good-naturedly. “Uh, Timothy,” he said. “Timothy Jackson, ma’am. But most folks just call me Slash.”

What an odd nickname, she thought. Allison took the hand that he extended toward her. His palm was hard and thick with calluses. “My name is Allison Walsh,” she said. “I’d prefer you call me that, instead of ‘ma’am’. I know it’s said out of politeness, but it makes me feel like my grandmother.”

Jackson laughed. “I get your drift…Allison.”

They drove a few more miles in silence, before the man spoke again. “Mind if I smoke?”

“No,” replied Allison. “I’m ready for one myself.” She reached up to the top of the dashboard and found the pack of Merits she had laid there.

Jackson bent down to open the trash bag that sat between his feet, apparently to get his own smokes. He was rummaging through the contents, when something dropped out of the breast pocket of his shirt. When he picked it up, Allison caught a glimpse of the object in the pale glow of the dashboard light. It was a small rectangle of smooth, gray stone.

"Oops," said Jackson with a mischievous grin. "You wasn't supposed to see that." He stuck the stone back in his pocket, then shook an unfiltered Camel out of its pack.

A red flag went up in Allison's mind. *What did he mean by that? I wasn't supposed to see it?* She didn't even know what the object was.

"Need me to open that pack for you?" he offered.

Allison had forgotten the Merits in her right hand. "Uh, sure," she said.

He took them from her, opened the pack, and stuck one of the cigarettes between her lips. "Here, I'll light it for you, too." There was the rasp of a thumb on the roller of a cigarette lighter, then, and instant later, the bluish-yellow flame of a Zippo was hovering before the end of her cigarette. She could feel its heat and smell the sharp odor of butane.

"Which hospital is your father in?" she asked, thinking that conversation might settle her nerves.

"Huh?" He turned and stared at her as if he didn't know what she was talking about.

"Which hospital?" she repeated. "In Chattanooga?"

"Oh," he said with a thin smile. "Memorial."

Allison nodded. She had no way of telling whether he was speaking the truth or not. She had driven through the Tennessee city several times, but knew practically nothing about it. And she certainly didn't know how many hospitals were there or even if one of them was named Memorial.

They drove on in silence. The radio was on low, set on a classic rock station. The Stones sang "Sympathy for the Devil". For some reason, Allison couldn't listen to the words without thinking about the man sitting next to her. The man that most folks just called Slash.

Slowly, the cross pinned to his shirt began to lose its innocence. She glanced over at him, hoping that he didn't notice.

Sometime between that moment and the first time she had seen him back at the gas station, the pin had changed its position. It now hung upside down. Inverted.

Allison's suspicions concerning hitchhikers began to creep back into her thoughts. She began to wonder if she had made a mistake.

They were halfway between Marietta and Chattanooga, when they approached a green and white exit sign.

"Adairsville," Jackson said softly. "Two miles."

Allison said nothing. She couldn't figure out why he had said that. But, on second thought, maybe she could.

"Yeah, Adairsville," mused Slash Jackson. "I think we'll get off there."

Allison's heart leaped in her chest. "What do you mean?"

"I said we'll be getting off at that exit," he told her.

She was about to protest, when she heard a crisp *snap*. Allison turned her head and caught a glimpse of polished steel gleaming in the dashboard light.

A knife! her mind screamed. *He's got a knife!*

She jerked the steering wheel to the right, throwing her passenger off balance. The Taurus veered toward the shoulder of the interstate, leaving the right lane and heading toward the dark grass beyond. The tires grated against gravel and, for a moment, she was afraid the loose rock would throw the car off its wheels and into a roll.

Then, suddenly, Jackson was close to her, his hand reaching beneath her chin. She felt something narrow and cold press against her throat and realized that it was the knife. Her heart thundered in her chest and she cried out in alarm.

"Put it back on the road, Allison," he hissed in her ear. "Now!"

She fought with the wheel and finally steered the car back into the correct lane again.

"Now take the Adairsville exit when it comes up," he instructed.

"Why?" she asked, her voice shaky.

"There's a place a few miles back in the woods," said Jackson. "An old house where no one will disturb us."

Allison Walsh recalled news stories she had heard on the radio during her drive to Florida. Stories of robbery, rape and murder along the same stretch of interstate that she now traveled. Feeling the knife blade against her throat, she was suddenly aware of who was responsible for those crimes.

A cold sensation settled in the pit of her stomach. She swallowed dryly. "What...what are you going to do to me?"

She could see Jackson smiling in the darkness, like a wolf bearing its fangs. "Everything," he whispered.

Allison moaned softly.

"Everything you've ever heard of," promised Slash. He turned the honed blade against her flesh, drawing a single drop of blood. "And some you've never imagined."

CHAPTER FIVE

"Keith! Over here!"

The boy left the crowd that had just departed from the Atlanta flight. He hefted a neon green backpack over this shoulder and searched for the one who had called his name.

"Keith!" came the voice again and he turned his attention to a line of people standing behind a roped barrier, waiting for friends and loved ones. Keith saw a tall, elderly gentleman with silvery-white hair and a leathery tan standing with the others, smiling and waving to him. He was wearing jeans, scuffed work boots, and a western-style shirt with pearl snaps and a yoke across the shoulders and back.

The 12-year-old groaned inwardly. Well, there was no turning back now; no appeals to be pleaded or tantrums to be thrown. His parents were on their way across the Atlantic and he was here in the Nashville Metro Airport, on the verge of the worse summer of his life.

Soon, he was past the barrier and standing before Jasper McLeod. Keith stared at his maternal grandfather through his Ray-Ban aviators and frowned openly. *Will you look at the old fart?* he thought to himself. *He looks like Jed Clampett on the Beverly Hillbillies.*

Jasper grinned and extended a wiry hand. "Howdy, Keith! Boy, it's sure good to see you again!"

Keith stared at his hand, then reluctantly took it. The old man's grip was strong and firm. "Uh, yeah," he muttered in reply. "You, too."

They finished shaking hands and stood there quietly for a long moment. Finally, Jasper broke the silence. "Do you have a suitcase with you?" he asked.

"Yep," said Keith. "It should be coming up soon."

They walked to the luggage carrousel and found the boy's suitcase waiting for them. It wasn't long before they had crossed the lobby of the huge terminal and was outside.

"I'm parked over yonder in that lot," he said. "You know, it cost me eight whole bucks to park there? Now don't that beat all?"

Keith simply nodded. *Not only is he an old fart, but he's a cheap old fart,* he thought.

A moment later, they were climbing into Jasper's Chevy pickup. Keith appraised the vehicle with a mixture of repulsion and amazement. He couldn't figure out how the old truck still managed to run. It looked like a prime candidate for the junkyard. And the interior was even worse than the exterior.

"I know it ain't much to look at," said Jasper almost apologetically. "It might be an old rust-bucket, but it's got 400,000 miles on the speedometer and it hasn't given up the ghost yet."

Keith felt around on the seat, but didn't find what he was looking for. "No seat belts?" he asked incredulously.

"Nope," said the old man. "This old Chevy is a B.S. model. You know, Before Seatbelts." Jasper laughed and gave the boy a wink.

Keith failed to crack a smile. *How corny! Am I gonna have to listen to his lame jokes the whole time?*

Jasper parked the boy's suitcase between them and closed his door. "Are you hungry?"

Keith looked at the Bulova diving watch his father had given him for his last birthday. The digital display read 11:37. "Uh, yeah, I guess so."

"We'll stop by Burger King and grab us a bite before we head to Harmony," suggested Jasper. "How does that sound?"

"Okay," said Keith. He slumped down a little in the seat, feeling embarrassed to be seen in such a junk heap of a truck.

As Jasper took the airport exit and hit Interstate 24, he glanced over at the boy's Atlanta Braves cap. "Did you know that you've got your cap on backwards?"

Keith rolled his eyes behind his shades. "It's the style."

"Oh," said Jasper with a nod.

They rode in silence for a while. Then Keith turned and looked at the man he would be spending the next month with. "Uh, what do you want me to call you?" he asked. "Mr. McLeod? Grandfather?"

"Grandpa will be just fine," said Jasper with a big grin. "That's what your cousin, Rusty, calls me." The old man reached over and turned on the truck's AM radio. Country music began to play through the speakers choked with scratchy static and interloping signals. "By the way, we're having supper over at your Aunt Susan's tomorrow after church. Your Uncle Frank is out of the state on a trucking job, so he won't be there. Do you remember much about them?"

Keith shrugged. "Kind of. Not very much."

"Well, we'll fix that up right fast," promised Jasper McLeod. "I know they'll sure be glad to see you. Particularly Rusty."

Keith tried to conjure an image of his red-headed cousin in his mind. No matter how hard he tried, though, he always came up with him looking like Opie Taylor on the old *Andy Griffith Show.*

"Do you like fried chicken?" asked Jasper.

Keith shrugged again. "It's okay, I guess."

"It's your aunt's specialty," he told him. Jasper's smile faded a little. "Don't talk much, do you?"

"Not much, no."

"I don't really blame you," he replied. "Way I figure, this wasn't your idea in the first place, was it? And you're none too happy about coming up her and spending your summer. Am I right?"

Keith turned and looked at the old man. "Yeah, that's pretty much it." The boy was a little surprised. *Old gramps isn't quite as dumb as I thought.* Something came to mind and he decided to test the waters a bit. "So how do you feel about my parents dumping me on you all of a sudden?"

Jasper laughed. "Well, now, that ain't how I look at it, Keith," he said. "To tell the truth, I've been looking forward to it. We ain't had much chance to spend any time together, have we? Well, this'll give us the opportunity. And you won't be disappointed, I swear you won't. Harmony ain't as bad as your folks have probably made it out to be."

I wouldn't bet my life on it, Gramps, thought Keith.

"You'll have a lot of fun, just wait and see," Jasper assured him. "Maybe not the kind of fun you're accustomed to, but it's good for a young fella your age to do new things every now and again."

"Yeah, right," said Keith, unconvinced. The country music that buzzed from the Chevy's ancient speakers was beginning to grate on the boy's nerves. "Uh, Grandpa? You mind if I listen to some of my sounds?"

Jasper turned and looked at him blankly. "Pardon me?"

Keith opened his backpack and took out an iPod with headphones. "Music. I just can't dig those tunes you're playing. They're just too sophisticated for my taste."

The old man detected the sarcasm in the boy's statement, but ignored it. "Why, sure. You just go on and help yourself."

"Thanks." Keith slipped on his earphones and cut up the volume, drowning out both the hillbilly music and any small talk his grandfather might want to subject him to.

Jasper McLeod stared at the boy for a moment, then turned his attention back to his driving. He was a little disappointed that things hadn't gotten off to a better start, but he knew he must be patient. They hardly even knew each other. It would take time for them to feel one another out and find some sort of common ground.

The old man just hoped that Keith got past the resentment he was so set on exhibiting. If not, Jasper was afraid it was going to be a long month.

A very long month, indeed.

An hour later, they were entering the town limits of Harmony, Tennessee.

Keith sucked on the straw of a fountain drink and stared out the side window at the rural community. The first thing they passed were fields of corn, soybean, and tobacco, as well as pastures of Holstein and Black Angus cattle. When the farms began to thin out, the town itself began to grow more apparent.

"That's my friend Edwin Hill's store there," said Jasper, pointing to the side of the road.

Keith looked at the weathered structure of planks and tin, but was far from impressed. It looked more like a firetrap than anything else.

They passed the general store and continued on. Next came shady, tree-lined streets with single and two-story houses of white clapboard and brick. Keith noticed several beer-bellied men in shorts mowing their lawns while their wives worked in flower gardens and their kids rode bikes or played freeze tag in the empty streets.

Then came the town itself. It was a slow-paced, sleepy place that looked nearly deserted, even though it was Saturday afternoon. A line of small shops and businesses sat to the left of the main street, while to the right stood a white-brick courthouse with a gazebo standing out front. To the rear of the courthouse, amid a grove of oak trees, stood a tall, steel water tower painted an ugly sea-green color. Across the sphere-like reservoir at the top were painted the words WELCOME TO HARMONY—THE NAME SAYS IT ALL!

Keith smirked and began to whistle the theme from *Green Acres.*

Jasper McLeod cocked his head like a dog and frowned. "What is that? Sounds kinda familiar."

"Beethoven," said Keith. "Concerto Number Three."

"Oh," said his grandfather, looking a little confused. "Right."

Keith caught himself before he could laugh out loud. Then he looked at the extent of the town, which they were quickly nearing the end of, and his humor died down. "What do you do for kicks around here, Grandpa?" he asked.

"Oh, all kinds of things," said Jasper.

"Like what? Got a mall or a video arcade?"

"Uh, no," admitted the old man.

"How about a movie theatre?"

"We used to. It burned down six years ago."

"Fantastic," groaned Keith. "So what do the kids do around here for fun? Swat the flies off the cow's tail and watch the corn grow?"

There was that sarcasm again. Jasper wasn't sure he liked that side of his grandson, but he refrained from mentioning it. "Mostly they ride their bikes, play ball on the diamond out back of the elementary school, and explore the woods south of here."

"Whoopee," said Keith with a bogus yawn. "I can hardly wait."

Jasper couldn't hold his tongue any longer. "Are you going to do this the whole time you're here, son?"

"Do what?" asked Keith with mock innocence.

"Make wise-ass comments like the ones you just made?"

Keith shrugged. "I don't know. Probably. That's just the way I am."

"I'd really prefer that you keep your opinion of Harmony to yourself from now on," Jasper told him, trying to keep a firm reign on his temper. "I know you're not crazy about this arrangement, but you're stuck here and that's just the way it is. I just hope you get rid of that chip on your shoulder and try to relax and enjoy yourself. This doesn't have to be as bad as you think it's going to be. It's entirely up to you."

"Thanks for the lecture, Gramps," said Keith. "But if you don't like the way I talk and the way I act, then you can always buy me a plane ticket home."

Frustration showed in Jasper's eyes. "You know I can't do that. It's too late."

"That's right," snapped Keith. "So don't try to push your hick-town-ways on me. Just stay off my back and we'll get along just fine. Comprende?"

The old man clutched the steering wheel tightly, his face red with anger. "If you were just a couple years younger, why, I'd turn you across my knee and whale the living tar plumb outta you!"

"Now it's child abuse, huh?" asked the boy smugly. "You're not racking up any points with me, Gramps."

Jasper glared at the boy. "Your mother mentioned that you had an attitude, but I figured she was just exaggerating."

"Afraid not," said Keith with a grin.

"That's clear enough to see," Jasper muttered beneath his breath, then said nothing else to antagonize his grandson. This wasn't how he had wanted their first day together to turn out. Not by a long shot.

Keith stared at his grandfather through the dark lenses of his Ray-Bans. He congratulated himself, feeling a cruel satisfaction at having bested the old dude. Part of him knew that it was wrong to feel that way, but that part was vastly overwhelmed by the stronger aspects of his character, mainly arrogance, ego, and self-importance.

He sat back against the truck seat and propped his Nikes on the dashboard of the old Chevy, hoping it would piss the old man off even more. *Maybe this won't be as bad as I first thought,* he told himself. *If I can play everyone here in Hootersville like I just played Gramps, I might just end up having myself a helluva lot of fun.*

CHAPTER SIX

Jasper McLeod pulled his pickup truck into the gravel drive of a farm a mile south of his own place. Sitting on the seat next to him, looking none too happy, was Keith. He sat there, still dressed in his Sunday clothes, with his arms firmly crossed and a sullen expression on his face.

"Well, we're here," said his grandfather. "Your Uncle Frank and Aunt Susan's place."

"No kidding," said the boy quietly.

Keith glared through the windshield. The house was a traditional two-story farmhouse with a shady front porch. To the rear of the structure was made up of a huge red barn, a concrete grain silo and several smaller outbuildings. It didn't look much different than Grandpa McLeod's farm, except that the old man's house was single story and there was no silo next to the barn.

Jasper looked at the boy and felt a little sad. Keith had scarcely said a dozen words to him since their argument the day before. Jasper didn't think it was because the boy was angry with him. No, indifferent was more like it. Keith seemed to be deliberately ignoring him.

If Keith was miffed about anything, it was the fact that he had been forced to attend services at Harmony Holiness Church that morning. Keith hadn't wanted to get out of bed early that morning. Jasper had woke his grandson up at 6:00, two hours later than he himself had risen. The boy had grumbled and frowned through his breakfast of scrambled eggs, country ham, white gravy, and buttermilk biscuits. When Keith had made a move toward his bedroom, intending to sleep the rest of the morning away, Jasper had collared him and steered him toward the shower. They had bantered a few unpleasant words back and forth, but Jasper had put his foot down. Still half-asleep, Keith had grouchily agreed to accompany his grandfather to church. Jasper knew he had been lucky. If they boy had been a little more alert, there would have been a good chance that the old man would have ended up going to church by himself.

"Keith," Jasper said, drawing the 12-year-old's attention. "Try to behave yourself, all right? Your aunt and cousin are looking forward to seeing you and if you end up sitting in there like a lump on a log, looking mad enough to chew nails, then it's gonna make everybody feel uncomfortable. Can't you get over this ugly mood of yours and try to enjoy yourself?"

The boy turned and regarded his grandfather. "Oh, you want me to crack a big smile and act like all is right with the world, like those yokels at church, is that it?"

Jasper sighed. "Well, it'd sure be an improvement over how you're acting now." The elderly farmer sat there for a moment, letting his temper settle. "Please, Keith. Susan and Rusty have been looking forward to seeing you for over a week now. Try to be civil, okay?"

Keith flashed a bogus smile that did little to match the contempt in his eyes. "Is this better?"

"Not much," said Jasper opening the door of his truck. "But I reckon it'll have to do."

Together, they left the truck and started up the sidewalk for the house. Jasper was dressed in a gray pinstripe suit from J.C. Penney, with a starched white shirt and burgundy tie. Keith wore a pale blue short-sleeved Arrow shirt, navy slacks, and black leather shoes that probably cost more than his grandfather's entire outfit. He had worn a tie and jacket during church, but they had been abandoned the moment he had left the building. They were now lying in an untidy heap in the middle of the truck seat where Keith had tossed them after changing.

Halfway to the house, Keith smelled the rich aroma of food. The only scent he recognized was that of fried chicken. But the others—while unfamiliar—smelled just as appetizing. His stomach growled in anticipation.

The front door opened and a woman stepped out on the porch. "Ya'll come on in," she called, waving to them. "Dinner's already on the table."

A moment later, they had let themselves into the farmhouse and made their way down a hallway decorated with antique furniture and family photographs on the walls. Keith soon found himself in a cheerful kitchen decorated almost entirely in a black-and-white cow motif. *How sickeningly cute*, he thought with mild amusement. But then he figured it was bound to be either that or homemade crafts bearing quaint sayings and loads of cream and mauve lace.

The woman who had greeted them from the porch was taking Blue Willow plates from an oak cupboard. She was overweight, with curly black hair and a sweet, moon-like face. She reminded Keith of pictures he had seen of Elvis Presley's mother, except that her eyes weren't quite as sad. In fact, they twinkled in delight the moment she turned and saw Keith standing there.

"Well, howdy, nephew!" she said cheerfully. She laid the stack of plates on the checkered cloth of the long kitchen table and headed toward him. The image of a charging rhino flashed through Keith's mind as she came closer. A moment later, she had him in an affectionate bear-hug that threatened to smother the breath plumb out of him.

"You remember your Aunt Susan, don't you?"

"Uh, sure," said Keith, his face nearly plastered against the woman's ample bosom. For a second all he could see was the front of her flower print dress and the white cotton straps of the apron she wore over it. She smelled cloyingly of Avon perfume and baby powder.

"My, my! I haven't seen you in a coon's age, Keith," said Susan McLeod, pulling away from her nephew. She stepped back and took a good, long look at him. "And don't you look sharp, too!"

"Thanks," was all that Keith said. He stood there for a moment, feeling a little disoriented by his aunt's show of affection. He couldn't figure out why she was so happy to see him. He hadn't seen her in a couple of years and he sure didn't feel the same toward her.

She stepped over and hugged Grandpa McLeod the same way. He smiled and patted her on the back, seeming more accustomed to her smothering embrace than Keith was.

"How're you doing today, Papa?" she asked.

"Fit as a fiddle," he declared. "Missed you at church, didn't we?"

Susan nodded. "Me and Rusty went for Sunday school, but we left before preaching, on account I had a mess of cooking to do. How was the sermon?"

"Boring," volunteered Keith, back to his old self again.

Jasper shot him a look of disapproval. "Oh, it was okay. It was Pastor Wilkes' specialty, of course. Fire and brimstone, with a dash of brotherly love thrown in for good measure."

The woman nodded in understanding. "He can tend to be a little repetitive. As I recall, he preached the same lesson Sunday before last."

"Where's that other grandson of mine?" asked Jasper.

"Here I am, you ol' stump turtle!" came a voice from the direction of the hallway.

Keith turned and regarded his cousin. Rusty McLeod was a good six inches taller than he was, but leaner and lankier. He had a bushy head of orange red hair, dark freckles on his face and bare shoulders, and bright blue eyes. He was fastening the straps of a pair of faded Duckhead overalls that looked as if they bore a variety of different stains; grass, mud, motor oil, and maybe even a few drops of blood, perhaps from a scratch or scrape. And, to top it all off, he was barefooted.

What a rube, Keith thought to himself.

Jasper McLeod laughed and soon had the red-headed boy in a playful headlock. Rusty giggled and tried to break the hold, without luck. "Old stump turtle, eh?" asked the old man. "Grizzly bear is more like it!"

"Okay, I give up!" yelled Rusty as the old man rubbed his knuckles across the boy's scalp. "Let me loose before you wear the hide plumb off my skull!"

Keith watched the horseplay between the two and, for a second, found himself feeling just a tad jealous, although he had no idea why he should.

"You two cut out your monkeyshines now," said Susan, setting a steaming bowl of creamed corn on the table. "You end up knocking all this food in the floor and both your hides will be nailed to the barn door out yonder."

"We'd best straighten up," said Jasper, looking a little out of breath. "Your ma is a notorious hide-nailer, you know."

Rusty stood up straight and rubbed his sore head. "That's right. And Daddy's even worse, when he's here to do the nailing." The boy turned and grinned at Keith. He extended a friendly hand. "Put 'er there, cousin," he said.

Keith shook Rusty's hand and tightened his grip a little. "Howdy, Hiram," he said with a smile of his own.

Rusty didn't flinch, however. He increased his pressure, until both boys had to withdraw their hands at the same time. "Hiram?" said Rusty, letting out a mule bray of a laugh. "That's hilarious. You're a right funny boy, cousin."

"My name's Keith," said the 12-year-old. "Not cousin."

"Uh, right," said Rusty, his grin still firmly in place. "Keith."

"You gentlemen sit yourselves down and we'll say grace," said Susan, pouring iced tea into jell jar glasses.

"Who?" asked Keith.

"Grace means a prayer," said Jasper. "Not somebody."

Keith nodded. "I knew that."

They all sat down and joined hands, then Jasper McLeod said a short prayer. During the blessing, Keith and Rusty increased the pressure of their interlocked fingers, testing each other's strength and endurance until both suffered white knuckles and grimaces of pain. When their grandfather said "Amen!", the contest came to an abrupt end. They boys traded challenging glances. They called it a tie, if only temporarily.

A moment later, they were helping themselves to the feast laid out on the table. Keith took a couple of pieces of fried chicken and a yeast roll and set them on his plate.

Susan held a bowl toward him. "How about some butter beans? They're fresh from the garden."

Keith shook his head. "Uh, I don't like butter beans."

"Then try some of this sweet tater casserole here," offered Rusty.

"I don't like that either," said the boy.

"You ever ate it before?' asked his cousin.

"Nope."

"Then how do you know whether you like it or not?" Rusty snickered and scooped out a heaping spoonful of the casserole. "Here, just try it. Mama makes it with brown sugar and marshmallows melted on top."

Rusty was swinging the spoonful Keith's way, when the boy suddenly pulled his plate away. The heap of syrupy yams ended up landing on the checkered tablecloth instead of on patterned china.

"I said I don't like it," said Keith, giving his cousin a warning look.

"For goodness sakes, Rusty," said Susan with a laugh. "If Keith don't like sweet potatoes, then that's all right. Nobody's making him eat them." She smiled at her nephew from across the table. "How about some of this creamed corn?"

"Betcha a nickel he don't like that either," said Rusty.

Keith hated corn, but he wasn't about to let Rusty get the better of him. "To tell the truth, I *love* creamed corn," he boasted. Then he spooned several servings onto his plate, just out of spite.

A half hour later, dinner was finished. Jasper and Rusty sat back in their chairs, patting their swollen bellies. "That sure was good, daughter-in-law," said the old man. "I pity Frank being on the road so much. I'm sure he misses your home-cooking something fierce."

"You really outdid yourself this time, Ma," said Rusty. He unleashed a belch that sounded like the croak of a bullfrog, then smiled sheepishly. "Pardon me."

Susan seemed pleased by the compliments. "Did you enjoy yourself, Keith?' she asked her guest.

"Uh, yeah," said Keith, trying not to show just how much he had enjoyed the meal.

"It was okay."

"Well, ya'll let your food settle a while," she said, getting up and starting to clear the table. "Because later we're gonna have homemade ice cream."

"Why don't you just get it at the store?' asked Keith. He couldn't comprehend why someone would go to the trouble of making ice cream when they could simply buy it.

"Aw, homemade is a thousand times better'n store-bought," said Rusty. "Besides, there ain't no place to buy it at. All the stores are closed in Harmony on Sunday."

"You're kidding me," said Keith.

"No, he's right," explained his grandfather. "Folks around here treat Sunday like a day of rest. And that means no shopping and such. Just sitting on the porch and taking it easy."

Cripes! thought Keith. *I am in Mayberry.*

"I'm gonna help Susan clean up here," said Jasper. "Rusty, why don't you give Keith a tour of the farm?"

Rusty grinned mischievously. "Yeah, I think I'll do just that." He stood up from the table. "Come on and I'll show you around."

"Lead the way, Goober," said Keith.

Rusty didn't laugh that time. He simply smiled. "Yeah, you're a right funny fella, that's for sure."

Then, together, they left through the back door, letting the screen slap loudly behind them.

"This here is the barn," said Rusty.

"Well, I sure didn't think it was the outhouse," replied Keith. The tour of the McLeod farm was beginning to bore him. He had already been shown the chicken coop, hog pin, smokehouse, and the 50-foot silo. The barn was just as unimpressive. It looked about the same as the inside of his grandfather's did. The interior was dark, musty with the smell of hay chaff and dried manure. There were several stalls to one side of the barn, all empty. Their occupants were more than likely standing in the pasture out back of the big structure. The other side sported a long workbench cluttered with woodworking and mechanic's tools. Overhead was a partial hayloft bearing stacks of bales held together with binder's twine.

"Well, what do you think?' asked Rusty, throwing his arms wide with pride.

"You seen one barn, you've seen 'em all, Mortimer," said Keith.

Rusty's smile lost some of its friendlessness. "Anyway, me and some of my friends play here a lot," he told his cousin. "Sometimes, when there's a haystack here in the floor, we climb to the loft and swing down by that rope hanging up yonder. Other times we just play cowboys and Indians. You like to play cowboys and Indians, Keith?"

"I used to play cops and robbers," said his cousin. "I kind of outgrew it, though. But then, I suppose that's about all you hicks have to do around here, isn't it, Bubba?"

Rusty's smile faded completely. "You know, I'm getting sick and tired of that."

"Tired of what?" asked Keith.

"Them names you keep calling me," said the farm boy. "You know, Hiram and Goober and Bubba."

"I guess I was just mistaking you for someone else," said Keith.

"And another thing. It wasn't polite you putting down my mama's cooking like that. It was downright disrespectful. She put a lot of time and effort into fixing something special for you and you just about thumbed your nose at her."

"Hey, man, I wasn't dissing your old lady," Keith told him. "It's just that my digestive system is a little more attuned to filet mignon and lobster, then grits, redeye gravy and possum meat."

Rusty's eyes sparked with anger. "You know what you are, cousin? You're a dadblamed smart-ass, that's what. I should've known you'd turn out to be one. A lot of city folks are like that."

"So what?" challenged Keith, stepping forward. "You aiming to do anything about it?"

"Yep," said Rusty, walking up lazily. "I figure you're just begging for an attitude adjustment."

"Attitude adjustment?" said Keith with a look of mock surprise on his face. "That's some mighty big words for you, isn't it, Gomer? Maybe you ought to stick to simpler ones...like Dick and Jane, dog and cat."

"We'll see how funny you are with a black eye and shy a few teeth," said Rusty coming nearer.

"In your case, it'd be an improvement," returned Keith. He raised his fists and prepared to teach the country boy a lesson. One of the major disciplinary problems Keith had racked up on his school record was fighting. He preferred to cut down his classmates with insults and wit, but he wasn't above using his fists. His Uncle Richard in Boston had taught him the fine art of boxing and he was pleased to say he was pretty darned good at it.

Rusty broke into a big grin and shock his head. "You gotta be kidding."

"Come on and I'll show you who's kidding," said Keith. He ducked his head a little and brought his fists to shoulder level, the right to punch and the left to block.

Rusty laughed that goofy laugh of his. Enraged, Keith took a couple of steps forward and sent a jab straight at his cousin's face. But the blow didn't connect. Rusty bobbed his head easily to the left. Then, with one lanky leg, he kicked Keith's feet out from under him. Keith lost his balance and fell to the dusty barn floor, flat on his back.

"Aw, you're a real pro," said Rusty with a snicker.

Keith caught his breath and slowly got to his feet. He bushed off his clothes then glared at the boy who had tripped him.

"Looks like you got some cow manure on the back of that fancy shirt there," pointed out Rusty.

"You son of a bitch!" growled Keith, starting forward.

"It ain't nice cussing on Sunday," laughed Rusty taking a step backward.

Keith closed in and concentrated on the grinning face before him. He already knew what his cousin's next move would be. When he jabbed with his right, Rusty would pull the same dodge and swing his head to the left again. But Keith wasn't going to let him get away with it twice. This time, he faked a right jab and, when Rusty made his move, delivered a solid left hook. His fist connected with Rusty's nose. The skinny boy in the overalls flailed backward and landed on his butt on the ground.

"How'd you like that, bean-picker?" asked Keith with satisfaction.

Rusty put a hand to his nose and found blood flowing from his nostrils. "Damn. I reckon I misjudged you a bit." Then he stood up and grinned. "But that don't change nothing."

The two boys squared off. When Keith came in again, Rusty was prepared. He blocked an overhand right, delivering a solid punch to his cousin's stomach. Keith doubled over with a groan and Rusty followed up with a jab to his face. The farm boy's knuckles crashed into Keith's lower lip.

Keith staggered back and touched his mouth. His lip was already swelling. Angrily, he threw himself at Rusty. In response, Rusty let out a rebel yell and did the same. The force of the impact knocked both boys off their feet. Soon, they were rolling across the dusty barn floor, kicking and punching, scratching and gouging.

They had been going at it maybe 30 seconds, when they met an obstruction and their rolling brawl came to an abrupt halt. Puzzled, the two looked at each other then stared upward.

Their grandfather stood over them, looking none too pleased.

"I do declare!" snapped Jasper McLeod. He reached down and, with little effort at all, snatched the two boys up by their arms. "Cousins at it, tooth and nail...and on the Sabbath besides!"

The two boys looked at one another again, this time trading a mutual understanding. "Uh, we weren't really fighting, Grandpa," said Rusty.

"Oh, yeah? Well what would you call it then?"

"We were just wrestling around a little," said Keith.

"Yeah," said Rusty. "Just wrestling. Maybe it got out of hand, but that's all it was. Wrestling."

Jasper stared at the two boys, his anger settling a little. "Okay then. But ya'll listen up. Any more wrestling of the kind I just saw and both of you will have your turn with me in the woodshed. You understand?"

"Yes, sir," piped Rusty respectfully.

Keith hated to say it, but knew he had no other choice. "Yes, sir."

The two boys dusted themselves off and turned toward the barn door. Susan McLeod stood there with her flabby arms crossed, her eyes dark and accusing. Back in the kitchen she had looked as if she didn't possess an unkind bone in her body. But now she looked as though she could bit through iron chains and snap 2-by-4s in half with her bare hands.

"Rusty," she said sternly. "Get to your room and don't come out for the rest of the afternoon."

"But Ma—" he began to protest.

"I don't wanna hear it," she told him. "Now do as I say."

Rusty shot an almost apologetic glance at Keith. In turn, Keith simply shrugged his shoulders. With his head hanging low, Rusty ambled toward the barn doorway. As he passed, his mother gave him a sharp swat on the seat of his britches. It picked up his pace a bit and it wasn't long before they heard the slamming of the back door.

"Keith," said Susan, just before she turned and left. "I'm very disappointed in you."

The 12-year-old stood there and swallowed nervously. He didn't know exactly why, but her words embarrassed him. He couldn't figure out why he really cared one way or the other, but he did.

"You oughta be ashamed acting like that, and you a guest at your aunt's house!" said Jasper, his face ruddy with anger. "I was a little careful about saying anything yesterday, but I ain't now. I'm not gonna tolerate any more of your lip, boy. You might be able to brow-beat your mama and daddy back home, but I'm your grandpa and while you're in my care, you'll do as you're told and not backtalk me. Do I make myself clear?"

Keith felt none of the confidence he had felt the day before. Apparently, his fight with Rusty had taken some of the arrogance out of him. "Uh, yeah," he mumbled.

Jasper glared at him sharply. "What was that?"

"Yes, sir," replied the boy, unable to meet his grandfather's eyes.

"Good," said the old man, looking a little weary. "Now, you go on out to the truck and wait for me. I'm gonna say goodbye to Susan, then we're heading home."

Keith nodded, then started for the barn door. *I guess that means homemade ice cream is out of the question*, he thought. But he didn't say it out loud. He didn't dare, not in front of Grandpa McLeod.

When he reached the truck, he sat and looked out the bug-speckled windshield. On the second floor of the farmhouse, Rusty stood in his bedroom window, looking down at him. He was dabbing at his nose with a piece of toilet paper. When he pulled the bloody tissue away, he grinned lopsidedly and shook his head.

Keith touched his lower lip. It was swollen to about twice its normal size. He also felt a few scrapes and bruises that he hadn't noticed until now. Still, he couldn't help but smile.

Despite their differences, he knew that he had developed a grudging respect for his cousin. And, judging from the look on Rusty's battered face, Keith could tell that he felt the same about him as well.

CHAPTER SEVEN

The next morning, Keith walked the mile of rural back road that stretched between his grandfather's farm and that of his Uncle Frank. When he arrived at the farmhouse around 9:00, he found himself a little winded. He was accustomed to walking the streets of Atlanta, at least those in the vicinity of his own neighborhood. Walking in the country was different, however. There were no traffic lights or street signs to mark your progress. You just set your sights on a distant hill or a far away grove of trees and headed for it. Also, he wasn't all that used to walking on clay dirt or soft grass. Hard concrete and asphalt was all he had traveled on for as long as he could remember.

He saw his Aunt Susan standing in the backyard, hanging sheets and pillowcases on a clothesline with wooden pins. When she spotted Keith coming up the drive, she smiled cheerfully. The boy could detect none of the anger and disappointment that she had shown yesterday afternoon. Oddly enough, she seemed as good-natured and happy as she had the first time he had met her.

"How are you doing this morning, Keith?' she asked her nephew.

"Okay, I guess," he replied. That wasn't entirely true. Keith hadn't gotten much sleep last night. For some strange reason, his behavior of the day before, both at the dinner table and in the barn, had nagged at him, preventing him from falling to sleep. That was part of the reason he had made the long trek to the McLeod farm that morning.

"Uh, Aunt Susan?" he began uncomfortably.

The woman smiled at him. "Yes, sweetie?"

"I just wanted to say I'm sorry," he said. "For being such a jerk yesterday. Lunch was good. It really was."

Susan's smile brightened. "Well, now, I'm sure glad you enjoyed it. And don't worry about the other. Your grandpa told me about how you feel about spending the month here. Can't say I really blame you. I'd be peeved if someone was to send me away like that, without giving me much time to get used to the idea."

"Really?" Keith was surprised that his aunt actually understood what he was going through.

"Why, certainly," she said as she finished one basket load and started hanging another.

"But you know something? I don't think it'll be much longer before you forget what you're mad about. You'll get to enjoying yourself and, by the time the summer's over with, you'll be dreading the trip back home."

Keith shrugged. "Maybe." But he doubted it.

He looked around the yard. "Is Rusty here?"

"He's upstairs, cleaning his room," she said. "You can go on up and see him if you want. It's upstairs, last door to your left."

Keith stood there for a moment longer, watching the woman pin bed linens on the heavy cotton line. "Tell me something, Aunt Susan?"

"What's that, dear?"

"Why are you hanging your clothes out here? Don't you have a dryer?"

Susan laughed. "I surely do. But things just seem to smell better if you hang them out in the fresh air."

"Oh." Keith shook his head and started for the back door of the house. If you tried that in the middle of Atlanta, you would likely discover your wash covered with bird droppings and spray-paint graffiti, and smelling like car exhaust fumes.

A minute later, he was on the second floor of the farmhouse, heading down the hallway for Rusty's bedroom. The entire house smelled of potpourri and cinnamon. The aroma was alien to the 12-year-old, but far from unpleasant.

"Rusty?" he called as he neared the end of the hall.

Abruptly, his cousin bounded into the hallway and aimed a slingshot at him; the kind made of crooked steel and yellow rubber tubing. Keith stopped dead still, startled by the contraption that was aimed his way. From where he stood, he could see that Rusty held a ball bearing in the cradle of the sling. If he were to let go at such a close range, the projectile could end up hurting him bad, or even worse.

But, an instant later, Rusty relaxed his grip. He lowered the slingshot, his eyebrows cocked. "Oh, its you."

"Yeah," said Keith, breathing a sigh of relief. "Couldn't beat me at wrestling, so now you're figuring to put out my eye with that thing, huh?"

Rusty laughed. "No fighting today. That's why Ma's got me working the chain-gang this morning." He nodded toward the door he had emerged from. "Come on. I'll show you my room."

Keith followed his cousin inside. The room was decorated with a simple oak bed, desk, and six-drawer bureau. The floor was cluttered with dirty clothes, comic books, and all manner of junk. The bedspread and curtains were tan and bore images of cowboys riding bucking broncos and roping unruly calves.

"Love your décor," said Keith with a chuckle. "Bet you have pajamas like this, too."

Rusty's oversized ears bloomed bright red with embarrassment. "Aw, I've had this stuff since I was a kid. Ma's gonna buy me something different this Christmas."

Keith realized that he had embarrassed his cousin and, for once, he found that he derived no pleasure from the put-down. "Don't sweat it," he said. "I was just picking at you."

Rusty tossed his slingshot on the desk and grinned. "Well, at least you ain't called me Hiram...yet."

Keith walked over and took a look at the walls of Rusty's room. They were decorated with posters of John Wayne as Rooster Cogburn and Clint Eastwood as the Man With No Name, as well as reproductions of famous wanted posters, offering cash bounties for Jesse James and Billy the Kid. On the desk sat a row of westerns by Louis Lamour and Zane Grey, held together by six-shooter bookends.

"Really into this cowboy stuff, aren't you?" he asked.

Rusty shrugged. "I reckon so. But I'm most interested in gunfighters and U.S. marshals and such as that. Grandpa says I should've been born back in the days of the Old West, I like that kind of stuff so much." The farm boy eyed his cousin. "You into anything like that?"

Keith thought for a moment. "Yeah, I'm into police and detective stuff. You know, private-eyes and gangsters and hard-boiled cops."

The lanky boy with the fiery red hair grinned appreciatively. "You see? We ain't that different after all. Our interests are kind of the same, except you like that crime stuff and I like the West."

"Yeah. I guess you're right."

Rusty began to pick the clutter from off the floor. "You know, if you help me clean up this place, we can get outta here and do some stuff."

"What kind of stuff?" asked Keith curiously.

"Help me pick up this mess and I'll show you."

They worked on the room for another 15 minutes. When Rusty was satisfied that it would pass inspection, he and Keith scrambled downstairs and shot through the kitchen. Susan McLeod had finished her laundry and was washing the breakfast dishes in the sink.

"Ya'll hold up a minute," she called out before they could reach the back door. "Did you finish your room, Rusty?"

"Yes, ma'am," he said. "All squared away."

"Where are you boys going in such a hurry?"

"Thought I'd take Keith over to Chuck's house for a while," said her son.

Susan nodded. "All right. Get back by 12:00 and I'll have tuna fish sandwiches and tater chips ready...and that apple pie I cooked early this morning for dessert."

"Then we'll be back by high noon," said Rusty with a grin. "Right, pardner?"

Keith nodded. "Right, Kemosabe."

A second later they were sprinting out the back door and leaping off the porch. Keith let his cousin take the lead, having no earthly idea where they were going. As it turned out, they headed straight for the barn.

"Who's Chuck?" he asked as they made it through the structure's open door and entered the musky, shadowy interior.

"He's a friend of mine," said Rusty. He headed for a stall at the far end of the barn.

"Thought we might ride over there and see him."

"What do you mean 'ride'?"

A moment later, Keith found out. Rusty went to a wall cluttered with leaning boards and farm implements, and returned with a bicycle. The bike was a ten-speed with a bright red frame and dusty rubber tires. There were playing cards stuck in the spokes for making a racket when the wheels spun. Keith thought that was just something kids did in books and movies, but he guessed he was mistaken.

"Got ol' Cyclone here," he said. "Faster than a Texas twister, she is."

"If you expect me to ride on the back of that thing, you're crazy," said Keith.

"Shoot naw!" said Rusty. "I got another one for you, if I can find it."

He searched through one of the rear stalls for a moment, tossing aside old milk cans and mangled parts of kerosene lanterns. "Bingo!" he finally yelled, tugging something free from the clutter.

It took a while for Keith to realize that it was actually a bike. It was an old Schwinn ten-speed that looked a good 10 years older than Rusty's. The frame was rusty and cobwebs clung to the handlebars and the spokes of the wheels. One of the tires was flat while the other looked as if it had been patched a half dozen times.

"Ain't much to look at, but it'll get you where we're going," said Rusty. "A little oil here and there, some air in that tire and we'll be ready to roll."

Rusty fetched an oil can and a hand pump from near his father's workbench, then set to work. Ten minutes later, the bike was in working order. At least that's what Rusty claimed.

The farm boy hopped on his bike and headed for the door. He was almost there when he noticed that his cousin wasn't following. He stopped and looked over his shoulder. Keith was standing there with his hands on the handlebars, studying the older bike with a critical eye.

"Don't worry," Rusty called. "It ain't gonna fall apart on you."

"That isn't it," said Keith.

Rusty turned his bike and rode back to where his cousin stood. "So what's the problem? Don't tell me you don't know how to ride."

"Well, it's been a while," Keith admitted. "I had a bike when we lived in the suburbs, but when we moved uptown, my parents wouldn't let me have one. They were afraid I'd get run over by a bus or something. "

"You know what they say...once you learn you never forget."

"I guess you're right," nodded Keith, although he looked doubtful.

They started out the barn door. Keith was a little shaky and off balance at first. But it didn't take but a few minutes for him to get the hang of it. By the time they reached the road, his confidence had built enough that he was able to keep up with Rusty.

"See?" Rusty told him with a grin. "I told you!"

Together, they headed down the rural stretch of Sycamore Road. Soon, they were riding north, in the direction of town.

A couple miles later, Rusty and Keith stopped to take a breather.

"You hanging in there, cuz?" asked the farm boy.

"Don't worry about me," gasped Keith, catching his breath. "I'm keeping up, aren't I?"

Rusty nodded, breathing just as hard as the other boy. Half of their fatigue was from exertion. The other was due to the heat. It was a little past ten o'clock and already the temperature was well into the mid-90s.

"It's a real scorcher today," he said. "You could roast a pig on a flagpole, it's so blamed hot."

"We should've brought us something to drink," said Keith.

"I could sure go for a cold Nehi right about now," agreed Rusty. "But Hill's store is all the way on the far side of Harmony. We'd pass out from heat stroke before we even got there."

"Maybe your friend Chuck has something cold in his fridge."

"More'n likely." Rusty sat atop his bike and stared thoughtfully at his cousin for a moment. "Tell me something?"

"Sure. What?"

"You don't make a habit of picking fun at crippled people, do you?" asked Rusty quite seriously.

Keith wondered why he was asking such a question, then recalled how much of a smart-ass he had been the day before. Maybe he had good reason to ask, after all.

"No, not really."

"Good. 'Cause if you get a wild hair to when we get to Chuck's, I swear I'll open a can of whup-ass on you that you ain't ever gonna forget."

Keith couldn't understand the nature of the threat. "What are you talking about?"

Rusty's face was solemn. "You'll find out soon enough."

Fifteen minutes later, they were walking their bikes off the sun-baked earth of the road and into the shade of a green yard thick with black walnut trees. When they reached the front porch, they parked their bikes next to the steps, then went up and knocked on the door.

A moment later, a thin, blond-haired lady with glasses appeared at the screen door. "Well, hi there, Rusty," she said.

"Howdy, Mrs. Adkins," replied the boy.

"Who's this you've got with you?"

"Oh, this here's my cousin, Keith, from Atlanta," said Rusty. "He's staying the rest of the summer with Grandpa, on account his folks went on a trip overseas."

The woman smiled. "Well, ain't that nice? I'm sure it'll do your grandfather a world of good, too. He's been awful gloomy since your grandmother passed on, God bless her soul."

"Is Chuck around?" he asked. Keith could tell that Rusty didn't want to discuss their grandmother's death.

He had gotten a little pale in the face when Mrs. Adkins had mentioned it.

"He's back in his room," she said. "I tried to get him to come out on the porch and get some fresh air, but you know him. He's in one of those funky moods of his again." She opened the door. "Ya'll come in. Maybe you can cheer him up a little."

"We'll sure see what we can do," said Rusty. He mustered one of his best good-ol-boy grins, although it looked as if it took some effort on his part.

"You boys look hot," she said. "There's lemonade in the refrigerator and clean glasses in the dish drainer. Ya'll help yourselves if you want."

"Yes, ma'am!" replied Rusty gratefully.

They went to the kitchen and fetched their lemonades. As they were walking down a dim hallway toward the back of the house, Keith stopped him for a moment. "Hey. Exactly what's wrong with this friend of yours? What'd his mom mean by his 'funky mood'?"

Rusty's face grew serious again. "Chuck ain't like other kids. He gets depressed sometimes." A warning look came into the boy's eyes. "Remember what I said before."

"Sure," said Keith, still confused. "I swear, I'll be a perfect gentleman."

A second later, they were standing outside a door with an American flag pinned to the outside with thumbtacks. From the other side, Keith could hear a slow, syrupy melody made up entirely of brass instruments. He turned and looked at his cousin.

"What kind of music is that?" he asked. "I don't think I've ever heard it before."

Rusty frowned. "It's called Big Band. Chuck listens to it all the time."

"Weird," said Keith. "It sure isn't Aerosmith or Guns N' Roses."

"And it sure as spit ain't Hank Williams either," said Rusty. "But don't say nothing about it. Chuck can be kinda touchy sometimes." He reached out and knocked lightly on the door.

There was the click of a boom box being turned off and then a thin, high voice came from the other side of the door. "Yeah? Who is it?"

"Rusty," he said, then added "Reporting for duty."

"Enter," called the boy.

Rusty turned the knob and the two stepped inside.

Chuck Adkins' room was a lot like Rusty's except for one distinguishing factor. Where Rusty's room was decorated entirely in Western memorabilia, Chuck's walls were covered with pictures and posters having to do with war. Or, more precisely, World War II. On one wall there was even a shelf bearing a German helmet with a bullet hole in the crown, a rusty bayonet, and a couple of hand grenades, hopefully defused. Hanging from the ceiling by transparent fishing line were dozens of plastic models: bomber planes, battleships, and Nazi submarines, all painted to the minutest detail.

After he had gotten an eyeful of the room, Keith turned his attention to the boy who lived there. Chuck Adkins sat at his desk, working on a model of a B-17 bomber. The boy was about their age, overweight, with curly black hair and glasses. It was a moment before Keith realized that Chuck wasn't sitting in a normal chair.

Now he knew what Rusty's warning meant. Chuck Adkins was handicapped. He was confined to a wheelchair.

"What're you looking at?" asked the boy. There was a trace of hostility in his shrill voice.

Keith swallowed nervously and took a sip of his lemonade. "Nothing, man. Nothing at all."

Chuck pulled his chair away from the desk and turned toward Rusty. "Who is this rude dude?"

"Aw, he's okay," said Rusty with a big smile on his freckled face. "This is Keith. He's my cousin from Atlanta."

The boy studied Keith for a moment. "Sure didn't think he was from around here," he said. "Dig that crazy haircut he's got."

"Yeah, it's a hoot, ain't it?" laughed Rusty.

Keith ignored the remark and stepped forward. "How's it going?" he asked, extending his hand.

Chuck stared at his hand, then finally took it. Keith found the boy's palm soft and moist. "Okay, I reckon. Of course, today's just like any other day for me."

"Your mom said you were feeling down," said Rusty. "How come?"

"Crap!" said the boy. "Why's everybody fussing over me all the time? Just 'cause I can't walk doesn't mean everybody has to pamper me like some kind of baby." The anger in his tiny eyes suddenly bled away into sadness. "Well, everybody fusses over me, except my dad, that is."

Keith could tell that it pained the boy to even talk about his father, although he couldn't imagine why, unless he was dead or something like that.

Rusty walked over to the desk, as if trying to conjure some other subject to talk about.

"Whatcha putting together here?"

"It's the Memphis Belle," said Chuck. "You know, the Flying Fortress that flew all those bombing missions. Mom got it for me at Walmart yesterday."

"Looks pretty rad," said Keith.

Chuck frowned. "What'd he say?"

"Some kinda city lingo, I think," replied Rusty.

Keith pointed to the shelf of collectibles. "Is that stuff for real?"

Chuck seemed to relax his guard a bit. "Yep. My Grandpa Adkins was in World War II. Stormed Normandy Beach with General Eisenhower's troops. He brought that stuff back with him. The helmet belonged to a real Nazi soldier that he killed himself."

"Wild," said Keith, impressed.

"Got something else of his, too," said Chuck. He opened one of the desk drawers and brought out a black velvet case. "It's his medals. A purple heart and a bronze star."

When Chuck took out the ribbons and displayed them on the desktop, Keith stared at them reverently. "Man, I don't think I've ever seen real medals before."

"My grandpa was a great guy," said the handicapped boy. "Told me all kinds of stories about the War when I was little. He died when I was seven." He looked a little sad. "You know, you guys are lucky you still have your grandfather around."

"You got that right," said Rusty.

Keith simply nodded. He didn't know exactly what to say about a man he hardly even knew.

Abruptly, a streak of green motion shot across the desk. Keith cried out and stepped back, startled. He watched as a green lizard scrambled up Chuck's arm and perched on his right shoulder. "What the hell is that?" he asked.

Chuck's stoic expression vanished and he laughed. "This here's my pet iguana," he explained. "His name is Churchill."

"After the fat English dude with the cigar," said Keith.

The boy was surprised. "Right. You know much about World War II history?"

"Just what I've picked up in school. I'm more into stuff like John Dillinger and Al Capone."

They visited with the boy for a while, then left Chuck to finish his model. Both Rusty and Keith felt as if they had helped lift Chuck's spirits a little. But, once outside the house, Rusty claimed that it wouldn't last for long. Soon Chuck would start thinking about his limitations again and his depression would be back in full swing.

They were on their bikes and heading back down Sycamore Road, when Keith asked a question that had been on his mind since meeting Chuck. "Tell me something? What happened to your friend back there? How'd he end up in that wheelchair?'

Rusty thought about it for a second. "He had an accident when he was 10," he finally said. "Went duck hunting with his daddy over at Willow Lake. They were going to a blind hidden in a clump of trees. Chuck climbed over a barbwire fence. His daddy was carrying a twelve-gauge shotgun when he was swinging over and he lost his balance. The gun went off and the shot hit Chuck in the small of the back."

Keith grimaced. "No kidding!"

"Yeah," agreed Rusty. "Scared his poor daddy half to death. He had to walk a couple of miles through the woods with Chuck bleeding all over him. We thought Chuck was going to die for a while. But the folks up at Vanderbilt Hospital in Nashville did surgery on him and he pulled through. But the gunshot severed his spinal cord. He's pretty much dead from the waist down."

"Ain't that a bitch," said Keith. "There's nothing they can do for him?"

"Nope. Ol' Chuck will be stuck in that damned chair for the rest of his life," said Rusty. "The worst of it ain't his injury, though. It's the way his old man acts toward him now."

"What do you mean?"

"Well, he just kinda ignores Chuck. Acts like he's not even there half the time."

Keith frowned. "How come?"

Rusty shrugged his freckled shoulders. "Who knows?" He glanced over at Keith. "What time have you got on that fancy watch of yours, cuz?"

Keith looked down at his diver's watch. "About twenty minutes till noon."

"If we lay the pedal to the metal, we might just make it home for them tuna sandwiches and that apple pie. I'm hungry enough to eat a Black Angus bull, horns, balls and all!"

"Well, I'm hungry, but not *that* hungry," said Keith with a laugh.

As the two boys sped down the rural road, leaving clouds of powdery clay dust in their wake, Keith thought about Chuck Adkins. He couldn't imagine how the boy could stand being confined to that wheelchair, unable to do all the things that normal kids could. He pictured the boy sitting in his curtained room, putting together his models, his only constant companion being his pet lizard. No wonder he was so down all the time. Keith didn't think he could stand it if he were to ever suffer the same fate.

He thought about it as he strained to keep pace with his cousin. Keith had come to Harmony pissed off at the world and feeling sorry for himself. But now he realized that he had absolutely nothing to complain about. In comparison to what Chuck Adkins had to endure from day to day, he had nothing to complain about at all.

CHAPTER EIGHT

Allison Walsh opened her eyes.

For a long time she had thought that she was dead. She should have been, considering what she had been through.

Then, slowly, her unconsciousness began to lift. The turbulent darkness of her dreams began to thin and she sensed a source of light to her distant left. Her eyes focused and found that it was a standing lamp in the far corner of the room.

But what room? It certainly wasn't the one she had come to know so well during her ordeal. The room that had seemed like Hell.

She groaned and tried to sit up. She was lying in a soft bed covered with white linen and blankets. As she moved her left arm, Allison discovered that something was tugging against her inner forearm. Hazily, she looked down and found that the needle of an IV was anchored beneath her skin midway between wrist and elbow, held firmly into place with surgical tape. Confused, she glanced over and saw a metal stand with a plastic IV bag hanging from its hook. The fluid inside the bag was as clear as water.

"Oh God," she muttered. "What's wrong? What happened?"

But she knew what had happened. Abruptly, her mind cleared and the terror came rushing back into her. Adrenalin pumped through her veins as that leering face with the ugly, serpentine eyes leaped into her thoughts. The face of a hitchhiker named Slash.

She opened her mouth and screamed.

The next few moments were full of shrill horror and confusion. She remembered clawing at her face and the material of her hospital, and wrestling with two nurses and a doctor who rushed to her bedside. Then one of the nurses injected something into the IV and Allison felt her terror begin to dissolve. That grinning face she now associated with torment and humiliation slowly began to fade. Eventually, it vanished completely. But she knew it was still there, hiding somewhere in the back of her mind, waiting to emerge again when she least expected it.

The tension drained from her body and, with a whimper, she sagged back against the raised mattress of the hospital bed. She cried softly. Through her tears she saw a tall black man take a handkerchief from the front pocket of his white smock. Tenderly, he dried her eyes.

"Ms. Walsh," he said quietly. "I'm Doctor Alan Matthews. I'm attending to your case."

"Where am I?" she asked feebly. She felt as if all the strength was slowly draining from her body. It must have been one strong sedative they had just given her.

"You are at University Medical Center in Rome, Georgia," he said.

"How did I get here?"

"A couple of kids found you while they were out playing," said Matthews. "From what I hear, you gave them quite a scare."

Allison had difficulty focusing her thoughts. "I remember an old house."

The doctor nodded. "Near Adairsville. That's where he took you."

Suddenly, the fear was back. She sat up stiffly. "Where is he now?"

Matthews gently pushed her back to a prone position. "Far from here, I would guess. I just hope the police track down the son of a bitch." He paused for a moment. "He was a sadistic bastard, wasn't he?"

Allison didn't have to concentrate to remember. It all came back to her; the countless rapes, the torture, the beatings. She closed her eyes and saw him standing before her, naked in candlelight. He was sharpening the blade of the folding knife against the gray rectangle of the whetstone. The gold cross pin, still inverted, pierced his left nipple. Allison's blood marked his face and body like Indian war paint.

She jerked her eyes open and the doctor came back into view, studying her with concern.

"Yes," she said hoarsely. "He was." Her body felt sore and heavy, used up. "Exactly what did he do to me?" she wanted to know.

Matthews hesitated. "I'd prefer to go into that when you're better rested and a little stronger."

"No," she said firmly. "Tell me now."

The doctor looked at one of the nurses who had remained, then turned uncomfortable eyes back to his patient. "Frankly, you've suffered more than any human being should be able to tolerate," he told her. "You've been sexually assaulted multiple times, beaten brutally about the face and abdomen, and subjected to numerous acts of mutilation."

"Yes," she whispered. "I remember." She pressed a hand to her chest and found a thick bandage covering her from her collarbone to just below her breasts. "He carved something in my chest. A word."

The doctor nodded silently. There was rage in his dark eyes.

Do it to me again, bitch! Do it to me good or I'll make you scream!

Tears began to well in Allison's eyes. "Now I know." She shifted her position in the bed and felt a twinge of agony sear her pubic area. "It hurts down there."

"He burnt you severely," said Dr. Matthews. "With a cigarette."

Allison nodded. The tears began to roll down her bruised face, but she uttered no sound.

Matthews patted her gently on the hand. "You rest up and try not to think about what happened. It's over. It's time to heal now."

As the doctor started toward the door, she called out. "What day is this?"

"It's Monday night," he replied.

"He abducted me on Thursday," she said, stunned.

"What he did to you took several days," said Matthews. "Even after he left, you were out there by yourself for a while. Now, please, try to put it out of your mind and rest." He gave her a smile of reassurance, then turned off the light and left her in partial darkness.

Allison laid in the sterile comfort of her bed and cried. The sedative began to take a firmer hold, turning her arms and legs heavy, as well as her eyelids. But she fought against closing her eyes. Every time she did, *he* came back to haunt her.

Look, Allison. Look at it bleed. Red is my favorite color, you know. And blood is as red as it can get.

"You bastard," she whispered. "Why did you pick me of all people?"

The face simply grinned cruelly and laughed. She remembered that godawful laugh. She was certain that she would never forget it.

Allison laid there for a time, her body slowly giving in to the sedative. She fought to stay awake, however. There was something else she needed to think about. Something she needed to deal with. Something she had needed to deal with for a very long time... years before she had known a sicko like Slash Jackson even existed.

She closed her eyes again. A face came into view, but it was not that of her most recent tormentor. Rather, it was the face of a devil from thirty years ago. A face she both loved and hated at the same time.

Put it in your mouth, Allie. Do it nice or I'll kill your mother. I swear to God I will.

The voice was similar to Jackson's, but it was more familiar—the voice of a loved one.

That's what made it so horrible. So very shameful.

Allison sobbed quietly. She could still feel his hands on the back of her head, pressing her downward. She could still smell him—*taste* him—just as she could still taste Jackson.

"Oh, Dad," she whimpered. "Why?"

She had been five-years-old then. He had done it to her only that once, but that had been enough. She had told no one about what had happened. She had been afraid, both for herself and her mother. She had locked the incident away inside her somewhere, all the pain and anguish and humiliation. When she had become a teenager, Allison had rebelled against her father's authority, although she never understood why. It wasn't until Slash Jackson had assaulted her in the very same manner that the wall gave way and it all came flooding back.

Allison lay there and wondered why her father had never attempted to molest her again. Perhaps he was scared to do it a second time. Or perhaps he had just wanted to know how it felt.

Slowly, the sedative won against her tormented thoughts. The images grew fuzzy and distorted. But before she drifted off, Allison promised herself something. Something she wished she had promised herself 30 years ago.

He won't get away with it this time. I swear to God he won't.

Then, an instant later, she was completely under. And this time, fortunately, she did not dream.

CHAPTER NINE

The day following their visit to Chuck Adkins' house, Keith and Rusty worked most of the morning and afternoon on the old Schwinn. They sanded the rust of the frame away with fine-grit emery paper, then painted it a glossy electric blue with spray paint they found on a shelf above the workbench. Next they polished the handlebars and spokes until they gleamed like new chrome. There wasn't much to be done for the tires and they had no money to buy new ones, so they simply scrubbed them the best they could and applied a generous coat of Armor-All to make them shine. Keith christened the bike Blue Fury, then the two set out on the dusty backroads once again.

By three in the afternoon, the heat of the blazing August sun got the better of them. They had brought along a canteen of cherry Kool-Aid this time, but it was gone before they knew it.

"Man, it's hotter today than it was yesterday," complained Keith. He pulled at the front of his Braves shirt. It was so drenched with sweat that it clung to his chest and back like a second skin.

Rusty wiped sweat from his forehead with a red bandanna he carried in the hip pocket of his overalls. He looked toward a heavy thicket at the side of the road and grinned. "I know how we can beat it," he said. "Let's park our bikes under that maple tree yonder and I'll show you."

As they left their bikes next to the shade tree, Keith looked worried. "Aren't you afraid someone might swipe them?"

Rusty laughed. "Here in Harmony? Folks would just soon jump in front of a tractor-trailer truck than steal another man's property. And they'd likely be hung up by their thumbs in town square if they were to try. Besides, who in tarnation would want to rip off these old junkers?"

"Yeah, I guess so," said Keith. He cast one last glance at Blue Fury before following his cousin through the tangle of milkweed, honeysuckle vine, and pink-headed thistle.

Once they were past the brush, the ground began to angle toward a shady hollow thick with weeping willow trees. Keith paused for a moment. "Do I hear water?"

"Right as rain," declared Rusty, unbuckling a strap of his overalls. "Goose Creek is just below us. And it's got the coolest water this side of Hawkshaw County."

"But we didn't bring any swimming trunks," said Keith.

Rusty snorted. "You are right citified, ain't you? Around these parts, kids don't need trunks. You just shuck off your clothes and jump in buck naked."

It wasn't long before they were standing on a bank above the languid channel of Goose Creek. Crystal-clear spring water trickled over smooth stones 30 feet to the south, then bled into a widening pool. "This is the deepest point here," said Rusty. He unbuttoned the other strap and let the overalls fall around his ankles. "It's a good 15-feet-deep in one spot. But watch out for turtles and crawdads, though. They'll latch onto your pecker quicker than lightning and it'll take a hammer and wire pliers to get 'em loose."

Keith stared at his cousin skeptically. "You're pulling my leg, right?"

Rusty simply laughed, shucked off his white Fruit-of-the-Looms, and dove in, head first.

He stayed down for a couple seconds then bobbed to the surface. "Lordy Mercy, this feels good!" He parted his red bangs, which were plastered damply across his eyes. "Well, what're you waiting for, cuz? Strip down and come on in. Or are you embarrassed to show yourself? Maybe the Almighty neglected to bless you with the same sized pump handle I've got."

"My pump handle's long enough, thank you," said Keith. He pulled off his shirt and kicked off his Nikes. "Matter of fact, Tarzan could swing through the jungle on mine, if he couldn't find himself a grapevine."

Rusty unleashed a bray of laughter. "Give me a break!"

Soon, Keith was unclothed. He took a couple of steps back then launched himself toward the middle of the pool. He hit the water a second later and it was so cold it nearly knocked the wind plumb out of him. Goosebumps prickled his bare flesh and, with a splash, he broke the surface. "Now that's what heaven's like!" he yelled out.

"I was afraid maybe you didn't know how to swim," said Rusty. "Expected you to end up on the bottom with the minnows."

"Fooled you, didn't I?" Keith spun, head over heels, then emerged once again. "I do a lot of swimming at the health club where my dad's a member. They have a big, Olympic-sized pool."

"I'll take Goose Creek any ol' day," said Rusty. "Besides, you can't do *this* in a swimming pool." An expression of blissful relief crossed the boy's face. "Ahhh!"

Keith felt the water grow a little warmer near his knees. "That's gross!" he bellowed, swimming away from the vicinity of his cousin.

"When nature calls, I answer," said Rusty with a big grin.

They had swam the length and breadth of the swimming hole, when a voice suddenly came from the direction of the bank. "Looks like ya'll are having fun."

Keith whirled in the water, startled. Startled not because someone was there, but because that someone was a girl.

Rusty swam in closer to his cousin. "Oh, I forgot to tell you I've got another friend I've been meaning to introduce," he said. "This here's Margret Sutton. But we just call her Maggie."

Keith swallowed nervously and stared up at the girl on the bank. She was short and lean and tanned, and had long honey blond hair pulled back into a ponytail. She wore denim cut-offs, a red top tied into a knot just above her bellybutton, and blue rubber flip-flops. It was her eyes that held Keith motionless in the water. They were emerald green, the prettiest shade that the city boy had ever seen in his life.

"Howdy, Rusty," she called, smiling brightly. "Who's your friend there?"

"This here's Cousin Keith from Atlanta, GA," said Rusty.

Maggie's smile widened a bit. "Hi, Keith."

Keith felt his heart quicken. "Uh, hi."

"I saw your bikes out by the road and figured you were down here skinny-dipping," she said. "Mind if I join ya'll?"

"Help yourself," said Rusty, seemingly unperturbed.

A jolt of panic shot through Keith. He turned toward his cousin. "Are you nuts?" he whispered. "We're *naked*!"

Rusty shrugged, his shoulders bobbing above the water. "So? She'll be just as raw as we are in a minute."

Keith looked back toward the bank. Maggie had already kicked off her sandals and was about to untie the knot of her top. "Ya'll turn around now," she said. "And stay that way till I'm in."

Both Keith and Rusty turned and faced the far side of the creek. "Don't fret so much," said Rusty. "Maggie's just an ol' tomboy. It'll be like swimming with another guy."

"Yeah, sure," said Keith doubtfully.

They waited until they heard a huge splash. When they turned around, they saw Maggie stroking her way toward them. Keith looked toward the bank and saw the girl's clothes dangling from the branches of a mulberry bush. Among them was a pair of frilly pink panties.

Keith felt himself stir down under the water, but it wasn't any crawdaddy tugging at him, that was for sure.

A moment later, Maggie was no more than a few feet away from them. "Lordy Mercy, this feels good," she said, smiling. She looked even prettier up close than she did from a distance.

"Just what the doctor ordered," replied Rusty. He ducked under the surface, then emerged and spit a stream of water straight at Keith's face. Maggie and Rusty laughed, while the 12-year-old sputtered.

"You turd!" growled Keith, then joined in their laughter. "You know what turds do?

They float. Unless they're full of crap. Then they sink." Without warning, he jumped on top of his cousin, dunking his head under.

Rusty came up blowing water out his nose. "Then that oughta make you the Titanic of turds," he told Keith.

The three suddenly got into a splashing fight, kicking and flailing, drenching each other with creek water. When they finally stopped, Keith found Maggie right next to him. She was so close, in fact, that he could have reached out and touched her. The thought aroused him even more.

"You know what would go good after a swim like this?" asked Maggie. "A nice, juicy slice of watermelon, that's what."

"Are you ever right about that!" said Rusty with a grin.

"Do you like watermelon, Keith?" Maggie asked him.

Just looking at her face made a shiver run down his spine. "Uh, can't say that I ever ate any."

Maggie's eyes widened in surprise. "You're funning me, ain't you?"

"Afraid not, little lady," said Rusty. "My poor cousin here is something of a virgin when it comes to the ways of the country."

The girl giggled. Keith turned beet red and kicked at Rusty beneath the water, but missed. "I've eaten cantaloupe," he said.

"Yeah, probably diced up into little cubes at some swanky restaurant," said Rusty. "Anyway, cantaloupe comes in a poor second to watermelon. Watermelon's got juice to make your fingers good and sticky, and seeds to spit out. It's messy, but it's pure paradise in a green rind."

A mischievous look sparkled in Maggie's eyes. "Let's go swipe us one," she said.

Rusty grinned. "Where from?"

"How about Old Man Perry's patch out back of his barn?" she suggested. "I saw some big'uns sitting out there, looking fit to bust."

"Sounds good to me," said Rusty. He turned to Keith. "How about it, cuz? Up for some patch-raiding tonight?"

"Sure," agreed Keith. "But nobody's going to end up shooting at us, are they?"

"Heck naw!" said Rusty. "If the kids around here didn't make away with a watermelon or two in a summer's time, the folks hereabouts would think we were going to the dogs. It's kind of a tradition."

After a while, they grew tired of swimming. Rusty and Keith turned their heads, while Maggie climbed from the swimming hole and dressed, putting her dry clothes on over her wet body. When she was through, she called out to the boys. "After supper we'll meet in that pine grove just south of Old Man Perry's watermelon patch."

"We'll be there," promised Rusty.

Maggie smiled at the dark-haired boy. "Bye, Keith."

Keith felt as if he had swallowed a bullfrog. "Bye."

After the girl had left, Rusty and Keith swam toward the bank. "Well, what did you think of 'ol Maggie?" asked the farm boy, reaching up and pulling himself onto dry ground.

"She's all right," said Keith, distracted. "Kind of pretty, too."

Rusty frowned. "Really? Can't say I ever thought of her in that way." He was stepping into his overalls, when he noticed that his cousin was still up to his waist in the water.

"You coming out?"

Keith blushed. "Uh, just give me a minute."

"Well, hurry up," urged Rusty, fastening the brass buttons of his overall straps. "It's getting late and we have a ways to ride before we make it home to supper."

"Okay," said Keith. Reluctantly, he pulled himself onto the bank and stood there.

Rusty's eyes widened. "Appears that she gave you quite a rise, that's for sure. Of course, it looks more like a soda straw than a pump handle, if you ask me."

"Well, who's asking you?" growled Keith as he hurriedly pulled on his underwear and tucked himself in.

Rusty couldn't hold out much longer. He threw back his head and brayed like a hysterical mule. Keith scowled at his cousin as he finished dressing, hoping that Maggie Sutton didn't overhear Rusty's laughter over his lack of control. If she did, he thought he might crawl under a rock and never come out again.

A moment later, they were scrambling up the hill toward their bikes, Rusty still snorting and snickering. Keith ignored him, however. He thought of Maggie and realized that he was looking forward to seeing her again.

But he didn't tell Rusty that. Given his cousin's current mood, he didn't dare.

CHAPTER TEN

After a supper of roast beef and stewed potatoes, Keith and Rusty headed back down Sycamore Road on Cyclone and Blue Fury. It was still light when they left the McLeod farm, but by the time they reached their destination the sun had set and twilight had fallen.

Rusty had removed the playing cards from the spokes of his wheels and tied a plastic milk crate to the front of his handlebars, to help tote the fruit of their evening raid. He held up his hand in the moonlight and silently glided to a stop at the side of the road. Keith followed. "Keep low and keep quiet," whispered the farm boy. They left their bikes parked next to a split-rail fence, with the front wheels pointed toward home. Then, cautiously, the two boys climbed the fence and started through the dark grove of long-leafed pines that stretched to the south of Lucius Perry's farm.

The night was alive with the chirring of crickets and the peeping of tree frogs. Halfway through the grove, Rusty paused and let out the low hooting of an owl. After a few seconds they were answered by the cooing of a dove 50 feet to their right.

"That's her," said Rusty. "Let's go."

They made their way through the grove as quietly as possible. The ground was flat and carpeted with dead needles and fallen pine cones. Rusty had slipped on a grungy pair of high-topped canvas sneakers before leaving the house. It was a good thing he had. If he had relied on his bare feet, Rusty wouldn't have gotten 10 feet without stepping on a sharp branch or spiky cone. And that was no fun at all, matter how tough the soles of his feet might be.

They were nearing the edge of the grove, when they saw the faint shine of blond hair in the moonlight. Rusty crouched down and motioned to his cousin to do the same. "Maggie?" he whispered.

"Over here," she said softly.

The two boys crept beneath some low-hanging boughs that were bristly enough to comb their hair. Soon, they were crouching next to the girl. Maggie glanced over at them with irritation. "Took ya'll long enough."

"Mama had peach cobbler for dessert," said Rusty. "And you just don't rush peach cobbler."

Maggie nodded, forgiving them for being late. The three stared across the uneven ground north of the pine grove. A small, white clapboard house with a tin roof stood a hundred yards away. Two of its windows glowed with dim yellow light.

"Old Man Perry uses 40-watt bulbs in all his light sockets," Rusty told Keith. "He's a notorious skin-flint. He'd swim to the bottom of Willow Lake for a nickel if he knew it was there."

"I saw him walk by the kitchen window a couple minutes ago," said Maggie. "I think he's in his front parlor now. Listen." From the direction of the house came the low melody of bluegrass music. From the scratches and pops, Keith gathered that the old farmer was listening to a record player. More than likely it was his only form of entertainment, if he was as miserly as Rusty claimed.

"What's the plan?" Keith asked.

"I've got a big one already picked out," said Maggie. "It's over yonder in the very center." She pointed across the dark patch of vegetation. "See it?"

The boy peered into the darkness. The leafy vines and oval fruit of the watermelon patch were etched in silvery moonlight. He had to search for a moment before he finally located it. The watermelon was every bit as big as Maggie claimed. It stood out among the others, ripe and green, a good two feet in length and 16 inches in diameter.

"I see it," he said. "Now what?"

"We just sneak out there and get it, silly." Maggie's green eyes twinkled in the pale glow of the half moon.

"But be careful," warned Rusty. "Old Man Perry is right proud of his melons. Treats 'em like the young'uns he never had."

"Got your pocketknife, Rusty?" Maggie asked him.

Rusty dipped into the side pocket of his overalls and produced a multi-bladed Case with staghorn grips. "Right here."

"Good." She turned to the boy in the Nikes and the Braves t-shirt. "Ready, Keith?"

He swallowed dryly and nodded.

"Then let's do it." Maggie crept out of the pine grove on her hands and knees, and began to make her way through the maze of vines toward the center of the patch.

"Got a lot of balls to be a girl, doesn't she?" whispered Rusty.

"I'll say," said Keith.

The two boys followed her example, keeping close to the ground. It took them a couple minutes before they finally made it to the melon they had set their sights on. Maggie crouched next to it, grinning from ear to ear.

"A real beaut, ain't it?" she boasted.

Rusty looked on the verge of salivating. "If it taste anything as good as it looks, we're in for a treat," he said. "Well, I reckon I'd best get to work." He unfolded the longest and sharpest of the pocketknife's blades then began to saw at the thick vine at the very end of the melon.

Keith crouched in the dark vegetation, his heart beating like a jackhammer. He had never felt such a rush when he shoplifted at the mall and he wasn't sure that it was a very pleasurable one. He raised his head a bit and looked toward the farmhouse. Sitting in the middle of the patch, he felt a little like Linus waiting for the Great Pumpkin to arrive.

Abruptly, a hoarse barking erupted from the direction of a lopsided barn that stood a few yards from the house. "What the hell was that?" whispered Keith, nearly jumping out of his skin.

"Old Man Perry's dog, Big Red," said Maggie, her bravado swiftly fading. "He must've caught wind of us." She looked over at Rusty. "Hurry up, will you?"

"I'm doing my best," he snapped. "This danged vine is thicker than a mule's ankle. I'm halfway through it, though."

Light suddenly splashed across the far end of the patch as the porch light of the house came on. The screen door was flung open and they saw the silhouette of a man standing there looking their way. "Who's out there?" he demanded gruffly.

"Hurry!" whispered Maggie.

"Almost there," replied Rusty, his hand working furiously.

"Answer me, you hear?" yelled Old Man Perry. "Who's there?"

The three children remained silent. They crouched low, hoping the farmer wouldn't see them amid the leaves and melons. Finally, the blade of the knife passed completely through. "Got it!"

"How're we gonna carry it?" said Keith. "Looks like it weighs a good 20 pounds."

"I'll tote it, just don't you worry," said his cousin. He hefted the watermelon in the crook of his arm. The weight of the melon rocked Rusty back on his heels, nearly throwing him off balance.

They were turning toward the pine grove, when an explosion boomed in their ears. It was the thunderous report of a shotgun being fired.

Keith elbowed his cousin in the ribs. "I thought you said we weren't gonna get shot at?"

Rusty grinned nervously. "I reckon I lied."

The mournful howling of the dog grew closer. "Let's skedaddle," said Maggie, picking up her speed. "Big Red's got our scent!"

The three scrambled through the melon patch, heading back the way they had come. The pine grove was only a few yards away, but it seemed more like miles.

"Go, boy!" urged Old Man Perry, approaching the far end of the patch. "Flush 'em out!"

After what seemed like an eternity, Maggie, Keith, and Rusty made it into the dense cover of the grove. They left their hands and knees, taking the rest of the distance on foot.

"Give me your hand," said Maggie, grabbing Keith and linking her fingers with his own. "You'll get lost if you don't stick close."

Keith said nothing. He simply let her pull him through the grove of close-grown pines. He certainly didn't want to get separated from Rusty and Maggie. The thought of being trapped in the grove alone with Old Man Perry and Big Red was enough to make him want to pee his pants. Besides, he didn't mind holding the girl's hand. Despite his terror, he was rather enjoying it.

A minute later, they were past the pines and at the split-rail fence. They scaled the barrier and ran for their bikes. Maggie's was parked a couple yards further down, hidden in a tall clump of Queen Anne's Lace. "Can you manage okay?" she called out to Rusty.

The farm boy hefted the watermelon and deposited it into the plastic tote that was lashed to Cyclone's handlebars with his right hand. "I'll be a little off balance, but I'll manage. Let's go!"

The three headed their bikes southward down Sycamore Road and began to pedal away furiously. Soon, the baying of Big Red grew distant and the threat of capture had left their minds. They began to laugh with triumph, slowing their pace a bit when they were half a mile away.

"We did it!" squealed Maggie.

Keith let out a sigh of relief. "I just hope it's as tasty as you say it is," he said.

"Oh, it will be," promised Rusty. "But there ain't no call to keep the spoils of victory all to ourselves. Follow me!"

The farm boy took the lead. Maggie and Keith grinned at each other, then increased their speed, falling in behind Rusty as he shot down the dusty stretch of rural road.

Chuck Adkins sat in his wheelchair on the front porch of his house. He waited quietly, patiently, for the hovering beacons of fireflies to grow near. The bugs clung mostly to the open yard, winking like Christmas tree lights in the summer night. But, occasionally, one of the fireflies would stray from the others and Chuck would reach out and snatch it with his fingers. He would then deposit it in a glass mason jar with a collection of others. Either that or he fed it to Churchill, who sat atop the boy's right shoulder.

He remembered once, when he was a couple years younger, running through the yard, jumping high and catching the lightning bugs by the dozens. But he would never do that again. He set his jar aside and sat there in the darkness. Those memories of life with motion always dragged his spirits down; a constant reminder of those simple little things he no longer had the ability to do.

Chuck stared into the night and thought he heard the metallic spin of bicycle gears. A moment later, he heard an owl hoot down by the mailbox next to the road. He smiled and, raising his hands to his mouth, let loose with the lonesome call of a whippoorwill.

Forms emerged from out of the darkness. "Whatcha doing out here, Chuck?" asked Maggie.

Chuck pointed to the mason jar. "Thought I'd catch some fireflies, but didn't have much luck." He looked over at Rusty and Keith. "What're you guys up to?"

"Been on a covert operation," said Rusty. He hefted the big watermelon above his head. "Over at Old Man Perry's place."

"We thought you might want to share it with us," said Keith.

Chuck's dark mood passed. "Boy, would I! I love watermelon."

Rusty looked toward the house with suspicion. "Where's your folks?"

"They're in the living room, watching TV."

"How about going in and fetching a knife to cut this sucker with?" he suggested. "I'll split it four ways and we'll chow down."

"Sure," said Chuck, spinning his chair toward the door. "Be back in a jiffy."

He wheeled through the front door, then started down the hallway. He passed the living room. His mother was dividing her attention between a situation comedy on TV and a historic romance novel. His father, a big man with thick black hair and grim eyes, sat on the couch beside her. Joe Adkins was a mechanic at the Shell station in town and his hands were a perpetual dirty gray from years of earning a living in grease and oil.

"Did I hear someone outside, hon?" asked his mother as he rolled past.

Chuck paused for a second. "Uh, yeah. It's Rusty and the guys. They brought over a watermelon."

"Oh, that's nice," she said, failing to pull her eyes from the page she was reading.

"I'm going to fetch a knife to cut it with."

"Fine," she said. "Be sure to take some newspaper with you, so it won't leak all over the porch."

"Yes, ma'am," said Chuck. He looked toward his father. The mechanic simply sat there, staring at the television. He had said nothing to his son during the entire conversation. He hadn't even acknowledged that Chuck was there. But the boy tried not to let it bother him. His father had treated him that way for two years now...ever since that fateful day at Willow Lake.

Chuck went to the kitchen and got a long-bladed butcher knife from a wooden block on the counter. Then he grabbed that morning's edition of the *Tennessean* from off the kitchen table. A moment later, he was back on the porch with his friends.

Chuck handed the knife and newspaper to Rusty. "So, did you have any trouble getting it?" he asked curiously.

"Big Red got after us," said Maggie.

"And Old Man Perry shot at us, too," added Keith.

The boy's eyes widened. "You're kidding!"

"Nope," said Rusty. He set the watermelon on top of the newspaper and quartered it with the knife. "He fired over our heads with that old twelve gauge of his. We were lucky to get outta there with our hides intact."

Chuck accepted his slice and took a big bite. "Tell me all about it, from start to finish," he urged. "And don't leave nothing out."

As they sat in the muggy darkness and feasted on watermelon, Rusty told the story of their clandestine journey into enemy territory. He embellished the escapade as only he could, throwing in the baying of Big Red and the crotchety voice of Old Man Perry for good measure. But also kept his voice low, on the chance that Chuck's parents might overhear.

Chuck grinned with admiration and spat a watermelon seed into the darkness of the front yard. His eyes gleamed dreamily behind the lenses of his glasses. "Man, I wish I could've been there with you. I would've given anything."

Rusty and Maggie looked at one another and grew silent. Keith studied the boy in the wheelchair and felt badly for him. He could imagine how frustrating it must be to have to live your life through the actions of others. If there was only some way he could tag along, just get away from that confounded house, even for a little while.

Keith glanced toward the road and saw the gleam of moonlight on the bikes down by the mailbox.

Suddenly, an idea hit him. A hell of an idea. But he said nothing about it, not until he discussed it with Rusty and found out whether it would actually work or not.

Keith concealed a smile as he took another bite of his watermelon. Maybe he had been wrong. Maybe he wasn't as much of a self-serving jerk as he first thought he was.

CHAPTER ELEVEN

For the second time in the span of a week, Jasper McLeod found himself in the center of a dark dream, experiencing a time of heated emotion and vengeance through the eyes of a small child.

The wind was cold against his face. He felt as if the chill might blister his flesh, it was so biting. But he said nothing, uttered not one word of complaint. He was in the company of men that night and, therefore, would act accordingly.

The boy clung tightly to his father, his hands grasping fistfuls of his woolen coat, drawing himself closer to the man's back. His father was quiet, as were the other citizens of Harmony who rode alongside them on fine horses and sway-backed plow mules. Their silence was due mostly to anger, as well as a grim sense of purpose they felt morally bound to. Their thoughts were divided between those who had died horribly only hours before, as well as the one who had been responsible.

That was where they were headed that frosty autumn night; to settle a score with the man who had concocted the poison that had stricken down 12 of their neighbors and loved ones, seven of them innocent children who had committed no crime other than suffering from colic or the croup. Those were the lost ones who preyed on their hearts the most...those babies who had trustfully taken the black medicine their parents had spoon-fed them and died violently because of it.

The 5-year-old glanced around him, although the cold wind stung his eyes, bringing involuntary tears. He knew all of the men in the posse, knew them by name and by face.

Cranston, Hill, Abernathy; all were well liked and respected men of the community, as was his own father. One of the town merchants, Wilbur Hill, rode his big chestnut roan, cradling a twelve-gauge shotgun in the crook of his arm. His son—who was scarcely 8 years of age—rode along side him, looking just as scared as the 5-year-old was. Or was it guilt the two boys felt? Guilt for neglecting to warn the town of Harmony of the medicine show man's potential for evil?

The boy looked up at his own father. The tobacco farmer rode with his shoulders hunched against the wind, one hand grasping the reigns of his horse, while the other was tightly fisted around the Winchester rifle.

They had ridden only a few miles, when they left the hard-packed clay of the roadway and entered a small clearing surrounded by thorny blackberry bramble. Curses mingled with clouds of frosty breath when they discovered the clearing to be empty. One of the men hopped down from his horse, hogleg pistol in hand, and walked to the gray ashes of an abandoned fire. He shucked off the glove of one hand and tested the dregs with a finger. He withdrew it swiftly, the tip blistered.

"He's just left," the man called out, hurrying back to his mount and swinging up into the saddle.

Almost immediately, they heard sounds carried to them by the night wind. The crack of a buggy whip and the pounding of horse hooves. "He's heading south!" yelled the boy's father. "Let's go!"

Flanks were spurred and soon the horses were on the road again, sprinting southward along the lonely length of Sycamore Road. Low-hanging tree branches whipped at hats and raked across the faces of the riders, but they paid no attention.

Their thoughts were focused on the dark shape that moved a quarter mile ahead of them. Desperation urged them forward. They all knew they must not fail at the task they had come to do. They must not lose the monster who attempted to escape them.

Moments later, the gap was closed between the hunters and the hunted. The boy looked past his father and, in the frigid moonlight, saw the vehicle that they pursued with such a vengeance.

It was a brightly-painted wagon drawn by two coal black geldings. Perched on the seat of the wagon was a skeletal form decked out in a black broadcloth coat and a tall stovepipe hat.

A form that laughed fiendishly as it cracked the whip wildly over the heads of the frantic team, driving them onward into the wooded darkness.

Jasper awoke, breathing hard, the bed sheets in a tangle around him. As the disturbing images of his dream faded, he almost felt as though he could still feel the chill of the night air against his face, as well as the fluid motion of the horse beneath him.

The elderly man sat up and turned on the nightstand lamp. Light hit his eyes, causing him to squint. But even still, Jasper continued to see that last shred of dark dreamscape.

The bearded man in the stovepipe hat, brandishing his whip with urgency and, yes, even pleasure.

Gradually, his breathing slowed and his heartbeat resumed its normal pace. This dream had been even more disturbing than the one he had experienced several nights before. Jasper thought of those he had dreamt of. There had been all the men he had grown up with during his childhood, as well as the 8-year-old Edwin Hill. And the farmer he had shared the horse with had possessed the face of Charles McLeod, Jasper's own father. The tobacco farmer had died of pneumonia in 1929 and there were times when

Jasper's failing memory couldn't even recall how he looked. But his face had reappeared clearly during the course of the dream...as well as the expression of grim rage that had shown in every line and crease of his weathered skin.

Jasper sat on the edge of his bed for a very long time, considering the dream he had just been a part of. In reality, he could remember accompanying his father on no such nighttime ride. But it had seemed so *real*. Like he had actually been there in the flesh.

But that wasn't what bothered Jasper the most. What clung to his thoughts the most was the one they had pursued. The lanky, bearded man in the black coat and hat. The old man shivered, despite the warmth of the summer night. Except for his dream, he had no earthly recollection of the man on the wagon, no name to call him by. All he knew—and somehow he knew it completely and without doubt—was that the dark man was evil. He could tell that by the cruelty of his laughter and the way he had laid the leather of the whip across the flanks of his team, bringing blood, fear and speed.

And there was another thing about that awful scene that disturbed the elderly man. And that was *where* the self-appointed posse had been chasing the dark man. Straight into the black heart of the South Woods.

Straight for the place known as Hell Hollow.

Was there some connection between the two? Jasper had no reason to believe so. Since he was a lad of 10 or 11, Jasper had heard whispered tales of the backwoods hollow being haunted, by what or whom he had never known. And whenever he had asked his father or the other adults in town about Hell Hollow, all had remained tight-lipped and refused to answer his questions.

With a sigh, Jasper turned the lamp off and laid back down on his bed, leaving the covers bunched around his ankles. It had only been a stupid dream, that was all. Familiar players in a theatrical production of the imagination. He hadn't thought of Hell Hollow for years, but for some reason it had come back to haunt him, conjuring old fears that reached clear back to childhood. And, as a result, his subconscious had conjured the disturbing image of that sinister man in the black stovepipe hat.

As he drifted back to sleep, he wanted to convince himself that that was all there was to it. But, for some reason, he found it difficult to do so. Deep down in his mind, he knew the incident that he dreamed of was somehow responsible for the carefully-veiled legend of Hell Hollow.

And, although he had long since forgotten it, he knew that both he and his father had somehow been involved. In a very crucial way.

CHAPTER TWELVE

Early the following morning, Jasper McLeod opened the door to Hill's General Store. As usual, the copper cowbell jangled loudly overhead, startling the elderly man.

"Land sakes alive, Edwin!" he declared, turning a contemptuous eye toward the contraption hanging over the doorframe. "Why don't you take that darned thing down?

You know it scares the crap plumb outta me!"

His friend grinned from where he stood behind the counter. "That's why I keep it up there, Jasper. To let me know when undesirables walk in."

"Then I'll just take my undesirable business elsewhere," grumbled Jasper with an expression of mock hurt.

Edwin laughed. "So, what can I do for you today?"

Jasper handed him a handwritten list. "Just need a few odds and ends," he said. "Couple pounds of boloney, bag of cornmeal, and a couple of candy bars for Keith."

The storekeeper nodded and eyed the paper through the lenses of his spectacles. Edwin Hill was probably one of the few merchants in the state of Tennessee who still adhered to the old-fashioned practice of gathering his customer's groceries for them. "Who wrote this?" he said with a frown. "You or that old bantam rooster of yours? Looks like chicken scratch more'n anything else."

"You're right funny this morning," Jasper said. He walked to the soda pop cooler and retrieved himself a Sun Drop. "Oughta start a comedy club here in Harmony."

Edwin ignored the farmer's remark. He walked to a refrigerated display case at the end of the counter and took out a long, thick tube of bologna. He carved off a slab of the luncheon meat, slapped it on the scale, then began to wrap it in clean, white butcher paper. "So, how is that grandson of yours doing?"

"Okay, I reckon," replied Jasper. "I admit, it was a little rough to begin with. He was fit to be tied and really gave me a hard time of it. But I think he's settled down a little, kinda gotten used to being here." The old man grinned. "Of course, Rusty might've had something to do with that. I think he and Keith butted heads last Sunday afternoon. That probably helped to knock him off his high horse a bit."

"How are they getting along now?" asked Edwin. After finishing with the bologna, he walked to a shelf behind the counter and took down a 5-pound sack of fine-ground yellow cornmeal.

Jasper took a long pull on his soda pop. "Oh, they're like blood brothers now. In fact, Keith's been spending more time over at Rusty's place than he has at the farm with me. Rusty even fixed him up an old bicycle so they could ride the back roads together."

Edwin turned and regarded Jasper curiously. "You sound sort of resentful of that."

"Naw, I'm tickled to death those boys have taken to one another," he said. "To tell the truth, I was afraid they might start out feuding, them being so different from one another."

The merchant wasn't fooled, though. "Now, admit it, Jasper. Something about it is sticking in your craw."

A hangdog look crossed Jasper McLeod's long face. "Well, dagnabbit, Edwin…I reckon I am kinda disappointed in a way. Here I thought Keith would be spending a lot of time with me on the farm, but instead he ends up roaming all over Hawkshaw County with his cousin."

"Well, you should've known he'd prefer the company of those his own age over you,"

Edwin told him. "It's only natural, especially it being summer and all."

"I understand that," said Jasper. "I reckon I just had this crazy idea about him and me working on the farm together. You know, doing things that might draw us a little closer."

"Forming a bond, so to speak?"

The farmer nodded. "Right. But it looks like I ain't gonna get much of a chance, if he ends up spending all his time away from me. Heck, he still treats me like a perfect stranger, even though he isn't quite as bratty as he was a few days ago."

"Well, I suppose that's because, in his eyes, you still are a stranger," said Edwin. "Give it some time. He's only been here a few days. You've still got the rest of the summer to do your best at winning him over."

Jasper's gray eyes were laden with doubt. "But what if that never happens?"

Edwin took a couple of Snickers from the candy counter out front and tossed them in a brown grocery bag, along with the bologna and cornmeal. Then he turned and regarded his checker-playing partner seriously. "Well, I won't lie to you, Jasper. You two might never grow any closer than you are right now. Take it from someone who knows."

Jasper's expression softened a little. "You're talking about Aaron, ain't you?"

The storekeeper nodded solemnly. "Yep. I reckon I'll always regret losing that chance for closeness with my only son. Never knew why we didn't get along, either. Whenever we were together, we mixed about as well as oil and water."

Jasper said nothing. He knew the pain that his friend had carried around for years. Aaron Hill had been a strapping young man when he was drafted into the Army back in 1968; someone with his whole life before him. But that life had been cut tragically short by a Viet Cong mortar at Khe Sanh. As a result, Edwin had always blamed himself for not being as close to his son as he thought he should have been.

Edwin leaned against the counter, supporting himself with an elbow. "When they sent Aaron back home sealed in that plastic coffin, I knew I'd lost my last chance to make amends with him." The old man's lips trembled. "Dammit, Jasper, I don't believe I ever even told him that I loved him."

Suddenly, the owner of the general store lapsed into a fit of coughing and gasping. His face turned alarmingly gray in color and his knees sagged a little. Luckily, Jasper was there to support him before he could lose his balance entirely.

"Is your heart acting up on you again?" he asked with concern.

Edwin nodded. "Just help me over to that chair yonder and let me sit down for a spell."

Jasper did as he requested. Soon, Edwin was sitting in a rocking chair next to the potbelly stove. A minute passed, but he didn't seem to improve any. "Where's your medicine?" asked the farmer.

"It's in my shirt pocket," said Edwin. He lifted his right hand, but it seemed listless, unable to rise more than a few inches.

Jasper took the amber vial from the breast pocket of Edwin's long-sleeved shirt and grappled with the child-proof cap for a frantic moment. Finally, he got it open, exposing the tiny pills inside. He laid the proper dosage of medication beneath his friend's tongue.

"Just settle back and relax," he said soothingly. "Drive that old guilt out of your mind and think of something pleasant."

Edwin nodded and breathed deeply. A few minutes later, the color slowly seeped back into his wrinkled face. He opened his eyes and managed a little grin. "That was a bad one."

"Want me to call an ambulance?" asked Jasper, placing a liver-spotted hand on his friend's shoulder.

"Hell, no!" snapped Edwin. "I'll be all right in a minute." The heart medicine was already taking effect. He could feel his pulse slowing and the tightness in his chest beginning to ease.

"One of these days I'm gonna walk in here and find you dead on the floor, harder than a carp," said Jasper, shaking his head. "You know you upset yourself something awful whenever the subject of Aaron comes up."

Edwin smiled feebly. "More than likely, it was God paying me back for giving you such a hard time about Felicia the other night."

Jasper handed him the bottle of Sun Drop. "Here take a swallow of this. Maybe it'll make you feel better."

The old man accepted the drink without protest. He took a couple of small swallows, then handed it back to his best friend.

"Aw, I feel like some old fool, letting myself get wound up like that," he muttered, looking a little embarrassed.

"Don't worry about it. I'm just glad I was here to get that medicine out for you."

"I know you've got better things to do than nursemaid me," said Edwin. "Why don't you ring up your sale and be on your way. I'll just sit here for a spell and regain my bearings."

"I can stick around a little longer," offered Jasper.

"Naw, you go on. I'll be just fine."

Jasper knew that the elderly man was too proud to show his weakness. The greatest respect he could show Edwin would be to just leave him alone and not fuss over him too much. "Okay, but I aim to call and check up on you later this afternoon."

"You do that," Edwin replied. He looked much better than he had 10 minutes before, although he still appeared uncommonly pale.

Jasper McLeod rang up his groceries on the antique cash register at the center of the long, wooden counter, put a $20 bill in the till and then counted out the change that was due him. As he headed for the door, sack in hand, he turned to study his friend once again. "You be sure to give me a ring if you need me, okay?"

Edwin smiled wearily. "Stop your nagging, Jasper. I'll be alright."

Jasper nodded and left the store. When he reached his pickup truck, he sat in the cab for a few minutes, finishing his drink and letting his nerves settle. Edwin's episode had scared the hell out of him. After Gladys had passed away, the country merchant had become the closest person in Jasper's lonely life. He knew if Edwin kicked the bucket that would leave him all alone with absolutely no one to lean on. And, if that was the case, Jasper knew he would follow soon afterwards. Those weekly checker games were much more than a pleasant form of recreation. In a sad way, they were almost a reason for living from one week to the next. Without companionship of some form, Jasper knew he had very little to live for.

The old farmer shook off the melancholy mood that threatened to overtake him. With a sigh, he tossed the empty pop bottle on the truck's cluttered floorboard, cranked up the engine and then started back through Harmony toward home.

CHAPTER THIRTEEN

Rusty thought the idea was terrific.

A big grin split his freckled face as he stared at Keith in amazement. "You know, you ain't half as dumb as I first thought," he said.

Keith knew his cousin was paying him a compliment, but he wasn't sure exactly how to take it. "Thanks. I think."

"And it's right nice of you, to boot. I know Chuck'll sure get a kick out of it...if we can make it work."

Keith reached into the back pocket of his denim shorts and handed Rusty a folded sheet of notebook paper. "I fooled around with it last night," he said. "What do you think?"

Rusty studied a detailed drawing that Keith had sketched. "Sure looks possible to me. In fact, I'd go as far as to say it'll work just fine."

"The only thing that's stumped me so far is where we're going to find the materials to build it."

"You just leave that to me," said Rusty. He jumped on Cyclone and steered it toward town. "Come on and I'll show you."

Keith hopped aboard Blue Fury and, together, the two boys coasted down the McLeod driveway then headed up Sycamore Road for town.

They reached Harmony 20 minutes later. The town square with its family-owned businesses and tall, brick courthouse seemed as lazy and laid-back as usual. There were only a few cars and pickup trucks parked along the main street, and the only movement Keith could detect on the sun-baked sidewalks was a couple of little girls playing hopscotch and a stray dog licking at a wad of bubble gum some kid had stuck to the side of a telephone pole. Other than that, Harmony looked more like a well-kempt ghost town than anything else.

They rode past the grassy yard of the courthouse with its tall oak trees and white gazebo, heading in the direction of a narrow side street that ran along the town's western side. They crossed a line of railroad tracks that possessed only warning signs and no caution lights. The intense heat of the August sun had already infected the polished rails. Shimmering waves radiated up from the steel tracks, blurring the landscape to north and south. Riding past them, Keith felt as if he were pedaling through the middle of a desert mirage.

The two boys headed down a dusty back road past a couple of weedy vacant lots. To their right loomed the Harmony water tower. It stood a good 80 feet in height; a huge sea-green sphere on three support-pole legs. A single pipe led from the belly of the reservoir to the ground underneath, hooking into a network of pips and spigots that linked into the community's water supply. Keith's gaze rose skyward, following a single steel ladder that traveled along one of the tower's foremost supports. A narrow catwalk surrounded the big water tank and, as far as he could tell, the only access to the inside was a single trapdoor on the very top, secured with a circular locking handle, sort of like the kind you find on submarine doors.

Rusty noticed his cousin's interest. "Kinda looks like one of them Martian spaceships in that *War of the Worlds* movie, doesn't it?"

Keith knew the film Rusty was referring to. "Yeah, it does. Have you ever climbed up there?"

The farm boy grinned. "Sure have. But don't tell my mama. If she ever found out, she'd whale the tar plumb outta me!"

It wasn't long before they reached their destination. "Here we are," called Rusty. "If anybody can help us, Big Jake can."

They coasted past a 12-acre lot surrounded by a tall, chain-link fence and scrubby stands of tall weeds and thistle. As they rode through an open gate, Keith read the sign overhead: JAKE ABERNATHY—AUTO PARTS, COLLECTIBLES, & SALVAGE—WE BUY, SELL OR TRADE.

Once inside the boundaries of the junkyard, Keith understood why Rusty had brought him there. If they were to find the materials to turn his idea into a reality, it would be here. To one side of the junkyard stood tall stacks of wrecked vehicles: cars, vans, jeeps, and pickup trucks, even an old rusty school bus or two. On the other side were mounds of garbage and scrap metal—everything from limbless baby dolls to copper tubing and cracked porcelain toilets. The ground underfoot was dusty clay earth with a few patches of crabgrass and ragweed sprouting up in spots.

"Come on," said Rusty, heading toward a barn-like structure at the rear of the property.

"I'll introduce you to Big Jake."

As the boys came to a halt a few yards from the weathered building, a huge black dog with a bright pink patch around one eye, lunged from where he had been lying on the ground. He barked and snarled viciously, his fangs flashing milky yellow teeth in the mid-morning sunlight. The only thing that separated them from the fury of the junkyard dog was a sturdy length of logging chain. One end was secured to the bumper of an old '72 El Camino, while the other was fastened to the back of the animal's thick leather collar.

"Don't worry about old Loco there," assured Rusty. "He's just showing off, that's all."

"He sure is a big one," said Keith, keeping his distance. "Looks like a cross between a Rottweiler and Greyhound bus."

"If you think Loco's an eyeful, wait till you get a load of Jake," said Rusty.

A moment later, Loco's owner appeared, drawn out of the shade of the building by the commotion his dog was making. Even after Rusty's warning, Keith was still surprised by the man who stepped into the sunshine. He was a good 6-foot-6 in height and probably weighed well over 300 pounds. All in all, with his shaggy blond hair and beard, Jake Abernathy resembled a Viking warrior dressed in grungy camouflage overalls and a white and orange UT Volunteers cap.

"Well, howdy there, Rusty!" he said with a tobacco-stained grin. "Whatcha doing way out here bright and early this morning?"

"Came to see if you could help us with something," said Rusty. He nodded toward the boy on the blue bike. "This here's my cousin from Atlanta, Keith Bishop."

"Nice meeting you, Keith," rumbled Big Jake in a thunderous voice.

"Same here," said Keith as the junkman's huge hand swallowed his own. He kept a friendly smile on his face, fighting against the impulse to gage at the horrendous odor the big man emitted. He smelled strongly of unwashed clothing and perspiration, but that wasn't the worse of it. Jake's breath was the most repulsive Keith had ever encountered. It was a sickening mixture of raw onions, sardines and beer.

The black dog continued to snap and snarl, thick runners of white saliva dripping from his toothy jaws.

"He isn't rabid, is he?" asked Keith.

The junk dealer laughed. "Well, he might be a little screwy in the head, but he don't have the hydrophoby. He just slobbers a lot when he gets excited, that's all."

"Is he dangerous?"

Big Jake nodded. "Sure is. If it wasn't for that there chain, you boys would likely be in three or four pieces right about now."

Keith swallowed nervously, praying that the logging chain didn't have any weak links in it.

"So, how can I be of assistance?" Jake asked, turning back to Rusty.

The lanky farm boy handed the man Keith's drawing. "We're aiming to build that contraption. We were wondering if you might have the parts in stock?"

Jake's sunburned brow creased in concentration. "I believe so." He glanced over at Keith with a grin of admiration. "You come up with this?"

"That's right."

"Pure genius, that's what it is!" said Jake with a hearty laugh. "You boys wouldn't mind if I helped you put this thing together, would you?"

Rusty grinned from ear to ear. "I was hoping you'd make the offer."

"Which bike are you figuring on attaching it to?" asked the junkman.

"Mine," said Rusty. "I don't think that old bike I fixed up for Keith would hold up."

Jake studied Blue Fury, his eyes lingering on the patched and bald tires. "You're probably right. What do you say we take a stroll around the yard and see what we can find?"

A matter suddenly came to Keith's mind; one he figured they ought to discuss before hand. "Uh, what are you going to charge us for the parts to build this thing?"

Jake laughed. "Charge? Hell, I ain't figuring to charge you nothing. Just the challenge of helping ya'll build this thing and seeing if it'll actually work...that's payment enough for me."

As the junkman led the way, Rusty turned and gave his cousin a wink. "Just you wait and see. If anybody can help us make this invention come to life, it's Big Jake here."

Keith simply nodded. Anxious to get to work, he followed Rusty and Jake into the cluttered maze of trash and debris.

Later that afternoon, Keith, Rusty, and Maggie showed up at the Adkins residence. Chuck was sitting in his wheelchair on the porch, reading a war novel, while his mother occupied a rocking chair nearby, snapping green beans into a large Tupperware bowl.

When Chuck looked up from his book and saw the grins on the faces of his three friends, he immediately knew they were up to something. "What's going on?" he asked.

"We kinda got a surprise for you," said Rusty, looking fit to bust.

"What sort of surprise?" asked the handicapped boy with suspicion.

"It's down by the road," said Keith. "Why don't you come and take a look?"

Chuck strained forward in his chair, trying to see what they had brought to show him. He could only see the handlebars of the three bikes past the white picket fence at the far edge of the front yard.

"You can't see it from up here," said Maggie. She jumped up on the porch and stepped behind the wheelchair, taking a handle in each hand. "Come on and we'll show you."

"But what is it?" demanded Chuck with a puzzled frown.

Mrs. Adkins laughed. "Why don't you just go down and see what your friends have brought you? If nothing else, it'll do my heart good to see you out yonder in the yard. You haven't been off the front porch in a couple of weeks."

"Okay," agreed Chuck, releasing the brake on his chair. "Let's go."

Maggie steered him down a ramp at the far end of the porch, then along the sidewalk that led to the gate of the picket fence. When they reached the edge of Sycamore Road, Chuck stared at the three bikes that were parked next to the mailbox. Keith's and Maggie's bicycles looked the same as usual, but the right side of Rusty's 10-speed was obscured by a threadbare horse blanket. There seemed to be something large and bulky hidden underneath.

"So what's the big surprise?" he asked.

Rusty looked over at Keith. "It's your baby, cuz. You do the honors."

Keith smiled. "Okay." He walked over and, taking a corner of the blanket in hand, yanked the cover away with a dramatic flourish. "Ta-daaaa!"

Chuck couldn't believe his eyes. Rusty's bike had a strange-looking contraption bolted to its frame. To put it simply, it was a modified metal trashcan with the lid riveted securely in place. A hole had been cut in the uppermost side and, in its hollow, was a padded seat from a fishing boat. A bicycle wheel was connected to an axle at the side of the can opposite the 10-speed. Chuck had seen similar vehicles in his history books, mostly affixed to the sides of German motorcycles. This was a crude imitation, but theoretically practical.

"Is this what I think it is?" he asked in amazement.

"It sure is," said Rusty.

"A sidecar. You built a freaking sidecar." Stunned, Chuck looked around at his friends. "For me?"

"That's right," said Maggie. She regarded the boy from Atlanta with undisguised admiration. "You've got

Keith to thank for it. He was the one who came up with the idea."

"Is that right?" asked Chuck.

"Yeah," said Keith. He felt his face grow hot and red with sudden embarrassment. "Anybody could've done it."

"But you hardly even know me," said the boy in the wheelchair. "Why would you want to do something nice for me?"

Keith shrugged. "I guess I just figured you deserved to have as much fun as the rest of us, that's all."

The skepticism in Chuck Adkins's eyes faded. "Well thanks. It's really great." He wheeled his chair closer and inspected the sidecar. "Does it actually work? It's not going to fall apart when I get in, is it?"

"I sure hope not," said Keith. "We've already tried it out with me and Maggie, and it worked like a charm."

"Climb on in," said Rusty. "Let's take her for a spin."

"Okay, let's do it," said Chuck anxiously.

Together, the three lifted the overweight boy from his wheelchair. Taking great care, they slid his lifeless legs through the opening and sat him inside. Chuck settled against the boat seat. "Feels comfortable enough." He immediately noticed a handle attached to the inside of the sidecar, connected to the wheel's stubby axle. It resembled an oversized crank, sort of like the kind on the side of an antique coffee grinder. "What's this for?"

"It helps turn the side wheel," explained Rusty. "You know, when we're trying to pull a steep hill." He frowned at his friend. "You didn't think I was gonna do *all* the work, did you?"

Chuck laughed. "I reckon not. Hop on and let's see what it does."

Rusty mounted his bike, careful to stick his right leg between the heavy steel brackets that secured the sidecar to the frame.

"Hey, Mrs. Adkins!" Maggie called up to the porch. "Come down and take a look at this!"

By the time Flora Adkins made it to the mailbox, Rusty and Chuck had made their way 50 feet down Sycamore Road. She watched in amazement as they made a U-turn in the road then started back. "Well, I'll be!" was all she could manage to say.

"Look, Mom!" Chuck called out happily. "Ain't it great?"

"Is it safe?" she asked.

Chuck pounded on the body of the sidecar with his fists. "It's solid as a rock!"

"Why don't we all go out and take us a ride?" Rusty suggested.

"Can I, Mom?" the boy asked excitedly. "Can I go with 'em?"

Doubts and fears nagged at Flora Adkins, but she didn't have the heart to say no. It had been a long time since she had seen her son so happy. Two long, difficult years, in fact.

"Well, it's fine with me, if you be extra careful and don't go too fast," she told him. "But you'll have to get your father's permission, too."

Chuck's spirits plummeted. "Aw, do I have to."

"I'm afraid so," she said. "He's in his workshop. Why don't you go and ask him?"

Chuck's expression darkened. "Oh, all right." He looked around at his friends. "Can you help me back into my chair for a minute?"

It wasn't long before the three were wheeling Chuck back up the sidewalk and around the side of the house. Joe Adkins' workshop was located in a small room that adjoined the two-car garage. The door was open and they could hear the shrill whine of a belt sander echoing from the shadows within.

"Want us to go with you?" asked Rusty.

"Naw," sighed Chuck. "I'll ask him myself."

The boy in the wheelchair left his pals and propelled himself along the paved driveway, toward the dark square of the open door. His father had arrived home from his job at the Shell station a half hour ago. He had mounted the porch in that solemn, preoccupied way of his, kissed his wife on the forehead, then walked through the house and out the back door, heading straight for his workshop. He hadn't said a single word to Chuck—just ignored him as if he weren't there.

Chuck hesitated just before he reached the doorway. He found himself afraid to even approach his father. Sometimes it was simpler—and less hurtful—if he ignored his father the way he himself was ignored. It pained the boy deep down inside to exist in a vacuum completely devoid of his father's love and affection. Of course, it hadn't always been that way. They had been the best of buddies once...back before the accident had happened.

Chuck glanced back at the others and cleared his throat. "Dad?" he called.

The sander continued its high-pitched whine.

"Dad?" he said louder. This time the noise came to a halt and an awkward silence hung in the air. Chuck could see his father sitting on a stool in front of his workbench in the shadows of the workshop, staring at the shelf he was working on.

"Yeah, son?" replied the man. There was no emotion in his voice, no hint of feeling at all.

"Uh, I was wondering if it'd be okay if I went riding with Rusty and the gang?" he began. "They rigged up this neat sidecar onto a bike and it really works great."

Joe Adkins continued to stare at the piece of maple that was secured to the edge of the workbench with C-clamps. "What'd your mom say?"

"She said it was fine with her," said Chuck hopefully. "She said you'd have to okay it first, though."

The mechanic shrugged his shoulders. "Do whatever you want," he said, his voice sounding incredibly tired, like that of an old man instead of a man who was scarcely forty years of age. "It doesn't matter to me."

Chuck swallowed dryly. "Okay," he said, feeling a little sad. "Thanks."

When the boy returned to his friends, Rusty frowned at the troubled look on Chuck's face. "What's wrong? Did he turn us down?"

"No, he said it was okay," said Chuck. "Said he didn't care one way or the other."

Rusty traded uneasy glances with Keith and Maggie. "Well, come on, guys," he said.

"Let's hit the road!"

A few minutes later, they were back down at the road. Chuck was helped into the sidecar, then Rusty, Keith and Maggie climbed onto their bikes.

"Ya'll don't stay out too long," Flora Adkins told them. She checked her watch. "It's a little after 3:30 now. Make sure you get him back home by six, okay?"

"Yes, ma'am," promised Rusty. "We sure will." He turned and smiled at Chuck. "Are you ready to roll, pardner?"

"You betcha!" said Chuck, his spirits soaring once again. "Bye, Mom."

"Bye, sweetheart," said his mother, feeling both elated and a little scared. After all, this would be the first time her son had left the Adkins' property in two years, not counting trips to the doctor and the hospital. "Have fun."

A moment later, the four were heading southward down Sycamore Road. Chuck Adkins settled back in the makeshift sidecar and closed his eyes. He relished the warmth of the late afternoon sun against his face, as well as the rich aroma of honeysuckle blossoms growing along the roadside and the rush of the wind blowing through his curly hair. For a very long time, Chuck had felt like a prisoner, not only in the wheelchair, but also in his own failing body. But now, due to an act of ingenuity and compassion on the part of his friends, he felt as if he had finally broken free of those restrictive bonds.

What he experienced at that moment, riding down the country road, was freedom, pure and simple. After a long absence, he was part of the gang again. And that was better than any medicine or physical therapy that he had been subjected to since the unfortunate incident at Willow Lake.

Away from the limiting confines of his wheelchair, Chuck felt like a true—and whole —boy once again.

CHAPTER FOURTEEN

Slash Jackson had put some serious mileage between himself and Atlanta during the past several days.

After his session with Allison Walsh at Adairsville, he had taken the woman's car and driven the rest of the way through northern Georgia, across the Tennessee line to Chattanooga. Feeling that he was pushing his luck, he ditched the Taurus in a Denny's parking lot and began to hitchhike. The brunette from St. Louis had probably been discovered by now. Whether dead or alive, Slash had no idea. In any event, the Georgia state police had probably alerted the authorities in Tennessee and provided them with a description of Walsh's car and, perhaps, of Jackson himself.

Slash brooded over the lenience he had shown toward the woman. Had he screwed up in the shack near Adairsville? Had he been too soft and merciful? He was beginning to believe so. In hindsight, he knew he should have taken care of business the same as he usually did. He should have slit Allison's throat when he had the chance, instead of leaving her naked and half-dead on the dusty floor of that abandoned house.

"So, has your father had a problem with his heart for a while now?" asked the man next to him.

Slash pulled his thoughts away from what he should and shouldn't have done, and focused on the driver of the big Lincoln Continental. He was a businessman from Lexington, Kentucky named Larry Bell. Bell was overweight and balding, with a ruddy face and a nervous tick at the corner of his right eye. The salesman was returning from a computer software convention at the Hyatt in Atlanta. Slash had approached him at a Burger King near Monteagle and given him the same song and dance he had pulled on Allison Walsh. Bell, a trusting and friendly man, had bought the sob story hook, line and sinker.

"Yeah, for about 15 years," liked Slash convincingly. "I wasn't aware of how serious it was until my mother called and told me was laid up in the hospital waiting for a triple bypass."

"Well, don't you worry," assured Larry Bell. "It shouldn't be more than an hour and a half until we reach Nashville. I'll even take you as far as the hospital, if you'd like."

"I really appreciate the ride, Mr. Bell," he replied, putting as much humility into his voice as he could muster. "It's really important to me."

"No need to thank me, son," said the computer salesman. He smiled assuringly at the man in the black Grateful Dead t-shirt and faded jeans. "I'm just glad I could help out."

Slash studied the middle-aged man from Kentucky. Larry Bell looked to be doing well in his career. He appeared well-groomed and the nails of his chubby fingers had been recently manicured. The gray suit he was wearing was custom-tailored, not off the rack, and his shoes were Italian loafers that had probably cost him $100. All that Slash was interested in, however, was the man's wallet. He was sure Bell carried a wad of cash on him, as well as some valuable credit cards—probably all platinum with impressive limits.

Slash settled in the Lincoln's leather-upholstered seat and relished the smoothness of the car's suspension. They passed over a pothole in the road, but barely felt it. Slash hoped to hold onto the luxury car for at least a couple of states before he was forced to abandon it. Hopefully, Bell's automobile, cash and plastic would sustain him until he reached Detroit where he had friends. He planned to hole up there for a couple months until things cooled off, then head back to Georgia where he belonged.

"Yeah, it's a real shame," continued Bell. "You know, my old man died of a stroke five years ago. He passed away while my wife and I was on a trip to Hawaii. I sure hope you get to see your father before it's too late."

Slash played the part subtly. He nodded quietly, allowing an expression of anxiety and sadness cross his face. Inwardly, however, he was amused. Slash's real father was already dead. When Slash was 14 years old, Bud Jackson had mysteriously disappeared after years of drunkenness and cruel abuse, both physical and mental. Everyone, including Slash's mother, was certain he had abandoned them. But that wasn't the case. Not by a long shot.

Unbeknownst to family and friends, Slash had been the one responsible for Bud Jackson's abrupt absence. In a fit of rage, he had split his father's skull in two with the edge of a shovel and buried him in an apple orchard out back of their house. It was not something Slash was ashamed of. In fact, it was one of the fondest memories he possessed of his dear old dad, particularly the look of complete bewilderment that had crossed his face when the shovel crushed his skull and cleaved his brain cleanly in half.

Absently, Slash glanced in the Lincoln's side-view mirror. His heart leapt into his throat when he saw a Tennessee state trooper cruising a few yards behind them. At first, Slash wondered if the trooper was onto him; if he knew that it was Slash who rode shotgun in Larry Bell's white Lincoln. But his fears subsided as they neared the Manchester exit. The patrol car put on its turning signal and left the interstate. Slash turned and watched as the car made its way up the ramp and headed for a Texaco station to the right.

As they continued northwestward along Interstate 24, Slash knew that it was time to make his move: It was time to take Larry Bell out of the equation while he still had the chance.

He let the computer salesman drive five miles further until he spotted a green sign up ahead. It read: EXIT 105—FAIRFIELD, BUGSCUFFLE, HARMONY—2 MILES.

Slash let Bell pass the exit sign before he made his move. He dipped his hand into his pants pocket and withdrew the folding knife. "Pull over," he instructed.

"Pardon me?" asked Bell, totally unaware of what was going on.

Slash extended the blade of the Buck knife with a practiced flip of his thumb. A metallic click rang throughout the interior of the car as it locked securely in place. Slash raised the knife to the row of double chins beneath Bell's ruddy face. "I said pull over," he instructed. "Nice and slow, right over here."

Larry Bell was no fool. He put on his turning signal and slowly eased onto the shoulder of the interstate. A moment later, they were sitting there with the engine idling.

"Turn it off," said Slash. "Then give me the keys."

The salesman nodded. He cut the engine and pulled the key from the ignition switch. The air conditioning died as well and, almost immediately, the heat of the August afternoon closed in on them, turning the interior of the car muggy and uncomfortable.

"Now what?" asked Bell.

Slash smiled. It was a smile he kept hidden from his victims until just the right moment. That awful moment when they realized that they had made the worse mistake of their entire life.

"Now we take a little walk into those woods over yonder."

Bell's frightened eyes shifted toward the side of the interstate. Beyond the guardrail was a steep embankment and a stretch of tall oaks and maples along with heavy underbrush. It was the type of thicket that ran for miles. The type where someone could vanish and no one would find him for a very long time.

"No," gasped Bell. "I'm not going."

"Yes, you are," said Slash. "You're gonna do whatever the hell I tell you to do."

"I've got a family," pleaded the salesman. The tiny muscles at the corner of his eye ticked with the precision of a fine watch. "I've got a wife and two teenage daughters."

"Too bad they're not here with us," said Slash, his voice soft and oily. "Then I could do all three of them while you watched. I reckon you'll just have to settle for watching your own self die instead."

"No," whispered Bell. Tears bloomed in his eyes. "Please."

"We ain't got time for groveling," snapped Slash. He increased the pressure of the blade, picking the folds of tender flesh beneath the man's chin. "Now, move your ass!"

Larry Bell moved, but not in the way Slash wanted. The pain of the cut, as well as the trickle of warm blood running down this throat, caused the salesman to panic. He grabbed Slash's hand in his own and attempted to wrestle the knife away from his attacker.

Slash couldn't help but laugh out loud. "What the hell do you think you're doing?" he asked.

Bell screamed hoarsely and struggled to pull the knife toward the dashboard as if he hoped to batter Slash's fist against the padded console and force him to drop the knife.

Slash's grin broadened. "This is downright funny; you know that?" He allowed the man to think that he was winning for a moment, but there was little chance of that. Muscles grown flabby and weak by a life of easy living were no match for those hardened by years of road-crew work. The sinew of Slash Jackson's forearm flexed like steely cords beneath tanned skin. Without effort, the blade of the knife began to inch back toward the salesman's throat.

"No!" croaked Bell, his eyes bright with alarm and hopelessness.

"Afraid so," said Slash. Then he plunged the blade deeply into the man's Adam's apple and with a sideward motion, sliced Bell's throat open. The big man let out a strangled cough, sending droplets of blood spraying onto the inner windshield and the top of the dashboard. He shuddered violently, his eyes bulging as he drowned on his own blood. A moment later, he was dead.

Slash withdrew the blade, feeling the honed edge grate against the salesman's neckbone. Then he wiped it clean on the material of Bell's trouser leg.

"Dumb bastard," he said, unlocking the blade and returning the knife to his pocket. He rummaged through Bell's jacket and found his wallet. Just as he had hoped. There was $400 in cash and four gold cards—enough to get him to Detroit and back several times over.

A flash of sunlight in the Lincoln's rearview mirror drew Slash's attention. He glanced up to see a car coming down the interstate at a steady speed. Again, sunshine gleamed off the car—or rather off something on top. Suddenly, Slash realized what it was. It was a bank of emergency lights.

It was the state trooper. He had filled his tank at the gas station and was back on patrol.

"Shit!" growled Slash Jackson. He stuffed the wallet in his hip pocket, grabbed the garbage bag of belongings from the floorboard and opened the Lincoln's passenger door. As he jumped the guardrail and slid on his butt down the embankment to the woods below, he caught a glimpse of the police cruiser from the corner of his eye. It was still a good distance away—perhaps a hundred yards or so—but it was gaining ground fast. In a matter of seconds, it would be there.

He wasted no time. When his feet hit level ground, Slash plunged headlong into the thicket, seeking the shelter of close-grown trees and heavy stands of honeysuckle and kudzu. He paused for a moment, catching his breath and hoping that the trooper would drive on without stopping.

His luck had turned sour, though. The state cruiser began to slow, then eased to a halt at the shoulder of the road, scarcely 12 feet from the rear bumper of Larry Bell's Continental.

Slash Jackson turned to leave, aiming to put as much distance between him and the state trooper as possible. In his haste to get away, he ran into a clump of blackberry bramble. The thorns snagged his clothing, refusing to let go. As quietly as he could, Slash struggled until he finally pulled free of the barbs.

He glanced back toward the interstate. A husky trooper dressed in a tan and brown uniform, mirrored sunglasses and a Smoky Bear hat was walking toward the driver's side of the Lincoln.

Slash didn't stick around to witness the patrolman's discovery. He escaped into the Tennessee forest, mingling with the summer greenery, as well as the deep shadows that lay in between.

CHAPTER FIFTEEN

It was a glorious ride for them all. Especially for one in particular.

"Faster!" urged Chuck as they headed along the southernmost stretch of Sycamore Road. They passed the Hadley place, the last farm before the rural road gave way to deepening thicket and tall stands of oak and birch.

"Sorry, pal," said Rusty. "I promised your mom that we'd take it easy."

"Aw, she won't know," he said. "I'm tired of dragging around at a snail's pace. Let's turn on the afterburners!" He grabbed the handle in the inner hull of the trashcan sidecar and began to crank it furiously.

Rusty felt the bike gain speed, despite his wishes. Soon, the pedals of Cyclone were whirling so swiftly that it was hard for his legs to keep up. "Slow down, Chuck! Dadblame it, what if we miss the next turn and end up tumbling head over ass into a ditch?"

Chuck merely grinned. "It's been a helluva long time since I've had a scraped elbow or bruised knee, Rusty. To tell the truth, I'd kinda welcome it."

"Speak for yourself! Now slow down a bit and I promise we'll pick up the pace. Okay?"

The overweight boy laughed and cut down his cranking to half its urgency. "Oh, all right, you lily-livered coward!" said Chuck.

"What time is it?" asked Rusty after they had made a rather precarious bend in the road and, fortunately, survived.

Keith checked his diver's watch. "It's half past five."

"Then we'd better get back," said the lanky farm boy. "I promised that I'd get Chuck back by six."

"I know what you promised," said Chuck. "But you can't take me back now. Shoot, we haven't even made it into the woods yet. And you know how much I always liked the woods."

Rusty recalled how he, Chuck and Maggie used to explore the green expanse of the forest south of Harmony, back before their friend's tragic accident. "But what about your folks? They'll have our hides for sure!"

"Aw, Mom won't mind if we stay out a little later," Chuck said, aware of the white lie he was concocting. "And, as for my dad, he wouldn't much care if I sailed off to China in a leaky rowboat."

"Oh, Chuck!" said Maggie. "You know that's not true."

Chuck Adkins thought of the way his father couldn't even look him square in the eyes. He said nothing in reply, but didn't seem very convinced of the girl's assurance.

"I don't know," said the normally reckless Rusty.

"Come on, buddy," moaned Chuck. The boy donned his best hangdog look, trying to appear as forlorn as he possibly could.

Rusty frowned. "Oh, all right! I can't take your blasted pouting. You look sadder than a basset hound with a bad case of hemorrhoids."

The others laughed as they continued onward along Sycamore Road, past the last boundaries of small town civilization and into the five-mile stretch of tall trees and dense underbrush known simply as the South Woods.

It wasn't long before the sun-baked blacktop eventually gave way to rutted clay earth. The sun was setting to the west, throwing long shadows across their path. Abruptly, the sunny cheerfulness of the summer day was gone. In its place, lurked something less comforting, less familiar to them.

"Hey!" called Keith. "Where'd the road go?"

Rusty and Maggie slowed their bikes and braked to a half just short of the gloom that choked the woods just beyond. Keith rode onward a few yards then stopped, suddenly aware that his friends were no longer with him. He looked back at them, puzzled at the expressions of hesitation on their faces.

"What's wrong?" he asked.

Rusty looked at Maggie and Chuck, then back at his cousin. "Uh, we'd best not go in there."

"Where?" Keith wanted to know.

"*There*," explained Maggie pointing ahead of the boy from Atlanta.

Keith turned and looked southward. The dirt trail—which became narrower and choked with weeds—began to gently slope downward. From what he could tell, the road grew steeper, plunging into a dark, wooded hollow that seemed to be more the size of a small valley than anything else.

"Huh?" Keith shook his head in confusion at the strange way they were acting. "I don't understand."

"Nobody goes down there, Keith," Chuck told him. "*Nobody*."

"Why not?"

Rusty and Maggie shifted uncomfortably on their bikes while Chuck hunkered a little lower in the hand-built sidecar. "'Cause it's Hell Hollow, that's why," said Rusty.

"Hell Hollow?" laughed Keith. "Why is it called that?"

"Just look at it," said Maggie.

Keith turned and appraised the hollow again. This time it seemed different than before. The trees seemed closer together and the lush carpeting of broad-leafed kudzu and blossoming honeysuckle appeared much thicker. Also the darkening shadows of evening seemed denser, almost sinister in a way. In fact, there were places deep in the backwoods hollow where he could see nothing at all. Only inky pits of darkness.

"It's just an old hollow, that's all," scoffed Keith. "It's nothing to get spooked about."

"That's easy for you to say," said Chuck. "You're not from around here. We are. We've heard the stories all our lives."

"What stories?" asked Keith, intrigued.

Rusty cleared his throat nervously. "Uh, you're gonna think we're crazy, cuz, but there's something you oughta know."

"What?"

A heavy silence hung between them for a long moment. Then Rusty continued. "Well, this place, Hell Hollow," he said. "It's haunted."

Keith snorted loudly through his nose. "Yeah! Right!"

The other three simply stared at him, their faces solemn.

"Aw, come off it, will you?" said Keith. "I know I'm a little green out here in Hootersville, but I'm not stupid enough to swallow this kind of bull. Next you'll be taking me snipe-hunting."

"We're not pulling your leg, cuz," said Rusty.

"Wish we were," Maggie added.

Keith began to feel a little angry. "Well, I'm not buying it. Is that why you came out here in the first place? So you could try to scare the crap out of the poor city boy?"

"No," said Chick. "Honestly, we didn't."

Keith looked from one face to the next. No matter how hard he tried, he could detect no deception in their eyes. They were sincere about what they were telling him. They genuinely believed that the vast hollow in the center of South Woods was haunted.

The boy laughed, but the sound was oddly humorless. "You're not kidding, are you?"

"No, we're not," said Maggie.

"Serious as a banker on foreclosure day," Rusty replied.

Keith turned and looked back into the hollow. For some strange reason, it seemed darker and deeper, as though the shadows were expanding and creeping out of the vegetation toward them.

"I thought you said you guys have been all over these woods."

"We have," said Rusty. "All except this hollow here."

"You mean you've never been down there?" he asked.

"Hell no!" said Chuck.

Keith shook his head in disbelief. "I thought you country folks were fearless. And here you are shivering and shaking at a bunch of trees and ivy." He looked back into the hollow. The shadows were even darker than before. He had to admit, it certainly *looked* spooky.

"Let's head on back," said Chuck, who, a moment ago, had thumbed his nose at the prospect of returning home.

Maggie and Rusty began to steer their bikes around, back toward the blacktop of the rural road.

"Hey, hold up for a sec," Keith called out. "Why do you think this place is haunted?"

"'Cause it just *is*, that's why," said Rusty. "Everyone in Harmony knows that. And they know to stay clear of it, too. Especially after dark."

"*Why* is it haunted?" asked Keith, unable to leave it alone.

"Nobody really knows," said Maggie. Even from where he was, Keith could see the goosebumps on her tanned arms. "It's just a common fact."

"What are you saying? That people have seen ghosts down there?"

Rusty shrugged his freckled shoulders. "Well, not exactly. It's more like *sounds* folks have heard down there."

"What kind of sounds?" In spite of him, Keith felt the fine hairs on the nape of his neck began to stand.

"Strange sounds. God-awful laughing. Like somebody who'd gone mad."

"Evil laughter," said Maggie softly.

Keith turned back toward the dark hollow, feeling a delicious thrill of pure terror run down his spine. His friends were right. There was something *wrong* with the place. It wasn't something you could actually see, however. Rather, it was something you felt...deep down in the marrow of your bones.

Still, he couldn't help but be intrigued. "I think we oughta go down there and check it out."

Rusty's eyes widened. "Are you crazy? I wouldn't set one foot in that place."

"Chicken, eh?" taunted the boy, hoping to shame his cousin into complying.

He had no such luck, however. Rusty's Adam's apple bobbed nervously. "Well, yeah. If you want to know the truth of it...I reckon I am."

Rusty's admission of fear brought no satisfaction to Keith. Instead, it merely reinforced his own uneasiness. "Just how long has this place had this rep?"

Chuck shrugged. "Ever since anyone in town could remember. We don't know how it got started. We just know it's true."

Keith snickered. "I can't believe you guys! Scared of some place for no good reason."

The three said nothing. No shame shown on their faces—only a grim certainty of things they had been taught since birth.

"Well, maybe we could come back and explore it tomorrow," suggest Keith. "In broad daylight."

"No way!" declared Chuck Adkins. "I wouldn't go down there with a whole platoon of Marines."

"Come on," said Rusty, turning his bike around. "Let's get out of here."

"I'm with you," said Maggie.

Reluctantly, Keith did likewise. As he pointed his blue Schwinn northward, he turned and studied Hell Hollow one more time. With the gradual setting of the sun the hollow had lost all color and contrast. It was a pit of solid blackness now.

A moment later, a breeze blew up from out of the hollow. An uncommonly cool breeze for such a hot and humid summer evening. A breeze that carried with it a strange and sinister odor.

An odor like medicine gone wrongfully bad.

He turned to find the others already starting back up Sycamore Road. Suddenly, being there alone was the last thing Keith wanted.

"Hey!" he called out, his voice higher than he would have liked. "Wait for me, guys!"

Then he headed back up the road as fast his feet could pedal.

CHAPTER SIXTEEN

It was after dusk—as well as the deadline of six o'clock—when they arrived back at the Adkins residence.

They glided into the driveway to find Chuck's mother standing on the front porch, arms crossed, a highly peeved look on her face. Rusty knew at once they had screwed up.

"I thought you said it'd be okay with your Mom if we stayed out a little later."

Chuck looked up at his mother's tense silhouette in the pale porch light and felt his stomach sink. "I reckon I underestimated her," he replied.

"Come here," demanded Flora Adkins. "All of you."

The four looked at one another suddenly aware of the trouble they were in. Slowly, they hopped off their bikes, helped Chuck back into his wheelchair, and, together, went to the porch to receive their punishment.

The woman glared at them, her eyes hard. "What time is it?" she asked.

Rusty swallowed dryly and glanced over at Keith. His cousin studied the face of his watch. "Uh, a quarter past seven," he said.

"And what time did I ask you to bring Chuck home?"

"Six o'clock, ma'am," said Rusty politely.

"It seems like someone got their signals crossed," said Mrs. Adkins. "Or else, no one really cared."

"It was my fault, Mom," admitted Chuck. "I told them you wouldn't mind. Guess I was wrong."

"You're right about that," she said. The anger in her face slipped a little, revealing the hurt and fear underneath. "I was worried sick about you, Chuck. And not just because you were out riding around only God knows where. Have you forgotten about your medicine?

The doctor specifically said that it had to be taken at six every night. And it's already more than an hour overdue."

"I'm sorry, Mom," stammered the boy. "I guess we were just having so much fun, that I kind of hated coming back home." He looked down glumly at the wheelchair he sat in. "Especially this blasted chair here."

"Go to your room, Chuck," she told him firmly. "I'll bring your supper and your medicine. Then you're to go straight to bed."

"But, Mom—" he began, but then thought better of it. He hadn't been punished so severely since he was six or seven-years-old, but he figured that he probably deserved it now. Although he certainly hadn't intended to, he had frightened his mother with his reluctance to return home on time.

"You heard me," she said.

Chuck nodded sadly. "Help me up on the porch, will you, Maggie?"

"Sure," said the girl. She took the black rubber handles of the wheelchair and steered him up the ramp onto the porch. She stood and watched as Chuck wheeled his way past his mother and through the front door of the house. Then Maggie jumped off the porch and rejoined her friends.

"We really are sorry, Mrs. Adkins," said Rusty. "We didn't mean to worry you none."

Flora's face failed to soften. "I'd suggest you three get on home. I've already called your folks. I'm sure they'll be wanting to talk to you."

A sensation of collective dread filled them. "Yes, ma'am," said Maggie. "Come on guys. Let's go."

Flora Adkins watched as Rusty, Keith, and Maggie climbed onto their bikes and headed back down Sycamore Road. Part of her felt ashamed for making the calls that would cause them so much trouble. But, for the most part, she felt satisfied by her actions. No matter whose fault it might have been, the four had scared her very badly. She had enough to worry about without having to agonize over whether or not her crippled son was laying in a drainage ditch somewhere, the victim of a bad bicycle accident.

After the clattering sound of baseball cards in bicycle spokes faded into the summer darkness, she took a deep breath and went inside. Chuck had obeyed her order and gone directly to his room. But he wasn't the one she was the most upset with. Not by a long shot.

She walked through the foyer and entered the living room. Her husband sat in his easy chair, his eyes glued to the television screen. Joe Adkins was obviously aware of his wife's presence, but chose to ignore it. He took a long sip from a can of Budweiser and, lazily pointing the remote control, began flipping from one channel to the next.

"Joe," she said, trying her best to contain her anger. "I could've used a little help out there."

The mechanic belched and took another swallow of beer. "I reckon you did good enough for the both of us."

"It shouldn't have been my place," said Flora. "You're Chuck's father. You should've been the one waiting for him on that porch."

Joe shifted his gaze from the television and stared at his wife. "Don't you think you overreacted just a little? The boy and his pales were just late getting home, that's all. It wasn't like they were out committing armed robbery or something like that."

Flora's thin lips grew thinner. "The *boy*," she said. "You mean Chuck."

A twinge of pain seemed to surface on the man's strong face, then give way to bland apathy just as quickly. He turned back to the TV and continued channel surfing.

"I'm getting sick of this," said the woman.

"Sick of what?" asked Joe absently.

"This stupid attitude of yours," she said in frustration. "This self-pitying guilt trip you've been on for the past two years. I'm tired of it, Joe."

He simply shrugged and took another sip of beer.

"For goodness sakes! You can't even bring yourself to call your son by name," she snapped. "It's the boy this or the boy that. His name is Charles Emery Adkins. Named after your father and mine, remember?"

"There's nothing wrong with me," Joe assured her. "I'm the same man I always was. It's you who got to be such a worrywart. If he so much as farts, you're there with a thermometer and a bowl of chicken soup. Leave the boy alone, Flora, or you're going to end up mothering him to death."

"At least I care about him," she said. "You don't seem to give a damn."

"That isn't so," said Joe with no sign of conviction in his voice.

"I'm beginning to wonder," she said, feeling her contempt bleed away into despair.

"Joe, sweetheart, ever since that blasted accident, you've been punishing yourself. Feeling guilty about something you had absolutely no control over."

"I shot my son," he told her. "I blew his spine in half, for God's sake!"

"It was an accident, Joe! You tripped. The gun went off. You didn't do it on purpose."

Joe Adkins lifted his eyes. They were full of torment and self-loathing. "Didn't I? He didn't want to go hunting that day. I wanted him to go. I *shamed* him into going. I picked and picked at him, making him feel like less than a man until he felt obligated to go with me. So don't tell me that it wasn't my fault. I acted like some macho redneck and ended up crippling my son for life."

"You're wrong," she said.

"No, I'm not," he told her flatly. "And you know it. *He* knows it, too."

Flora simply stood there and stared at her husband of 15 years. She was tired of hearing his self-incrimination. He had made it perfectly clear to her time after time. Shaking her head, she turned and headed for the kitchen to warm up Chuck's supper and fetch his medicine.

Sometimes she felt as if she had two invalids living in the house with her. One was a physical cripple, while the other was an emotional one.

Keith stood outside the back door of the farmhouse for a long moment, dreading to step inside. He could see his grandfather clearly through the fine mesh of the screen and he looked none too happy.

Apparently, Jasper McLeod knew his grandson was there lingering in the darkness just outside the glow of the kitchen light. "Come on in," he said sternly.

The boy took a deep breath and stepped inside, careful to prevent the screen door from slamming shut. He didn't want to make it any worse than it already was.

His grandfather sat at the kitchen table, half a cup of black coffee sitting before him. His eyes were as hard and gray as flint. "Have a seat," he instructed.

Keith did as he was told. "Now what?" he asked. "Are you going to chew me out?"

"That was what I was aiming to do," said Jasper. He stared at the 12-year-old for a moment. "What I want to know is what you young'uns were thinking? Mrs. Adkins let Chuck go with ya'll on the condition that you get him home by six. But ya'll disregarded the promise you made and that upset her something awful."

"We're sorry about that," said Keith. "Time just got away from us and besides, Chuck said his mom wouldn't mind."

"But the fact of the matter was, she did," said the elderly man. "Keith, that boy has had a hard time of it in the last couple years. He is paralyzed from the waist down, won't walk another step again in his entire life. His mother was just afraid for him. Don't you understand that?"

"Sure," allowed Keith. "But I think everybody's making too big a deal out of this whole thing."

Jasper took a long sip of his lukewarm coffee and sighed. "So, where'd ya'll go anyway?"

"We just rode down Sycamore Road a couple of miles," said the boy. "Went out into the woods, that's all. Rusty and the others got spooked over some place called Hell Hollow and we came on back."

The old man seemed to stiffen in his chair. Something other than anger suddenly shown in his eyes. "Ya'll didn't go down in there, did you?"

"Nope," said Keith. He could detect the old man's uneasiness. "Don't tell me you believe it's haunted, too."

"Just stay away from there," warned his grandfather. "Take it from me...that's not a place for kids to mess around with. Adults, either."

"Why not? It's just an old patch of woods and weeds."

"Just stay away from it," said Jasper. "Understand me?"

Keith suddenly felt his temper rise. "I'm tired of this third-degree you're putting me through. I'm going up to my room."

"I'm not through talking to you, young man!" Jasper told him. "Now, sit back down."

"You're not my father," snapped the boy. "So you don't have any business telling me what the hell to do."

"Don't cuss at me!" bellowed the elderly man. Before he knew what was happening, he reached out and grabbed his grandson by the arm.

Keith's face turned pale with rage. "Let go of me, you old fart!" He jerked away from the old man's grasp and backed toward the hallway. "Don't you *ever* touch me again, you hear? If you lay your hands on me one more time, I'll have your wrinkled ass tossed into jail for child abuse. Don't think I'm bluffing either."

Jasper could tell by Keith's expression that he wasn't. "Please, son, just sit down and let's—"

"No!" yelled Keith, nearly in tears. "I hate being here, you know that? And I hate you, too! Just stay away from me, okay? Just leave me alone!"

The elderly farmer sat at the kitchen table and listened as the boy's footsteps mounted the stairs. When he heard the slamming of the bedroom door, a cold sensation of hopeless dread ran through Jasper's gut, from breastbone to stomach. He had wished for a greater closeness with his grandson, but instead his anger had gotten the better of him. As a result, the gap between them had probably stretched further than before Keith had even arrived in Harmony.

He thought of the way the boy had trembled in his grasp, not out of fear, but pure rage.

"You old fool," he grumbled, staring glumly at the stained top of the kitchen table and the cup of coffee that sat before him, growing cold.

"But, Mama—!" began Rusty.

"Don't you 'Mama me', young man," said Susan McLeod. She stood beside the fireplace in the living room, while her son sat slumped on the couch. "You're going to have to learn to stop doing whatever pops into your head at the time and show a little responsibility. This isn't the first time you've pulled a stunt like this. God knows you've given both me and your daddy enough guff lately."

"But I don't do it purposely, Mama," Rusty tried to explain. "It just seems to work out that way for some reason."

Susan studied her son. He looked like a smaller, younger version of his truck driver father: whipcord lean and lanky with sharp green eyes and a shock of orange-red hair the hue of rusty barbed wire. And that wasn't all. He possessed much of the same personally that Frank McLeod had, both positive and negative.

"You're a carbon copy of your papa, you know that?' she said. "High-spirited and independent, full of energy. But you've gotta learn not to let those things get in the way of doing right. You've got to learn to stick to the rules, son. If you don't, you'll end up on the county work farm before you reach 20. I've seen it happen before."

"Aw, Mama, you're exaggerating," Rusty half-laughed.

The rigid look on her plump face told him that she, for one, didn't believe so. "Don't you sass me, boy. I'm the one talking here. You just keep your butt glued to those seat cushions and listen to what I have to say. Understand?"

Rusty swallowed dryly. "Yes, ma'am."

"I just want you to take a moment and think of what you did this evening," she explained. "You didn't just go for a longer stretch of joyriding than you promised Flora Adkins you would. You betrayed her trust and ended up scaring her half out of her wits. She's been taking care of Chuck since that accident at Willow Lake. She's waited on him hand and foot, built up his spirits and never let him out her sight. When she finally decided to give him that first bit of freedom away from her, she put her trust in you and the others to give her peace of mind. And how did you repay that trust? You let her down. You acted as if it didn't mean anything."

"Mama," ventured Rusty, knowing that he was treading on treacherous ground.

"Chuck isn't as bad off as Mrs. Adkins makes out. He can't walk, but he's sturdy enough. He just wanted it to be like old times again, if only for a little while."

Susan McLeod knew what her son was driving at. "And you kind of found it hard to disappoint him by taking him back on time, is that it?"

"Sort of," said Rusty.

The woman sighed, feeling as if she couldn't fault him much, particularly since his indiscretion had been out of loyalty to a friend. "Your supper's on the table. You can heat it up in the microwave. We'll discuss your punishment later."

"Yes, ma'am," he said, leaving the couch. As he passed her, he paused. "I'm sorry, Mama."

When Rusty had left the room, Susan sat down on the couch, emotionally drained. She was glad that the confrontation was finally over. She didn't mind bearing the responsibility of raising her son to be the best person possible, but at times she felt as if she had been branded the villain of the McLeod household. She knew that Rusty understood the responsibilities she had to shoulder in his father's absence, but she was afraid that in time that he might come to resent her role of disciplinarian. Susan just wished Frank was around more often to share such difficult times. Rusty was at the age where he needed a firm hand to keep him in line. And Susan wasn't at all certain that she was strict enough to do the job effectively.

Maggie Sutton was relieved when she discovered that her parents' car was not in the driveway. Her brother's black Mustang was there, but the burgundy Altima was nowhere to be found.

As the girl parked her bike next to the garage and cautiously entered the side door, she remembered that it was her mother and father's night to go out. They were probably at the Cracker Barrel in Manchester, chowing down on chicken and dumplings, hash brown casserole and fried okra.

She entered the house and made her way down the hallway, toward the family room. A glance at the light on the answering machine told her that no messages had been left. That gave her some small shred of hope. Perhaps Mrs. Adkins had been unsuccessful in reaching Maggie's parents and exposing their neglect in bringing Chuck home on time. That was, unless her brother had answered the phone.

Maggie paused and listened. Tom was home, that was for certain. She could hear his stereo booming from the upper floor of the house. Her 17-year-old brother had some heavy metal band cranked to maximum volume: something he was only allowed to do when their parents were out of the house.

Perhaps Tom had not heard the phone ring due to the decibel level of his stereo. And maybe, if she was very careful, she might just be able to sneak up the stairs to her room without alerting her arrival home. If he got an inkling that she was in the house, he wouldn't be able to resist engaging in his favorite pastime: tormenting her. Since he was twelve, Tom Sutton had made a hobby out of teasing and picking at his little sister, generally making life difficult for her—especially if she was attempting to keep something from her parents. That alone brought out a particularly sadistic side of his personality.

She climbed the stairs and cautiously made her way along the hallway. A moment later she had reached the door of her bedroom. Maggie breathed a sigh of relief. She knew Mrs. Adkins would reach her parents eventually and that she would have to face the music sooner or later, but hopefully tonight she would escape punishment.

Maggie knew that she was wrong the moment she laid her hand on the doorknob. As her fingers touched metal, the chaotic thumping of bass and crescendo of percussion ended in mid-note. She whirled and, there, standing in the open doorway of the adjacent bedroom, was her brother. Tom Sutton was tall, handsome, and athletic; three attributes that he was well aware of. He was also the star of the high school football team and the most popular buy in his class. He wasn't very successful academically and struggled to keep a steady C average—much to Maggie's secret delight—but that didn't seem to bother him any. He had his obnoxious friends, a string of air-headed girlfriends, his car, and his sports, and that was all that was necessary to make him happy. To tell the truth, if Maggie could think of one word that might best describe her older brother, it would undoubtedly have to be 'asshole'.

Tom leaned against the doorframe and smiled at her. "I thought I heard you come in," he said, then added "Margret" as an afterthought. Maggie didn't mind people calling her by her proper name, but for some reason when Tom used it, it completely drove her up the wall.

"I don't see how you heard anything with all that noise, Thomas," she said in retribution.

Her brother's smarmy grin almost faltered. "What are you doing sneaking down the hall like that? Trying to hid something?"

"Of course not."

Tom's smile broadened. "Nope. Wrong answer. The patented Sutton Lie-O-Meter just went way off the scale, little sister."

"You're a jerk, you know that?" she snapped, turning the knob of her bedroom door. If she could just get into her room, she could lock him out and she wouldn't have to listen to his stupid remarks.

"Just hold up, squirt," he warned her. "You know, I got an interesting call tonight."

Tom's eyes sparkled cruelly.

Maggie froze in her tracks.

"Yeah, it was Mrs. Adkins out on Sycamore Road calling to let Mom and Dad know what kind of irresponsible little brat their darling daughter is. Of course, luckily, I was here to take a message."

The girl turned, her eyes pleading. "Tom...please don't tell them. At least not until tomorrow."

Her brother threw up his hands. "Hey, why put off till tomorrow what you can do today, that's what I always say." He glanced at the hall clock. "And I'd say the folks should be home in an hour or so."

"There's really no need to tell them tonight," Maggie urged. "It'll just upset them, that's all."

"Sorry, kid. I've already made up my mind to tell them the minute they step through the front door." Tom Sutton grinned devilishly. "This is what I live for, Margret. The times that their precious angel screws up."

Maggie stared at her brother. "Why are you so mean to me all the time?" she asked, unable to understand the nature of his viciousness.

Tom shrugged his broad shoulders. "It just comes natural, I guess. Now you go on in your room. I promise to send Mom and Dad in to see you just as soon as they get here."

Maggie knew no further pleading on her part would dissuade him. When her brother got an urge to make life miserable for her, there was absolutely nothing she could do to change his mind.

The girl stepped into her bedroom and closed the door behind her. She felt her heart sink, knowing that she was in for a good talking-to when her parents arrived. And she was sure that Tom would have his slimy ear glued to the other side of the door the whole time, relishing every word.

Maggie kicked off her flip-flops and lay down on her bed. She stared at the things that decorated her room: the Ringling Brothers and Barnum & Bailey posters on the walls, as well as the collection of porcelain clowns that graced her mirrored dresser. There was even a Barbie doll dressed in a bright pink leotard and a feathered headdress perched on the edge of her chest-of-drawers like an acrobat balanced precariously on a tightrope. When she wasn't hanging around the guys being a tomboy, that was the thing Maggie enjoyed most of all—the circus with its glitz and glamour. The cotton candy and roasted peanuts, the lions and elephants and seltzer-spraying clowns. And—most of all—the ones who defied death at the height of the big top on the tightrope and the flying trapeze.

With a sigh, Maggie closed her eyes and imagined herself in a sequined leotard, holding a balancing pole in one hand and waving to the cheering crowd with the other. For a little while at least, she would be that lovely daredevil of her dreams. But, sooner or later, Maggie knew her fantasy would fade with the sound of her parents' car pulling into the driveway and the excited drumming of her brother's feet as he rushed downstairs to meet them at the front door.

CHAPTER SEVENTEEN

"Where the hell am I?" wondered Slash Jackson as he stumbled through the treacherous darkness of the Tennessee backwoods.

It seemed as though he had been walking for hours. After leaving the interstate and the blood-splattered Lincoln behind, he had headed eastward through the forest as quickly as the uneven terrain would allow. As the evening drew on and he became convinced that no one was immediately on his trail, Slash slowed his pace a bit. Using the sun that peeked through the heavy foliage as a reference point, he turned northward, hoping to make a gradual swing west again and meet up with Interstate 24 some 10 or 15 miles further on.

By the time the sun had set and the shadows had thickened into total darkness, Slash had lost his bearings. He found himself wandering aimlessly through the dense thicket of close-grown trees and knee-deep undergrowth, searching for some sign of civilization. But the further he descended into the forest, the darker and wilder the wilderness became. He saw no electric lights or even the sign of a deer path, let alone an actual road. Crickets sung in the thicket around him, as well as an owl or a distant whippoorwill every now and then.

He continued on, afraid to turn back. He knew eventually that he would have to come across a farm or town. The woods wouldn't go on forever. If he lost his head, there was a better chance that he would be caught for what he had done to Allison Walsh and Larry

Bell. And, as a result, would end up paying for all the other crimes he had committed and probably spend the rest of his life behind prison walls.

He wasn't prepared to surrender his freedom quite so easily. Slash continued through the deepening darkness, near exhaustion and feeling weak from lack of food and water. Breakfast at an interstate truckstop had been his last meal. Nearly 14 [yours] had passed since then and he was ravenously hungry. He was thirsty, too. Strangely enough, he had failed to come across a single backwoods creek during his escape through the forest and his mouth and throat were paper dry. He would have settled for drinking out of a stagnant mud puddle if it were to come down to that. But, so far, he hadn't even been lucky enough to find that.

Slash was pushing his way through a wall of honeysuckle, when he saw a patch of moonlight shining through the open treetops ahead. Hoping that it would give him a clearer sense of where he was, he stepped through the fragrant vines, expecting to meet solid ground on the other side. Instead, his foot swung into open air. He clutched handfuls of honeysuckle hoping to correct his balance but it was too late. He pitched headfirst down a steep embankment. With a grunt, Slash tumbled down a high grade covered with moss, ferns and sharp rocks. By the time he finally reached the bottom and landed on his back in a bed of soft kudzu, Slash was a mass of bruises and abrasions.

Shakily, he got to his feet and was relieved to find that he had suffered no broken bones. His ears rang from a glancing blow to the side of his skull, probably on one of the jutting stones, but there was no blood. His probing fingers found a good-sized knot beneath his oily black hair, but fortunately that seemed to be the extent of the injury.

After a spell of dizziness had passed, Slash studied his surroundings in the pale glow of the moon. He had fallen into a large hollow of some sort. Looking up at the honeysuckle patch he had stepped through, he figured he had fallen a good 50 feet down a very steep incline. It was a wonder he hadn't broken his fool neck in the process.

Slash stood there and looked around. The hollow was a deep basin choked with heavy underbrush and tall pines. The opposite side of the valley ascended in a steeper slope than the one he had just fallen down and he groaned at the prospect of having to climb back up to level ground. Nevertheless, he knew he had to get moving. If he could find a secluded farm nearby he had a chance of getting back on track. He might luck upon food or water and maybe even some spending cash and a vehicle. And, if he was fortunate enough, perhaps some fun of the kind he had enjoyed with that brunette back in Georgia.

He started northward across the floor of the hollow, stepping high to keep from getting snared by the creeping ivy that grew heavily above the earth. Halfway across, he spotted something in the moonlight. At first he thought it was an old shack covered with green ivy. But, upon closer inspection, he discovered that it was not that at all.

It was a wagon. An ancient 4-wheeler that resembled a western stagecoach. Or, on second thought, it looked more like an old-time circus wagon, the type that traveled from town to town back in the late 1800s and early 1900s. Its wheels had collapsed beneath the weathered hull and it was almost entirely obscured from view by a heavy blanket of dark, clinging ivy.

Curiously, Slash approached the wagon. As he neared the rusty iron tongue of the front axle, the toe of his boot bumped into something below the kudzu. He bent down and dug through the undergrowth until he found what he was searching for. It was the bleached white skull of a horse. One that looked to have been there for decades.

Intrigued, Slash reached the front of the ivy-covered wagon. He climbed upon the broken bench of the front seat surprised at how sturdy the ancient vehicle still seemed to be. On either side of a narrow doorway leading into the back were the shattered globes of lamps secured just below the lip of the overhang. One still held the stub of a candle. Slash wrestled the tapered length of wax from its mounting and, taking the Zippo from his jeans pocket, attempted to light it. It took four tries, but eventually the wick ignited and held its flame.

Slash moved around to the side of the wagon. Beneath the mass of clinging vines, he could detect a trace of writing. He pulled the stubborn strands of kudzu away, then stepped back and read the elaborately-lettered words that covered the side panel. They were badly weathered and faded, but he could still make out what they said.

DOCTOR AUGUSTUS LEECH'S TRAVELING MEDICINE SHOW—MAGIC, MUSIC, & MUSE—FEATURING THE GOOD DOCTOR'S PATENTED CURE-ALL ELIXIR!

After reading the inscription, Slash turned toward the rear of the wagon. Maybe there was something in the back that might be of interest or value. Maybe some antiques that he could pawn for traveling money.

When he reached the back of the medicine show wagon, he found that the twin doors were caved inward. Vines obscured most of the entrance while pitch-blackness lurked beyond. Slash tugged the ivy away and cautiously stepped inside. It was the height of summer and the woods he was lost in were bound to be crawling with snakes. He would hate to walk blindly into a den of timber rattlers or copperheads. He had enough trouble to contend with already.

Upon entering the cramped hull of the wagon, he stood still and listened. He heard nothing stirring in the darkness. As a matter of fact, since he first fell into the hollow, Slash hadn't heard much of anything. No chirring of crickets, no peeping of tree frogs, no distant call of a lonesome night bird. All that had greeted him was complete silence. That should have unnerved him, but he was too intrigued by the discovery of the wagon to give it much thought.

He crept into the dark belly of the wagon, holding the moldy candle ahead of him. The interior was musky and cluttered with all manner of junk: wooden cases marked ELIXIR, and old cherry-wood wardrobe, a fancy dressing table with a cracked oval mirror and an ancient 5-string banjo with a broken neck. And there was something else at the foremost end of the cramped cabin. Something Slash Jackson certainly didn't expect to find.

It was a skeleton. The skeleton of a rather tall man, from the looks of it. It was dressed in a black coat and Abraham Lincoln hat, the material of both mildewed and crumbling into dust. A tarnished gold pocket watch with the leering face of a devil hung from the fob of a satin vest that had split at the seams, revealing the skeleton's naked ribs.

Slash suppressed a shudder of fear that threatened to run down the length of his spine. His curiosity far outweighed his uneasiness. He drew nearer and examined the skeleton that sat with its back to the front wall. Both of its legs were shattered. They were nothing but jagged shards of white bone from the knees down.

That hadn't been what had killed the man, however.

He lifted the candle, letting the flickering light play upon the grinning face of the skull. In the center of the bony forehead, directly between the gaping, black eye sockets, was a single bullet hole. A rifle bullet from the size of it.

"Somebody sure had it in for you, didn't they?" said Slash. He studied the grinning skull for a long moment. "Just who were you, anyway? The fella that ran this traveling show? Doctor Leech?"

The skeleton simply smiled back at him almost teasingly—a mystery in time-bleached bone.

"Yeah, I bet that's who you were," he said. "What the hell did you do to get somebody that pissed off?"

Again, the earthly remains of the traveling medicine man held no answers. Only grim and sinister possibilities.

Slash was about to turn back to the junk that littered the wagon floor, when the candlelight played across the skeleton's right hand. Clutched in the bony claw was a skinny, long-necked bottle. A cork was jammed firmly in its mouth, but slightly askew. Almost as if it had been sealed in haste, at a second's notice.

"Let's see what you got there, partner," said Slash. He pried the bottle loose from the skeleton's hand, snapping a couple of brittle bones as he did so. He blew dust from the paper label. It was faded from age, but Slash could make out what it said. It read: DR. LEECH'S PATENTED ELIXIR—CURES A VARIETY OF PHYSICAL ILLNESSES—GOUT, ARTHRITIS, HEADACHES, IRREGULARITY, & CHILDHOOD AILMENTS.

Intrigued, Slash uncorked the bottle and lifted the mouth to his nostrils. At first, the scent of the bottle's contents repulsed him. It smelled like a combination of sulfur, urine, and dried snakeskin. But, when he took another whiff, the aroma somehow smelled entirely different. It smelled like the finest Tennessee sipping whiskey, like Jack Daniels Old Number Seven aged to a delectable vintage.

"Don't smell half bad," said Slash. His throat yearned for a drink of anything liquid, his thirst nagging at him like a dull ache. "Well, let's see if it tastes any better than it smells."

The aroma of the dark and ancient elixir curled through his nostrils, drawing him like a fish on a hook. Unable to resist the temptation any longer, he lifted the bottle and took a long swallow.

The liquid went down smooth, as if possessing more oil content than water. Slash expected it to burn going down his gullet, like good whiskey should. But it didn't. Instead, it seemed as cold as ice. The elixir flowed through him like a swallow of Death itself, chilling him from head to toe.

"Gaaaah!" chocked Slash, flinging the bottle into the lap of the grinning skeleton. "No wonder they iced you! That's some evil hooch you brewed there!"

The skull with the bullet hole between its empty eyes simply stared at him and grinned, as if privy to some dark secret Slash had no earthly inkling of. Not yet at least.

Slash coughed and gagged, but the damage had been done. The swallow of nasty elixir had already reached the pit of his stomach. He felt it settle in his belly like a ball of ice and slowly expand. Frightened, he crawled toward the back entrance of the wagon but suddenly found himself barely able to move. His limbs grew sluggish and heavy, as though he were attempting to swim through a sea of road tar and molasses.

"Damn!" he groaned as his arms collapsed beneath him and he fell flat on his face amid the clutter of the wagon floor. "What have I done? Poisoned myself?"

Using the last bit of strength he possessed, Slash turned his head and stared at the skeleton who sat a few feet away. Its toothy grin almost seemed to have broadened, grown more wicked and satisfied. *It knows,* he thought to himself numbly. *It knows what it's done to me.*

Unfortunately, Slash Jackson had no earthly idea of what he had just gotten himself into. The terrible coldness engulfed him like the cloak of a black cocoon, dragging his consciousness into its dark and frigid depths. A moment later, he had fallen into a deep slumber.

A slumber possessed of frightful sounds and disturbing images that had long since been forgotten with the passage of time.

CHAPTER EIGHTEEN

They were nearly upon him.

In defiance, he cracked the whip. It broke the hide of the right-hand horse, drawing dark blood and sending him at a faster pace than before. The other animal caught the rich scent of his partner's blood, surging forward as well. Soon, they had sped from a trot to a full gallop. Their shod hooves drummed on the hard clay dirt of the road that stretched into the dark forest ahead of them.

He couldn't help but laugh. His mirth climbed into the cool night air, brimming with arrogance and cruel humor. His black eyes sparkled wildly as he considered the purpose of their pursuit. He recalled how they and their wives had watched him with rapt fascination as he expounded eloquently on the virtues of his wondrous elixir. In all, they had purchased two cases of the bottle medicine, anxious to return home and try its miracle properties on ailing kin and sickly children. The fools! So gullible and full of blind trust. If they had tested his elixir on their livestock before they offered it to their loved ones, they would have seen it for the poison that it was. But they had not and, as a result, twelve had died horribly.

The traveling medicine man's laughter grew louder and bolder. He considered the children that had suffered and his smile broadened, framed by his waxed mustache and goatee beard. He could imagine their pain, their bright and lasting agony. The convulsions, the vomiting of blood, the sensation not unlike hot needles piercing internal organs...the side-effects were truly horrendous. They were more intense the younger the child, of course. He had done much research to ensure its potency, going as far as adopting children from local orphanages and testing his deadly concoction upon them.

Pleasure filled him at those cherished memories of watching them writhe and scream, timing the length of their torment with the assistance of his devil-faced watch.

His elixir worked on adults, as well, but in an entirely different manner. It was not as immediate or obvious. Sometimes, after ingesting the concoction, they would go unaffected for days or weeks at a time. Then tragedy would befall them. They would die of cancer or failure of the heart, or some horrible accident would befall them: a farming accident, a buggy wreck, or an unexplained fall from a railroad trestle. Sometimes they simply went insane. It didn't really matter to him. Eventually, it always came down to the same end result.

He thought of how long he had sold death and despair to the God-fearing folk of the South. He had peddled his lethal wares for nearly seven years and, in all that time, had never been caught. He had never been made to pay for the evil he had brought upon the rural communities he frequented. And it would be the same that night. He would elude his most recent pursuers, vanishing into the darkness of the Tennessee forest before they could they overtake him.

"Faster, you black bastards!" he laughed. His whip cracked the autumn air like tethered lightning. Blood blossomed from dark hide once again and the geldings, already lathered with the sweat of exertion, pushed their stamina beyond the limit. The brightly-painted wagon rocked from side to side, its red wheels spinning as swiftly as the roulette wheel of a Mississippi River gambling boat.

A gunshot cracked from behind him, striking the edge of the seat and sending splinters flying into the night air. He grinned and looked around the corner at the advancing posse. Another gunshot rang out and a revolver bullet tugged at the crown of his stovepipe hat, nearly knocking it from his head. He caught the edge of the brim in time to save it then turned back to his escape, cackling all the while.

Deeper into the forest he drove. Soon, the treetops mingled above the roadway, forming a canopy dense enough to shut out the glow of the full moon. The candles of the wagon's lamps cast some illumination on the earthen trail, but not enough to light the team's way. They galloped onward blindly, afraid to let up lest they suffer the agony of the whip of their slowness.

Then, suddenly, the medicine man knew that he had made a fatal mistake. The road abruptly vanished and both team and wagon lurched into open space. The horses wailed in fright, their thin legs flailing through empty air, as they soared into a deep backwoods hollow. A moment later the animals and the vehicle they pulled hit the earth with a tremendous and devastating crash. The black geldings collided with the ground first. One died immediately, while the other's legs snapped like matchsticks. The wagon's wheels collapsed upon impact and the medicine man suffered similarly. The front end of the wagon plowed into solid earth, snapping the seat in half and driving him violently downward. Both of his legs shattered with the force of the fall. Sharp spikes of gleaming bone jutted from the cloth of his black trousers as he screamed in agony and defeat.

When the wagon had finally settled in a fractured heap amid the bed of stones and kudzu, he struggled against his suffering, knowing that fate had finally dealt him a losing hand. He could hear the excited yells of the horsemen as they carefully made their way down the steep slope of the wooded hollow toward him. With difficulty, he pulled himself upward and squeezed through a narrow entrance that led into the belly of the wagon's cabin. He dropped to the floor with a jolt of white-hot agony and sat there against the back wall, breathing raggedly, fighting against unconsciousness.

He knew the end was inevitable. They would finally have their retribution this time, burnished with hatred and rage for the poison he had knowingly peddled for the supposed benefit of them and their precious children. But he did not want to face his demise in a stupor. He wanted to look them square in the eyes and let them know, in no uncertain terms, that he did not fear them. He wanted them all to know the extent of his contempt for them, as well as for the virtues of faith and goodness they held in such high regard. He wanted to curse in the face of their Almighty Savior, the way he had all the days of his adult life.

Outside the wagon, the group of angry farmers and townsmen had arrived. Their horses snorted and shied at the agonized cries of the injured gelding. The boom of a shotgun thundered through the night and the animal's hoarse bellowing ceased. The medicine man fought against his own torment, listening as they dismounted and approached the wagon. He knew he had little time to spare. He reached into the inner pocket of his black frock coat, produced a bottle of his deadly elixir, and pulled the cork free.

He heard them as they surrounded the wagon, searching for him. "Let's see if the son of a bitch is hiding inside," one suggested. He knew they would be through the back entrance and upon him in a matter of seconds. He closed his eyes and chanted something in a language that was far removed from the country he now traveled in. Then he lifted the bottle to his mouth. But he did not drink.

The pounding of rifle butts against the back door barely came to him as he lowered the bottle and pushed the cork firmly into place. An instant later, the partition caved in and the dark forms of several men squeezed through the open doorway. He could smell the anger rolling off of them like the pungent scent of a polecat.

"He's poisoned himself with his own medicine!" exclaimed a mousy fellow with round, wire-rimmed glasses; the town banker from the looks of him.

A tall, rawboned farmer with a leathery face led them. "Well, it won't kill him quick enough, that's for sure!"

The medicine man felt the coldness engulf him, sensed the darkness closing around him like a smothering blanket. Soon, he would be gone. But, before that happened, he summoned the strength to utter one last curse. "Damn you all to hell," he rasped, his lips curling into a grin of pure wickedness.

He watched as the big farmer lifted a Winchester rifle to his shoulder and placed a calloused finger upon the trigger. The man glared over the sights as he settled them on a point squarely between the murderer's eyes. The lanky man in the black coat and hat closed his eyes and smiled almost smugly as darkness surrounded him, pulling him further into the void.

"No, Pa!" came the voice of a child—a small boy. "Please, don't!"

But the farmer would not listen. His finger tightened on the rifle's trigger. A single shot cracked through the night...and it was over and done with.

Or so they thought.

He opened his eyes and lay there for a long time. Eventually, the awful coldness left his body and the warmth of life and vitality surged through him. Slowly, he sat up and stretched, as if awaking from a long and restful sleep.

The candle lay on its side, its wick still lit. He picked it up, found a tarnished brass candleholder lying amid the rubble of the floor, and secured it firmly into the socket of the base. He set the candle on the dusty surface of the dressing table and pulled himself to a standing position. He had to steady himself, for he felt as week and unbalanced as a baby taking its first faltering steps. That would pass, however. The vessel he occupied was strong. Its muscle and sinew were toughened from years of grueling labor and its brain was certainly compatible, well accustomed to the same dark thoughts and sadistic pleasures he had once relished. It was as though he were home once again following an extremely long absence.

He walked shakily to the cherry-wood wardrobe and, after a couple of tugs, firmly pulled the warped door free. There, hanging on the wooden rod, was a black frock coat with wide lapels and a long, narrow tail. And, perched on the shelf above, was a tall, stovepipe hat of jet-black silk.

Taking the ancient, but durable articles of clothing from the wardrobe, he put them on. Soon, he stood before the cracked and cloudy mirror of the dressing table. The coat fit perfectly, as if it had been tailored for the body they now covered. He decided to keep the Grateful Dead t-shirt. He rather liked the chorus line of dancing skeletons that adored the front. It seemed to fit his dark mood appropriately.

Picking up a rickety stool, he sat before the shattered mirror and ran an exploring hand along his gaunt and whiskered face. The eyes were a shade lighter and the complexion a bit darker from exposure to the sun, but, other than that, the resemblance was quite amazing.

"Yes," whispered Augustus Leech, adjusting the brim of the stovepipe hat rakishly, his eyes gleaming with renewed malice. He flexed the muscles of his new body, feeling the power as it began to return. "This will do. This will do rather nicely indeed."

Outside the ivy-covered wagon, the creatures of the forest sat perfectly still and listened. Their tiny eyes twinkled with fright and they cowered further into the black shadows as a sound rang throughout the length and breadth of Hell Hollow. It was a sound their kind had heard only once before, and that had been over 80 years ago.

Laughter.

The sinister laughter of one who was truly and undeniably evil at heart.

PART TWO

DREAMS & NIGHTMARES

CHAPTER NINETEEN

"There you go, Ms. Walsh," said Doctor Matthews as he signed the release form. "As of this moment, you are a free woman."

Allison wasn't so certain, however. "Physically maybe," she half-joked. "But mentally? That's another matter entirely."

The doctor smiled at her sympathetically. "Of course, it's natural for you to continue to harbor feelings of fear and anxiety, considering the ordeal you suffered. That's one of the biggest shortcomings of my profession. We can mend broken bones and suture wounds, but we're totally powerless to heal the human soul."

"You did more than you let on," said Allison, taking his hand. "And I really appreciate it. I guess there's still some things I'm going to have to work out on my own."

"Preferably with the help of a good therapist," suggested Matthews. "I hope your sessions with Ms. Prentess were of some value."

He was referring to Elizabeth Prentess, one of the hospital's psychologists. A nice lady, but a little too smug and self-absorbed for Allison's taste. "Yes, she helped me a lot," she lied.

"Good," said the doctor. "But, remember, to get back on track for keeps, you really should see someone on a regular basis."

"I'll certainly keep that in mind," replied Allison, although she had already abandoned such an option. She had never had much faith in shrinks or their methods. She felt that whatever healing was to take place deep down within her, would be of her own making.

But, before that could happen, she had several difficult issues to work through. Issues that dealt with both the present and the distant past.

"Good luck, Ms. Walsh," said Matthews. "And, please, try to put this behind you, all right?"

"Thank you, Doctor," she replied, mustering her most hopeful smile. "I certainly intend to."

A moment later, a nurse was wheeling her off the elevator and through the spacious front lobby of Rome's University Medical Center. She felt sort of silly and self-conscious being escorted to the front entrance in a wheelchair, especially when she was well enough to walk on her own. But it was merely a policy of the hospital, as it was with most medical facilities.

"Do you have a way home, Ms. Walsh?" asked the red-haired nurse, whose name was Nadine.

"Yes, I'm supposed to have a rental car delivered here by 10:00," she said. "The police haven't located my car yet. The bastard has probably abandoned it in another state by now. Either that or dumped it in a lake somewhere."

"Well, I certainly hope they find it soon," said Nadine.

Allison looked down at the clothes she wore that morning. The modest peach blouse and white slacks, along with the canvas sneakers, was her one and only outfit. She had been brought to the hospital completely naked. The clothing she had worn at the time of her abduction had been too torn up and bloodstained to be of much use. The blouse, slacks and shoes had been generously purchased for her at the local Wal-Mart by some of the nurses on her floor.

"I really do appreciate the clothes, Nadine," she said, a little embarrassed. "It was very nice of you all."

"Don't mention it, hon," said the nurse, her sunny smile vanishing. She placed a supportive hand on

Allison's shoulder. "It's the least we could do...given the circumstances."

"Yes," said Allison. And what horrible circumstances they had been.

Once again, she fought against that ugly image that threatened to fill her thoughts—Slash Jackson coming toward her in the dim glow of a candle, his naked body painted crimson with her blood, armed with a knife, a hard-on and an expression of pure, undiluted evil. She closed her eyes and breathed in deeply, counting backward from 20 to one. Eventually, the image of her attacker faded. But she knew that it would be back to haunt her sooner or later, both during her waking hours and in her nightmares.

Allison and Nadine said their goodbyes in the hospital lobby, where the brunette waited for the arrival of her rental car. The rental agent had promised to meet her in the front lobby, but, so far, he was nowhere to be found.

She waited fifteen minutes then decided to find a vending machine. The pain medication she was on tended to make her mouth dry and she could sure use a soda at that moment. She left the lobby and started down a central corridor that led past the bank of elevators. Soon, she found an area that had several vending machines.

Allison took a purse from her shoulder—also purchased by the nurses—and dug some loose change from the bottom. Fortunately, Slash Jackson had neglected to use any of her credit cards so far. She had withdrawn $500 dollars of emergency cash from her American Express account, which was more than enough to get her back to St. Louis with no hassle.

After purchasing a soda and popping the tab, she left the vending area and started back for the main lobby. But, several minutes later, she found herself in an entirely different part of the hospital. It wasn't long before she pushed through a set of swinging doors and found another entranceway. But it was not the one she had been looking for.

She could tell by the pneumatic doors, reception desk and narrow waiting area, that she had stumbled onto the emergency ward. To her left was a large, windowed room with partitioned areas for treating everything from cut fingers to severe trauma.

"Excuse me," she asked the nurse at the desk. "Could you tell me how to get back to the main lobby?"

The woman regarded her indifferently. "You go back through those doors, take a left, go down to the next corridor and make another left. That should take you right there."

Allison was about to follow her directions, when the pneumatic doors opened with a whoosh and a paramedic team rushed in, wheeling an adjustable gurney. One of them performed CPR on the bloody man on the gurney, while another held an IV bag and propelled the cart forward. Close on their heels was a police officer, his eyes frightened and his face as pale as flour.

"Hey, we need some help here!" yelled the patrolman, his voice cracking with emotion.

A lean doctor in green scrubs and a white lab coat appeared from the emergency room. "What have we got here?"

"A police officer," replied one of the paramedics. "Shot twice with a twelve-gauge shotgun; once in the stomach, once in the right side of the chest. His vital signs are unstable and he's presently in cardiac arrest."

"Let's get to work people," he called to a team of nurses and residents. "Pronto!"

Allison stood there, dazed, as the doctors wheeled the injured officer into the examination room and began to attend to him. She watched as they removed his navy uniform shirt—which was no more than bloody, shredded cloth—as well as his Sam Browne gun belt. A nurse hurriedly deposited the two items on a small table next to the open doorway then returned to assist with the battle to stabilize the wounded man.

Allison stared past the others, at the face of the gunshot cop. His skin was clammy and gray, his eyes unresponsive. *He's not going to make it*, she told herself. Then she shifted her eyes to his chest and abdomen. They were little more than bloody, open holes.

Instantly, Slash intruded on her thoughts once again. She felt herself slipping back to a single horrible moment when she thought that she would die for sure. Allison had been naked and bound on the dusty floor of the abandoned house, blood flowing from the deep cuts in her chest. She had stared pleadingly up at a grinning face as bright and wicked as a clown from Hell. Allison had searched for a shred of decency and compassion, but realized that he possessed neither.

Aw, what's the matter, Allison baby? asked Slash, his tone full of mockery. *Are you bleeding too much? Can I do anything for you? Call 911 maybe? Or how about a Band-aid?* He had laughed long and loud. *Hell, we'd have to buy a couple dozen boxes to fix you up, wouldn't we?*

Allison drove the ugly memory from her mind and again focused on the dying police officer. *Someone like him did this to you,* she thought. *Someone exactly like Slash.*

Abruptly, she knew what she had to do. To heal herself, to make herself feel fully whole again, she must rid herself of the demon who had taken her so brutally and without mercy.

Allison calmly surveyed her surroundings. The doctors and paramedics were focused on the man on the gurney. The other police officer—apparently the victim's partner—stood a few feet away, overcome with shock. The nurse at the reception desk had left her post to assist the trauma team.

She turned her attention to the table by the doorway, or more precisely, on the bundle of bloody items that rested there, forgotten.

It was perfect. A once-in-a-lifetime opportunity that would be gone at a moment's passing.

She acted while no one was watching then left the emergency ward. Allison pushed through the swinging doors and into the corridor she had left scarcely 45 seconds ago, her purse two pounds heavier than before.

It wasn't until she reached the hospital's main lobby that she allowed herself to breath easy. Allison walked to the big glass windows that looked out onto the single lane of the building's covered entranceway, as well as the parking lot beyond. Her heart began to pound. *Where is he?* her mind screamed, near panic. *He said he would be here at 10:00!*

She stood there aware of what she had just done, as well as the jeopardy she had put herself in. She felt no guilt for her actions, only the fear of being caught.

"Oh...ma'am?" called a male voice from behind her.

Allison froze. She could imagine the other police officer standing directly behind her, his buddy forgotten for the moment, his face stern and uncompromising. Had he noticed her? Had he witnessed her little slight-of-hand act?

She took a deep breath and turned around. Fortunately, her fears were unfounded. Instead of the policeman, a curly-haired man in a white shirt and tie stood there.

"Are you Allison Walsh?" he asked, referring to a clipboard he held in his hand.

"Uh, that's right," she said.

"I'm Wayne Billings from Avis," he said. "Sorry I'm late, but traffic was kind of heavy."

Relief flowed through Allison. "That's okay. I was just released a few minutes ago."

"Got a real nice car for you," he said. "A Nissan Altima with the works. It's parked in the lot outside. Just sign here and we'll have you on your way."

Allison signed the paperwork and took the keys he offered. A moment later, she was sitting in the burgundy sedan with the engine running and the air conditioner cranked up to full blast. She made sure that no one was looking, then opened her purse and removed the object she had stolen from the table in the ER.

The revolver was a .38 Smith & Wesson with a six-inch barrel and black neoprene grips. It felt heavy in her hand, but not uncomfortably so. She pushed the cylinder release and checked the loads. There were five hollow-point cartridges, with an empty chamber behind the hammer. Whatever had happened to the policeman that day, the poor guy hadn't even gotten the chance to draw and fire his weapon before being gunned down.

Allison snapped the cylinder back into place then stashed the gun back in her purse. She no longer felt totally helpless. Instead, she felt a peculiar sense of empowerment. Empowerment to shift the odds in her favor and pay her tormentor back for those long hours of constant agony and terror.

As she put the car into drive and left the hospital parking lot, Allison Walsh considered the fate she had planned for Slash Jackson. When she caught up with him—and she assured herself that she *would* locate him eventually—she intended to make him pay dearly for the pain and humiliation he had caused. And, in the process, instantly heal a hurt that would otherwise take years of therapy to cure.

CHAPTER TWENTY

"There ya go, pal," said Big Jake Abernathy. He rammed a barbecue fork through a charred steak and, lifting it from the flames of the grill, flung it in the dust a few feet away. "Just the way you like it. Burnt blacker than the inside of a coal miner's asshole."

Loco was up from his prone position in a flash. The black dog with the pink patch around his eye pounced on the piece of meat as if it were the first morsel of food he had been offered all week. That wasn't the case, however. The junkyard dog had downed two heaping bowls of dog food earlier that morning, as well as several pans of cold water from a spigot that protruded from the cinderblock foundation of the barn-like building that served as Jake's office, residence, and workshop. Of course, that mattered very little. Loco was like his master in several respects. He possessed an almost insatiable appetite, as well as a cast-iron stomach that could digest nearly anything it was subjected to.

Jake smiled in satisfaction as he watched the big dog grip the slab of black beef between his massive paws and began to tear into it with his sharp, yellow teeth. "Does my heart good to see a dog eat," he said to no one in particular. Then he turned back to the charcoal grill and threw his own sirloin on the flames. His taste for steak was the complete opposite of Loco's. He barely left the meat on the grill long enough to sizzle before he tossed it on a plate with sautéed onions and peppers, as well as a mound of greasy potatoes he had deep-fried only a short time ago. The steak was nearly as raw as it had been when he bought it at the grocery store in town, seeping a puddle of blood that mingled with the grease of the seasoned fries. If it had been any more raw, it would have been chewing its cud and mooing.

The junk dealer took his plate in hand, sat down in a lawn chair with frayed nylon webbing, and picked up a quart bottle of Miller High Life from where it stood on the ground. A cheap stereo system blared Led Zeppelin from a couple of speakers sitting in the building's open doorway and an electric fan in the nearest window circulated the warm air around him, making the heat of the summer night seem less sticky and humid than it should have. Jake sighed in contentment and settled back in his chair, then sliced himself off a hunk of bloody steak that would have choked a humpback whale. Unlike some folks, it didn't take very much to make Jake Abernathy a thoroughly happy man.

"This is the life, ain't it, Loco?" he said, wiping his greasy whiskers with the back of a tattooed forearm and taking a swig of cold beer.

The Rottweiler answered with a muffled grunt, his slobbering jaws chocked full of scorched meat.

Jake had finished off half of his Miller and most of his meal, when Loco suddenly lifted his head from where it rested on his paws. The dog's stubby ears pricked and a low growl rumbled deep down in his gullet.

"What's wrong, boy?" asked the junkman. He followed Loco's gaze into the shadows, but could see nothing. The sky was cloudy that night, sealing away any light from moon or stars. The junkyard was blanketed in pitch darkness.

Loco's agitation increased. His dark lips trembled until they parted at the corners, revealing clenched teeth. Slowly, he dog stood. His legs locked, his muscles quivering beneath his glossy black coat.

Jake slowly set his plate and bottle aside. He knew Loco as well as he knew himself. The dog had heard something, that was for sure. He leaned forward in the lawn chair and strained to hear it himself. The hard rock strands of "Communication Breakdown" drowned out any sound he might have caught. He left his chair, stepped inside and cut off the stereo, then went back outside.

He listened, but heard nothing. Literally nothing. Other than Loco's deep-throated growling and the soft buzz of the electric fan, the night was completely silent. There were no crickets singing in the tall weeds or anything else for that matter. Only thick, oppressive silence.

Loco's black eyes narrowed and he took a few steps forward. He would have taken off, but the logging chain he was tethered to prevented him from advancing any further.

Jake stood perfectly still, holding his breath for a few seconds. Suddenly, he heard it. It was the sound of movement in the junk heaps at the foremost boundary of the salvage yard. The sound of rattling cans and old inner tubes being shifted to one side. The furtive noises of a scavenger.

Slowly, the junk dealer walked over to his dog. Loco pulled against his restraint until the links of the chain were taut. Jake sucked his greasy teeth and listened for a moment longer. The noises came again, louder this time, as if the intruder didn't give a damn whether he was heard or not. And it wasn't the rats that made their home in the heaps of trash and metal, either. Jake knew how his rats sounded and it certainly wasn't they who were on the prowl that night.

A grin shown through Jake's blond whiskers as he stooped down and laid his hand on the snap clasp that was the sole link between the logging chain and Loco's heavy leather collar. "Okay, boy," he said, easing back on the release with his thumb. "You heard him before I did, so you get first shot."

Loco trembled in anticipation, leaning forward, his muscles bunched into tight coils. A runner of thick saliva dripped from the corner of this mouth and splattered into the clay dust of the yard.

A second later, Jake let him go. "Get him, old bud!" he yelled, laughing. "Tear his thieving butt clean off!"

The dog wasted no time. He shot away from the light of the building's security lamp, his dark form instantly merging with the darkness that stretched beyond. Jake stood there and grinned, listening to the quick padding of Loco's feet crossing the earth, as well as the fit of throaty barking that had replaced his growling.

"That's it, boy!" called Jake, loud enough for the unwelcome scavenger to hear. "Show 'im he can't rip off Big Jake Abernathy and get away with it!"

As Loco tore across the junkyard, Jake thought of the rash of thefts that had plagued Harmony during the past couple of days. Fletcher's Hardware had been broken into the night before last. The only items that had been stolen were a few cans of paint—red, yellow and blue—as well as a couple of brushes. And that wasn't all. Just that morning, a local carpenter named Ben Allen had gone out to his pickup truck to find most of his tools gone, along with several sheets of heavy plywood and a box of [ten-penny nails].

Staring into the darkness, Jake wondered if the same thief was out there at the edge of his property, attempting to pull another late-night raid.

Jake crossed his brawny arms over his chest and waited for the first scream of alarm. But, for some strange reason, it failed to come. Instead, Loco's ferocious growling came to an abrupt halt. One second, the dog was zooming in for the kill and then the next there came a sharp, high-pitched whine, followed by total silence.

The sudden absence of noise startled Jake. Loco basically had two moods; threatening and non-threatening. When he was on the offensive, he was vocally loud, with throaty growls and coarse barks. When he was passive, he was completely silent. In all the years Jake had owned the dog, he had never once heard him whine even when he was a puppy. Loco was either rowdy or quiet. There had never been any middle ground. Or at least not until that night.

Concerned, Jake backtracked to the office. He reached through the doorway and took a gun from a rack next to his cluttered desk. It was a Mossberg pump shotgun with eight inches sawed off the barrel. He stepped back into the yard, jacked a 12-gauge shell into the breech and peered into the darkness.

"Loco?" he called. "Boy, where are you?"

The dog neglected to answer. But he did hear something. Something that caused the hairs to stand up on his tattooed forearms.

A low, snickering laugh.

For a long moment, Jake Abernathy felt rooted to the spot, unable to move. Something about that laughter bothered him. Or, rather, frightened him. Yes, he had to admit it. He was scared for both Loco and himself. And that was quite an accomplishment on the intruder's part, considering that Big Jake hadn't been scared of anything or anyone since grade school.

The junkman gathered his nerve then started forward. He gripped the shotgun tightly, ready to fire at the first flash of motion ahead. Halfway to the edge of the yard, he heard a faint clinking, as if someone were climbing the tall chain-link fence that surrounded the property. For some reason, his mind conjured the image of a dark form—a decidedly *human* form—scurrying up and over the barrier like an oily black lizard. Spooked, he swiftly shook the thought from his head and continued onward.

When he reached the end of the junkyard, he found no evidence of anyone having ever been there. Worried, he looked around. "Loco?" he called out. "Where are you?"

At first, he heard nothing. Then, from the shadows beneath the rusty hull of a wrecked school bus, Jake caught a faint noise. A low, squealing whine more reminiscent of a whipped poodle than that of a 150-pound ferocious Rottweiler.

Jake crouched down on his haunches and peered into the darkness beneath the junk heap. "Loco? Is that you, boy?"

The thing cowering in the shadows unleashed another shuddering whimper. In the dim light that drifted from the direction of the office, Jake could barely see the shine of the dog's eyes peering fearfully from out of the shadows.

"What the hell's the matter, Loco?' he asked, trying to inject some gruffness in his tone, but unable to pull it off. "Did that lousy burglar scare the piss clean out of you?"

Another pitiful whimper from the animal told him that he was correct in his assumption. But who could do that to a monster like Loco? Or *what*?

Jake attempted to lure Loco from beneath the bus for a half hour that night, but to no avail. Finally, he gave up and, returning to the apartment at the rear of his office, retired for the evening.

The next morning, the junk dealer walked his property and took a mental inventory of his clutter to see if anything was missing. There was. Oddly enough, the only things missing from the 12-acre lot were four antique wagon wheels. Sturdy oak wheels with hammered iron rims.

Exactly how the culprit had managed to tote four 150-pound wheels over an 8-foot fence was totally beyond him. Jake decided to call the county sheriff and report the theft. But first, he tried his luck with Loco one more time.

The dog wouldn't budge, however. He continued to cower in the shadows of the school bus's undercarriage, whimpering in terror and refusing to venture into the open sunlight.

CHAPTER TWENTY-ONE

Keith couldn't seem to get it out of his head.

Since that evening when he and the others had ended their ride along Sycamore Road on the edge of the South Woods, he had thought about that dark valley choked with shadows and secrets. He recalled the expressions of uneasiness and fear on the faces of his friends, the way they had balked at exploring the place, giving some lame excuse about it being haunted.

Their hesitancy hadn't dissuaded his curiosity, however. Several days had passed since Keith had laid eyes upon the mysterious spot called Hell Hollow and, still, he could close his eyes and feel that spooky chill run down his spine at the thought of a legend whose origin had long ago been forgotten, but was still taken very seriously by those who resided in the rural community of Harmony.

He had to go back and check it out, see for himself if there was actually something there to fear or if everyone was just shivering in his or her shoes over nothing. But, deep down inside, Keith knew he would never go back to the South Woods alone. Despite his swaggering attitude, he was secretly afraid to go there on his own. Part of him scoffed at the stupid ghost stories about evil laughter in the darkness, but another part couldn't help but wonder if they were really true.

Keith had to convince Rusty and the others to accompany him to Hell Hollow...but how? He had considered his options carefully and had come to a conclusion. There were only two ways he could hope to coerce them into returning to the forbidden hollow. He could humiliate or shame them into going there, something he wasn't sure he could pull off. Or he could go another route. He could make a dare on an entirely different subject; hit a raw nerve that couldn't be ignored, and then stack the stakes in his favor.

The day was scorching hot. Despite the trouble they had gotten into several nights ago, they had been forgiven and set loose once again. Rusty was perched atop Cyclone, Keith was on Blue Fury, and Maggie was straddling her neon pink ten-speed, which she called Hot Mama.

Surprisingly enough, Mrs. Adkins had consented to letting Chuck tag along, perhaps feeling upon hindsight that she had reacted too harshly. The boy had moped in his room for two days, his spirits at rock bottom and that was something Flora Adkins couldn't bear. Reluctantly, she gave in and was amazed at how fast Chuck had abandoned his depression when she granted him permission to accompany his friends on their wanderings along the dusty backroads of Hawkshaw County. The handicapped boy rode in the sidecar that was attached to Cyclone. Much to his delight, Rusty and Keith had painted it olive drab green with a fanged mouth and leering eyes just behind the nose, much like the fighter planes of World War II. Chuck wore mirrored aviator glasses and a John Deere cap. His iguana, Churchill, accompanied him, perched lazily atop his right shoulder.

They decided to explore the northern edge of Harmony, a mile or so past Hill's General Store. They had stopped at the little store along the way and bought a few snacks to take with them. By the time they reached the steel and concrete bridge of the Duck River bridge, they were hot and exhausted. They parked their bikes in the shade of a big hickory nut tree, thankful to get away from the blistering eye of the August sun for a while. They pulled out their snacks, which consisted of Royal Crown Colas, banana moon pies, salty Tom's peanuts, and two-penny bubble gum.

The four lounged around the base of the tree, eating and joking around. They discussed some things that had been on their minds lately: who would win that year's World Series, a gruesome murder that had taken place on Interstate 24 scarcely 10 miles away, and a rash of petty thefts that had hit Harmony out of the blue.

It wasn't long before Keith had finished his peanuts and soda pop. He reached into the back pocket of his shorts and brought something out into the open.

"What's that?' asked Chuck as he poured a little soda into the cup of his palm and held it up to Churchill. The green lizard dipped his wrinkled head and began to lap at the beverage, his tiny pink tongue darting eagerly.

"Just some baseball cards," said Keith, tearing open the foil pack.

Rusty eyed his cousin with suspicion. "I didn't see you buy that back at the store."

"I didn't," grinned Keith. "I lifted it."

Maggie's eyes widened. "Keith! That's stealing!"

"What's the big deal?" he asked. "It didn't cost more than a dollar."

"That's not the point," said the girl, seeing genuinely disappointed in him.

"She's right," said Rusty. "You oughtn't have ripped off Mr. Hill like that. He barely makes a living off that place as it is."

Keith rolled his eyes. "It's just some stupid cards, that's all," he said, unable to understand their outrage. "Besides, what's the difference between stealing this and swiping a watermelon out of someone's patch?"

"There's a big difference," said Rusty.

"Yeah? And what would that be?"

"Like I said before, swiping a melon is sort of a tradition around these parts," proclaimed the lanky boy. "Kids have been doing it for ages."

"Right," nodded the city boy. "And where I come from, kids have been palming baseball cards since they first came out. So what's the difference?"

Rusty opened his mouth, but found that his argument was losing steam. After considering the comparison for a moment, he discovered that, in reality, there really was no difference between the two at all.

"I think you ought to go back and pay Mr. Hill for what you took," said Maggie.

"Yeah, right!" snorted Keith. "And have him rat on me to Grandpa? That's just what I need right now, to have the old man on my back even more than he is now." He stuck the cards in his hip pocket and looked over at the girl with the long blond hair. For some reason the expression of deep disappointment on her pretty face bothered him. He felt his heart sink. For the first time since he could remember, he actually felt guilty for taking something that wasn't his.

"Aw, come on, guys," said Chuck, stretched out in his garbage can sidecar, his hands folded behind his head. "Cut the dude some slack. He's not from the Bible Belt, you know. He's from the wicked old city. It's an urban thing, ain't that right, Keith?"

Keith laughed and traded a high-five with the boy. "See, the man here sees me for what I am. Besides, it's just a misdemeanor at best. It's not a major crime like bank robbery or murdering someone with an axe!"

Maggie frowned. "I still don't think it was very nice."

The boy felt that nagging sensation of shame tug at him again. Why did he care what Maggie thought of him anyway? He remembered her skinny-dipping in Goose Creek with him and Rusty, as well as the soft feeling of her hand in his as she led him through the dark pine grove during their escape from Old Man Perry's watermelon patch. Suddenly, he thought he knew the true reason why her disappointment bugged him so. He was developing a crush on Maggie. Just the thought of it made him feel a bit queasy, as well as more than a little scared.

Quickly, he knew he must change the subject. He looked over at the Duck River Bridge. The narrow bridge was painted the same dull green as the Harmony water tower, its framework of riveted steel girders resting atop thick pillars of water-stained concrete. Below it ran the muddy channel of the Duck, winding its way toward Normandy Lake, then eastward to the mighty Tennessee River.

"Rusty," he said, "how long would you say that bridge is?"

His cousin shrugged. "I dunno— a hundred and fifty feet. Maybe two hundred. Why?"

"I bet I could beat you across it," he said with a smug grin. "Blue Fury against Cyclone. One on one."

"You're on, cuz!" said Rusty without hesitation. He spat on his palm and traded a handshake with the city boy.

"Wait just a second," said Chuck. "There's got to be something at stake here. What are ya'll betting?"

Rusty thought for a moment then eyed the iPod clipped to Keith's belt. "If I win, I get to borrow that fancy music machine of yours," he said. "Chuck can download me some Southern rock and bluegrass, and give it a taste of some good music for a change."

Keith cringed at the thought of country music twanging through his headphones, but didn't let it show. His smile only broadened as he made his wager. "Okay. And if I win, we go to Hell Hollow and take a look around. All of us."

The red-headed farm boy turned as pale as a bed sheet. "Uh, no deal. I'm pooped anyway. Wouldn't be a fair race, me being so tuckered out and all."

Both Maggie and Chuck seemed relieved that Rusty had backed off from the challenge. But Keith wasn't about to give up so easily.

"I knew you wouldn't do it," he said, leaning back against the trunk of the tree. "You brag about how fast that crummy bike is, but when it comes down to putting up or shutting up, you chicken out. I guess you know I'd leave your butt in the dust."

Rusty's face reddened and his eyes narrowed. "Oh, yeah? Well, you're wrong about that, cuz. I accept your challenge!"

"And what about our wagers?" asked Keith. "My iPod against a trip to Hell Hollow?

With no backing out on either one?"

Chuck and Maggie looked on the verge of protesting, but Rusty wasn't about to be called a coward again. "You got it! But ol' Cyclone's gonna be the winner by a yard, maybe even more."

"We'll see about that," said Keith, getting up and stretching.

Using tools they kept in the bottom of the makeshift sidecar, they disconnected the contraption from the frame of Rusty's bike. A short while later, they approached the bridge, leaving Chuck and Churchill sitting in the shade of the hickory tree. Maggie rode her bike to the other side of the bridge, where she would determine the winner. "You guys be careful," she called back to them as she pedaled across. "If somebody decides to cross over while ya'll are on it, you're dead meat."

Both boys knew what she was referring to. The Duck River Bridge was one of the few one-lane bridges left in rural Tennessee. There was a flashing yellow light at both ends of the bridge, as well as boldly painted sign that read SINGLE LANE—PROCEED WITH CAUTION. If a car or pickup truck decided to cross the bridge while they were racing, they would barely be able to squeeze by on either side of it. There was scarcely 14 feet of asphalt from one railing to the other.

"This ain't gonna take but 30 seconds at the most," said Rusty. "We'll be okay."

Keith looked across the bridge and saw the worried look on the girl's face. He felt that fluttery sensation in his stomach again. "Yeah, don't worry about us," he said.

"Are you guys ready?" called Chuck, loading his mouth with three pieces of bubble gum.

Keith hunched over Blue Fury like a dirt-bike rider at the starting gate. "Let's go."

"Ready when you are," added Rusty. His lanky frame hugged that of Cyclone, as if boy and bike were a part of one another."

Chuck nodded. "Okay, let's do it. On your mark...get set..." He stretched the gum with his tongue, then blew a pale pink bubble as big as a softball. The bubble swelled until it burst with a loud *pop*. "Go!"

Together, the two started forward. Heat waves shimmied from the cracked asphalt of the bridge, as well as the framework of girders above and around them. Gears clashed and pedals pumped, building speed and propelling the boys and their bikes across the rural bridge like stones from a slingshot.

"Come on, Rusty!" yelled Chuck, so psyched that he would have leapt to his feet if he had been physically able. Churchill left his master's shoulder and scampered to the top of his John Deere cap, as if seeking a better vantage point.

On the far side of the bridge, Maggie found herself torn between the two boys. She was an old friend of Rusty and certainly didn't want to venture into the dark heart of Hell Hollow. But, on the other hand, she desperately wanted the boy from Atlanta to win, although she didn't understand why. She saw him speeding across the bridge, hunched low over the handlebars, putting everything he had into it and she couldn't help but root for him. "Come on, Keith!" she laughed, feeling kind of giddy. "You can do it!"

"Traitor!" Rusty yelled back at her. He looked over and, much to his surprise, found that he and his cousin were running neck and neck. "You'd best just slow down before you sprain something important, city boy. You ain't gotta chance in hell of winning."

"We'll see about that when we cross the finish line, Hyram!" replied Keith. "Now if you're aiming to beat me, I'd suggest that you quit talking and save your energy for that last twenty feet."

The two boys reached the halfway point in the center of Duck River Bridge. Keith poured on the speed and pushed it to the limit using muscles he never knew he had. He looked over and saw that Rusty had slipped back a couple of feet. *I'm doing it!* he thought in amazement. *I'm actually gaining on him!*

A big grin split his face and he looked to where Maggie stood waiting for them. But, strangely enough, she was no longer watching them. Instead, she was looking down the road toward the direction of the interstate. *What's she up to?* he wondered.

Then she turned around and looked back at them, her face full of alarm. "There's a truck coming!" she yelled. "A *big* truck!"

Keith didn't dare slow down. He had gained a lead over his cousin and he wasn't about to relinquish it. He continued to pump the pedals of Blue Fury, even though the muscles in his calves burnt with the effort. *Probably just an old pickup truck, anyway,* he told himself. *We'll get by it just fine.*

Then, when he and Rusty were scarcely 60 feet from the other end of the bridge, a noise became apparent. It was low at first then it grew in volume, eventually drowning out their grunts of exertion and the machine gun clatter of playing cards in the spokes of their bicycles. Puzzled, Keith glanced over at Rusty. The farm boy looked back at him, equally perplexed. Then the rumble turned into a roar as the vehicle up ahead appeared around a bend in the road and, neglecting to slow down, drove onto the one lane bridge.

It wasn't a pickup truck. Far from it. Instead, it was a big Peterbilt tractor-trailer truck, hauling a long silver tanker with a yellow Shell emblem on the side. Apparently, it had just left Interstate 24 and was heading into Harmony to fill the tanks at the gas station in town.

"Oh shit!" yelled both Keith and Rusty at the same instant. As the big truck blasted its air horn, the two parted, each heading for an opposite side of the bridge. The Peterbilt's brakes hissed, but it was still coming at them at 50 miles per hour, seeming to fill the width of the narrow bridge with only inches to spare. They looked up past the chrome grill of the big truck and saw the driver staring down at them from the windshield. His eyes were obscured by sunglasses, but they could do little to hide the expression of horror on his face.

Then, suddenly, the truck was upon them. Keith rode the edge of the bridge as closely as he possibly could, praying that it was close enough. He saw the Peterbilt's left fender and tire heading straight for him and he squeezed his eyes shut. He lifted his legs taking his feet off the spinning pedals, but Blue Fury refused to slow down. It sped forward even faster than before.

Keith braced himself, expecting to feel the impact of the fender smashing into him, as well as the tug of the big tire jerking him under its massive tread. Terrified, he could imagine himself being squashed by the tanker truck until there was nothing left of him and Blue Fury but an ugly smear of blood and bike parts.

Abruptly, he felt a warm wind sweep past him. He smelled the gassy odor of diesel fuel as well as the stench of hot rubber. He felt steel strike his knee, bringing a burst of pain, but it came from the opposite side. He had veered too close to the bridge railing and bumped his leg.

He opened his eyes just as a blur of silver passed him, followed by a dense cloud of sooty exhaust fumes. He was through the diesel smoke in a flash and, a few seconds later, past the last girders of the bridge and into the open roadway again.

Almost afraid to look, he glanced over, expecting to see his cousin several feet ahead of him. Instead, Rusty was a good two yards behind him. He sped past Maggie—who stood with her hands plastered over her eyes—and laughed in triumph, his hands off the handlebars and his arms raised in the air.

"I did it!" he screamed at the top of his lungs. "I won!"

A second later, his feet had found the pedals of the bike and he came to sliding halt in the road. Maggie and Rusty soon joined him. His cousin, for one, looked none too pleased with the race's outcome.

"You won!" squealed Maggie, jumping up and down. For a moment, Keith half-expected her to wrap her arms around his neck and give him a big kiss, but she didn't. After the thought had passed, the boy found himself feeling both relieved and just a little disappointed.

"You bet I did!" he said with a grin. "I knew Blue Fury wouldn't let me down."

"I reckon I fixed up that pile of junk better than I first thought," grumbled Rusty. Keith expected him to gripe about the truck ruining the race and promptly demand a rematch, but he didn't. He accepted his defeat honorably. "Congratulations, cuz," he said, extending his hand.

Keith reached out and shook it. "Thanks," he said. "Close call, eh?"

"I'll say," Rusty agreed with a big sigh. "I thought we were roadkill for a moment there."

"Me, too," admitted Keith.

Maggie looked across the bridge. The diesel truck was long gone, probably past the Harmony town limits by now. "I think we oughta get back over to Chuck. I bet he freaked when he saw that truck bearing down on you."

Soon, the three were on their bikes and heading back across the Duck River Bridge. They took it slower this time and much more cautiously, glancing over their shoulders every few seconds to make sure a convoy of Peterbilts weren't dogging their taillights.

When they reached the other side, Chuck was waiting for them. "Man!" he said. "I just about peed my pants when I saw that gas truck come across. I figure you two were strawberry jam for sure."

"It was close, but we squeezed past," boasted Rusty.

"So who won?" asked the handicapped boy.

"I did," said Keith with a gloating grin.

Chuck looked uneasy. "So you mean to tell me—?"

"That's right," Keith said. "We're all going to Hell Hollow...this afternoon."

"Hold on, pardner," said Rusty, holding up his hands. "By the time we get all the way back across Hawkshaw County and to the end of Sycamore Road, it'll be going on five o'clock. And I sure ain't going down in that blasted hollow with the sun going down."

"Me neither," said Maggie. "Couldn't we go tomorrow, early in the morning maybe?"

"Or high noon at the very least?" put in Rusty.

Keith rolled his eyes in disgust, although secretly he too thought it best to explore Hell Hollow in broad daylight. "Okay, Gary Cooper. High noon it is. But a deal is a deal. And that means nobody chickens out. Comprende?"

"Si, señor," said Chuck.

Suddenly, Maggie gasped in alarm. "Keith! You're hurt!"

"Huh?" Keith glanced down and saw that the side of his right knee was badly skinned up. "Aw, it's nothing."

"But it's bleeding," she moaned. "Doesn't it hurt?"

"Not at all," claimed the boy, his chest puffed out a couple of inches. He didn't dare tell her, but the abrasion burned like pure fire.

"Come on," she said, climbing back on Hot Mama. "We'll go to my house. I have some peroxide and Band-Aids. I'll doctor it up for you."

"Hey, why does he get special treatment?" asked Rusty. He raised his arm, showing off a bloody gash on the knob of his left elbow. "I'm wounded, too."

"Okay, I'll fix you up, too," said Maggie, although her concern seemed to be centered more on Keith than anyone else.

"What a couple of babies!" laughed Chuck. "The way ya'll are carrying on, you'd think you've got a couple of sucking chest wounds."

"Just the same, I think they ought to be cleaned up," Maggie told him. "Now come on."

Rusty and Keith took a few minutes to bolt the sidecar back onto Cyclone then the four headed back toward town.

On the way, Keith felt smugly satisfied. His plan had been a success. He had challenged Rusty to the race, won it fair and square, and was awarded the prize he had sought. The others had grudgingly agreed to accompany him to Hell Hollow, despite the spooky rumors of ghosts and disembodied laughter.

Just thinking about it made him feel both triumphant and uneasy. On one hand, he had gotten his wish. They would venture into wooded hollow and see what they could find. But, on the other hand, it was what they might possibly find that sent a shiver through him.

What if the legend was right? What if what they found was something supernatural and potentially dangerous?

Keith swallowed his nervousness and followed his friends back down the road toward Maggie's house. He guessed they would just have to wait until tomorrow to see if his fears were on target or totally off course.

CHAPTER TWENTY-TWO

Jasper McLeod moved his checker to the wrong square...for the fourth time that night.

Edwin Hill shook his head and skipped his opponent's piece, adding it to the growing stack that sat at the corner of his side of the checkerboard. "What's with you tonight, Jasper?" he asked. "You ain't playing worth a crap."

The elderly farmer leaned back in his high-backed chair and sighed. "I reckon you're right." He took a long drink of Sun Drop, then sat the bottle back on the floor next to his feet.

"What's the matter? Still worrying over that grandson of yours?"

Jasper nodded. "Partly. He hasn't said two words to me since the other night, when I grabbed hold of his arm. I didn't mean to do it, Edwin. It's just that I was raised to respect my elders and not sass them. I lost my temper and now he won't have nothing to do with me."

"Aw, he'll get over it," Edwin assured him. "You gotta remember, he's been raised differently from most boys. Rusty's used to getting a good butt-whupping when he misbehaves. But Keith probably hasn't had one lick of discipline since he was born. More'n likely his mama sits him on the couch and psycho-analyzes him, instead of laying a belt to his backside."

"You're probably right about that," said Jasper. "That's why his manners are so God-awful bad." The old man paused, staring absently at the lack of his checkers on the playing board. "But that ain't what's weighing on my mind tonight."

Edwin cut off a thick shaving of chewing tobacco with the blade of an old Case pocketknife. He poked it into the pouch of his left jaw and began working on it. "So what *is* eating at you, Jasper?"

Jasper ran a liver-spotted hand along his lean jaw. "Well," he said. "It's this dream I had a couple nights ago."

"A dream? You mean to tell me, a blasted dream has got you on edge?" chuckled the storekeeper.

The farmer's face reddened a bit. "Yeah, believe it or not. Anyway, the more I turn it over in my mind, the more I wonder if it was really a dream at all."

"What do you mean?"

"Well, it seemed more like a memory than something my imagination conjured up," explained Jasper. "Like something I should've recalled from my childhood. But, for the life of me, I can't remember nothing of the sort."

Edwin turned his head and forcefully sent sprits of tobacco juice toward the floorboards of the general store. The glob of brown spittle hit the coffee can at the base of the potbelly stove with a metallic clang. "So what's this cotton-picking dream about?"

Jasper took another sip of Sun Drop, then proceeded to tell Edwin Hill about his dream. He told him every detail that he could remember; the night ride on the back of his father's horse, the other men of Harmony armed with pistols and rifles, the presence of Wilbur Hill and eight-year-old Edwin. He also told him of their discovery of the abandoned campsite, followed by the pursuit of the brightly-painted wagon drawn by two coal black horses.

And, with a trace of hesitation, he also mentioned the one who had occupied the seat of the wagon. The skeletal man in the black frock coat and stovepipe hat, laughing sinisterly and cracking the coach whip wildly overhead.

When he was finished, he looked across the table at his friend. Edwin sat there for a long moment, staring at a red checker he turned over and over between his fingers. "Well, what do you think?" he asked anxiously.

Edwin shrugged. "A right peculiar dream, I must admit."

"Does any of it sound familiar?" pressed Jasper.

"No, can't say that it does."

"Are you sure? None of it?"

Edwin lifted his eyes and stared at the man sitting across from him. "You and me on horseback, armed to the teeth, chasing some skinny fellow on a painted wagon? Now, Jasper, don't you think I'd remember something like that?"

"I might not, if I were four or five," said Jasper. "But there's a chance you could, if you were eight years old."

"Well, I'm pretty clear on what happened during my eighth year," Edwin replied. "And riding with a vigilante mob just don't come to mind. I'm sorry, Jasper, but this dream you had was just a dream. Nothing more."

"But it seemed so damned *real*," declared the elderly man. "I could feel the chill of the night air and hear that fella's laughter. It sank clean down into the marrow of my bones. It was evil, Edwin. As dark and depraved of soul as any sound I've ever heard in my life."

The store owner raised his hands. "Sorry, but if it happened, it didn't happen in my lifetime. My memory is as crisp as a saltine cracker, and I just don't recollect any of it at all."

Jasper smiled sheepishly. "Yeah, it does sound kind of farfetched, especially to have happened in a peaceful little town like Harmony."

"That's right," Edwin assured him. "It was just your mind playing tricks on you. You were worrying over Keith and it concocted that silly dream."

Jasper nodded. "I reckon you're right. There is one thing that still needles me, though. The direction we were chasing that fella...it was straight for the South Woods. And Hell Hollow."

Edwin said nothing in reply. He simply chewed his tobacco and stared uneasily at the checker between his fingers, avoiding his friend's eyes.

Thirty minutes later, they had finished their fifth and final game. Edwin accompanied Jasper out into the muggy summer night and watched as his long-time friend waved goodbye, climbed into his rattletrap pickup, and headed down the road toward home. But, even after Jasper had been gone for several minutes, Edwin continued to stand on the high porch of the general store. He stared aimlessly into the starry sky for a long while, before finally going back inside.

Edwin closed the door behind him and then did something he hardly ever did—he engaged the lock. The rash of nighttime burglaries came to mind, but that wasn't why he locked the door. He had another reason.

He was spooked. Jasper McLeod's unexpected telling of his mysterious dream had dredged up fears that Edwin hadn't felt in a very long time. And, as for the dream itself, there was actually no mystery to it at all. Despite Edwin's dismissal, the details of Jasper's nightmare had been eerily familiar. Frighteningly familiar, in fact.

It had pained him to do so, but Edwin had deliberately lied to his best friend. It had startled him when Jasper had brought the subject up, then his surprise had instantly turned into defensiveness. He wasn't sure why he had decided to convince his checker-playing partner into thinking that no such incident had taken place. After all those years, it couldn't have hurt to tell him the truth; a truth that Jasper had apparently either forgotten or completely cast from his mind.

Edwin Hill walked behind the counter and took a brown paper sack from a shelf beneath the cash register. He went to the table, cleared away the checkers and board and sat down heavily in his chair. He took a bottle of Jim Beam from the sack, unscrewed the top and took a swig of the amber liquor. After his heart doctor had read him the riot act as to what he could and could no longer indulge in, Edwin had sworn off beer and hard spirits. But he still kept a bottle of Beam around, for those times when the grief of losing his son became too difficult to handle. That and bad memories such as the one Jasper McLeod had just awakened.

The storekeeper set the liquor bottle on the tabletop and thought of that night some 90 years ago. Jasper's dream had been like a dark and grotesque photograph that Edwin had never wanted to lay eyes upon again. Every bit of it—the pursuit of the medicine showman, as well as what had happened to him shortly thereafter—had come back to haunt him, as crystal clear and unsettling as it had been when he was a lad of 8-years-old.

And, along with it, surfaced that oath he had taken after the incident in Hell Hollow: an oath sworn upon by the men of that secret posse. All of them—Jasper included—had promised that not one word of what had happened to Doctor Augustus Leech would ever be mentioned within the God-fearing boundaries of Harmony, Tennessee. Edwin was the only one who still held that oath to heart. All the others had carried the ugly secret to their graves.

Apparently, Jasper had somehow repressed the memory of that night. It was understandable. After all, it had been Jasper's father, Charles McLeod, who had pulled the trigger and put a rifle slug between the eyes of the murderous peddler who had deliberately poisoned twelve citizens of Harmony, among them innocent youngsters who had been ailing from one childhood sickness or another.

The act of vengeance itself didn't bother Edwin. It had been justified. It was what had taken place following the killing that still sickened him deep down in his soul.

They had left him down there in the dark pit of that backwoods hollow. There had been no burial of the body and nary a word was uttered over his earthly remains. Rather, they had simply turned and gone home, leaving Augustus Leech and his poisonous legacy to rot away with the erosion of time and nature.

But now both of them—murderer and memory—had returned in the form of a dream.

Or had it been more of a premonition?

Edwin Hill drove the thoughts from his mind. He took another drink of liquor then capped the bottle. The deadening effect of the alcohol failed to smother the guilt he felt over lying to his friend, however.

And, as the night drew on, neither did it quell the fear that remained with him. A fear that clung to his heart like a shadow dogging one's heels on a lonely, moonlit country road.

A shadow that disturbingly resembled that of a lean, mustachioed man clad in a long black coat and a tall stovepipe hat.

CHAPTER TWENTY-THREE

"What'll you have, dear?" asked the waitress that appeared beside her table.

The nametag on her uniform blouse identified her as Lucille and she looked as if she had been an employee of the Tank & Tummy Truck Stop since it first opened for business. And considering the amount of cigarette burns and coffee stains on the table's acrylic surface, the combination greasy spoon and gas station had probably been in operation for twenty or thirty years.

Allison Walsh studied the menu, the pages of which were covered with clear plastic, also stained. After a restless night of little sleep and too many nasty dreams, she found herself famished. "I'll have the Tummyful Country Breakfast," she said. The special consisted of three eggs sunny-side-up, hickory-cured bacon, a side of grits, two cathead buttermilk biscuits and sorghum molasses. A near-lethal dose of cholesterol and calories to be certain, but Allison didn't care.

"Want coffee with that?" asked Lucille. She looked bone-tired and old before her time. A double application of Nice & Easy and too much makeup attempted to hide gray hair and crow's feet, but failed miserably.

"Yes," said Allison. She folded her menu and placed it back in its wire holder amid a gathering of condiments in the center of the table. "The blacker the better."

Lucille scribbled the order on her pad and nodded. "Have it to you in a couple minutes," she said then walked back toward the eating counter. Several burly truckers sat on padded stools there, choking down ham biscuits and syrup-drenched pancakes. One reached out and swatted the waitress on the fanny as she walked past, but she totally ignored him. It was a little past nine a.m. Lucille was too bummed out from starting her shift at four o'clock to pay much attention to the customer's playful gesture. Besides, considering the way he seemed to make himself at home, he was probably one of the Tank & Tummy's regular customers.

Allison sat at her table, anxious to be back on the road again. She had covered few miles the day before, stopping at every interstate exit between Rome and Chattanooga. Allison had questioned the clerks of convenience stores and gas stations concerning the one she was looking for. But, so far, she had hit one brick wall after another. No one had remembered seeing the lean, dark-eyed man with the stringy black hair and goatee beard. From the curt replies she had received, Allison couldn't tell whether they had actually told her the truth or simply didn't want to get involved.

She had crossed the Tennessee state line late last evening and checked into a room at a Best Western. She ate a couple of chicken burritos she had bought at a Taco Bell, then undressed and took a shower. Allison still recalled the pain that had pulsed through her abused body as the warm spray engulfed her, particularly from the word that had been carved deeply into her chest. She hadn't shied from the discomfort, however. Instead, she embraced it. Upon her release from the hospital, she found that she actually *wanted* to remember what had happened to her during those horrible days and nights in the abandoned house near Adairsville. Until she found the bastard, she intended to keep the agony fresh, both in mind and body. That way, when she finally confronted her tormentor, there would be no hesitation. Not one second's worth.

Her food arrived ten minutes after she had placed her order. She thanked Lucille, then dug hungrily into the plate of eggs, grits and bacon. It didn't take long to polish off the Tummyful Country Breakfast, including the biscuits and molasses.

She was finishing her coffee when a stocky fellow dressed in a NASCAR t-shirt and a black Harley-Davidson cap walked in and took a seat between the two truckers.

"Well, if it ain't the prodigal son!" greeted the man who had slapped Lucille's sagging caboose. "How's it going, Jerry?'

"Alright, I reckon," he replied. "Lucille, honey, are you going to stand over yonder gabbing with that short-order cook back there, or are you going to feed a hungry man?"

The waitress pulled herself away from the narrow window that provided access to the kitchen. She smiled when she saw the truck driver sitting on the other side of the counter.

"Look what the cat dragged in," she said, taking her pencil from behind her ear. "What can I get for you this morning, Jerry?"

"I'll take a stack of cakes with pecan syrup," he said, not bothering to even pick up a menu. "And a side order of link sausages, too."

"You got it," said Lucille. She poured Jerry a cup of black coffee from a big Bunn coffee urn, then pinned the order slip on the stainless steel carrousel that hung inside the access window. The cook—a tall, skinny man wearing a bandanna headband—ignored the slip on the carrousel and went to work pouring dollops of pancake batter on the hot griddle.

Allison went back to her coffee, eager to finish her meal and hit the road again. Then she caught a snippet of conversation that instantly drew her attention.

"Hey, did you hear about what happened up the road a piece?' asked the trucker named George. "About that guy getting murdered?"

"Hell, no," said Jerry. "I've been hauling swinging beef down in Texas for the past ten days. What happened?"

"A state trooper came across a car parked at the side of the interstate and, when he took a look inside, found the driver sitting there with his throat cut clean open. And, from what I heard, it hadn't happened two minutes before that trooper showed up. Whoever killed and robbed the poor bastard got away by a hair. They're still looking for him, but so far no dice."

"Who got killed?' asked Jerry.

"Some businessman from Kentucky," said George. "They found him near a place called Harmony, about eighteen miles north of Manchester."

"Well, ain't that a damn shame," grumbled Jerry. "Goes to show that nobody's safe on the road anymore. They'll kill you for a pack of smokes these days, they surely will!"

Allison finished her coffee, a small grin lurking beneath the rim of her cup. Her hands trembled with a mixture of excitement and fear as she left a generous tip for Lucille. Then she paid her check at the register and left the truck stop.

When she reached her rental car, Allison sat there for a long moment, her eyes closed. She couldn't be sure, but somehow she felt that Slash Jackson was the one the state police were looking for. It was the fact that the businessman's throat had been slashed that caused her to believe so. Allison remembered how many times Slash had laid the honed blade of his knife against her throat during the duration of her abduction, threatening to cut her clean down to the neckbone if she didn't do something he wanted her to. If she didn't scream louder or perform one of the many acts of perversion she had been forced to commit, the blade was there as a persuader.

She opened her purse and, slipping her hand inside, found the gun tucked between her wallet and a pack of Merits. She felt a strange comfort—as well as a thrill of anticipation —as she ran her fingers along the length of cool, blued steel. It was almost like a sexual hunger in a way, her burning need to confront him. And she was certain the release she would feel upon pulling the trigger would be just as sweet and powerful as any orgasm she had ever experienced.

Reluctantly, Allison Walsh let go of the .38 revolver and closed her purse. Then she started her car and, hitting Interstate 24, headed north for a place called Harmony.

CHAPTER TWENTY-FOUR

In silence, they traveled the dirt road that cut through the center of South Woods. They had departed from Chuck's house around 11:30 and, by the time they left the vast acreage of farmland behind and entered the shadowy stretch of the forest, it was nearly noon. Keith was anxious to get there, but he was the only one. Rusty, Chuck and Maggie didn't come right out and say so, but they weren't very happy about breaking a local taboo and visiting the place known as Hell Hollow.

"Come on, guys," said Keith as the earthen trail grew less defined and more choked with weeds and encroaching underbrush. "Don't be such wimps. You three look like you're on the way to the electric chair instead of some stupid old hollow out in the middle of the woods."

"It's been worse than that for some folks, or so the stories go," said Maggie.

"What do you mean?" asked Keith with interest.

"There's been tales about folks going hunting out in these woods and never being seen alive again," explained Rusty. "Or even dead, for that matter."

"I heard that way back in the early '60s some city fellas came down from Nashville, aiming to do some coon hunting," put in Chuck. "There were four of them, along with three redbone hounds. The fools headed into these woods at sundown, but didn't show back up in town the next morning. The county sheriff came out here to look for them. He only found their station wagon. He and his deputy followed their tracks to Hell Hollow.

That's where the footprints just disappeared, both human and dog. It was as if the hollow just swallowed them up whole."

"And nary a one of them city-slickers were ever found, either," added Rusty, looking spooked.

"Aw, what a load of crap!" laughed Keith.

"Well, folks around here don't think so," said Maggie. "There *is* something weird out there. And we're warped for even agreeing to go."

"Hey, a bet is a bet," the boy reminded them.

"Like you haven't already told us that a zillion times already today," said Chuck. He reached over and punched Rusty in the arm hard. "And you could've pedaled a little faster and beat him, too. Then we'd be sharing that iPod instead of riding out here!"

Rusty grimaced painfully. "Heck, you trying crossing that bridge with a big-ass truck heading straight for you. Then maybe you wouldn't be so quick to lay the blame on me."

"I still think you could've stomped him," grumbled Chuck. "I mean, you grew up on a bike. He's only been riding one for a few days."

"Just shut your hole, will you?" said Rusty, feeling bad enough.

"I can't believe how chicken-livered you guys are," said Keith with a big grin on his face. "Or how gullible you are for believing such bull in the first place."

A few minutes later, the road became almost non-existent. There were only a couple of dirt ruts lined with tall weeds and little else. The dark forest, choked with shadows, pressed in on them from both sides, the limbs of the trees even merging overhead. Only a few specks of light filtered through the thick foliage. Otherwise, the noonday sun was almost completely blocked from view.

A moment later, the road vanished entirely and the ground suddenly dropped away. They stopped their bikes at the edge and peered down a steep slope covered with thick, leafy kudzu. Below stood a grove of cedar and birch trees, as well as heavy stands of honeysuckle vine and thorny blackberry bramble. The shadows were so thick at the bottom that very little could be seen from their vantage point.

"Well, here we are," said Rusty. Despite the hot August day, goosebumps stood out visibly on his freckled arms.

"Listen," said Chuck softly.

Keith frowned. "What? I don't hear nothing."

"That's it," said Maggie, looking uneasy. "It's *too* quiet. No birds or bugs. No wind blowing through the trees. Nothing at all."

Keith listened for a moment. She was right. The hollow was completely silent. The sounds of nature he had grown accustomed to since his arrival in the country seemed to be nonexistent here. It was so silent that, for a second, he wondered if he had suddenly been stricken deaf.

"Well, if we're going down there, let's go on and get it over with," said Chuck. He raised his arms. "Ya'll are going to have to help me, though. I sure can't get down there by myself."

Rusty nodded and looked over at Keith. "I reckon we'll have to tote him on our shoulders," he said. "You figure you're up to that, cuz?"

"Don't worry," snapped Keith. "I'll do my part."

The two boys engaged the kickstands of their bikes, then walked over and lifted Chuck out of the makeshift sidecar. After several attempts, they finally hefted the overweight boy onto their shoulders.

"Lordy Mercy, Adkins!" groaned Rusty, nearly collapsing. "You're heavier than I thought. You'd best start lying off the chicken and dumplings come suppertime. And your mama's strawberry cheesecake, too, come to think of it."

"Screw you!" said Chuck. "Quit your bitching and moaning, and let's go. I want to get this over and done with."

"You're not scared, are you?" asked Keith.

Chuck looked down at the boy from Atlanta. "Heck, yeah, I'm scared. And you would be too, if you'd grown up hearing the stories we've been told."

"Come on," urged Maggie, leaving Hot Mama and joining them. "But be careful. It's pretty steep."

Keith and Rusty shifted Chuck's weight more securely on their shoulders, then

Cautiously started down the slope of the hollow. They had to step high, for the lush carpet of kudzu was deceptively deep in places, nearly up to their knees at times. Also, the converging vines underneath tended to snag their feet and ankles, threatening to trip them up several times.

"Are there snakes out here?" asked Keith. The only snakes he had ever laid eyes had been safely confined behind glass at the Atlanta Zoo.

A mischievous grin crossed Rusty's freckled face. "Sure are, cuz," he said. "There's all manner of snakes out in these woods. Rattlers and copperheads mostly. Probably a next of 'em hiding beneath these vines at this very moment."

Maggie looked over to see that Keith's face had turned a shade paler than it had been a second ago. She couldn't help but smile. "Aw, cut it out, Rusty. I know he deserves to have the crap scared out of him, but lay off, will you?"

Rusty arched an eyebrow, regarding the girl cautiously. "You ain't getting sweet on him, are you, Maggie?"

Maggie's face turned beet red. "No! Of course not!"

The farm boy looked past Chuck's knees at his cousin. Keith's face had grown even redder than the girl's. "So, when's the wedding?" Rusty asked. "Can I be your best man?"

"I think you'd better shut up," warned Keith. "Right *now*!"

"Yeah, put a sock in it, Rusty!" said Chuck. "If you two start fighting, I'll end up stuck square in the middle. I might even get hurt...and you know how my mom is." He paused for a second. "You don't want my mother to get pissed at you *again*, do you?"

The two boys shook their heads. After their altercation in the barn last Sunday afternoon, neither feared the other. But they did fear Flora Adkins. Silently, they called a mutual truce and continued their way down the northern slope of Hell Hollow.

When they reached the floor of the valley, they found it to be eerily still. Nothing seemed to move; not the branches of the trees or even the air around them. They looked for some sign of the bugs that had constantly pestered them during the muggy days of August—swarms of gnats, dive-bombing mosquitoes or troublesome flies—but none abided in the shadowy basin of Hell Hollow. Neither did they see any birds or squirrels in the tall cedars that stretched before them.

And there was something else; something that became apparent almost immediately. It was much cooler in the hollow than it was anywhere else. The summer heat didn't seem to reach the depths of Hell Hollow. In fact, it felt a good 10 or 15 degrees cooler there than where they had left their bikes parked only a few yards away.

Maggie rubbed the goosebumps on her arms. "This is creepy," she said. "Can we go now?"

Keith felt a chill run through him as well, but didn't let it show. "Fat chance! Everybody goes...just like I said when I made the bet."

"What do you expect to find down here?' asked Chuck.

Keith grinned wickedly. "Who knows? Maybe the bones of those lost hunters and their dogs."

Maggie shuddered. "Stop it, Keith!"

"Aw, don't give him the pleasure of seeing you squirm," Rusty told her. "We ain't gonna find nothing down here anyway."

Keith and Rusty rested for a moment, then, toting Chuck on their shoulders, started into the shadowy depths of the cedar grove. The leaves of the trees and underbrush seemed much darker there in the hollow, and the bark seemed almost tar black in hue.

When they had gone only a few feet, Maggie suddenly raised her hand. "Hey! Listen to that."

They paused, standing as still as statues. Faintly, they heard the melody of a musical instrument drifting from further back in the hollow. It was the half-strumming, half-picking of a banjo.

"Now who would be out here in the middle of nowhere?" asked Chuck.

"I think we oughta get the hell outta here," mumbled Rusty beneath his breath.

Keith looked over at his cousin. "What did you say?"

Rusty swallowed his uneasiness. "Nothing. Nothing a'tall."

Slowly, they continued onward. Not far from the slope of the hollow, they suddenly found themselves in a small clearing. But it was what they found in that backwoods glade that surprised them the most.

Standing in the center of the clearing was an old cabin wagon like traveling peddlers drove in those old western movies. It was undoubtedly ancient, but it was hard to really tell. The sides were painted in brilliant shades of red, yellow and blue, and majestic letters spelled out a single inscription. DOCTOR AUGUSTUS

LEECH'S TRAVELING MEDICINE SHOW—MAGIC, MUSIC, & MUSE—FEATURING THE GOOD DOCTOR'S PATENTED CURE-ALL ELIXIR.

The presence of the wagon surprised them, but the man sitting near the rear of it was an even bigger shock. He sat before a campfire, picking an old 5-string banjo whose neck had been repaired with silver duct tape; a tall, slender man dressed in faded jeans, a Grateful Dead t-shirt, a long black coat, and a high stovepipe hat. He had long black hair, a scraggly mustache and a pointed goatee beard, and his complexion was pale and waxy, as if he were feeling poorly. Dark shadows highlighted his sunken cheeks and the sockets around his eyes.

As they stood there staring at him with their jaws unhinged, Keith tried to identify the tune the man was playing. It wasn't bluegrass and it wasn't one of the old standards like "Camptown Races" or "Buffalo Girls". No, it had a definite edge to it—a frantic, dangerous edge—that the boy couldn't quite identify. It was familiar, though. Keith knew he had heard it somewhere before.

Abruptly, the man stopped playing and looked up. His eyes widened with sudden delight and a big grin split his lean face. It reminded Keith of an illustration he once saw in a children's book. The wolf smiling at Red Riding Hood, dressed in the gown and cap of her devoured grandmother.

"Well, now!" he said. "Company's come to call!"

The four simply stood there, staring at him. Of all the things they had expected to find in the wilderness of Hell Hollow, the man in the top hat and tails was the last thing on their list.

"Howdy," said Rusty warily.

"Hi," echoed Maggie, standing slightly behind the others.

"There's no need to be frightened of me," he said, setting down his banjo and standing up. "I'm as harmless as a ladybug. Please, sit down an visit for a while."

When they made no move to do so, he laughed. "Come on now. I'm just a traveling salesman and showman. I know I look kind of scraggly and suspicious, but I assure you, I'm no child molester or serial killer. You have my word of honor."

There was a way in his expression and speech that seemed to put Rusty, Chuck and Maggie at ease. But Keith wasn't so sure about the stranger. *This is all wrong,* he thought to himself. *He shouldn't be down here.*

"Well, okay," said Rusty. "Besides, much more of toting this lard-ass around and my arm is gonna pop clean out of its socket."

"Hey!" protested Chuck with a frown.

"He's right, dude," admitted Keith as they lowered Chuck to the ground. "I've got to put you down, too. No offense."

Gently, they helped Chuck over to the log of a deadfall and sat him down. The other three sat around him, quiet, both unsettled and intrigued by the man who camped in the center of Hell Hollow.

The man smiled at them and then squatted next to the fire. Two feet above the crackling flames hung the skinned body of a jackrabbit on a spit. He seasoned it with salt and pepper, then turned it a little to cook the other side.

"What are you doing out here?" Rusty finally asked. "Are you some kinda hippie or something?"

The tall man laughed uproariously, as though Rusty's question was the funniest thing he had ever heard in his life. "No," he answered. "No, my good man, I'm just a weary traveler, as I said before. I strayed from the main road and wound up stuck down here in this hollow. I let my horses loose for a stretch of the legs and, when I awoke early this morning, they were gone. Just ran off and left me. The ungrateful beasts!"

Chuck looked puzzled. "But what are you doing driving this old wagon around? The

Only people who drive wagons around these parts are the Mennonites who live out near Bugscuffle."

The man laughed again. "Believe me, I am *not* of their religious sect." He stood up from his place beside the fire and, taking the tall hat from his head, bowed elegantly. "Allow me to introduce myself. May name is Leech. Doctor Augustus Leech."

"A *real* doctor?" asked Maggie.

"Well, that's a matter of opinion to some," he admitted. "Mostly that's just a theatrical title. I travel the country in this wagon, selling my medicinal wares and entertaining those who will but grant me a moment of their precious time. Dramatically, I'm a jack-of-all-trades. I am an accomplished magician, ventriloquist, juggler, musician, comedian, and thespian. I prefer to present my performances the old-fashioned way, journeying from town to town in this wagon I have restored. Sounds sort of nuts, huh?"

The four nodded.

"Purely eccentric, I assure you," he said.

"How come we've never heard of you before?" asked Rusty.

"Oh, I'm no stranger to these parts," Leech told them. "I've visited your quaint town of Harmony before." His dark eyes sparkled. "A very long time ago."

Keith studied the man and his brightly-painted wagon. He felt as if reality had unexpectedly taken a hike on them. As if they had all stepped smack dab into the middle of the Twilight Zone.

The man suddenly looked down at the rabbit roasting over the fire. "Where is my manners? I was just sitting down to lunch. Will you join me?"

"Yuck!" said Maggie with a scowl of disgust. "Poor little bunny!"

Augustus Leech seemed to see his catch in a brand new light. "Oh, how terribly insensitive of me!" He reached down and, taking the spit from the fire, withdrew the wooden rod that impaled the steaming body of the rabbit. Reverently, he laid its carcass on the ground at their feet. "Poor creature! His existence was once full of happiness and freedom, and here I come along and, out of blatant hunger, have callously deprived him of his simple life. Well, what has been taken away can be restored once again."

The kids watched as Leech took a large red handkerchief from the breast pocket of his coat and, unfolding it, laid it gently over the cooked animal, covering it completely.

"Jesus once raised Lazarus from the dead," said Leech with a strange grin. "I'm not quite in His league, but I do have a few tricks up my sleeve."

"What are you going to do?" asked Maggie, mesmerized.

"Watch!" the man instructed.

He swept his pale, long-fingered hands over the lump beneath the crimson hanky. At first, nothing happened. Then the cloth began to twitch. Leech took the edge of the handkerchief between thumb and forefinger, and, with a dramatic flourish, whipped it away.

Maggie gasped. "Look!"

Where the half-roasted body of a skinned hare once lay, there now crouched the frightened form of a brown jackrabbit. The animal trembled on a bed of soft clover, its eyes bright with fear. The scent of cooked flesh was gone. In its place was the faint, musky smell of the rabbit's furry coat.

"Scat!" said Leech, scooting it away with his hands. "Be gone, little one. Back to the carefree existence you once cherished."

The rabbit wasted no time. It bounded off into the dark thicket that surrounded the backwoods clearing. Soon, it was completely out of sight.

"How'd you do that?" asked Rusty, his face slack with amazement.

Leech raised his hands. "Please. A good magician never reveals his secrets."

"But there's no way you could've done it," said Chuck, clearly impressed.

"Oh, but I did, didn't I?" replied Leech.

Rusty, Maggie and Chuck smiled and laughed. Keith was the only one who saw the doctor's magic trick in a different light. Something about the resurrection seemed unsettling and wrong, although he couldn't put his finger on exactly why he should react in such a negative way.

For the next hour, the four sat there, totally enraptured while Augustus Leech entertained them with feats of magic, ventriloquism, and juggling. He chilled them as he produced a live tarantula from his open mouth, threw his voice above, behind, and below them, and juggled the live coals of the campfire without burning his hands. Leech's tricks were bizarre and far removed from the norm, but they held a certain appeal for the four twelve-year-olds. Anybody could see a rabbit pulled from a hat. But to see one brought back to life...well, that was something different.

Toward the end of their visit, Doctor Leech pulled a wooden case from an inside pocket of his black coat. The box was about the size of a DVD case, the wood dark and gummy with old vanish, the brass hinges tarnished with age.

"What's that?" asked Keith.

"Something special," he told them. "Something *magical.*"

He opened the case and withdrew its contents. It was a deck of oversized cards. They looked to be as old as the box that held them. The pasteboard was brown and frayed around the edges, and they smelled musty, like the yellowed pages of old books. The illustration on their backs was the same; a sleeping half-moon and a scattering of stars against a pitch black background.

Chuck watched as the man shuffled the deck in his skinny hands. "What are they?

Tarot cards?"

"Similar in a way," said Leech. "But these deal more with dreams than with the telling of futures."

"Interpreting dreams?" Maggie wanted to know.

"No, my dear lady," said the man with a smile. "The giving of dreams."

"What do you mean?" asked Rusty.

"Everyone has a secret fantasy; a private world they yearn to explore. You four are no different than anyone else."

Intrigued, they watched as his pale hands fluttered like night moths, cutting the deck and shuffling it with a grace that was nearly hypnotic. When he finally stopped, he stared at the uppermost card of the big deck.

"Maggie Sutton," he said softly.

The girl jumped. The mention of her name startled her, for she could not recall having introduced herself to the man. Come to think of it, none of them had.

When Leech lifted his eyes to her, they were soft and dreamy. "I know where your heart lies. Sawdust and dusty canvas. The rich scent of cotton candy, buttered popcorn, and roasted peanuts. Bareback riders, lion tamers, a tiny automobile disgorging a multitude of clowns. Pink spandex and lace, the feeling of open air on all sides. And adoring audience, their eyes transfixed skyward. On you."

He peeled the top card off the deck and handed it to her. Maggie stared at the rectangle of pasteboard. It had no numbers or letters in its corners. Rather, the face of the card depicted a single illustration. A lovely, blond woman tiptoeing across a taut high wire above the distant earth of a circus arena. Staring up at the lovely performer were the faces of the crowd, hazy and unidentifiable, yet full of wonder.

Leech shuffled the deck once again. When he stopped, he peered at the card that ended on top. "Rusty McLeod," he whispered.

The farm boy's Adam's apple bobbed nervously.

"Your heart belongs to the Old West. A hot sun blazing down on an Arizona desert. Sagebrush, tumbleweeds and thorny mesquite. A narrow dirt street lined by false-fronted buildings, horses tied to the posts, drinking from watering troughs. A tied-down holster, a shiny Colt .45 and a polished brass star. Both respect and contempt from those within your midst. And always the challenge of a gunfight just beyond the horizon."

Rusty took the card that was handed to him. It depicted a frontier town with a U.S. marshal standing in the center of its single street, his hand hovering over the handle of a pearl-handled six-shooter, ready to draw.

Again the brittle fluttering of cards. "Chuck Adkins."

Chuck nodded and waited, his face pensive.

"Your heart is that of a warrior," said Leech. "A desolate landscaped blasted and burnt by shell-fire. The stench of cordite, blood, and wholesale death. An earthen trench filled with men clutching M1 carbines, waiting for the order to attack. And order that can only be given by you. A strong and courageous leader who would lead his platoon through the very gates of Hell if need be."

Chuck took the card. On it was a drawing of a machine-gun wielding sergeant leading a wall of soldiers across a battlefield, bombs bursting all around them.

Doctor Leech shuffled the cards, his eyes moving toward the last one of the four. "And now for you...Keith Bishop."

Keith held his breath. The revelations that Leech had revealed about each one of his friends had been mysterious and fascinating. But when it came to be his turn, he felt a strange sensation build down deep in his belly. A sensation very much like dread.

"Your heart is dedicated to the eradication of evil," said Leech, his voice holding a trace of amusement. "A city of skyscrapers and rain-soaked streets. Crime reigns supreme. Speak-easies and mobster dens, pay-offs and corruption. But above it all, an unstoppable champion of law and order. A trench coat, a gray fedora, and a .45 automatic holstered beneath your armpit. Prepared to hit the streets and force the power of good upon those who thumb their noses at it."

Keith knew what he would see when he looked at the face of the card. A handsome cop in a hat and raincoat standing on a dark city street, a badge in one hand and a blue-steeled .45 automatic pistol in the other.

The clearing was thick with silence for a long moment. Then Leech spoke. "These are your secret dreams. Your secret *lives.* To live them, you only have to place these cards beneath your pillows at night and you shall be transported there. To experience the exhilaration and glory, the thrill and wonderment of being swept away from this dismal town and into the dreamscapes you so strongly desire to explore."

Keith looked skeptical. "Oh, you're just pulling our legs!"

"No, I'm not," assured the lanky wanderer. "All you need do is try them out and you will see that what I say is true."

The four looked at Augustus Leech and saw that he was dead serious. He actually believed that the cards had the power to transport a person into the depths of their most cherished dream.

"I guess it wouldn't hurt to try," said Rusty.

"My gift to you *will* work," said Leech. "You have my word on it."

The four sat there and stared at their individual cards, hoping that what he promised was true, but afraid that it was merely an illusion, like the resurrected rabbit or the spider-out-of-the-mouth trick.

Doctor Leech suddenly laughed. "Come now! Don't take it all too seriously. It will be fun, you shall see. Like a rollercoaster ride at the county fair. No true danger or peril. Only adventure."

His words seemed to break the spell that had transfixed them. They laughed and smiled, again entertained by their host's unusual brand of theatrics.

"Well, we'd best get going," said Rusty almost reluctantly.

"Farewell, my young friends," Leech said. He returned the wooden case to his coat pocket and stood. "It has been a pleasure meeting you all."

"Same here," said Chuck, as the tall man helped him effortlessly onto the shoulders of Rusty and Keith.

"Yeah!" agreed Maggie. "Wait till everyone in town finds out about you!"

A guarded look crossed Leech's gaunt face. "Not quite so fast, young lady. I must ask you to keep my presence here a secret for the time being. You must promise to tell no one, not even your own families."

"How come?" asked Keith, suddenly suspicious.

"I need ample time to prepare for my grand entrance," he told them. "I want my visit to Harmony to be a surprise. How can I mystify and delight those who have already been heralded of my impending arrival? Besides, I must first locate a couple of sturdy horses to replace those who abandoned me."

"Amos Hadley has horses for sell," suggested Rusty. "His farm is the first one you'll come to down the road here."

"Then I shall see if I can make a deal with the honorable Mr. Hadley," said Leech.

"Now, remember, not a single word about me to anyone. Give me a few days for preparation and, I promise, I will put on a show for the citizens of Harmony the likes of which they have not known for a very long time."

"That sounds great!" said Rusty with a smile. "I can hardly wait."

A broad grin crept across the man's whiskered face. "Neither can I."

After saying their goodbyes, they left the backwoods clearing and left the cedar grove. Soon, they were trudging back up the northern slope of Hell Hollow, their hands clutching the cards Leech had given them and their lightened by their unexpected encounter.

All except Keith, that was. "Doesn't it kind of seem strange, him being down there like that?" he asked when they reached the rim of the hollow.

"He explained what happened," said Chuck as they sat him back in the sidecar. "It does sound sort of weird, but he seems like a nice enough fella."

"Yeah," said Rusty. "So what's bugging you?"

Keith shrugged. "I don't know. He just doesn't seem kosher."

"I thought he was right entertaining, if you ask me," claimed Maggie. "You're just being a stick-in-the-mud, that's all."

"All these city-slickers are overly paranoid," explained Chuck. "It's just their nature to be suspicious."

"And these stupid cards," continued Keith. "What a load of bullshit!"

"Aw, it was fun, Keith, and you know it," the girl admonished. "Besides, I'm going to try mine."

"Me, too," said Rusty as he climbed on his bike. "Who knows, it might just work like he promised."

"Suckers!" snickered Keith. He felt like throwing the card away, but he didn't. He stared at the picture of the police detective and felt something nag at him. A strange feeling of longing. Puzzled, he stuck the card in his back pocket. If nothing else, it would make a neat souvenir of his one and only trip to Hell Hollow.

On their way back down Sycamore Road, the banjo tune they had heard upon approaching the clearing came back to Keith. He ran it through his thoughts several times, before he finally realized what the tune had been.

It wasn't a bluegrass or pop song at all, but good old rock and roll.

The tune Doctor Leech had been playing on his five-string banjo was an unlikely choice. An old cut off Van Halen's debut album.

A song called "Runnin' with the Devil".

CHAPTER TWENTY-FIVE

That night as he prepared for bed, Keith heard the phone ring down the hallway. A moment later, his grandfather called out to him. "Keith, it's for you," he said.

Puzzled, Keith left the spare bedroom and went to where Grandpa McLeod stood with the receiver in his hand. "Who is it?" he asked.

"Rusty," said the old man. "But keep it short. It's already past your bedtime."

Keith rolled his eyes. "Aw, it's only 10:30!" he said. He studied the expression of disapproval on his grandfather's face. "Okay, okay. Just a couple minutes."

Jasper handed the boy the phone, then went back to the kitchen, where he had been drinking coffee and flipping through a copy of *The Progressive Farmer.*

"Yeah, it's me," said Keith into the receiver. "What's up?"

"You getting ready for bed?" asked Rusty.

"Sure. Why?"

"Are you going to try out that card Doctor Leech gave you?" he wanted to know.

"Come on!" laughed Keith. "You're still not swallowing that crap about it making you dream, are you?"

"Who knows? I've heard of weirder things before. Besides, what harm is it gonna do?

Just slip it under your pillow and go to sleep. If it works, it works. If it don't, then you were right, and I reckon you'll let us hear an earful in the morning."

"You better believe it," said Keith. "Are Maggie and Chuck going to do it, too?"

"Yep. I've already talked to them. So, are you?"

"Maybe," Keith told him. "Seems pretty stupid to me. Like sticking your molar under the pillow for the Tooth Fairy to swap out for a quarter."

"Could be a heckuva lot more interesting than a quarter," said Rusty. "If it works like that fella promised."

"Well, I wouldn't hold my breath if I were you." Keith considered it for a moment, then sighed. "Okay, I'll go along with this kooky experiment. We'll compare notes in the morning."

"Sounds good," said Rusty. "Goodnight, cuz."

"Sleep tight," replied Keith. "Don't let the bedbugs bite." He hung up the phone and started back toward his room.

"Goodnight, Keith," Grandpa called from the kitchen.

The boy considered ignoring him, then changed his mind. "Yeah, goodnight." The tension between them had eased a little, but not so much that you could really notice.

A moment later, he was back in his room with the door closed behind him. He undressed, changing into a pair of pajama pants and an old Atlanta Braves t-shirt. He pulled back the covers of the big feather bed then turned to where his clothes laid on the floor.

He dug the oversized card out of the back pocket of his shorts and studied it. The drawing of the hard-nosed detective was kind of neat, done in shades of light and shadow like an old '40s art-deco illustration. But that was all it was, in his opinion. Just a silly card with a picture on the front. Not some mysterious portal to a universe of secret dreams.

"Well, here goes nothing," he said, then reluctantly stuck the card beneath the big goose down pillow he had slept on since arriving at his grandfather's farm.

Keith turned off the lamp on the nightstand, then laid down, leaving the covers pooled around his ankles.

He settled into the soft depths of the feather mattress, listening to the sounds of crickets in the yard beyond the bedroom's open window. It was warm that night. A little humid, but no all that uncomfortable.

It wasn't long before he had fallen fast asleep.

And began to dream.

He found himself stepping from a gray brick doorway, taking a bank of concrete steps two at a time. Disoriented, he looked around and saw that he had just exited a tall building that looked more like a fortress or a prison than most. Two lighted globes at either side of the entrance read POLICE.

As he moved away from the precinct building and into the misty rain of a late summer evening, his surroundings became more defined. Old Fords and Packards drove up and down the street, while a paperboy across the street hawked the evening edition of the local newspaper. The boy looked odd, dressed in his flat cap, striped shirt and knickers, but somehow Keith knew that the clothes were acceptable in the place where he now existed. He studied his own attire. He wore baggy gray pants, a pinstriped shirt and dark tie, a tan trench coat and a gray felt fedora cocked at a rakish angle. He felt something heavy beneath his left arm and found it to be a Colt .45 semi-automatic pistol in a leather shoulder holster. In the side pocket of his coat was a black wallet with a brass badge and a card identifying him as a detective, first-class.

As he reached the curb, he breathed deeply. The air reeked of leaded exhaust fumes, wet asphalt, and Chinese food from a joint a half-block down the street. He wasn't there a second, when a navy blue sedan pulled up next to him. A fresh-faced rookie cop hopped out, leaving the engine idling.

"I brought your car around like you asked, Detective Bishop," he said.

"I owe you one, Muldoon," he said, not surprised that he knew the beat cop by name.

He slipped into the driver's seat and closed the door. Although he had never driven a car in his entire life—and particularly not an old car like this—Keith found himself fully capable of handling the vehicle. He shifted into gear and, pulling away from the curb, merged with the traffic. Soon, he was cruising down the rainy street, heading east for the far side of the city. Although the metropolis of bustling streets and tall skyscrapers was alien to him, he seemed to know precisely where he was headed.

He arrived at the waterfront a few minutes later. The streetlights were few and far between as he cut the sedan's engine, as well as its headlamps. He sat in the car for a moment, studying the area. Long warehouses of corrugated steel stood on both sides of the street and, a few yards away, the avenue came to a dead end. Beyond it he could see the shine of the moon on dark water. A light fog began to roll in off the harbor and, before he knew it, the piers nearby were choked in mist.

Keith left the car and stood there for a second, listening. A foghorn bellowed in the distance, but that was all he heard. The air smelled different there—salty with the odor of fish. Probably from the cannery that stood down the street a few yards away.

He reached past the lapels of his trench coat and withdrew the .45 from its holster. He cocked the slide back and checked the breech. There was a single brass cartridge there, just behind the barrel. He knew there were others waiting patiently in the slender clip that filled the hollow of the pistol's thick butt. Keith returned the gun to its holster, the started down the street, toward the waterfront.

He clung to the shadows that choked the wet avenue. Keith passed a couple of seedy brick buildings' the Seaman's Hotel and Rocky's Gym. Soon, he reached the waterfront with its deserted docks and tall stacks of wooden crates and chained bundles, waiting to be picked up by ships. He moved silently among them, alert, listening for the least little sound.

It came a moment later. The crisp strike of a sulfur match against the heel of someone's shoe. He turned to see a face briefly illuminated in the square of a shadowy doorway, followed by the glowing tip of a cigarette in total darkness.

"That you, Lester?" he asked, taking a couple steps forward.

"Keep your voice down, copper," rasped the man in the doorway. "This place has ears. Big ears. And if they don't like what they hear, you could end up at the bottom of the bay in a pair of cement galoshes, feeding your face to the fishes."

An instant later, Keith was in the cover of the doorway, standing opposite the man he had come to see. In the faint glow of the cigarette, he recognized the pale face with its weak jawline and nervous twitch at the corner of the right eye. It was Lester, one of Keith's stool pigeons. Lester had spent several stints in the Big House, but had lived comfortably there, squealing on one convict after another. That seemed to be his calling in life, both inside the joint and out. Lester would spill the beans on anyone, from the lowest pickpocket to the biggest crime boss…for the right price.

"What have you got for me, Lester," Keith demanded. "I haven't got all night."

"Just hold your horses!" hissed the stoolie, glancing around nervously. "First the cash."

Keith peeled a bill off a bankroll and slapped it in the man's sweaty palm. "There you go. Now sing."

Lester cleared his throat. "The one you've been looking for is called the Big Man. Deals in everything you could imagine...gambling, prostitution, gun-running. Drugs and booze, too. Reefer, heroin, cocaine, bathtub gin. But he's a mean son of a bitch. Many have crossed him, but few have lived to tell about it."

"Where's his operation located?" Keith asked.

Lester was about to let the cat out of the bag, when a sound caused him to flinch. The scrap of shoe leather against pavement, only a few yards away. "That's all for now, flatfoot," he said. He ground his cigarette butt against the palm of his hand, plunging the doorway into darkness. "I gotta run."

Keith reached out and grabbed the man by the lapels of his navy pea coat. "Not so fast, Lester," he growled. "Not until I get my money's worth."

"You'll get it later," said Lester, pulling away and glancing around nervously. Then he stepped out of the doorway and headed along the dock, toward the darkness of an alleyway.

As Keith himself stepped from the doorway, two gunshots rang out. He saw Lester clutch his chest and fall to the wet pier, dead before he hit the boards. Keith drew his gun and started toward the stoolie's body. Two men stood next to a tower of packing crates; a small, rat-like fellow in a zoot suit and a big goon of a bruiser in an overcoat and black hat. The bigger thug raised his arm, aiming a Saturday Night Special straight at the cop. Keith stepped back into the doorway, dodging a bullet that glanced off a corner of the brick wall. He reappeared a second later, his own gun extended at arms length.

"Freeze!" he warned, steadying his aim.

The big fellow ignored his warning. He cocked his piece and prepared to fire again. Keith beat him, squeezing the trigger first. The big automatic bucked in his hand. Blood blossomed on the goon's chest, squarely above his heart. He fell like a brick wall, facedown into a puddle of water.

The ratty guy turned and fled. Keith caught up to him before he could reach the open street. He laid his hand upon the man's narrow shoulder and spun him around on his heels. "You're coming with me," he said.

"Not on your life, gumshoe!" squealed Ratface. He whirled, the gleaming blade of a stiletto in his hand. Keith leaped back, dodging the switchblade. Skillfully, he managed to block the man's flailing knife and countered it with a solid haymaker. The little man succumbed the instant the detective's knuckles connected with his chin. He dropped his knife and fell on his back in the wet street, throwing up his hands in defeat.

"I give up, copper!" he cried. "You got me!"

Keith grabbed the criminal by his necktie and hauled him to his feet. "Okay, who sent you?" he demanded. "Who put the hit out on Lester the Stool?"

"I ain't squealing!" said Ratface. "No way. I'd be a dead man if I did."

"You may end up in worse shape if you don't," threatened Keith. He took a pair of nickel-plated cuffs from his pocket and snapped the bracelets around Ratface's skinny wrists. "Come on! We'll see if you're more cooperative once we get back to the station."

A few minutes later, Keith had piled the thug into the back of the sedan, then slipped behind the wheel. With squeal of tires on wet pavement, he made a sharp U-turn, then headed away from the waterfront and back toward the heart of the city.

Rusty found himself on horseback in the middle of a burning desert.

The earth was hard-baked and cracked beneath the gelding's faltering hooves. The blinding eye of the noon sun glared down at him, mercilessly, filling the air around him with waves of shimmering heat. He took a canteen from where it hung from the saddle horn, but immediately knew that it was empty. It had been for a day now.

Rusty ran a hand over his blistered lips and peered ahead of him. In the distance stood tall buttes, followed by more scrubby desert. The horse beneath him snorted feebly. "I know, Cyclone," he told the animal soothingly, reaching down and patting it lovingly on the shoulder. "I'm mighty thirsty myself. But we'll come to a waterhole before long. I promise we will."

Comforted by his master's words, the horse trudged onward. An hour later, they crossed a drywash and came upon a small grove of barrel cactus. Rusty swung down from the saddle and stumbled to the biggest of the bunch. He took a Bowie knife from his gun belt and sawed the flowered top off the stubby cactus. He then sliced a clump from the soft, white meat of the plant and squeezed droplets of moisture into his mouth. He cut another piece and did the same for Cyclone.

"Maybe this'll do us till we can get to town," he said. The horse snorted and seemed to hold his head up a little higher than before.

Later that evening, they spotted something upon the horizon, silhouetted against the backdrop of a brilliant western sunset. A scattering of false-fronted buildings standing in the middle of nowhere. "There it is, boy," he said, his voice full of relief. "Canton City. Our new home."

It was dark by the time they rode past the town limits. The place was far from being a city. It was no more than a dozen buildings surrounded by a few tarpaper shacks that served as homes. Rusty's attention was drawn by the clink of a hammer against iron. He rode over to the livery stable and saw a big, burly man standing at an anvil just inside the doorway.

The man noticed him, laid down his mallet and walked over. "Howdy, stranger," he greeted, although his eyes were a shade suspicious. "Can I help you?"

"I need to find a place for ol' Cyclone here," said Rusty. "A clean stall and a bate of oats. Maybe a grooming every day or so."

"How long are you figuring on staying?" asked the blacksmith.

"As long as you folks aim to have me around," said Rusty. He pulled back the front of his duster, revealing the brass star pinned to his vest.

The liveryman's ruddy face brightened. "Why, you're the new marshal!"

"That I am," replied the lawman. "And your name would be?"

"Sanderson," said the blacksmith. "John Sanderson. I own the livery here in town."

Rusty swung down from his horse and handed Sanderson the reigns. He took his saddlebags and rifle in hand, while the liveryman escorted the gelding through the big doorway of the stable. "Take care of him and I'll settle with you later. Right now I'm going to the saloon yonder for a drink and a bite to eat."

"You be careful though, Marshal," warned Sanderson. "Kid Calhoun is over there and he ain't in the best of moods. He's all liquored up and itching for a fight."

"We'll see about that," said Rusty, heading down the dusty street toward the oasis of light that was the Wagon Wheel Saloon.

A moment later, he was pushing through the batwing doors into the saloon. A piano player was tickling the ivories in the corner, while a bald bartender with a handlebar mustache and garters on his sleeves served drinks. Rusty stepped up to the bar, setting his gear on the floor beside him. He nodded at the two men who stood at the bar next to him; a gold miner and a cowpoke. They nodded back then shifted nervous eyes behind him, toward a table in the far corner of the room.

Rusty glanced over his shoulder. Sitting at the table was a young man dressed entirely in black from head to toe. He wore a smart-alec grin on his handsome face and a brace of silver Colts around his waist. On his lap, giggling and drinking from a bottle of whiskey was a buxom, red-haired saloon girl dressed in red silk and black lace.

"What'll you have, stranger?" asked the bartender, stepping up to the bar. "Beer? Red-eye maybe?"

"Buttermilk," drawled Rusty. "A tall, cool one."

The bartender nodded and went to fetch Rusty's order. A loud guffaw abruptly split the air. "Buttermilk!" roared the man in black. "The man's got a craving for buttermilk of all things!"

Rusty turned and eyed the gunslinger sharply. "What of it?" he asked.

The humor in the gunslinger's face suddenly faded. In its place grew something dangerous and volatile. "Do you know who I am, mister?"

Rusty nodded. "Some sawed-off blowhard named Kid Calhoun, I reckon."

Rage suddenly filled the young man's dark eyes. He stood up, dumping the girl onto the saloon's sawdust floor. "I don't take kindly to being called such," he said. He stepped away from the table and spread his arms, positioning his hands loosely over the butts of his forty-fives.

"It's the plain and simple truth," said Rusty. "Take it or leave it."

"Oh, I'll leave *you*...lying stone cold dead on this floor," said Kid Calhoun. "Now step away from that bar and draw your gun."

The cowboy and the miner quickly took their drinks and left the establishment. The bartender stepped out of the line of fire as well. Slowly, Rusty turned around and swept the right side of the duster away, revealing his pearl-handled Colt. "You don't have to do this, you know," he warned. "It'd be much better if you just walked out of here, climbed on your horse, and rode out of town. Nice and peaceful like."

"Yeah, I reckon you'd like that," sneered the Kid. "But it ain't gonna happen that way. The only one who's gonna be leaving Canton City is you. Nailed inside a pine box, heading for a hole in Boot Hill."

"Then you won't listen?" asked Rusty with a sigh.

"Hell, no!" gritted Kid Calhoun. "Now do as I said. Draw!"

Rusty stood away from the bar, his hand hanging loosely next to the holster of his gun belt. He watched his opponent, while Kid Calhoun did the same. Tension hung heavily in the air of the saloon, thick enough to cut with a knife.

An instant later, the gunslinger made his move. Both hands swung downward, shucking the silver Colts from their holsters. But before he could thumb back their hammers, a single gunshot boomed throughout the saloon. Startled, Kid Calhoun stared at the six-shooter fisted in Rusty's right hand. It had miraculously appeared there; he hadn't even seen the twitch of a muscle or the flash of steel from leather. Then he looked dumbly down at the spurting hole in the center of his own chest.

"Sorry about that, Kid," Rusty said, twirling his Colt and slipping it neatly back into its holster. "But you made the call."

Kid Calhoun's guns dropped from his limp hands and he fell to his knees with a crash. A second later, he was lying facedown in the sawdust, sprawled out and still. Dead before he even hit the floor.

A stretch of silence rang throughout the Wagon Wheel. Then the batwings burst open and a flood of men rushed in; citizens of Canton City who had witnessed the confrontation through the panes of the saloon windows. A short fellow in a black coat and derby hat stepped up and shook Rusty's hand. "Thanks a million, stranger," he piped in a squeaky voice. "That killer has been a thorn in our side for a couple weeks now."

"Well, he won't bother nobody again, that's for sure," assured Rusty. He lifted the glass of buttermilk from the bar and took a long swallow from it.

"Exactly who are you, mister?" asked the town undertaker as he pulled a tape from his vest pocket and bent down to take Calhoun's measurements.

Rusty revealed his badge once again. "Rusty McLeod, United States Marshal, at your service, gentlemen."

"Welcome, Marshal McLeod!" said the short fellow in the bowler hat. "I'm Mayor Talbot, the one who requested you. And it looks as if they sent us an exceptional lawman to boot!"

"Glad to be here," said Rusty.

"Drinks are on the house!" called Mayor Talbot. "In celebration of the marshal's arrival!"

Rusty finished his buttermilk and set the glass down. "How about another one?"

"You got it, Marshal!" said the bartender.

The peace officer relaxed, basking in the admiration of those who had brought him there. As the body of Kid Calhoun was carried through the doors of the Wagon Wheel Saloon, he accepted another glass of cold buttermilk and sighed.

After a long, hard ride, he felt as if he were finally home.

CHAPTER TWENTY-SIX

Amos Hadley was startled from a sound sleep by silence.

He had lived on the rural farm at the far end of Sycamore Road all 68 years of his life, and, in all that time, he had made a habit of sleeping with his bedroom window open in the spring and summer months. He had also grown accustomed to the comforting night sounds of crickets and tree frogs, as well as an occasional dove or whippoorwill calling distantly from the heavy stand of woods that stretched for miles to the south. Over the years, that nocturnal symphony had become a part of him, just as much as the beating of his heart or the steady rhythm of his breathing.

Then, shortly before midnight of that warm August night, those noises stopped abruptly, rousing him from a deep slumber that only hard work and a clear conscience could provide.

Amos sat up in the brass bed he had shared with his late wife, Helen, until her death five years ago. The elderly man stared past the moonlit square of the open window, listening. His ears strained for sound; any sound at all. He heard none. The crickets that normally sang from the darkness of the grassy yard were eerily silent, as were the tiny toads that usually peeped from the limbs of the big sugar maple directly outside the house. A hush a choked the summer night. A hush so still and so complete that it seemed as though time itself had been frozen.

What's wrong with them? he wondered. *Either something out there has scared them plumb out of their wits... or stricken them dead.*

He figured the former assessment to be more likely. But what out there in the dark of night could have startled those creatures into total silence? Just the thought of such happening sent an involuntary shudder through Amos Hadley.

He sat there for a long moment, expecting the night chorus to resume, but it didn't. The silence continued. He waited for the sound of a soft summer breeze blowing through the maple's leaves, or perhaps the squeak of the iron weather vane shifting atop the roof of the twenty-stall horse stable out back of the house. But neither of those noises materialized either.

Cautiously, he climbed from the bed and, barefooted, walked across the hardwood floor to the window. He took a deep breath, trying to slow the quickening pace of this heart. Amos expected to smell the sweet scent of honeysuckle blossoms, as well as the pungent tang of wild onions, which grew plentiful in the horse pasture. Something else dominated the air, however. An odor that hung heavily, almost oppressively, in the night. An odor not unlike that of a burnt-out house, combined with an underlying touch of raw sulfur.

He looked toward the long, low structure of the stable, but there was no evidence of a fire. The windows remained pitch black. There was no tell-tale flicker of flames from blazing hay, and neither could he hear the frightened whinnying of panicked horses. Amos Hadley currently had 18 animals, all thoroughbreds, housed in the stable. If something had been wrong, they would have kicked up a ruckus that could have been heard clear to Harmony and back.

An unpleasant thought came to the old man. *Maybe they're like the crickets,* he told himself. *Maybe they've been scared silent, too.*

He felt his pulse climb another notch as he peered into the night.

But by what?

Amos was about to call himself a skittish old fool and climb back into bed, when a sound cut through the quiet. The high-pitched squeal of unoiled hinges. He identified its location at once; the big double doors of the stable's front entrance.

"There's something out there all right," he told himself, his uneasiness suddenly changing into angry suspicion. "A damn horse thief, more than likely." A week before, such a thought would have never entered his mind—not in a virtually crimeless community like Harmony. But, considering the rash of strange burglaries that had plagued some of the businesses in town, he couldn't help but wonder if the perpetrator had graduated from paint, tools and wagon wheels to something much more valuable.

Dressed only in a dingy V-necked undershirt and boxer shorts, Amos walked to his closet and opened the door. He found his old double-barreled Parker shotgun leaning against the wall behind his best Sunday suit, where it had stood longer than he could even remember.

He cracked open the double breech and checked the shells. There was no rocksalt or birdshot loads like some farmers tended to keep on hand. His gun was loaded for bear with double-aught buck. If the thief at the stable made one wrong move toward him, he would end up badly hurt and bleeding, or maybe even worse. Needless to say, when it came to someone stealing from him, Amos Hadley was not a very tolerant or forgiving man.

Cradling the scattergun in the crook of his arm, the horse-breeder left his house and started across the dark yard, toward the stable. As he grew nearer, he could see the big double doors standing wide open. *Cocky bastard,* thought Amos sourly. *Well, we'll see how cocky he is with a load of buckshot in his ass!*

He was halfway there, when dark motion showed just inside the stable doorway. Amos lifted his shotgun and curled his finger through the trigger guard, waiting for the thief to show himself.

A moment later, he emerged. Even in the light of a new moon, Amos could scarcely make out the trespasser. All he could distinguish was his basic size and shape. The man was rail-thin and tall, dressed almost entirely in black. And he wore a peculiar, high hat of some kind.

Amos's confusion turned into cold rage when he saw what the thief was leading from the stable. It was two of Hadley's finest roans. One was pitch black and named Charcoal. The other, Spitfire, was also black, but with three white stockings and a slash of white running down his slender forehead. The two were Amos's pride and joy, the sires of many a Kentucky racer during the past five years.

"What the hell do you think you're doing?" he demanded.

In the light of the moon, Amos detected the glint of amused eyes within the shadowy sockets of the man's gaunt face. "I'm stealing your horses, Mr. Hadley," he said. "Go on back to bed and I'll spare you. Refuse and you'll surely regret it." A wicked grin curled between dark whiskers. "Until your dying day. Or night, as it may be."

The threat stoked Amos's anger even more. "Don't see no gun with you," he said, raising the butt of the Parker to his shoulder. "But I've got enough here for both of us. Now let go of those horses, or I'll blow a hole through your belly big enough to pitch horseshoes through."

The man laughed softly. It was a hissing, serpentine sort of laugh that caused the fine hairs on the nape of Amos's neck to stand on end. Amos felt his hands begin to tremble slightly, making it hard to keep the shotgun squarely aimed.

"Don't say that I didn't warn you," whispered the thief. Then something strange happened. The man's hands began to crackle with what first looked like static electricity. The blue-white current intensified as it danced along the leather straps of the roans' bridles, immediately engulfing their narrow heads. The two horses stood stone still for a moment, their muscles taut and quivering. Soon, saliva began to seep from between their clenched teeth and their black eyes rolled up into their heads until only the whites could be seen.

Lord Almighty! thought Amos. *He's killing 'em both!*

But that wasn't what was taking place at all. The fingers of electricity culminated in a brilliant burst of light, nearly blinding the old man. When he finally regained his sight, he saw the two horses standing tall and darkly ominous on either side of the stranger. They pretty much looked the same as before, except for one aspect. Their eyes blazed fiery red, like the coals of a fire peeking through the slotted grate of a potbelly stove.

"Kill him," rasped the tall man, releasing their bridles and stepping away.

As the horses started slowly toward him, Amos aimed the shotgun between them and fired the load of one barrel at the thief. The big gun boomed, but its bee-swarm of buckshot parted only open air. Before the pellets could hit the dark man, he was gone, swallowed up by the blackness of the night.

Amos turned his attention back to the two horses that plodded toward him, their heads lowered, their red eyes glowing eerily. For the first time in his life, Amos Hadley felt an emotion he had never experienced in the presence of his beloved horses. Fear. Cold, undeniable terror. He could tell by the way the two roans were coming toward him that they had one intention in mind and one only.

The intended to murder him in cold blood.

The elderly man could think of nothing else to do but turn and run. He didn't start back for the house; instead he fled for the open pasture that lay just south of his property. As his bare feet pounded across grass, Amos turned and glanced behind him. The two horses were picking up speed, moving at a light trot. A cloudbank swallowed the moon, painting the night pitch black. Hostile red eyes pierced the darkness, as well as the coarse breathing of the two roans. Obscured from view, they sounded more like a pair of crazed, disease-ravaged beasts than the healthy, gentle-natured animals that Amos had raised from the time they were colts fresh from their mothers' wombs.

He ran past the smokehouse and chicken coop then hurriedly climbed the white board fence that stood beyond. A moment later, he was stumbling across the grassy pasture. He heard the drumming of hooves quicken and looked around to see both animals jump the four-foot barrier with no trouble at all. The clouds overhead seemed to tighten in density, shutting out every last bit of moonlight. In utter darkness, Amos ran across the open pasture, hoping to reach the cover of the South Woods. The horses pursued him, powering into a full gallop.

Is this really happening? he found himself wondering. *Or is this just some sort of horrible nightmare?*

A peal of evil laughter told him that, indeed, it *was* happening and, yes, it *was* truly a nightmare that he was caught up in. A nightmare that was frighteningly for real. The laughter seemed to swoop through the air above his head, encircling him, both receding and growing nearer at the same time. The ugly sound almost seemed to crawl inside his ears and enter his body, infecting every vein and artery, muscle and bone. He could feel the force of its wickedness thrumming throughout him, causing his blood pressure to rise and his breathing to grow labored and irregular.

Halfway across the pasture, his legs gave out. He dropped feebly to his knees, bright pinpricks of light dancing before his eyes. Amos felt as though he was on the verge of passing out, but he fought the sensation. If he fainted, he would die for sure. The only chance he had for survival was to keep a clear head and attempt to fight for his life.

He turned and feebly lifted the shotgun. From out of the darkness appeared an even blacker form. Angry red eyes glared at him as the beast stopped 20 feet away, its sleek muscles quivering in anticipation. A hideous sound rumbled deep down in the roan's throat; a low growling much like that of a mad dog, but a dozen times more terrifying.

"I'm sorry about this, Charcoal," moaned the old man. He steadied the sights of the gun on the heaving chest of the dark animal.

He was about to pull the trigger, when he heard soft movement from behind him. Amos turned his head just as a hoof caught him just behind the ear. The force of the blow knocked the elderly man sprawling and he felt his hands grow suddenly numb. Lying flat on his back, he stared at his fingers and found the shotgun gone from his grasp. Dizzily, he looked up at the night sky. The cloudbank moved onward and the moon appeared once again, bathing the pasture with a pale glow. Immediately, Amos saw that his predicament had taken a fatal turn.

Charcoal and Spitfire stood above him, their nostrils flared, drinking in the rich scent of blood. Amos knew where they smelled it from, too. The back of his head was warm and mushy where Spitfire's hoof had undoubtedly caved in a portion of his skull. The animals moved closer and, in the unnatural glow of their eyes,

Amos could see something other than hostility. Something much more horrifying in nature.

Pure, ravenous hunger.

Amos Hadley screamed as Charcoal's dark head dipped downward, his lips curled back and his huge teeth exposed. Agony coursed through the old man's body as the roan's teeth found his belly, slashing grinding, tearing past the flimsy cloth of his undershirt and rending the flesh underneath. The horse's muzzle burrowed deep into the pit of his innards; working, chewing, *devouring.*

Spitfire joined in the grisly banquet. The animal latched onto the flabby muscle of Amos's arm and, with a wrench of its powerful head, ripped the bicep from its moorings. The old man looked up in pain and terror as the roan tossed back his head and gobbled the hunk of meat down his gullet, then returned for more.

The horses fed with a hunger that could only be described as hellish. Soon, the pain grew so intense, that Amos could no longer hang on to consciousness. As darkness drew around him like a comforting blanket and the horrid sensation of teeth mangling flesh and bone grew less and less severe, Hadley weakly turned his head and looked back toward the farm.

Sitting on top of the white fence was the tall man Amos had encountered at the stable. He watched intensely from his perch, enraptured by the ferocity of the horses' bloodlust, his smile brimming with sadistic approval.

"Eat your fill, my children," he called out to the snarling animals. "We have much to do and you shall need your strength."

They did as their master requested, attacking the dying man with a renewed vigor. As they tugged and tore at his body, Amos Hadley felt his life slowly slipping away. Toward the end, a great sadness filled him more than anything else. For he knew, once the bellies of the two beasts were full, there would be very little left of him. Nary enough to be properly laid to rest and, more important, scarcely nothing left at all to warn the folks of Harmony of the horror that was about to be unleashed upon them.

CHAPTER TWENTY-SEVEN

Further along Sycamore Road, the dreams continued.

Maggie found herself sitting at a dressing table in a roomy circus trailer. She stared at her reflection in the mirror, marveling at the maturity that shown both on her face and in her body. Her face was clear and beautiful, and her breasts were full and round beneath her skintight suit of shiny pink spandex. In real life, she barely needed a training bra. In fact, she was still so flat-chested that her big brother loved to tease her about her "mosquito bites" when their parents weren't within earshot.

Someone knocked on the trailer door. "Five minutes till showtime, Ms. Sutton," called a voice.

"I'll be right there," she replied. She looked around the interior of the trailer, amazed at the abundance of colorful posters that covered the walls—posters that possessed her name and likeness. In this world, it was clear to see that she was a star.

Maggie finished applying pancake makeup, lipstick and rouge then placed a jeweled tiara atop her head of luxuriant golden blond hair. She closed her eyes, took a deep breath to focus herself and stood up. She was amazed at how tall and strong she was. The muscles of her arms and legs felt tight and evenly balanced. They were no longer the awkward limbs of a girl on the verge of puberty. She slipped her tiny feet into rubber-soled slippers, then left the trailer.

As she walked along the stretch of circus trailers toward the huge canvas tent of the Big Top, roustabouts and animal handlers called out to her, wishing her luck. She smiled and nodded her appreciation, then proceeded onward, her head held high.

A moment later, she arrived at the rear flap of the tent. A clown in a bright orange overcoat and floppy size 40 shoes politely pulled back the flap for her. "Knock 'em dead, kid!" he said.

"Thanks, Bobo," she said, stretching up on tip-toes and giving him a kiss on his white grease-painted jaw. The clown feigned exaggerated embarrassment then escorted her inside.

The interior was dark, except for a spotlight focused on the center ring. Maggie breathed deeply. The scents of sawdust, popcorn and cotton candy filled the air, as well as the excited rumbling of the crowd all around her. She felt her heart begin to beat faster, not in fear, but in happy anticipation. This was what she secretly lived for. The thrill of performing.

A tall, debonair ringmaster stepped into the spotlight, dressed in shiny black boots, white pants, a red jacket and a tall black top hat. The crowd launched into a burst of cheers and applause. He bowed gracefully and spoke into a microphone he held in his hand.

"Ladies and Gentlemen, Boys and Girls!" he called in a clear, crisp voice that would have put a radio deejay to shame. "Now for the moment you have been waiting for! The spectacle that has made this show the greatest in all the world!"

The crowd went wild. Whistles, cheers, and clapping burst from the audience, rising clear to the roof of the Big Top.

"That's your cue, sweetheart," said a dwarf wearing a red satin jacket with CIRCUS MAGNIFICENT in white letters on the back. He took her hand and led her to a tall steel pole with rungs bolted to the side.

She laid an affectionate hand against the side of the little man's smiling face. "Thanks, Max," she whispered. Then she took the rungs one at a time, ascending to a platform that stood a good seventy feet above the center arena.

In reality, Maggie had a secret fear of heights. Even when she climbed apple trees with Rusty back home she fought to remain calm and nonchalant, even though she was scared half to death. But here in her dream, she felt no such anxiety. As she climbed the rungs, pulling herself higher and higher, she felt relaxed and tranquil, like a fish in water. Before long, Maggie was stepping onto the small platform secured at the uppermost reaches of the pole. She looked up and saw that she could almost reach out and touch the ceiling of the Big Top. That in itself should have thrown her into a fit of panic, but it didn't.

"I wish to direct your attention to the spotlight high above the center arena!" continued the ringmaster. "There you will see the star of our show and the one you have all been eagerly waiting to see. The world famous high wire acrobat extraordinaire! Lady Margret!"

A cheer forceful enough to shake the poles of the Big Top exploded from the crowd as a spot suddenly illuminated Maggie. She squinted against the glare of the beam and smiled as she saw the audience—thousands of men, women, and children—rise to their feet and applaud. She waved cheerfully to them all and went to work. She took a long balancing pole from where it stood on the platform, then stood at the very edge, centering herself. The crowd fell into an immediate hush, their eyes glued to her graceful form directly overhead.

Maggie took a breath, then, for the first time, looked at the rope that stretched from her platform to the one directly opposite, a hundred feet away. The rope looked like a long, silver thread in the brilliant glow of the spotlight. Calmly, she took the pole firmly in her hands and placed a single foot upon the rope. Below, the crowd gasped loudly.

She felt no apprehension whatsoever. Confidence filled her as she mounted the rope and, gripping it with the curled soles of her feet, deftly traveled it, one step at a time. Her breathing was shallow, her balance perfectly centered, as if she had been born on the high wire. A minute later, she was stepping onto the other platform, raising her arms to the deafening cheers of her admiring fans below.

Maggie then tossed the pole away and, with no hesitation at all, returned to the rope. This time she somersaulted back across, doing death-defying flips and half-turns, landing firmly on the rope with hands and feet at all times. The spectators were ecstatic. They whistled, cheered, and stomped their feet, threatening to cave in the wooden bleachers around them. She ended her act with a triple backflip that brought her to a perfect handstand on the platform where she had originally started.

"Truly stupendous!" called the ringmaster over the roar of the crowd. "The one…the only…Lady Margret, Queen of the High wire!"

Maggie took a bow and blew kisses to those who cheered in the stands below. The ovation lasted for five minutes, eventually prompting an encore. She took a unicycle from a hook on the pole, as well as several balls from a wicker basket. Then she rode the unicycle across the rope, juggling as she went. She returned—backwards—eliciting more adoration from the appreciative masses.

She looked down at the center arena and saw that bouquets of roses were being thrown to her. With tears in her eyes, she spread her arms and soaked in the love that poured up from the stands. Yes, that was what she had craved for so very long. Total love and acceptance.

And, here in the circus of her dreams, she received all of that and more.

Chuck found himself sitting on a long bench in the fuselage of a World War II bomber plane. An Air Force lieutenant stood at an open doorway a few feet away, wearing an orange flight vest and white helmet. He peered into the fading light of dusk, the wind of the slipstream causing him to hang onto a handle bolted to the plane's inner wall.

"Only a few minutes until we reach the rendezvous point" he called to Chuck.

Another airman stood directly next to him, double checking the parachute pack that was strapped squarely to Chuck's back. "Everything's A-Okay, Sergeant," he said, giving Chuck a thumb's up. "Are you ready?"

Chuck suddenly knew what he was about to do. He was about to jump from the plane, like a paratrooper. He expected to throw a fit and refuse to go, but he did nothing of the kind. Instead, he nodded bravely and squared his shoulders. "Ready whenever you are," he said.

"Thirty seconds until the jump-out point," called the lieutenant at the door.

Chuck took a deep breath and felt for his weapons. They were all there; the K-Bar Marine knife, a bandoleer of pineapple grenades, a holstered .45 automatic, and an M1 carbine with a banana clip of .30 rounds. He wore olive fatigues with the stripes of a sergeant high on the sleeves, combat boots and a helmet with camouflage netting.

He felt something wiggle against his chest and looked down. From inside his flack jacket, he saw his pet iguana peering up at him. "Are you ready, Churchill?" he asked. The lizard clicked happily, the snuggled further into the vest for the duration of the ride down.

A red light on the wall suddenly turned green. "This is it!" called the lieutenant into the howl of the wind. He joined the other airman and, together, they lifted Chuck from the bench. Chuck felt a little disappointed that he was still crippled; he thought that he would have regained the use of his legs in such a detailed dream. But the regret lasted only an instant. He had more important things to think about, like his rendezvous in the heart of enemy territory, as well as the mission that would follow.

"Best of luck to you, Sergeant," said the lieutenant as they reached the open doorway.

"The fate of the Allied forces and the world are upon your shoulders, Sir," said the other one.

"I'll do my best to crush the enemy and end this damned war," Chuck promised. Then he nodded and felt himself being heaved into the open air.

The blast of cool air and the force of the gravitational pull nearly knocked the wind out of him. He recovered immediately, spreading his arms as he plunged earthward. Growing accustomed to the freefall, he turned his head and saw the dark silhouette of the plane making a sweeping turn, heading back toward friendly borders.

Chuck looked downward, the goggles over his eyes providing protection against the sting of the wind. The scarred landscape of a vast battlefield stretched beneath him for miles. Further to the north, he could see the flashes of violent explosions as the War continued on schedule. Even from such a lofty height, he could smell the odor of gunpowder drifting skyward.

War is hell, he thought to himself. *And I love it!*

Chuck found himself counting in his mind as he watched the earth of the desolate German countryside rush up to meet him. "Here we go, Churchill!" he called out. Then he grabbed the pack's ripcord and pulled.

An instant later, the chute bloomed overhead, jerking him upward. He felt his momentum slow, until he was drifting easily, heading toward a network of trenches that cut across a sprawling area of pockmarked pastureland. Chuck knew he was a sitting duck, sailing in the open air like that, but he hoped that the chaos of battle a mile or so to the north would prove to be a valuable distraction. Fortunately, he found that he was right. He reached the earth without drawing any attention at all. At least no hostile attention.

Chuck hit the earth with his dead legs and rolled, careful not to get entangled with the cords of his chute. The circle of dark nylon joined him on the ground seconds later. He wasted no time. Taking a folding trench shovel from his belt, he quickly dug a hole and buried the parachute, concealing it from view. Then shrugged out of the empty chute pack and, taking a pair of binoculars from a case that hung around his neck, trained them on the foremost trench that he had just passed over.

It wasn't long before dark forms climbed out of the foxhole and cautiously moved in a V-formation toward him. The leader of the platoon cupped a hand to his mouth and called out. "Those who seek guidance eagerly watch the skies," he said, giving the first code phrase. He stared through the gloom at Chuck's prone figure, his carbine at the ready, in case the enemy had pulled some clever act of deception.

"Their wait has ended, for the eagle has landed," replied Chuck in response.

A moment later, the platoon was across the field and gathered around him. "Right on time, Sarge," said the pointman.

Chuck reached out and shook his hand. "Good to see you, Corporal Steel," he said. "How far to the enemy line?"

"A mile and a half north," he replied, unfolding a map and showing their commander the lay of the land. "But before we can even get close to the real action, there's a Kraut machine gun nest blocking our way. We'll have to take it out."

Chuck opened his flak vest and took out a cigar. He bit off its end, then lit it with a Zippo lighter with the Marine Corp emblem stamped into the metal. "Then let's do it," he said gruffly. "Where is my Warchair?"

"We have it back here, Sir," said a buck private from the rear of the platoon.

"Bring it to me," he ordered.

A second later, the group of infantry soldiers parted. The private appeared, pushing the mighty Warchair. It was an armored wheelchair that looked more like a miniature tank with its heavy steel plating and iron treads. Chuck was lifted and placed into the seat of the chair, then handed a British-made Sten Mk2 submachine gun. He jacked a 9mm round into the breech and set the selector on "full automatic". Then he closed the Warchair's armored hatch and stuck the gun's barrel through a narrow slot in the front.

"You take point, Corporal," he said.

"Yes, sir," replied Steel. He worked the bolt of his M1 carbine, then started forward.

"Come on, men," said Chuck. "Let's kick some ass."

Together, they headed across the battle-scarred earth, their eyes glued to the brilliance of bursting bombs and tracer bullets that lit the gloom of dusk a mile and a half away. Churchill left the shelter of his master's flak vest and scrambled to the top of his helmet to get a better look. Chuck puffed on his stogie and worked the gears of the armored wheelchair, sending it onward at a slow, steady pace.

A short while later, Corporal Steel turned and silently held up his hand from a position 80 feet ahead. "Stay here, men," Chuck told those who stood around him. "I'll take care of this myself."

With a low hum, the wheelchair surged forward. Soon, he joined the soldier behind the shelter of a bombed oak tree. "How many are there?" he asked.

"A good dozen of the goose-steppers, Sarge," Steel told him. "There's four clustered around a heavy-duty Maxim, while the other eight are lined along the wall of the nest with their Mausers. Want me to come with you?"

Chuck thought about it for a second and shook his head. "No, I believe I can handle it."

"Good luck, Sarge," said Steel, heading back across the battlefield to rejoin the platoon.

Chuck wasted no time. He shifted his chair into high gear and, with a roar, powered around the blasted trunk of the tree. It wasn't long before he had closed the gap between him and the Nazis to only a few yards. Mausers cracked as he appeared out of the twilight. Their rounds merely glanced off the chair's armor plating. He heard a German curse rise from the trench, followed by a volley of fire from the 7.92 mm Maxim. The steel-plated wheelchair rocked on its treads with the force of the gunfire, but remained upright. Chuck continued onward, his teeth gritted around the stub of his smoldering cigar, his eyes full of steel and fury.

"Hang on, Churchill!" he called to his lizard. "We're going in!"

Thirty feet from the machine gun nest, a German potato masher spun from the trench, heading straight for him. He shifted the barrel of the Sten gun and sent a burst skyward. The slugs hit the grenade's handle, knocking it back into the foxhole from where it came. A second later, an explosion went off in the trench, filling one end of it with fire and smoke. A couple of Nazi soldiers were thrown from the nest, their bodies riddled with shrapnel. Chuck let out a loud battle-yell, then picked up speed and went over the edge of the trench, into the passageway below.

He landed atop the Maxim, crushing the German machine gun beneath the treads of the Warchair, as well as a couple of the soldiers who were manning it. A German major drew a Luger pistol from a flap holster, but it did him no good. A burst from the Sten nearly cut him clean in half. Four stormtroopers attacked Chuck from the right, their bayonets fixed. The top half of the Warchair pivoted and a swarm of 9mm slugs from the Sten mowed them down, leaving them in a twitching heap on the dirt floor of the trench.

The last three Nazis made a futile attempt to take him from the right. A bullet from a Mauser rifle ricocheted off the side of Chuck's helmet, knocking it slightly askew. "Hey, that smarted!" he growled. He pivoted to the right and, through the gun slot, tossed a couple of pineapple grenades beneath the soles of their jackboots. They went off almost immediately, tearing the soldiers limb from limb. One's head—wearing a German storm trooper's helmet and an expression of utter defeat—spun out of the trench and bounced several yards across the battlefield, before resting against a bullet-scarred boulder.

Chuck grinned around his stogie. He opened the armored hatch of the Warchair and took one of the mangled Mausers from the trench floor. He tied an American flag around the end of the barrel and held it high, so his men could see.

"All's clear!" he yelled out.

It wasn't long before the soldiers of his platoon were hauling the ton of steel-plated wheelchair to level ground once again. They smiled at him with admiration and respect. They knew they would be led to victory with Sergeant Adkins leading the way.

"Well, what are we waiting for, boys?' asked Chuck. "Let's have some real fun!"

A cheer rose from the ranks as they surged forward. They were ready to take on Hitler's warriors and win, no matter what the cost might be

CHAPTER TWENTY-EIGHT

Edwin Hill felt miserable.

He sat in his chair next to the potbelly stove, drinking from the bottle of Wild Turkey. Only the light over the front counter was on. The rest of the general store was cloaked in darkness.

Edwin took a sip of liquor and felt it burn its way down into his belly. Usually, he indulged in his secret vice due to a feeling of loss over the death of his son. But this time it was something else entirely. The emotion that dragged his spirits down that night was pure and simple guilt. He felt bad about lying to his best friend.

The storekeeper couldn't figure out why he had done it. The incident in Hell Hollow had taken place way back in 1917, nine decades ago. True, he had been sworn to secrecy concerning the killing of the murderous medicine man when he was 8 years old, but the need for secrecy had passed long ago, when most of the men of that vigilante posse had died. Now there was only he and Jasper McLeod left, and Edwin was the only one of the two who even remembered what had happened. Jasper had either been too young to recall the awful events of that night, or he had completely suppressed the memory.

"There ain't no need to keep it hidden away any longer," he told himself, screwing the cap back on the liquor bottle. "Jasper has a right to know, even if it does cause him pain."

The one memory of that night that stood out the strongest in Edwin's mind was the moment when Charles McLeod aimed the sights of his Winchester and put a bullet squarely between Augustus Leech's defiant eyes, followed by 5-year-old Jasper's cry of shock and disbelief. Seeing one's father kill another man is truly a traumatic experience, even if the bastard slain was responsible for the death of your baby sister and 11 others.

"Yeah, I'll do it tomorrow," he declared out loud, his words slightly slurred by the whiskey he had consumed. "I'll have Jasper come over first thing in the morning and tell him flat out. I owe him that much at least."

Edwin looked at an old Orange Crush clock that hung on the wall directly behind the counter. "Lord Almighty! It's done past one in the morning. I'd best close this place up and get on to bed."

He was getting up out of his chair, when the jangle of the copper cow bell over the front door drew his attention. He glanced over and saw someone stepping inside. Edwin tried to identify the man, but the light of the 40-watt bulb over the counter failed to reach the doorway. The customer closed the door behind him and stood there, cloaked in shadow, neglecting to move any further inside.

Edwin mustered an apologetic smile. "I'm sorry, sir, but we're closed. I know I should've put the sign on the door, but I had my mind on other things. We'll be open bright and early at seven o'clock, if you want to come back then."

The visitor said nothing. He simply stood there in the shadows and stared at the elderly shopkeeper.

Edwin frowned. He took a couple of steps forward, peering into the gloom. The fellow was tall and broad-shouldered, and was clad in an Army dress uniform. It had been years since Edwin had seen anyone decked out in military duds, particularly in Harmony.

"Uh, do I know you?" he asked.

The soldier nodded. "Yes," he said in a hauntingly familiar voice. "But not as well as I would have liked."

Edwin felt a jolt of cold dread shoot through him. He reached out and held onto a wire rack of potato chips to steady himself. "Who are you?" he asked hoarsely.

Slowly, the man stepped out of the shadows, into the dim glow of the counter light. His face was strong and tanned, his eyes clover green, and his dark hair was shaved close to the scalp in a military crew cut.

Edwin sharply sucked in a breath and took a stumbling step backward. "No!" he said, shaking his head.

"It's me, Papa," said the visitor. He walked toward the old man, holding his cap in his huge hands. "Your son, Aaron."

Edwin felt the strength drain from his legs. His heart began to race as the impossibility of what was taking place sank into his sluggish mind. "But it can't be! You're...oh, dear God in heaven, you're *dead*!"

"It was a mistake, Papa," explained Aaron Hill, that familiar country boy grin splitting his ruddy face. "They thought I was dead, but I wasn't. Somebody else got mistaken for me. I was captured by the Viet Cong and held prisoner all these years. I just now got home."

The elderly man struggled with what he was being told, attempting to judge whether it was fact or fiction. "But if that's what happened, why wasn't I told? Why wasn't I notified by someone?"

"I made them promise not to," said Aaron approaching his father. "I wanted it to be a surprise, Papa."

Edwin didn't quite know what to say. He felt his heart begin to settle down as hope began to conquer the horrible loss he had experienced for over forty years. To call the sudden resurrection of his only son a surprise was a gross understatement.

"It's a miracle," he muttered. Dazed, he let go of the chip rack and started toward his son.

"Yes, it is," said Aaron. The strapping soldier dropped his cap on the floor and raised his arms. "Papa—" he faltered, his eyes brimming with tears.

A joy unlike any Edwin hill had ever felt filled the old man. Tears of happiness bloomed in his own eyes as the distance between the two closed and soon they were in each other's arms. Edwin closed his eyes, thankful that he one he was embracing was solid. He wasn't a ghost or a figment of Edwin's inebriated imagination, that was for sure.

"I love you, Papa," sobbed Aaron, nestling his face against the old man's starched white shirt.

A pang of soulful relief swelled in Edwin's age-weakened heart. "Oh, I love you, too, son," he moaned, hugging the big man closer. "I've always loved you."

Aaron Hill clutched his father tightly and nodded silently. The gesture told the elderly man that his son had known that all along, even though he had never actually came right out and said so.

The blissful reunion lasted a few moments more. Then it abruptly went horribly wrong.

Edwin felt a dampness soak through the material of his shirt. At first, he thought it was merely his son's happy tears. Then the dankness grew heavier and warmer. Moisture trickled across the old man's shoulder, soaking the shirt all the way down his back to the waistband of his britches.

"What in tarnation—?" he asked, pulling away. As he did so, he glanced down at the floor and saw a thick pool of stark red blood forming around his and Aaron's feet.

Edwin's heartbeat began to quicken again. Although he didn't want to, he knew he had to look into his son's face and see what the nature of the bleeding might be. Slowly, he raised his head and stared at the things he had been fooled into believing was his son.

Most of Aaron's face was gone, as if having been blown away by the concussion of an enemy mortar. All that remained above his neck was a jagged fragment of jawbone, topped by a slender slice of face on the left side. Only one of the boy's eyes remained intact and it stared sightlessly at him, dull and totally devoid of life. Tatters of torn flesh clung loosely to the splintered bone, while jagged shards of dark shrapnel protruded from amid the gleaming viscera, an ugly reminder of just how hellish war could truly be.

Edwin screamed and stumbled backward, his face growing pale with shock. "No!" he wailed, witnessing the horrible devastation that Aaron's sealed casket had concealed during that funeral service so very long ago.

The dead soldier walked toward him, arms outstretched. "I love you," the thing rasped, blood bubbling thickly in its windpipe. The jawbone moved sluggishly with each word, expelling a couple of loose teeth from their cracked sockets. The teeth dropped to the floor and crackled across the hardwood boards. One landed on the toe of Edwin's patent leather shoe.

"Stay away!" screamed Edwin, feeling his left arm begin to throb with each jerk of his rising pulse. "Stay the hell away from me!"

"But…I love you!" pleaded the headless corpse, anxious for another embrace. A much more lasting embrace. "I love you, Papa!"

Edwin Hill took a couple more steps toward the back of the store, then succumbed to a burst of agony that totally engulfed the left side of his body. His arm and shoulder grew rigid and he dropped to the floor, hitting hard on his ancient knees. Edwin attempted to regulate his breathing and calm down, but the hideous apparition that approached him made it impossible to do so. He fell to his side, clutching his left arm tight enough to draw blood beneath the sleeve. His heart thundered crazily beneath his breastbone, gaining in speed, refusing to slow down. It felt as though someone were attempting to batter his way through the wall of his chest with a sledgehammer, from the inside out.

The elderly man closed his eyes, grimacing as bolts of debilitating pain coursed through every inch of his 98-year-old body. He lay there breathing raggedly for a moment, hoping that the awful specter of his slaughtered son would fade away. But it didn't. Past the roaring in his ears, Edwin could hear the sound of footsteps draw closer, until they finally stopped no more than a yard away from where he lay.

He expected the thing to speak again, to tell him that it loved him in that gurgling, blood-engorged voice. Instead, a snickering laugh filled his ears. A laugh full of contempt and sadistic pleasure. The laugh of someone who truly enjoyed the agony Edwin was experiencing.

Edwin opened his eyes, expecting to see the crisp uniform pants and shiny black shoes of the headless soldier. Instead, he saw only black trousers and mud-encrusted work boots with heavy rubber soles and rawhide laces. With great effort, the old man craned his neck, turning his face upward.

Standing over him was a tall, lanky man wearing a black t-shirt with dancing skeletons across the front, a black frockcoat and a dusty top hat. Edwin stared into the man's leering face. It was a different face from the one he had known 90 years ago; disturbingly similar, but not precisely the same. The glint of evil was there, however, gleaming deep from within those dark, smiling eyes. The same sparkle of sheer wickedness that had glared back at them from the seat of a medicine show wagon one windy autumn night an eternity ago.

"You!" he managed to croak, his jaw trembling. "It *is* you, isn't it?"

Augustus Leech simply smiled down at him, his eyes twinkling with sick amusement. “I couldn’t come back to Harmony without visiting my old friend Edwin,” he said. “So, how have you been doing all these years? Have you thought of me often or did you stash me away in that dark closet you call a conscience, along with all your other skeletons?”

Edwin could only gape at the man, caught between the agony that gripped him and the mortification of having Leech—or a startling incarnation of him—standing only a few feet away.

“Speaking of skeletons, how did you like ol’ Aaron?” he asked with a sly grin. “A real hoot, wasn’t he? That was how he looked when the medics found him in that rice paddy at Khe Sanh, you know. His head all burst open like that. Looked like a rotten melon laid out in the hot sun.”

“No,” groaned Edwin feebly.

“Oh, yes, dear fellow,” insisted Leech. “And another thing. He hated you. He utterly despised you from the day he was born until the day those gooks blew his head off. Even if you would have old him that you loved him, he would have spat in your face. Your only son loathed you, Edwin Hill. He cursed the earth you walked on.”

Hot tears spilled from the old man’s eyes as another explosion of agony wracked his chest. Slowly, he reached for his shirt pocket. But when his fingers dipped inside, he found that it was empty.

Leech hunkered down beside him and laughed. “Is this what you’re looking for?” he asked, holding a prescription vial between his thumb and forefinger. It was Edwin’s heart medicine.

Edwin’s mouth worked wordlessly, like a fish smothering in the open air. He reached out with a trembling hand, but the man in the stovepipe hat held it mere inches from his fingers.

"You know, I would be more than happy to give this to you, Edwin," he said teasingly. "But I'm afraid you've been a naughty boy. You were intending to tell your friend Jasper about what took place all those years ago down in that backwoods hollow." His dark brows arched in amusement. "What do you folks call it? Hell Hollow? How appropriate. In fact, much more appropriate than you could ever imagine."

"My medicine," whispered Edwin, feeling darkness begin to close around him. "Please."

"I'm afraid not," said Leech, sticking the plastic vial into his coat pocket. "You see, you simply must be punished for allowing your conscience be your guide, instead of your spineless fears. Believe me, under different circumstances I would have no objection to your telling Mr. McLeod everything; how you chased me down, ran me over the edge of that hollow, and then shot me down in cold blood. But if you were to do that, the element of surprise would be totally lost. He would undoubtedly alert the good citizens of Harmony and, before long, all my plans would be futile. They would likely band together and treat me in the same rude manner you and those vigilantes treated me."

"Your plans?" croaked Edwin. "What the hell have you come back for?"

"You expect me to say 'vengeance', don't you?" countered Leech. "Revenge for that night long ago. Well, I must admit, that does play a significant part in the scheme of things. But my motivation is much more complex than that, I'm afraid. You see, I'm doing this for the sheer joy of it. Just for fun. That's all."

"And that's why you murdered those people 90 years ago?" asked the storekeeper.

"Because it gave you *pleasure*?"

"See...you understand me much better than you thought," he replied. He moved in closer, until his face was no more than a few inches from Edwin's. "Did you really think I was satisfied by poisoning only a dozen adults and children? If so, you are sorely mistaken. I wanted you all. Every last soul in Harmony. I'd done it before, you know. Stricken entire communities with the help of my infamous elixir; poured that dark potion down their gullible throats and inflicted countless agonies upon both their bodies and minds. Before they died, they begged for mercy and, when it failed to come, they turned their backs on God. They cursed His name...as I intended they do. That made it much more easy. For the Master to step in and claim what was rightfully his."

"The Master?" asked Edwin.

A malicious smile curled across Leech's whiskered face. "I believe we both know who I'm referring to." The tall man pulled a pocket watch from his breast pocket—a watch bearing the face of a leering devil on its ornate lid—and appraised the time. "Well, I must be running along. It was nice chatting with you, but I do have much to do in preparation. I wouldn't want to disappoint the good folks of Harmony. I wouldn't want them to think that I have forgotten this hospitable village after all these years."

Edwin Hill suddenly got an inkling of what the man's sinister intentions might be. "Damn you to hell, you son of a bitch!" he growled weakly.

Augustus Leech turned as he was walking toward the front door. "I recollect promising you the same thing once," he said. "And, take it from me...I *always* keep my promises."

After Leech had departed, Edwin laid in the darkness, the pain in his chest waning until only a dull numbness remained. He knew that he must get to a phone and call Jasper; warn him about the disaster to come. But he was helpless to do so. Every ounce of strength and willpower had been wrung from his body by his chaotic heart.

All he could do was lay there on the hard boards of the floor and allow darkness to claim him, just as Doctor Leech would claim the souls of Harmony, both for his own wicked pleasure and for the benefit of the one he so loyally served.

CHAPTER TWENTY-NINE

Bright and early the next morning, Keith and the others met on the front porch of Chuck Adkins' house.

The city boy hopped off Blue Fury when he reached the driveway and pushed the bike the rest of the way across the dewy grass of the yard. Rusty, Chuck and Maggie had already congregated around the porch swing, talking excitedly.

"What's happening, dudes?" Keith asked, although he already knew what had them wound up.

Rusty grinned as his cousin climbed the porch steps. "Yeah, like you have to ask! Well, did it happen for you, too?"

Keith recalled the night on the rainy streets of a crime-ridden city. He could almost smell the salt air of the waterfront, as well as feel the heaviness of the .45 automatic cradled beneath his armpit. He couldn't help but smile to himself. "Yeah, it did. Just like that guy in the hollow promised."

"See? Didn't I tell you?" said Maggie, bouncing on the seat of the hardwood swing so forcefully that she sent it swaying back and forth. "Those cards were for real. They were some kind of magic!"

"Now hold on for a minute," said Keith, sitting down in a ladder-backed rocking chair and propping his feet on the ledge of a porch post. "The jury's still out on this mumbo-jumbo stuff, at least in my opinion. Could be we just dreamed what we did because we secretly wanted to. Those cards Doctor Leech gave us just stirred up our imaginations, that's all."

"Aw, I should've known you'd still be a doubting Thomas, even after it panned out," said Chuck, irritated at the city boy's skepticism. "I don't know about you, but my dream was just as real as if I'd actually been there.

It wasn't just some stupid dream like I usually have. I could even smell and feel in this one." He remembered how the right side of his head had been a little sore when he awoke that morning, in the same exact spot where the Mauser bullet had glanced off his combat helmet in the dream.

"Mine was like that, too," said Maggie. "I can still smell the sawdust and cotton candy."

"And I can still taste that buttermilk, too," proclaimed Rusty.

Chuck cut amused eyes his way. "Buttermilk?"

"Never mind," said Rusty. "The point is, these dreams were so blamed *real*, it wasn't like we were dreaming at all. It was like we were really there, in the flesh. Shoot, I woke up with my lips as dry as a cicada husk from riding through that desert half the night."

"You guys are warped to the max!" snorted Keith. "It wasn't *that* real!"

"Don't lie to us, Keith," said Maggie, looking upset. "Tell us about your dream. After you remember it all, I bet you'll change your mind."

Keith raised his Ray-Bans until they were perched on the top of his head. "Swear you won't laugh?"

"Scout's honor," said Rusty, raising his hand in the classic salute.

Keith proceeded to tell them about his journey to a city of tall skyscrapers, bustling streets and an undercurrent of crime and corruption. He told them of his role as a hard-nosed police detective in search of the elusive Big Man, as well as his encounter with Lester the Stoolie and his gunfight with the two gangsters. As he laid out every detail of his dream, Keith couldn't help but feel as though part of him was still there, continuing to live out the day-to-day routine of Detective Bishop.

After he was finished, the other three took turns describing their dreams. Rusty told of his life as a U.S.

marshal and his gunfight in the Canton City saloon. Maggie recounted her experience as a world-famous high wire acrobat, the star attraction for Circus Magnificent and the idol of thousands of spectators. Chuck told them of his mission behind enemy lines in the role of Sergeant Adkins, as well as his raid on the German machine gun nest with the help of the unstoppable Warchair.

"Admit it, Keith," said Chuck after he had finished. "It was pretty real, wasn't it? I mean, have you ever had a dream like that before? One with that much clarity and detail?"

"No, I can't say that I have," agreed the boy.

"Then you're willing to eat crow and admit that those cards Leech gave us were for real?" asked Maggie.

Keith shrugged. "Yeah, I guess so."

"Well, shit fire and save matches!" said Rusty. "I can't believe he actually admitted he was wrong. Better call *Time Magazine*. They'll want to save their cover for this one!"

"Aw, bite me!" snapped Keith, sliding his shades back over his eyes with a nod of his head. "I'm big enough to admit when I was wrong."

"Yeah, after we finally convinced you," said Chuck. He looked over at Rusty. "Man, you've got one stubborn cousin there."

"Don't I know it," said the farm boy.

"I heard it was a McLeod trait," said Keith with a sly grin. "Like sleeping under the porch with the hound dogs or wiping your butt with dried corn cobs instead of toilet paper."

"I suggest you shut your mouth up right quick, if you don't want me to wipe your butt with the toe of my shoe," snapped his cousin.

"Quit acting like a couple of Neanderthals!" said Maggie. "This is serious business."

Keith considered the four illustrated cards and the dreams they had apparently conjured. "Doesn't all this seem a little bit *wrong* to any of you?"

"What do you mean?" asked Chuck.

"I mean being able to mold someone's dreams and make them seem like real life?"

"I thought it was pretty neat," said Maggie.

"Yeah, it was neat... but it wasn't normal. If you ask me, we're messing around with something here that maybe we shouldn't be."

"Aw, don't be such a party-pooper," Rusty told him. "We had those dreams last night and it didn't hurt, did it? It's just plain old fun, that's all. There ain't nothing to worry about."

"Are you sure about that?" asked Keith. "I've heard if you dream of falling and you hit the ground before you wake up, you could die."

"That's just an old wives' tale!" protested Chuck.

"But what if it isn't?" Keith wanted to know. "What if something like that happens to one of us while we're living out our dream? What if Rusty gets gunned down by a gunslinger, or Maggie falls off the high wire, or Chuck gets blown to smithereens by a grenade? What if some gangster mows me down with a Tommy gun? Are we going to wake up like nothing ever happened...or will we even wake up at all?"

The other three stared at him for a long moment, considering what he had just said. Then Chuck scowled and shook his head. "That's stupid, Bishop! Dreams are just something your subconscious cooks up, not flesh and blood reality. There's no way they could end up hurting us physically. Right, guys?"

He waited for Rusty and Maggie to back him up, but they were slow in doing so. They hesitated a moment longer than he expected, giving him the impression that maybe they were swallowing the bull Keith was trying to feed them.

"We don't know that for sure." Keith showed them the knuckles of his right hand. They were pink and a couple had the skin scraped off them. "See this? My knuckles weren't like this before I went to bed last night. Then I dream about punching out that little rat-faced bastard and I wake up with my hand swollen and aching. What does that mean?"

Chuck shrugged. "Maybe you hit it on the bedpost in the middle of the night. I don't know." He absently lifted his hand and rubbed at the sore spot near his right temple. "Anyway, tell me one thing. Why are you so down on Doctor Leech? He seems like an okay guy to me."

Rusty and Maggie agreed.

"I don't know for sure," Keith admitted. "It's something I can't put my finger on. He seems like something more than some crazy performer riding around in an old-timey wagon, living out some weird fantasy. He seems like someone with a hidden motive."

"What kind of motive?"

"I'm not sure, but he's up to no good. I'd bet my life on it."

"Aw, come on, cuz—" started Rusty.

"I'm not kidding." Keith's face was dead serious. "The guy's not the righteous dude you make him out to be. He's like a bad apple. Shiny and delicious-looking on the outside, but full of worms inside."

"I didn't get that impression," said Chuck.

"You mean you think a guy who brings dead rabbits back to life and makes spiders crawl out of his mouth is *ordinary*?" asked Keith. "He's not like everyone else, that's for sure. And, besides, the guy's a thief."

"A thief?" asked Maggie. "What do you mean by that?"

Keith thought of his own shoplifting escapes and almost said *it takes one to know one*, but he didn't. "Well...duh! Who do you think has been stealing all this stuff around town? Wagon wheels, lumber and cans of bright paint? He used all that stuff to fix up that old wagon of his."

The three seemed startled. He could tell that they, too, had just come to that realization.

Chuck leaned back in his wheelchair and eyed the boy from Georgia. "So you're just going to stop this dreaming stuff cold turkey? You're just going to rip up that card Leech gave you and go on having the same boring, idiotic dreams as before?"

Keith thought about it. He considered the rain-soaked city and the prospect of never setting foot in it again. For some reason, he found himself feeling immediately homesick, as if tearing up the card would be an act of self-exile. Whether he wanted to admit it or not, the place of his dream had strangely seemed more like home than that brownstone condo he shared with his parents back in Atlanta.

"Well, I didn't exactly say that," he finally said. "I just think we oughta be careful. And we shouldn't trust this Leech fellow so much. I swear, there's something really bad about him. I can feel it."

"Okay," said Rusty. "We'll do it this way. The next time we go dreaming, we'll wake ourselves up the moment we think we could end up getting hurt or killed. Agreed?"

The other three nodded. "I don't know about you," said Chuck, "but I can't wait until I'm back where I was last night. I'm ready to get back on that battlefield and kick some Nazi butt!"

"Well, we could all go home and take a nice long nap," said Rusty. "But I ain't done that since I was in kindergarten."

Keith's eyebrows arched over the frames of his sunglasses. "Oh, last year, huh?"

Rusty grinned. "I don't care if you are some bad-ass police detective in your dreams, hotshot. Here in the real world you're just some skinny city kid with a smart mouth and little to back it up. Anytime you want to finish that wrestling match we started in the barn, you just let me know."

"Bring it on, Hyram," said Keith.

"Aw, give me a break!" snapped Maggie. "You guys and your macho bull! You're turning my sneakers brown with all the crap you're letting fly."

"Tell it like it is, Hot Mama!" laughed Chuck, giving her a high-five.

They all agreed to revisit their dreamscapes that night, then compare notes the following day. In the meantime, they decided to hang around Chuck's place and mess around in the workshop out back. Keith had found plans for a glider in an old issue of *Popular Mechanics* his grandfather had lying around the house and Chuck assured them there was enough plywood out back of the garage to build one. Of course, they had no expectations of actually getting it off the ground, but at least it was something to keep them occupied until nightfall came and gave them the opportunity to enter their individual dream worlds once again.

CHAPTER THIRTY

Allison Walsh reached the outskirts of Harmony around 7:30 that morning.

She crossed the Duck River Bridge and drove a half-mile before she came to the first business in the rural town. Allison parked her rental car in the lot of crushed gravel and cut the engine. She sat there for a moment, finishing off a cup of coffee she had bought at a McDonald's off the Manchester exit. When she was through, she stashed the empty cup in the white paper bag and climbed out of the Altima.

The old country store wasn't much to look at; an ancient structure with weathered walls, a tin roof and rusted tobacco and soda pop advertisements hanging here and there. She climbed the steps to the front porch. A hand-written cardboard sign taped to a glass pane of the door read "Yeah, we're OPEN. Ya'll come on in!" The invitation was a sincere one and Allison reached for the door knob feeling as though the proprietor of this place might possibly turn out to be a bit more friendly and a lot more receptive to her questions concerning Slash Jackson than the others she had talked to during the past few days.

She opened the door and walked in. Two things startled her almost immediately. The first was the jangling cowbell that had been rigged over the upper doorframe. And, secondly, was the body of an elderly man lying on his back on the dusty hardwood floor.

"Oh my God!" said Allison. She left he door standing open and rushed to the man's side. She set her purse aside then studied the elderly storekeeper. His face was ashen and slightly blue around the lips, and at first she was sure that he was dead. But when she took his hand in hers, she was relieved to find that he was still warm to the touch. Allison reached up and pressed a couple of fingers against the side of his neck. He had a pulse, but it was faint and irregular.

"Mister?" she asked, gently patting his hand. "Are you conscious? Can you hear me?"

A shallow whistle of breath exited his nostrils, but that was the only sound he made. Allison checked his pockets, but found no medicine that he might require. She left his side and went behind the sales counter. She searched the shelves underneath, as well as a couple of drawers below the cash register, but found nothing.

Allison was about to reach for a telephone that hung on the beam of a back wall, when the grumbling roar of an engine came from the road she had just traveled. She stepped from behind the counter and looked out the open doorway. An old red pickup truck pulled into the front lot with a crackle of near-bald tires on gravel. A second later, the truck lurched to a stop and a man climbed out.

She reached the porch by the time the fellow was on his way up the front steps. He was a tall, lanky old man, probably in his mid-90s, with a face like tanned leather and thick crop of silvery hair.

"You've got to help me!" she gasped, frightened for the life of the man inside. "We've got to call someone!"

"Just hold on there, little lady," he said. "What's the matter?"

"There's a man lying in the floor here," she said. "I think he's had a heart attack."

The expression on his face changed from curiosity to terror in an instant. "Damn!" he said, pushing past her and running to the unconscious man's side. From the way he had reacted, Allison could tell that the two were close friends.

"When did you find him?" he asked.

"Just a minute ago," she told him. "I walked in and there he was on the floor. I was just about to call 911."

A sad look crossed the elderly man's long face. "We're just a little mud hole in the road, miss. We don't have even have cable TV, let alone 911. We'll have to call the paramedics over at the fire hall."

He gave Allison the number and she quickly called it. A moment later, she hung up the phone. "They said they'll be here in two shakes of a lamb's tail, whatever that means."

A hint of relief crept into the man's wrinkled face. "That means they'll be here in about two minutes. The fire hall is no more'n a half of a mile from here." He stared at his friend helplessly and began to search through the pockets of his companion's shirt and pants.

"If you're looking for medicine, I already tried," she told him. "I couldn't find any."

"Damn!" he cussed, forgetting that he was in the presence of a lady for the first time in his life. "Edwin always keeps them in his shirt pocket."

"Is that his name?" she asked, standing there feeling fidgety and helpless.

"Yes, ma'am. Edwin Hill." He held out a big calloused hand. "I'm a friend of his. Jasper McLeod."

"Pleased to meet you," she said, shaking his hand. "I'm Allison Walsh. I was just passing through."

"You must've made a wrong turn and got lost then," he said, attempting wry grin and failing miserably. "The road through Harmony doesn't go much of anywhere. It hits a dead-end, smack dab in the middle of a patch of woods."

"No," answered Allison. "Harmony was where I intended to go."

Jasper McLeod turned his attention back to his friend. He lifted one of Edwin's eyelids with the ball of his thumb. The pupil underneath was unresponsive.

"You just hang in there, you old dog," he whispered, gripping the old man's limp hand in his own. "The cavalry is on its way."

"I'm sorry," the brunette said softly. "I'm so sorry."

A moment of silence stretched between them. Then Jasper spoke. "Are you here in Harmony to visit someone, Miss Walsh? Kinfolks?"

"No," she said carefully. "I just wanted to ask some questions. About something that happened on the interstate a few days ago."

"And what would that be?"

"A man was found murdered a mile or so from the Harmony exit," she explained. "His throat was slashed."

Jasper nodded. "Yeah, I heard about that. You a police lady or something?"

"A reporter," said Allison, not straying too far from the truth. "I was going to ask some of the merchants here in Harmony if they'd seen the man that was supposedly responsible."

"I didn't think the state cops had a description of the killer," said Jasper, puzzled.

"What does he look like?"

Reluctantly, Allison conjured the image of Slash Jackson in her mind. The way he had looked at the gas station outside of Atlanta, not naked and bloody in the candlelight of that abandoned house near Adairsville. "He's tall and thin, but muscular. Long black hair, with a mustache and chin beard."

Jasper shook his head. "I ain't seen no strangers like that around. But that doesn't mean that someone else hasn't. Drive into town and ask around. I'm sure folks'll be glad to help you out if they possibly can."

Allison was encouraged. "Thanks. I'll do that."

A second later, they could hear the shrill wail of a siren in the distance. By the time Allison stepped to the door and looked out, a white and orange emergency van was pulling into the gravel lot, throwing a cloud of gray dust in the air.

She watched as two paramedics worked over Edwin Hill, stabilized him, and then loaded him onto a stretcher and carried him from the general store to the back of the van. She walked to the front door with Jasper McLeod, watched him take a brass key from the sill over the doorway and lock up once they stepped outside.

"I'm gonna meet 'em over at the hospital in Manchester," he said, taking two porch steps at a time. "I appreciate your help, Miss Walsh."

"I just hope he pulls through okay," she offered, not knowing quite what to say.

Jasper forced a good-natured smile. "Aw, Edwin's a tough old buzzard. He'll be all right."

Allison could detect a tone of uncertainty in the elderly man's voice. "Well, I hope so."

She stood next to her car and watched as Jasper jumped into his truck and took off after the emergency van. When both vehicles were gone from sight, she sighed deeply, shaken by the events of the past several minutes. Then she climbed into her car and headed toward Harmony, to try her luck there.

Unfortunately, her luck turned out to be all bad.

Later that evening, Allison returned to her room at a seedy, 30-dollar-a-night motel off the Fairfield—Bugscuffle—Harmony exit. She closed her door and slid the security chain into its brass cradle. Wearily, she set a greasy paper sack on the nightstand next to the bed. It contained a BLT and an order of fries she had purchased at her last stop in Harmony; a little Mom and Pop café called the Friendly Corner.

Allison laid her purse on the full-sized bed then stepped into the bathroom. The citizens of Harmony had certainly been friendly, as well as cooperative. But they hadn't been the least bit helpful. According to everyone she had spoken to, no one had seen anyone who even remotely resembled Slash Jackson. By the time 5:00 had rolled around, she felt as though she had talked to every man, woman, child and dog in the little farming community and not received one shred of useful information in return. All had been kind and considerate, but that wasn't what she needed. She needed a lead that would eventually take her right to Jackson.

But, sadly, that lead hadn't presented itself that day.

Feeling lonely and depressed, Allison sat down on the commode, buried her face in her hands, and cried. She remained that way for a long time, venting her frustration in a torrent of angry tears. When she had finally cried herself out, she lifted her face and stared into the mirror over the bathroom sink. It was like looking into the face of a Holocaust survivor; hollow eyes, sunken cheeks, and the grim expression of one who had stared death square in the face and lived to tell about it.

Why are you doing this, Allie? she asked herself bitterly. *Have you gone completely crazy?*

She stared at her reflection again. All she saw there was a small, frightened child, not a hellcat avenger with a loaded gun and the nerve to pull the trigger.

With a shuddering sigh, Allison decided to take a hot shower. Maybe that would clear her mind and help her determine whether she was acting foolishly or not. She turned on the warm spray of the shower, undressed and folded her blouse and slacks over the bar of the towel rack.

It was when Allison turned back toward the bathroom mirror that the decision of whether to go home to St. Louis or continue with her search was made for her. Staring back at her starkly, in puffy pink flesh and ugly brown scabbing, was the word that Jackson had so meticulously and gleefully carved into the flesh of her chest, just above the swell of her breasts.

Rage suddenly rose from deep within her, screwing her tearful face into a mask of anguish. "You bastard!" she screamed shrilly, flailing out with her right hand. The heel of her palm struck the bathroom mirror forcefully enough to bring a pattern of spiderweb cracks to the steamy surface.

With the anger came pain. She turned her hand and found that she had cut herself. It was a shallow gash, but it was bleeding profusely. Breathing deeply, Allison turned on the cold water of the sink and held her injured hand beneath the icy stream until the flow of blood slowed to a trickle.

Allison wasn't regretful of her impulsive act. Instead, she relished the pain that throbbed through her hand. It reminded her of the not so distant past. Of similar and much greater pains administered by knife, fists, cigarette and teeth in the flickering light of a single candle. She found herself actually *wanting* to remember, not to punish herself, but to keep the hatred within her burning brightly.

She knew at that moment that doubt would never plague her again. She would find the demon that put her through hell and, when she did, she would kill him.

Or die trying.

CHAPTER THIRTY-ONE

When Keith returned to the McLeod farm after a day of messing around at the Adkins residence, he was surprised to find the house empty. Usually, Grandpa had already cooked and ate supper, saving him a plate to heat up when he came in from his ramblings with Rusty and the gang. But as he opened the kitchen door at seven that evening, he found himself completely alone.

"Grandpa?" he called. When the elderly man failed to answer, he checked the bottom rack of the refrigerator. Oddly enough, there was no china plate of food covered with aluminum foil waiting for him as usual. That scared him a little. *Where is he?* Keith wondered. *Did something happen to him?*

A sensation of dread joined his uneasiness as he quickly went from one room of the house to the next. His grandfather was in terrific shape for his age, but he was in his mid-90s and that was positively ancient in Keith's opinion. Grim scenarios began to play in the boy's mind. What if he had suffered a heart attack or a stroke? Or what if he had gone down to the cellar for some canned vegetables and fallen and broken his hip...or his neck?

Keith checked every inch of the house, including the basement, but could find no sign of his grandfather. He was near panic and heading outside to check the barn, when the phone rang. Keith ran over and snatched it up quickly, his heart pounding in his chest.

"Hello?" he croaked.

"Keith, this is Grandpa," came the old man's voice.

A wave of relief flowed through the boy. "Where are you?" he demanded.

"Sorry if it upset you coming home and finding me gone, but I've been at Coffee County Medical Center in

Manchester since early this morning. I know I should've called sooner, but it's been touch and go all day."

A jolt of alarm shot through the boy. "Are you okay?"

"I'm fine, son," Jasper assured, sensing the boy's concern. "It's Edwin Hill who's ailing. He had a bad heart attack and I've been waiting to see if he was going to make it. The doctors have him in intensive care right now."

Keith was happy that it wasn't his grandfather who was sick, but he was still sad to hear about what had happened to Mr. Hill. "Will he be alright?" he asked, feeling a twinge of guilt at the thought of the baseball cards he had shoplifted from the candy shelf of the general store.

"I don't know yet," Jasper told him honestly. "But they've got him stabilized." The elderly farmer paused for a second. "I know it ain't politically correct these days, but would you be okay staying by yourself tonight? I'd really like to be here when Edwin wakes up...if he wakes up. The doctors won't let me in to see him until he regains consciousness."

Keith didn't have to give it a second thought. "Sure, that'd be fine. I'll be okay."

He had had a lot of practice taking care of himself during those long hours of overtime

his parents put in at their individual careers.

"Are you sure?" asked his grandfather, sounding a little worried.

"Hey, no problem. I'll fix me something to eat, watch a little TV, then go to bed."

"Okay, but I ought to be home first thing in the morning," said Jasper. "Be sure to lick all the doors and keep the porch light on, okay?"

"Sure," said Keith. "And don't sweat it. I'll be just fine."

"Well, goodnight."

"Goodnight, Grandpa," he replied, then hung up the phone.

Keith walked to the kitchen pantry and checked out the shelves. He found a can of chili and decided that would satisfy him well enough. He opened it, dumped the contents into a pot and heated it on the eye of the gas stove. His grandfather was too old-fashioned to own something as modern as a microwave oven.

When the chili was hot enough, he poured it not a bowl, fetched some saltine crackers and a glass of sweet tea and sat down at the table to eat. When he was finished, he left his bowl and glass in the kitchen sink, then gave Rusty a quick call. He told his cousin of Edwin Hill's heart attack and their grandfather's desire to spend the night at the hospital, waiting for bad news, but praying for good.

"You can come over and stay the night here if you want," suggested Rusty. "Mama wouldn't mind a bit."

"I think I'll just hang around here," said Keith. "I was gonna watch some TV, but I'm beat. I think I'll just go on to bed instead."

"Yeah, me, too," agreed Rusty. "I'm itching to get back to my dream and see how it turns out."

"So am I," Keith had to admit. "What about Chuck and Maggie?"

"I just called 'em a few minutes ago. Chuck's already getting ready for bed and Maggie was about to. Maggie's folks are out of town on a trip for the next few days. She's having to stay at home with her brother. I don't think he likes her very much. He is a colossal dork...and a mean one, too. Especially to Maggie."

Keith felt his temper rise at the thought of *anyone* giving the blond-haired girl a hard time. But he didn't say anything to Rusty. If he did, he wouldn't hear the end of it from his rambunctious cousin.

"Well, have a good one, bud," said Rusty. "Remember, we meet back at seven sharp, just like this morning."

"See you then, dude," Keith said before hanging up.

He did as his grandfather had requested, locking both the front and back door, and leaving the porch light on. Then he went to his room, changed into his t-shirt and pajama pants and prepared for bed.

Keith dug through his backpack until he found the oversized card he had stashed there before leaving that morning. He sat on the edge of the bed and stared at the drawing of the police detective standing amid towering skyscrapers. A part of him couldn't wait to get back to that urban dreamscape, while another was a little hesitant about returning. He thought again about the mysterious stranger they had come across in the wooded wilderness of Hell Hollow. Doctor Augustus Leech and the wondrous gift he had given them had seemed too good to be true, and Keith suspected that his instincts were right.

But, so far, he had absolutely no evidence to support his skepticism.

"Maybe Chuck's right," he told himself. "Maybe I am being too paranoid."

Keith looked at the card one last time, then tucked it beneath his pillow and turned off the light. A short while later, he was asleep and on his way.

It was different this time.

He stepped out of the doorway to the stench of week-old garbage, chemical smog, and urine. The street that ran next to the station house was choked with traffic. Car horns blared loudly, the drivers waving their fists angrily at their fellow commuters and shooting them the bird. Down the street, a woman screamed. He looked over to see a skinny hooker in a tiger skin tank top, leather mini-skirt and fishnet stockings being manhandled into a long, white pimpmobile.

Confused, Keith looked around to see if he was at the right place. The precinct station was the same, except that the gray brick was nearly black with soot and the globes of the outdoor lamps had been shattered by the rocks of vandals.

He descended the steps, dodging a puddle of puke some wino had left as a calling card. As he reached the sidewalk, a rattletrap black sedan with a cracked windshield and numerous dents in the fenders pulled up to the curb with a squeal of faulty brakes. A lanky beat cop left the vehicle and glared contemptuously at Keith. He could tell it was Officer Muldoon, but not exactly the same one who had cheerfully retrieved his car the last time. This one was surly and subordinate, his lean face pocked with acne scars and his yellowed teeth gnawing the stub of a toothpick.

"Next time get your own damn car!" he spat, then stomped up the steps and entered the station house, slamming the behind him.

What's going on here? thought Keith. Before walking to the sputtering heap of his car, he looked down at his apparel. His trench coat and the suit underneath it were shiny and threadbare; more like something from a thrift store than clothes bought on a detective's salary. He checked his hat. It was stained from acid rain and its crown bore a bullet hole that was precariously close to the top of his head. He checked his gun and badge. The .45 automatic showed evidence of rust, due to poor maintenance and his detective's badge was tarnished an ugly green color.

Discouraged, he climbed into his car and shut the door. The car no longer possessed a smooth, powerful engine. Instead, it shuddered and backfired as he pulled away from the curb and merged with the oppressive wave of traffic. He had to pump the gas pedal continuously to keep the engine from dying.

This time, Keith took a different route than the one he had taken in his previous dream. He reached into his coat pocket and withdrew a slip of paper. Scrawled on it in black ink was a message: TONIGHT—CASSANDRA—PURPLE PASSION LOUNGE—9:00. The way to the nightclub was no mystery to him. He navigated the congested streets with more difficulty than he had before, but soon arrived at his destination.

He parked his sedan in a back alley, then walked around to the front of the Purple Passion. The lounge was a two-bit dive with a garish purple canopy over the doorway and a blank door with a small window set in its upper panel. Keith checked the loads in his gun. The parts of the pistol rattled loosely as he jacked the slide, and the bullets inside the breech and clip were tarnished and moldy, as if they had been there for years.

Feeling less sure of himself than he had during his last dream, Keith swallowed nervously and rapped his knuckles on the door. A moment later, the tiny door slid open, showing two beady black eyes beneath a gorilla-like brow. "Who the hell are you?" growled the man on the other side.

"Name's Bishop," Keith told him. "I'm here to see Cassandra."

The man on the opposite side of the door grumbled, then reluctantly disengaged a bolt. As Keith stepped inside, he found the doorman to be a grotesquely muscular bouncer who looked like he had been weaned on steroids as a baby. The brute scowled at the police detective and spat at the floor in disgust.

"The table in the far corner," he growled. "Sit tight. I'll get Cassandra."

Keith did as he was told. He crossed a dark lounge choked with cigarette smoke and the stench of hard liquor. A gathering of bums and losers sat at the bar, while the other customers occupied tables, enjoying the show that was taking place on a stage across the room. In the glittering light of a disco ball, three middle-aged women with sagging breasts, multiple stretchmarks, and plenty of cauliflower celluloid did an obscene striptease to lurid catcalls and peals of drunken laughter.

Feeling kind of sick to his stomach, Keith took a seat at the table in the far corner. He attempted to avoid looking at the naked women on stage, but found their bouncing boobs and shimmering fat to hold some sort of unwholesome fascination for him. He had only seen nude women in the few *Playboy* magazines he had lifted from convenience stores from time to time, but these hags looked nothing like the nubile, airbrushed beauties he was accustomed to fantasizing over.

"Enjoying the show, dick?" came a sultry voice from over his shoulder.

Keith turned to find a tall, leggy dame in a slinky silk dress and stiletto heels standing there. His eyes scanned her hourglass waist and perky breasts, finally settling on her face. It was the countenance of a goddess, albeit a naughty one. Her eyes sparkled with a dangerous light and her bee-stung lips were pouty and sensual. A thick mane of flowing copper red hair wreathed her face and spilled down across her milky shoulders, catching the spiraling lights of the mirrored globe like streamers of liquid fire.

"Are you Cassandra?" he asked, feeling a little warm under the collar.

"The one and only," she said in a low, husky voice. "Mind if I join you?"

Before Keith could answer, she took the chair opposite him. He watched as she snapped her fingers. Out of the darkness, two waiters appeared. One served her a dry martini on a small tray, while the other inserted a cigarette in a long holder between two of her outstretched fingers and lit it with a Zippo lighter.

"I have them eating from my hand," she cooed. "As well as other places."

Keith shifted uncomfortably in his chair. "I was told that you could tell me some things," he said. "About the Big Man."

Cassandra laughed. "All in good time, flatfoot," she said. "First let's get better acquainted." The woman extended a long, shapely leg underneath the table and rested her high-heeled foot in the detective's lap.

Keith felt himself stir immediately. Soon, he found himself even more aroused than when Maggie had gone skinny-dipping in Goose Creek with him and Rusty.

"My, my, Detective," she whispered, a sliver of pink tongue coasting across the edge of her upper lip. "What a big nightstick you carry."

Keith pushed her active foot from his lap and stared her square in the eyes. "I didn't come here to play footsy with some horny broad," he said, trying to sound tough. "Now are we going to talk about the Big Man or not?"

"Of course," she said, "but not out here in the open. Not with so many people around."

"Where then?"

"The back room," she suggested. "We'll have some privacy there."

"Okay," said Keith. "But no funny business."

"Sure," agreed Cassandra. She left her chair and led him toward a door at the back of the club. "But don't say that I never offered."

Keith had no idea that he was walking into a trap until the swinging door shut behind him and he found himself blinded by the beam of a bright light. *It's a set-up!* he thought.

He pulled the .45 from its shoulder holster and aimed it toward the light. But, unlike his last escapade, he didn't even receive the chance to fire.

The boom of a revolver rang throughout the back room. Keith yelled in pain as a bullet slammed into his hand, knocking the automatic from his grasp. In the brilliant light, he looked down and was shocked to find that two of his fingers had been blown away. Blood gushed from the ragged stumps of his knuckles, while white-hot pain coursed up his wrist, filling his right arm with agony.

Okay, that's enough! his mind screamed. *Time to wake up!*

Suddenly, a form slipped up from behind and brained him with the blunt end of a blackjack. His head exploded with darting white dots and a jolt of pain so severe that it drained all the strength from him. His legs betrayed him, dumping him in a heap on the cold concrete floor.

Dazed, he stared up to see that the light had been shifted. He saw Cassandra sitting on a whiskey keg, her luscious legs crossed, an expression of disgust on her lovely face. "A piss-poor excuse for a copper, if you ask me," she said, drawing smoke from her cigarette.

Then, from out of the darkness between two wine racks, emerged three figures. The one on the left was a tall, dark Jamaican complete with dreadlocks and a single gold earring. He wore a long overcoat and held a sawed-off pump shotgun in one long-nailed hand. The form on the right was a broad-shouldered Columbian with skin the shade of burnt umber and raven black hair pulled tightly into ponytail. He wore a gray Armani suit and cradled an Uzi submachine gun in his gold-ringed hands. Both men smiled cruelly, although no humor whatsoever shown in their dark and merciless eyes.

Although the two henchmen were threatening, they couldn't hold a candle to the man they served. His thoughts swimming from the blow to the head, Keith stared up at the last one to emerge from the gloom.

"You wanted to find the Big Man," he said. "Well, now you've found him."

A jolt of terror gripped Keith. For, standing before him, dressed in a pinstriped suit and gangster hat reminiscent of Al Capone or Bugsy Segal, was a tall, lean man with jet black hair and a neatly-trimmed mustache and goatee. He smiled fiendishly as he stepped forward and lowered the muzzle of a Thompson machine gun square at the police detective's forehead.

Keith couldn't believe his eyes. The crime lord he had gone in search of—the notorious Big Man—was none other than Doctor Augustus Leech.

As the mobster's laughter filled the room, Keith struggled to do what he had attempted before. *Wake up, Bishop!* he told himself. *Wake up, dammit!*

But no matter how hard he tried, he simply could not escape the nightmare that his perfect dream had unexpectedly become.

CHAPTER THIRTY-TWO

Rusty stepped onto the porch of the western hotel, surprised by the heat that radiated from the air around him. It had to be a good 120 degrees. As he left the shade of the covered walkway, something else hit him as well. The putrid stench of a dead animal.

Crossing the sun-baked street, he saw the source of the odor lying in the dirt a few yards away. It was the bloated body of a mangy yellow dog. Its eyes were glazed and sunken, its four legs jutting stiffly into the air, as if attempting to ward off the grisly fate that had befallen it. Apparently, someone had killed the poor mutt on purpose. Its brains leaked through a neat, round hole in the center of its forehead; a bullet hole from the size of it. A slew of scavengers had already arrived, preparing to take their share of the carcass. A swarm of green-tailed flies buzzed around the bloated dog, while high in the blazing Arizona sky above sailed the dark silhouettes of buzzards, cutting lazy circles and figure eights in the scalding air.

Rusty spat in disgust and looked around. The town he had called home during his last dream didn't seem so inviting this time around. The false-fronted buildings were weathered and peeling paint, the glass of their windowpanes shattered in places and the gingerbread trim of the eaves hanging in disrepair. Bullet holes were plentiful everywhere; in porch posts, slatted walls and the closed doors of the shops. Dark brown splotches stained the boards of the walkways and in the air lingered the coppery smell of old blood.

He turned and regarded the building he had just left. The sign over the doorway was different than it had been before. Instead of reading CANTON CITY HOTEL, it read CARNAGE CITY HOTEL. As he turned toward the drinking establishment across the street, he found that its name had also changed. Instead of the Wagon Wheel Saloon, it was now the Whipping Post Saloon.

"What the hell's going on here?" Rusty muttered. He walked across the dusty street, sidestepping the dead dog and starting for the saloon. Two children appeared from an alleyway, rolling a metal hoop with a wooden stick. When they saw the marshal, their eyes widened and they stopped dead in their tracks. The two abandoned their hoop, letting it roll into the open street as they turned and ran.

"Hey, you young'uns!" he called out. "What's the matter?" His voice only seemed to frighten them even more, though. They sprinted down the shadowy alleyway and disappeared from view.

Puzzled, Rusty stepped onto the boardwalk and pushed through the bullet-scarred batwings of the Whipping Post Saloon. Like the town itself, the interior of the bar was simply not the same. The big room was dark and dusty, its stale air reeking of rotgut whiskey, puke and piss. The piano stood silently in the corner. Its bench was empty and its wooden center had been split clean open by the blast of a shotgun. Dried blood speckled the ivory keys. Apparently, someone had not been all that pleased with the piano player's musical prowess, or, rather, his lack of it.

Rusty walked up to the bar and waited. The bartender spat tobacco juice into a shotglass and wiped it out with a dirty bar rag. He seemed to ignore the marshal for a while, then grudgingly flung the cloth across his shoulder and glared at the lawman. "Yeah, what the hell do you want?"

"The service ain't quite what it was last time I was here," said Rusty, disturbed by the man's insolence.

"Well, if you don't like it, you can go somewheres else." The bald bartender snickered.

"Of course, the next saloon is 200 miles away, so you'd best get to walking."

Rusty matched the barkeep's glare with one of his own. "Just quit your jawing and give me a buttermilk, will you?"

The man turned to fetch the marshal's order. He returned a moment later, setting the tall glass of milk on the counter with a bang. "Enjoy," he said with a sneer.

Rusty raised the glass to his mouth and took a big swallow. It wasn't the delicacy that he recalled it to be. Thick globs of clabbered milk moved sluggishly down his throat, causing him to gag. He coughed and sputtered until his face was red. "This is soured!"

The bartender laughed. "It's our vintage stock, Marshal. Ain't my fault that you can't handle the hard stuff."

Rusty's temper got the best of him. Before he knew it, he had the rude bartender by the bowtie and the muzzle of his six-shooter pressed firmly against his nose. "I don't think that was none too funny, you hairless polecat!"

The contempt that shown in the man's eyes suddenly changed into pure fear. "I'm sorry, Marshal," he stammered. "Honest! I'll fetch you a fresh glass right now."

"You do that," said Rusty. He released the man and watched him hurry to set things right. "And put it in a clean glass this time."

"Yessir!" said the barkeeper. "Anything you want, Marshal!"

As Rusty waited for his drink, he heard the drumming of horse hooves approaching from the direction of the open desert. They grew nearer, like the spreading thunder of a bad storm. A moment later, they stopped with a grating of iron shoes against dry earth.

Rusty waited for another sound, but it did not come for a long time. A tense silence seemed to envelope the desolate community of Carnage City.

Then a voice—half snake and half mad dog—cut through the hot, noon air.

"Rusty McLeod! Show yourself!"

The marshal felt a sinking sensation in the pit of his stomach; a feeling of uncertainty and apprehension he had not experienced when he had faced Kid Calhoun. He turned his eyes to the barkeeper. The man stared at the daylight beyond the batwings like a frightened jackrabbit. Obviously, he was more scared of the one out on the street than he was of Rusty.

"Oh God, it's *him*!" moaned the bald man. "It's Sidewinder himself!"

"Who the heck is Sidewinder?' asked Rusty. But the question was pointless. Rusty already knew who the desperado was. In fact, he had his wanted poster pinned to the wall of his office, offering a reward of $10,000 for bringing the gunslinger in dead, not alive.

"I said get out here, Marshal!" snarled the voice again. "Or are you too stinking yellow-bellied to face me?"

The challenge steeled Rusty's nerve. He took a gulp of the fresh buttermilk, then turned and walked across the sawdust floor of the Whipping Post.

"He'll gun you down, Marshall," called the barkeeper with a nervous giggle. "Just like he has a hundred men before."

"We'll see about that," said Rusty. Despite his bold words, the fluttering in his belly increased tenfold, as if he'd swallowed a nest of candle flies. *What's the matter with me?* he wondered, slipping the rawhide loop off the hammer of his Colt 45. *This is my dream. I'll do okay. I'll beat him to the draw, just like I did with Calhoun.*

Rusty pushed through the batwings, squinting against the sunlight. As he stepped into Carnage City's single dirt street, he faced east. Fifty feet away, silhouetted against the glare of the noonday sun, was the form of a tall, thin man dressed entirely in black. The gunslinger's clothing was much darker than Kid Calhoun's garb; as black as death itself. He tried to distinguish the man's facial features, but they were totally obscured by shadow.

"What do you want?" Rusty asked, although he was well aware of the shootist's intentions.

"I want *you*, Marshal McLeod," said the gunslinger with an oily laugh. "I've already killed every lawman in the Arizona territory. You're the only one left. That's why I rode all this way...to try my hand at you as well."

Rusty peered into the dark face of his opponent. A glint of steely eyes shown from the shade beneath his hat; eyes as cold and deadly as those of the gunfighter's namesake. They were eyes that had seen men sweat in fear, time and time again. They were eyes that had watched men die...and enjoyed it.

"What's this going to prove?" Rusty found himself saying. In the last dream, he had felt no mercy for the one he had faced, as well as no fear of being a fraction too slow on the draw. But this time, he possessed no such confidence.

"Nothing, except that I'm the fastest gun in the West," said Sidewinder. He dropped a skeletal hand easily to his holstered gun and slipped the thong from its hammer. "Now, are you going to stand there and try to talk your way out of dying? Or are you going to slap leather and test your skill against mine?"

Rusty swallowed nervously. He glanced down at his holstered Colt. Although his fingers hovered a mere inch from its pearl handle, it seemed miles away. He heard the snort of an animal and glanced to his left.

Sidewinder's horse stood tethered to a hitching post, every bit as black and bold as its master. Its eyes were the most striking features; they glowed a muted red like the lingering embers of a campfire. Rusty then looked to his right. Through the cracked panes of the hotel and the surrounding shops he could make out pale faces watching them. Faces with eyes that gleamed not with fear or concern, but anxiousness.

They want to see him kill me, Rusty thought. *They don't respect me after all. They'd like nothing better than to see me die in the dust with a bullet hole in my guts!*

Sidewinder spread his legs slightly, taking a wider stance, his right hand dangling loosely over the jutting handle of his six-shooter. "We're wasting time, Marshal. Are you ready to die like a man?"

Rusty straightened his shoulders and relaxed the muscles of his arm, ready to drop, draw and fire. "You're the one who's likely to die," he replied. "But not like a man. Instead, like the slimy snake you are."

The gunslinger laughed softly. "We'll see in a second or two. Now on the count of three..."

Rusty took a deep breath and held it.

"One," Sidewinder began to count.

The marshal splayed his fingers like the legs of a pale tarantula and waited for the moment to arrive.

"Two."

Rusty focused on the center of Sidewinder's black shirt, finding his target before he even took aim.

"Three!"

The lawman drew his Colt and fired, quicker and with more fluid ease than he had shown during his gunfight with Kid Calhoun. The .45 boomed in his hand, sending a jolt of recoil through the bones of his wrist and arm. He tensed, expecting to hear a similar gunshot ring from 50 feet away. But it failed to come. He watched in amazement as the dark form wavered on its feet, gun aimed impotently at the ground. Then it crumpled into a black heap on the sun-baked earth of Carnage City's main street.

I did it! thought Rusty in exhilaration. *I beat him to the draw!*

But his joy at having survived the gunfight was short-lived. A voice to his left suddenly rang out.

"Mighty fine shooting, Marshal. But there's just one little problem. You shot the *wrong* person."

Rusty turned his head and saw Sidewinder leaning against a post outside of the Whipping Post Saloon, a mug of cold beer in his hand. The outlaw's face was less obscure now. It was lean and whiskered, but the upper half was still hidden by the shadows of his broad-brimmed Stetson.

Confusion filled the lawman. "But if I didn't shoot you...then *who*?"

Sidewinder laughed, his mouth curling into a pearly grin. "Take a look."

Almost afraid to, Rusty turned and regarded the one who had fallen to his quick-draw. He was shocked to find a middle-aged woman dressed in a black mourning dress lying in the street, a bloody bullet hole piercing the center of her chest. It was the Widow Johnson, a respected citizen of Carnage City. Around her knelt her six children – orphans now—dirty-faced and shoeless. The brood cried in anguish, grieving over the murder of their poor, defenseless mother.

"No!" yelled Rusty. "It wasn't her. It was you!"

"Afraid not, McLeod," said Sidewinder. "You just screwed up, pardner. And not only will it cost you your badge...but your life as well."

Suddenly, all the doors of Carnage City opened, disgorging a stampede of outraged townfolk into the dusty street of the Arizona town. They converged on

Rusty before he could hope to react, knocking the Colt from his hand and assaulting him with rifle barrels and axe handles. The pain of the blows, the smothering crush of their bodies, the awful thrill of raw fear...all were incredibly *real.*

"Wake up, Rusty!" he found himself repeating over and over again. "Come on, it's time to get the hell outta this blasted dream!"

Beyond the angry faces of the townspeople, Rusty saw Sidewinder fling his beer mug aside and step into the open street. "Sorry, hoss, but this ain't a dream...not any longer. It's as real as real can be. And it won't be over till these good folks convict you of murdering poor Widow Johnson and hang you by the neck until dead."

Then Sidewinder lifted his face toward the sun and began to laugh. It was the most sinister, chilling laughter that Rusty had ever heard in his entire life.

But that wasn't what surprised him the most. It was the sight of the gunslinger's face that sent a jolt of alarm through his bruised and battered body. For it was a familiar face.

The face of Augustus Leech.

"I'll see you at the trial, Marshal," said Sidewinder with a sneer of contempt. Then he turned and went back into the saloon.

"No!" screamed Rusty, knowing that he had been lured into a clever, but horrible trap. He bit his tongue and clenched his fists until his fingernails drew blood from the palms, but neither did the trick. He failed to dispel the enraged mob around him and awaken in his bed back home. Instead, he was carried down the street toward the town jail to await trial for the crime of cold-blooded murder.

CHAPTER THIRTY-THREE

Jasper McLeod was sitting in a waiting room at Coffee County Medical Center, drinking a can of Sun Drop and brooding over a *Newsweek* article on the ecological hazards of a particular brand of fertilizer, when a nurse stepped inside and knocked gently on the doorjamb.

"Mr. McLeod," she said, "Dr. Jenkins wanted me to let you know that Mr. Hill has just regained consciousness."

Relief showed on the elderly man's face. "Thank God! So, how's he doing? Is he going to pull through?"

"That remains to be seen," the nurse told him truthfully. "His vital signs are improving, but he's had a massive coronary. His heart has suffered a lot of damage and that's very risky considering Mr. Hill's age. Presently, he's listed in fair condition."

"Would there be any chance for me to see him?" asked Jasper hopefully. "Just for a couple minutes?"

The nurse smiled and nodded. "Dr. Jenkins said it would be okay to allow you a short visit. No more than five minutes, though."

"I'd surely appreciate that," the farmer told her. He tossed his half-finished soda in the wastebasket, returned the magazine to the stack on a side table and followed the nurse from the waiting area.

A moment later, he was escorted into a room in the intensive care unit. Upon walking in, Jasper was sure that they had entered the wrong room. The sunken, old man who laid in the adjustable bed, linked to half a dozen high-tech monitors, possessed little resemblance to the wry, checker-playing storekeeper he had known all his life. But, as he drew nearer, he saw that it was, indeed, Edwin. Just looking at his friend with all those tubes and wires sprouting from his body both sickened and scared Jasper McLeod. Not that he was unaccustomed to seeing someone he cared for in such a pitiful condition. His beloved wife, Gladys, had looked much the same way, just before she died only a couple of floors away in that exact same hospital.

"Just take it easy at first and try not to excite him," advised the nurse. "He's still extremely weak."

As the woman left, Edwin opened his eyes and swallowed dryly. A feeble smile crossed his wrinkled face. "Should've known your ugly puss would be one of the first things I'd see when I woke up." He slowly lifted his hand and motioned for Jasper to come nearer. "Pull up a chair and sit a spell."

Jasper looked around the room and found a single padded chair against a wall. He took the chair and parked it next to Edwin's bed. "It's good to see you again, old man," he said, his voice breaking. "I was afraid..."

"Now, don't go getting sentimental on me, Jasper," Edwin said. "Next you'll want to give me a big hug and a kiss!"

"I wouldn't go that far," chuckled Jasper. He reached out and took his friend's hand. "But it is a load off my mind, seeing you up and talking like this."

A worried look came into Edwin's bloodshot eyes. "Jasper...there's some things I've got to tell you. Some right important things."

"What is it?" asked Jasper.

"First of all, I'm sorry," Edwin said softly, squeezing the elderly farmer's work-calloused hand. "Sorry for lying to you."

"Lying to me about what?"

"About that dream you had the other night," he said, his eyes flitting nervously toward the open doorway of the intensive care room. "About that fella in the stovepipe hat and Hell Hollow."

A cold sensation ran through Jasper's aged body. "What do you mean, Edwin?"

In halting whispers, Edwin told him of the incident that took place in the autumn of 1917. Of how a mob of angry vigilantes—Edwin and Jasper among them—had hunted the murderer of twelve of Harmony's citizens and, out of vengeance, shot him down in cold blood deep in the dark valley of Hell Hollow. He also told Jasper that it was his own father, Charles McLeod, who had delivered the bullet that had ended the life of the sadistic traveling medicine man.

Upon hearing that, Jasper leaned back in his chair, his face dazed, as if he had been struck by a physical blow. But Edwin knew it went much deeper than that. "Are you okay, buddy?" he asked.

"Yes," said the farmer, nodding slowly. "I remember now. What happened that night. Oh God, he really *did* do it, didn't he? Killed that fella in the wagon?"

"That's right," replied Edwin. "But it was out of love for his dead child—your sister—as well as all the others who died from that bastard's poisonous elixir."

"I understand that," said Jasper. He took a couple of deep breaths and wiped a film of tears from his eyes. "That's why I dreamed what I did. I reckon it was just a repressed memory coming to the surface. That's all there was to it."

"Or maybe not," said Edwin gravely. "Could be it was more like an omen of sorts. A premonition."

Jasper stared at his friend as though his heart attack had damaged his brain in some way. "A premonition? You know I don't believe in such foolishness, Edwin. I never have."

"Well, maybe it's about time you should," said the old man. "Because I didn't give myself this damn heart attack. It was given to me."

"By who?" asked Jasper, feeling that eerie sensation of dread close in on him once again.

"By that son-of-a-bitch your daddy killed ninety years ago," whispered Edwin.

A name suddenly popped into Jasper's mind, one he hadn't thought of since he was 5 years old. "Leech," he gasped. "Doctor Augustus Leech."

"That's right," said Edwin with a nod. "He's back, Jasper. Not in the same form he was before, but just as evil and dangerous as he was back then. Maybe even more."

"But that can't be. That's just plain craziness!"

"I would've said so, too, if he hadn't come to me in the form of Aaron last night," he replied. He closed his eyes at the image of his mutilated son. "Leech struck me down with emotion the same way another would use a gun or a knife. And, when he was done, he stood right there before me, laughing, dressed in that confounded stovepipe hat and black coat. The face was a little different, but it was him alright. I swear it was!"

Jasper couldn't believe such a thing was taking place. "But what does he want? Revenge for what we did to him?"

"That's one reason. But there's others as well. Part of it is pure pleasure; just the fun of watching someone die in horrible agony. But part of it is even more sinister in nature."

"What do you mean?"

Edwin hesitated. He turned his eyes toward the open doorway, as well as the dark window next to the bed. "God help us, Jasper, but I honestly believe he's in league with the devil. I think he poisoned those folks way back then to benefit his 'master', as he calls him. I believe he was harvesting souls for Satan."

Jasper couldn't believe what he had just heard. "Do you know how insane that sounds?"

"Yes," agreed his friend. "But it's true. Don't ask me how, but it is."

Their conversation was suddenly interrupted by the appearance of the nurse at the door. "Sorry, Mr. McLeod, but your five minutes are up. You'll have to leave and come back tomorrow morning."

Jasper nodded and left the chair next to the bed. The two old men stared at one another. "I'll see you later," said the lanky farmer.

"Be careful, Jasper," Edwin warned, his pale face grim. "And don't do nothing foolish. Nothing that might bring harm to you...or the boy."

"I won't," promised Jasper, although he didn't fully understand exactly what Edwin was referring to.

A moment later, he was walking down the outside corridor, moving away from the intensive care unit. He felt disoriented, as though he had talked to his friend during the course of a dream, instead of in the sterile environment of a hospital room. It was impossible, of course. No one could come back from the dead after 90 years. That was, unless, they had some help from the devil himself.

That's pure nonsense, Jasper, and you know it! he told himself. *Edwin was just out of his head, that's all. Affected by his illness and the medication he's on.* But despite all the self-convincing, he knew deep down that what his friend had said was true. Incredible, but true all the same.

Edwin's words came back to him. *Don't do nothing foolish...nothing that might bring harm to you...or the boy.*

Unexpectedly, a wave of fear hit the elderly man so forcefully that he nearly lost his balance. He suddenly felt as though Keith might be in grave danger, although there was no plausible reason to believe such a thing. He stood in the hallway for a long moment, attempting to quell that foreboding impression, but he simply couldn't shrug it off.

Shakily, he walked to a bank of pay phones next to the elevators. He found a couple of quarters in his pocket, dropped them into the slot, and dialed his home phone number. His heart pounded as the humming of the ring came once...twice...three times. When it reached its seventh try, he returned the phone to its cradle, took the quarters from the return receptacle, and attempted it again. He let the phone ring a dozen times and then hung up.

Keith wasn't there. Or he was and could not answer the phone.

A sensation of alarm like none he had ever experienced gripped him. He knew, down deep in his heart, that Keith was in trouble. Had the boy and his friends gone exploring down in Hell Hollow and come upon something more than empty wood? Had they met someone there that they had neglected to tell anyone about? Perhaps a tall, bearded man dressed in a long black coat and stovepipe hat?

Jasper rushed to an elevator. If what he suspected was true, Keith might not be the only one in peril. His other grandson, Rusty, might also be in danger, as well as Maggie Sutton and Chuck Adkins.

The steel doors slid open a moment later. Soon, he was crossing the deserted lobby of Coffee County Medical Center at a quick walk and the parking lot outside at a dead run. He knew he must get home...fast. He had to find out if he was merely overreacting, or if the evil that Edwin claimed existed was actually for real.

CHAPTER THIRTY-FOUR

The trailer was much smaller than she remembered.

Maggie had to duck her head as she walked to the dressing table and sat down. A single 60-watt bulb dangled from the center of the low ceiling, casting a dim glow throughout the cramped mobile home. Puzzled by the change of surroundings, the girl looked around. Above a small cot in the far corner hung a single poster. This one was different than the colorful banners bearing her name and likeness. The poster was printed in somber shades of black and gray, the lettering elongated, almost abstract in a sense. And there was one other variance that she could not understand. Instead of CIRCUS MAGNIFICENT, the show she was now a part of was called something else entirely. Something much more dark and mysterious; CIRCUS HORRIFIC. And in the place of her smiling picture were the leering faces of sideshow freaks. Pinheads, limbless wonders, bearded fat ladies and dog-faced boys.

She turned back to the task at hand. She stared into the mirror. Instead of the gaily-adorned outfit of sparkling pink spandex, Maggie found herself dressed in a black leotard with a garish spider web cape. Her jeweled tiara was gone, replaced by a jagged crown of black thorns with a black widow mounted in the center.

Why am I dressed like this? she wondered. *It wasn't like this before.*

As she applied white pancake makeup, gray eye shadow, and jet black lipstick, Maggie heard a sound at the trailer door. A click, followed by a metallic jangle...like a padlock being unlocked and slipped from its hasp. Had the door been locked? Had she been confined there like some sort of prisoner?

A second later, the door opened. "Get your butt out here!" growled a gruff voice. "Now!"

Confused, Maggie left the dressing table and walked to the open doorway. A white-gloved hand reached inside and, grabbing her by the wrist, dragged her outside. When she hit the ground, she looked at the one who held her. "Bobo?" she asked, her voice tiny.

But the clown who stood over her was not the sweet, good-natured performer she had met during her previous dream. Instead, he was a nightmarish jester from hell, dressed like a comedic vampire. He leered at her with fangs that looked too real to be mere props.

"That's Count Bobo to you, toots!" he snapped. He jerked her wrist and began walking, dragging her behind him. "It's five minutes till showtime. And do it right this time, or you'll have to answer to the Colonel!"

"The Colonel?" she asked shakily.

"Colonel Raven," said Count Bobo. His breath stank of liquor and decay. "The ringmaster and owner of this grand show. He didn't like it the last time you screwed up. If you do it this time, he'll tie you up and feed you to the lions. See? They're ready for you, in case you fail to deliver this time."

Maggie looked to where he pointed. A huge cage of emaciated lions stood at the iron bars, roaring loudly, their eyes burning with a mixture of hunger and madness. It looked as though had not been decently fed in several weeks.

"Yeah, I'd say they would gulp down a tasty morsel like you in a matter of minutes, costume and all," said Bobo with a dirty laugh.

On their way to a massive, black canvas tent, they passed several circus performers, or what passed for performers in this bizarre dreamscape of hers. They included a lion tamer missing an arm, a pair of Siamese twins that were both male and female, a scaly reptile boy who slithered on his belly, and a tattooed man with images that seemed to crawl and revolve along the surface of his skin. None greeted her or wished her well with her approaching performance. Instead, they glared at her with hatred and jealousy.

When they reached the flap of the Big Top, County Bobo released her wrist, leaving red marks that would eventually turn into bruises. "Now you go in there and give those slack-jawed idiots what they paid for!" he warned. "Or those lions back there will be wrestling over your liver by nightfall."

Prompted by a threat and a push, she stumbled through the dark portal of the open flap. As it closed behind her, Maggie peered into the darkness, disoriented, trying to regain her bearings. The interior of the Big Top smelled much different than it had before. Instead of the tang of sawdust and the delicious aroma of cotton candy and buttered popcorn, the stench of elephant dung and diseased animals filled the confines of the huge tent.

"Well, don't just stand there!" snapped a small form in the gloom. "Get your skinny carcass over here! The Colonel is about to introduce you."

Hesitantly, she walked toward the little man. It was the dwarf named Max. But he exhibited none of the charm and kindness that he had shown toward her in her last dream. Instead, he was insolent and surly, grabbing her roughly and shoving her to the metal pole that stretched upward into the darkness.

Maggie felt none of the confidence she had experienced before. Fear gripped her now, causing her cringe from the rungs of the ladder. "No," she protested. "I can't go up there. I just can't."

The dwarf grinned cruelly. "You *will* go up there," he said. "Or you'll get a taste of *this*." He took something from off his belt and with a snap, unfurled its length. In the gloom, Maggie could see that it was a black leather bullwhip.

"I'd hate to slice up the star attraction," chuckled Max, his voice low and taunting. "But I will if I have to. Now get up there!"

Maggie knew that she had no choice but to obey. Nervously, she turned to the metal post and began to climb, taking one rung at a time. During the journey upward, Maggie knew that something had gone terribly wrong. This dream wasn't the pleasurable, joyful experience she had lived before. It was no dream at all, but a nightmare.

Foot by foot, she climbed. Below in the darkness, she could hear the restless rumble of the crowd, waiting for the spotlights to reveal the next act. She kept expecting to reach the platform any second, but oddly enough it failed to materialize. Clutching tightly to the steel rungs with her sweaty hands, Maggie continued upward. It hadn't taken her nearly as long to arrive at the platform last time. She knew it hadn't.

After what seemed to be an eternity, Maggie finally arrived at her destination. She crawled onto the platform on her hands and knees. The self-assurance of a seasoned high wire walker was completely gone. Her old fear of heights was back in full swing again. Shakily, she rose to her feet, her legs feeling rubbery underneath her.

She waited in the darkness for a moment, attempting to catch her breath. Then, abruptly, a bright spotlight flashed on, exposing her to the gathering of spectators below. She raised her hand and shielded her eyes against the light, attempting to see the ground below her. Far away, another spot shown on the arena. It looked like the size of a pie plate; the audience around it appearing more like an army of ants than actual people.

How high up am I? she wondered. *A hundred feet up? Two-hundred? Maybe even more?*

Then, far below, a tiny black speck entered the illuminated arena. Maggie had to squint to make it out. It was a tall man wearing a black top hat. She knew it had to be the ringleader of Circus Horrific. The one known as Colonel Raven.

"Ladies and Gentlemen!" he bellowed, his voice rising faintly up to her. "Please direct your attention to the platform high above the center arena. There you will see the one you have all been waiting for! The most daring and death-defying high wire acrobat in the world today. The one...the only...Queen Margret, the Spider Woman!"

Maggie felt her head swim as she stared at the distance between the platform and the earth below. A fall from such a lofty height would mean an immediate and crushing death. She turned her attention to the rope that stretched between her platform and the one directly opposite. The width of the arena seemed to be triple what it had been before. Instead of 50 feet of space to travel, she now had a good 150.

"And to make the Queen's feat of daring even more spectacular," came the voice of the ringleader, "she will attempt to walk the wire, unaided by balancing pole or safety net, with nothing to break her fall but this vat of ferocious alligators!"

Maggie gasped as a team of clowns rolled a huge tank of water into the arena and positioned it directly below the high wire that stretched above. Even from that height, the girl could see the dark forms of alligators swimming from one side of the tank to the other. Several raised their leathery heads from the water and snapped savagely at her, showing their yellowed teeth and their soft, pink gullets.

"No way!" said Maggie, turning toward the ladder than had brought her up. "I'm not gonna do it!"

A snickering laugh sounded from the darkness beyond the steel pole and, suddenly, Max the dwarf appeared, brandishing his whip. "Oh, yes you are," he said, giving the whip a sharp crack. The tip caught Maggie across the left cheek, bringing a sting of pain. Shocked, she lifted her hand to her face. Her fingertips came away smeared with blood.

This isn't right! she thought. *This is just a dream. I'm not supposed to get hurt!*

She thought about the pact she had made with her friends at Keith's insistence. Maggie closed her eyes and concentrated, trying to wake up. But no matter how hard she tried, she remained rooted to the spot, unable to escape the dream.

"Get out there and walk that damn rope!" said Max. "Do it…or Colonel Raven will deal with you himself. And that'd be a helluva lot worse than falling into that vat of gators, believe me."

Looking into his tiny black eyes, Maggie knew that he was right. She had never met the infamous Colonel Raven, but she felt as if she already knew the kind of man he was.

Taking a deep breath, Maggie turned and stepped onto the rope. The soles of her feet curled inward, attempting to grip the cable. She stretched out her arms, but her balance was off. She nearly fell before she straightened herself. The security she had experienced during her previous dream was totally missing. Her legs trembled beneath her as she took one precarious step at a time.

By the time she reached the halfway point on the high wire, Maggie was a nervous wreck. Sweat rolled down her face and her muscles ached with the strain of maintaining her balance. She glanced down only once and was stunned to find herself directly over the alligator tank. The reptiles snapped and bellowed, their eyes hopeful. They seemed to smell her, despite the distance between them.

A few minutes later, Maggie reached the far side of the tent. She scrambled onto the platform, sobbing with relief. He muscles quivered as she sat down and attempted to catch her breath.

It's over! she told herself. *I made it!*

The crack of the whip brought her back to reality, so to speak. She yelped as it struck her again, skimming across her back, splitting the dark material of her costume and raising an ugly pink stripe across her skin.

"Not so fast, Queenie!" laughed Max, standing on the same platform she occupied. "Now you've got to go back across...on *this*."

Maggie got to her feet just as he tossed her the unicycle. She caught it and was shocked at its condition. The bolts of the frame were loose and the tire was low on air. "I can't!" she cried. "I'll fall off for sure!"

"Then you'll fall," said Max with a shrug of his stubby shoulders. "That's what the crowd came to see, after all. You plunging to your death."

Maggie looked off the edge of the platform and knew that he was right. Even from that height, she could barely make out the expressions of cruel anticipation on the audience's tiny faces. They were no better than a crowd staring up at someone on the ledge of a building, calling for them to give up all hope and jump.

She again tried to wake up, but no dice. She simply wasn't going anyplace. Maggie crept to the edge of the platform, positioned the flabby tire of the unicycle on the rope, and carefully climbed onto the seat. Slowly, she worked the pedals and started forward. The rope began to swing and sway before she even got a third of the way across. Then, abruptly, the wheel of the unicycle slipped off the rope, carrying her with it.

Maggie shrieked. She flailed out blindly, attempting to grab hold of something. Luckily, her fingers latched onto the rope and held on for dear life. It sagged with her weight, but held firm. The girl hung by one hand. She gasped as needles of pain skewered her shoulder. It felt as though her arm might pop clean from its socket.

Terrified, she looked down at the ground below her. The unicycle spun downward, finally hitting the surface of the tank with a splash. The alligators attacked it immediately.

Their powerful jaws ripped apart metal and rubber with the same ferocity they normally reserved for flesh and bone.

Maggie knew if she didn't do something fast, she would lose her grip and she too would fall. Using all the strength she could muster, she grabbed the rope with her other hand and held on. She saw the ringmaster below, glaring up at her with his hands planted firmly on his hips. She would have to continue, despite the danger of losing her balance again. Maggie let out a frightened sob, then hauled herself upward.

But, miraculously, she did not find herself with 100 more feet of rope to travel. Instead, she found the ledge of the platform within reach. Shuddering with anxiety, Maggie pulled herself onto the stand and lay there for a long moment, breathing deeply. Below her, a sound began to rise from the multitude of spectators. But it was not the cheers of adoration she had heard before. Rather, it was a mutual moan of disappointment. They had been cheated of the sight of her falling to her death, as well as being devoured by hungry alligators. They were booing at her for emerging from her performance alive.

It took a while, but she finally made it down the rungs of the pole to solid ground. When she got there, she found someone waiting for her. It was the ringmaster; tall and lean, wearing a top hat, red jacket, white slacks and shinny black riding boots. But it wasn't his attire that surprised her the most. It was his face. Pale and gaunt with a waxed black mustache and neatly trimmed goatee beard.

The owner of Circus Horrific, the dastardly Colonel Raven, was none other than the man they had met in the heart of Hell Hollow...Doctor Augustus Leech.

The man's dark eyes sparkled with pure evil as his gloved hand caught her by the throat and lifted her off her feet. She strangled, attempting to catch her breath, but his fingers tightened, cutting off her wind.

"I thought I told you there would be no more mistakes!" hissed Raven with a scowl. "Your stubborn desire for survival is ruining my show! Next time do what you were hired to do and give the crowd what they paid to see!"

Maggie suddenly realized that her job was not to succeed at traveling the high wire, but to fail at the treacherous feat. Colonel Raven expected her to fall to her death, simply to please the sadistic, ticket-buying public.

Raven shook her roughly, then flung her to the ground. "Well, this is the last time you will defy me! Your next performance will go as planned. And, unfortunately, you will not survive!" He motioned to two brawny roustabouts who stood nearby. "Take her back to her trailer!"

The two scooped her up and escorted her from the Big Top. A moment later, she was tossed back into the cramped trailer. She ran for the door, hoping to escape, but it slammed shut in her face. To Maggie, it sounded like the clang of a jailhouse door.

She stood there, trembling, as the padlock was returned to its hasp and snapped firmly back into place. As the receding steps of the roustabouts faded, Maggie went to the cot in the far corner. She sat on it, hugging her knees close to her body, tears shimmering in her frightened eyes.

She considered attempting to wake up again, but knew that it would be futile to even try. She was there to stay...and there was absolutely nothing she could do about it.

CHAPTER THIRTY-FIVE

Chuck stared into the first rays of dawn as he and his men trudged across the muddy battlefield, heading toward Berlin. He took a deep breath and nearly gagged. The stench of war surrounded them; an oppressive combination of cordite, burnt flesh and decay. The forms of soldiers, both American and German, laid strewn across the barren fields, their bodies torn and dismembered, their faces staring sightlessly into open space. The sights and smells had invigorated Chuck in his previous dream. But this time it sickened and disgusted him.

He shifted the Warchair into a higher gear and felt it lurch and grind. It moved with none of the fluidity of power that it had exhibited before. The same went for his platoon. His men plodded through the heavy mud, holding their M1 carbines as if they were heavy weights, their eyes peering dully ahead, leeched of emotion. "Thousand-yard stares" like the grunts in Vietnam had developed after several months in-country.

"What's wrong with the men, Corporal?" he asked. They showed none of the confidence or warrior spirit that they had expressed at the beginning of their mission behind enemy lines.

"Morale is low, Sarge," said Corporal Steel with a sigh. "That hit they took a few kilometers back really threw 'em for a loop. A lot of them were badly injured, too."

Chuck turned his attention back to his troop. Steel was right. Nearly all of them had suffered some injury or another. Some had mangled arms in dirty slings, some had bleeding head wounds, and others limped on shattered legs with the help of makeshift crutches fashioned from old Mauser rifles and the gnarled limbs of trees. Corporal Steel had even taken a load of shrapnel in his right side. His olive drab shirt was saturated with fresh blood and, through his splayed fingers, Chuck could see the ugly holes that had been blown through his flesh, as well as the glistening pulp of his organs just beyond.

"Are you going to make it, Corporal?' he asked, concerned.

"Don't worry about me, Sarge," he replied, grimacing with pain. "I'm tough as a—"

Before he could finish his sentence however, Steel's eyes rolled back into his head and he pitched face-forward into the mud.

A buck private with his left arm blown off at the elbow walked over. He flipped Chuck's second-in-command onto his back with the toe of his boot. "He's dead, Sarge."

Chuck stared at the face of violent death, finding no glory in Steel's lifeless eyes. War was hell and Chuck hated it.

"Come on, men," he said after they had buried the corporal beneath a mound of boulders. "We still have a mission to accomplish. Are you with me?"

He expected a cheer of enthusiasm, but instead heard only a half-hearted grumble from the ragtag platoon of infantry soldiers. As he sent his Warchair lurching forward, he looked down at the top of his flak vest. Churchill lay listlessly within the shelter of the bullet-proof garment. The iguana was sick. His color was alarmingly pale and his tiny eyes were coated with sticky yellow matter. Chuck rubbed a finger down its back, but the only response he received was a shuddering twitch.

This can't be happening, thought Chuck, feeling depressed and bewildered. *It was perfect last time. So why is everything falling apart?*

Suddenly, from over a rise on the horizon, came a jolting staccato of machine gun fire. Several of Chuck's men unleashed death shrieks and fell limply into the mire, riddled with bullet holes. Chuck looked ahead and saw a dozen Nazi storm troopers running toward them, firing German Schmeissers.

"It's an ambush!" yelled Chuck, feeling none of the courage he had felt during his last tour of duty. "Return fire!"

The infantrymen attempted to obey their sergeant's order, but they were too slow in acting. Two more waves of German soldiers, sporting Mausers with fixed bayonets, closed in from the east and west, taking them by surprise. The skirmish lasted for only a few minutes. When it was over, every last soldier of Chuck's platoon lay dead on the muddy earth.

Fear gripped Chuck as the enemy surrounded him. The bravado he had experienced back at the Nazi machine gun nest was absent. In its place was uncertainty, despair, and sheer terror.

A soldier ran forward, his rifle held like a lance before him. Chuck pulled the trigger of his Sten, but the bolt had jammed. The sergeant twisted his head to the side just as the edge of the Mauser's bayonet skimmed across his right cheek. With a shriek of pain and fright, Chuck discarded the Sten and, drawing his .45 automatic, fired through the gun slot of the Warchair's steel-plated door. The bullets slammed into the Nazi's stomach, driving him back. Shakily, Chuck reached up and felt his face. A deep, bleeding furrow had been carved into the flesh of his right cheek and lower half of his ear had been completely sliced off.

This is just a dream! he thought, stunned. *I'm not supposed to get hurt!*

He was about to turn his .45 on the other soldiers, when a potato masher was hurled from the rear of the crowd. Chuck attempted to deflect it back toward its pitcher like he had back at the machine gun next. But this time his bullets failed to hit it. The grenade struck the wet earth, bounced a couple yards, and disappeared beneath the iron treads of the Warchair.

Chuck was shifting the vehicle into high gear, when the explosion came. He screamed as a fiery flash engulfed him. A devastating concussion rose from beneath the Warchair like a mushroom cloud, blasting the rivets from their moorings and rending heavy steel plating. Chuck suddenly felt himself spinning through the air, his hair and uniform singed, his body stinging from a dozen shrapnel wounds. He landed 50 feet away, striking the earth with a thud. He lay there on his back dazed and unable to move.

He must have blacked out for when he regained consciousness, he found himself not on the battlefield, but lying on a canvas stretcher on the concrete floor of a German railway station. He groaned and opened his eyes as the toe of someone's boot kicked him in the ribs again and again.

"Wake up!" a stern voice demanded. "Wake up, you yankee dog!"

Chuck's vision focused. Around him stood several soldiers sporting Schmeisser machine guns, as well as three leather-coated members of the German Gestapo. But it was the one who brutalized Chuck's ribcage with the toe of his jackboot that startled the sergeant's mind back into full consciousness.

For the one who stood over him was a tall, lean version of Adolf Hitler, complete with a long woolen coat, decorated officer's hat and swastika armband. But there was one distinct and horrifying difference. The face that sported the arrogant eyes and vertical mustache of the Fuhrer belonged to none other than Doctor Augustus Leech.

"So, you thought you could defeat us, is that correct?' the Fuhrer growled, leering with contempt. "Well, we showed you, did we not, Herr Adkins?"

Chuck attempted to answer the commander-in-general of the Axis forces, but he was tongue-tied.

"I did not expect you to talk," said the Fuhrer, giving him one last kick to the abdomen. "Don't think you have won, though. We have ways of making you comply." The chancellor looked over at the Gestapo agents. "Take him to the train. I have important matters to attend to now. I will deal with him later."

The two thugs grabbed him by the arms, allowing his lifeless legs to drag on the ground. They carried him to the wooden cattle car of a long train. As they flung him through the open doorway, Chuck caught a stench he had never smelled before. The horrendous odor of feces, disease and human despair.

Chuck landed on a filthy, hay-strewn floor. He stared up to find dozens of men, women, and children standing around him. They stared at him sorrowfully, as if wanting to help, but possessing no power to do so.

The door of the cattle car was slammed shut and secured with a heavy padlock. Almost immediately, the locomotive unleashed a shrill whistle and belched sooty black smoke from its stack. With a lurch, the train moved forward, slowly gaining speed.

"What's happening?" Chuck asked those around him. "Where are we going?"

A small man of Jewish decent leaned forward, his face full of sadness. "This train is traveling to Poland," he said. "To a place called Auschwitz."

"No!" screamed Chuck. He crawled to the door of the car and, grabbing the wooden slats, stared at the countryside that sped by. He closed his eyes several times, attempting to break ties with the nightmare he found himself in. But release refused to come. He remained confined to the reeking cattle car packed to the rafters with the damned.

Chuck knew then that Keith Bishop had been right all along. Leech's gift to them had been more than the gateway to their fondest dreams. Instead, it had been a portal to their deepest, darkest nightmares.

CHAPTER THIRTY-SIX

Jasper McLeod pushed open the back door so forcefully that it slammed against the kitchen wall. “Keith?” he yelled, his voice edged with fear. “Where are you?”

He half expected the hall light to come on and his grandson to appear, groggy and irritated in the doorway of his bedroom. But as Jasper stepped into the corridor, the house remained dark and unsettlingly quiet. He strained his ears for sound, but heard nothing. Not the low moan of someone waking up or the faint squeak of creaking bedsprings. Only silence.

When he reached the spare bedroom, he hesitated at the open doorway for a moment, afraid to look inside. When he finally gathered the nerve, he stepped through and felt for the switch on the wall. The ceiling lamp blinked on, flooding the room with light.

His heart jumped in his chest. The covers of the bed were askew, the goose down pillow and feather mattress indented in the shape of a 12-year-old boy. But Keith was nowhere to be found. The bed was completely empty.

An emotion stronger than panic filled the elderly man. Quickly, he checked beneath the bed and in the closet. He found nothing. Jasper went from room to room calling Keith’s name, hoping for an answer, but secretly knowing that he would receive none. He even checked the root cellar and the barn outside, but both were deserted.

His grandson was gone.

Nearly out of breath, he returned to the farmhouse and made his way to the telephone on the hall table. Jasper caught his wind and then dialed a number he knew by memory.

"Hello?" answered the sleepy voice of a woman.

"Susan, this is Jasper."

"Papa?" she said, startled. "It's after midnight. Is something wrong?"

He took a deep breath, praying to God that his suspicions were false. "Susan, Keith ain't staying the night over there, is he?"

"No," said Susan McLeod. "Rusty asked him if he wanted to sleep over, but he said he'd rather stay at your place instead."

"Well, he ain't here," said Jasper. "He's gone."

"Land sakes alive! Where do you think he—?"

Jasper interrupted her. "I don't want to scare you none, dear...but could you go in Rusty's bedroom and see if he's there?"

"Of course he's there," said Susan. "I just tucked him in a couple of hours ago and you know how he sleeps. I doubt a tornado could wake him up."

"Just go check," repeated the elderly farmer. "Please."

He heard a rattle as Susan laid down the phone. A moment later, she was back on the line, her voice agitated. "He's not there, Jasper. His bed looks like it's been slept in, but I can't find him anywhere."

"He's not in the bathroom, is he?"

"No, I checked there. Do you think they could've snuck out to meet up somewhere? Kids have been known to do that, you know."

"Usually, I wouldn't put it past them. But tonight, I'm not so sure." Jasper stood in the hallway feeling that sensation of cold dread pass through him again. He closed his eyes and thought to himself for a moment. "Can I call you back in a minute, Susan? I've got to check on something."

He hung up the phone and then called the Sutton residence. The groggy voice of a young man answered irritably. "Yeah, what is it?"

"Is Mister or Mrs. Sutton there?' he asked, at first unable to identify the person on the other end of the line.

"No, they're out of town," the boy answered. "Who the hell is this, anyway?"

Jasper placed him now. It was the Suttons' arrogant cuss of a son. "Tom, this is Jasper McLeod. You know, Rusty's grandfather."

The teenager was silent for a moment. "Oh, yeah. So what the crap do you want?"

"Could you do me a favor?" said Jasper, attempting to hold firm to his temper. "Would you go to your sister's room and check on her?"

"Check on Maggie? Why would you want me to do that?"

"Could you please just do it?" snapped Jasper. "Now?"

"Okay, okay! Don't get your long johns in a wad, Gramps."

A short stretch of silence rang through the receiver. Then Tom Sutton came back on the line, sounding genuinely pissed off. "The little turd is gone! She must've ducked out of the house after I went to bed. Wait until I get a hold of her!"

"No, I don't think she did sneak out," Jasper told him. "She's vanished...just like Rusty and Keith."

"Vanished?" asked Tom, his anger seeming to turn into confusion. "What do you mean?"

"I'll call you back in a few minutes," said Jasper.

"But, wait—"

Jasper broke the connection, waited for a dial tone, then tried another number. It rang a couple of times before someone picked it up. "Hello?' answered the deep voice of a man. In the background echoed the soft sound of a television show—an old rerun of *Gunsmoke* from the sound of the voices.

"Joe, this here's Jasper McLeod," he said.

"Hey, Jasper," greeted Joe Adkins. "What can I do for you?"

"I know it might seem strange for me to ask, but could you go to Chuck's room and make sure he's in bed?"

"Huh? Why wouldn't he be there?"

"Please, just check."

Again that almost endless period of waiting. Then Joe Adkins was back on the line again. "Jasper, he's gone. His wheelchair is still beside his bed, so he couldn't have left the house." An edge of anger came into the mechanic's voice. "Your grandsons and that Sutton girl hasn't talked him into sneaking out after dark, have they? If so, they need the tar whaled plumb outta them!"

"No, Joe, that's not it," said Jasper. "God help us, I don't believe that's what happened at all."

Concern suddenly replaced the anger. "Then where is he?"

"I don't know, but I think he's in danger. The others are gone too, Joe. Wherever they are, I think they're all in a helluva fix."

"What are you talking about, Jasper?" demanded Joe, sounding frightened now.

"I'll call back and explain," he said, then hung up the phone once again.

Jasper stood in the hallway, debating on whether he should call Susan back first or check Keith's bedroom one more time. He elected to do the latter. A moment later, he was sitting on the edge of the feather bed, staring at the imprint of his grandson in the soft folds of the mattress. He reached out and laid a hand on the impression. It was still vaguely warm from the heat of Keith's body.

But when he tried the pillow, he found it to be ice cold to the touch. The chill did not seem to come from the bundle of goose feathers, however. Rather, it seemed to originate from something *underneath.*

"No," Jasper uttered softly. "No, it couldn't be."

Following Edwin Hill's confession at the hospital, bits and pieces of their lone visit to Hell Hollow as small children began to come back to him, bit by bit. The magic trick involving the toad, the mouse and the black dove. Jasper's sick puppy turned slavering mad dog.

And there had been the cards. The oversized playing cards that Leech had given them.

Jasper's had depicted a Confederate soldier, while Edwin's had shown a futuristic space man. Both boys had tried them out only once, then destroyed them, frightened at the wondrous, but unnatural dreams they had encountered.

Jasper lifted the pillow and was not surprised to find a similar card laying there, in the exact spot where Keith's head must have rested. His hand trembled as he picked up the card and studied it. On its face was a black and white drawing of a police detective in a moonlit city. As he stared at the illustration, the old man could swear that he felt a cool breeze drift from the face of the card, as well as the offensive odor of automobile exhaust and raw garbage.

Then Jasper turned the card over. From a black background of twinkling stars, a half-moon grinned at him, almost mockingly so. Staring at that lunar profile, he couldn't help but be reminded of a face he had seen in a recent dream. A leering, defiant face as darkly sinister as that of Old Scratch himself.

It was the face of the man driving the medicine show wagon.

The face of Augustus Leech.

PART THREE

DARK POISONS

CHAPTER THIRTY-SEVEN

Around 5:00 the next morning, Joe Adkins knocked on the back door of the McLeod farmhouse, feeling nervous and a little frightened. He had spent most of the night with his wife, Flora, trying to comfort her and prevent her from launching into a fit of hysterics over their son's puzzling disappearance. Joe also had a difficult time convincing her that it would be in their best interest not to alert the local sheriff. During his second phone conversation with Jasper McLeod, the elderly farmer had assured him the fate that had befallen Chuck, Rusty, Keith and Maggie was something beyond the law's ability to handle. He didn't know exactly what Jasper had been talking about, or even if he was correct in his opinion to keep the police out of it. After a heated discussion, Joe had reluctantly agreed to meet with Jasper before doing anything rash.

Before he could knock again, Jasper McLeod opened the door. The elderly man reached out and shook the mechanic's hand. "Howdy, Joe. Glad you decided to come."

"What choice did I have?" said Joe, stepping inside. "My boy's missing and you seem to be the only one who knows what's happened to him. Or *think* you know."

"Oh, I'm pretty sure about it," said Jasper grimly. He motioned toward the kitchen table. "I reckon you know everybody."

Joe turned his attention on the two who sat at the table. One was a heavy-set woman with shoulder-length black hair and a worried look on her face, while the other was a teenage boy with reddish-blond hair and a Hawkshaw County Hawks satin jacket. He recognized them immediately. Susan McLeod and Bill Sutton's boy, Tom. Both acknowledged him with a nod and he quietly returned the gesture. The housewife and the high school student looked as ill at ease as Joe did. And they looked scared as well, although the boy attempted to hide it behind a wall of attitude.

"Can I get you some coffee, Joe?" asked Jasper, stepping over to a coffee pot on the gas stove.

"Yes, please," he said, taking off his Texaco cap and pulling out a chair next to Susan.

Jasper poured a ceramic mug full and set in front of him. "There's sugar and cream on the table if you need it."

"I drink mine black," said Joe.

Tom Sutton rolled his eyes. "Let's screw the formalities, okay? The grease monkey's here, so why don't you tell us exactly what the hell's going on?

Jasper McLeod stood at the end of the table and glared at the young man for a moment. "You listen to me, you arrogant little cuss," he said, his words angry but restrained. "This is serious business we're discussing here. It involves the lives of four children. That includes you little sister. I'd much rather be dealing with your father or mother, but, lucky me, I'm stuck with you instead. So why don't you just shut your trap and listen up. Okay?"

The teenager's face turned a brilliant red and he opened his mouth, on the verge of telling the old man off.

However, Joe interrupted him before he could do so. He reached across the table and firmly laid his hand on the boy's forearm. "You'd best think twice before you fly off the handle, son," he said. "And watch your mouth, will you? There's a lady present."

Tom looked into the mechanic's eyes and saw a subtle threat there. He closed his mouth and slumped back in his chair, his arms folded across his chest.

Silence hung over the kitchen table. Then Susan spoke up. "So, what's this all about, Papa?" she asked. "What's happened to them?"

"Have they been kidnapped or something?" Joe wanted to know.

"Fat chance!" said Tom. "We're not exactly a bunch of Donald Trumps sitting here. They wouldn't get very much for my sister, I know that. Our folks have enough trouble making ends meet, let alone paying some sort of ransom."

Jasper ignored the boy's remark. "No, I'm pretty sure that's not what happened." He paused, choosing his words carefully. "But there is someone who I believe *is* responsible for their disappearances."

"Who is it?" Joe asked.

"A fella by the name of Leech," Jasper replied. "Augustus Leech."

The three stared at him blankly.

"I didn't figure ya'll would recognize the name," he said. "If you did, you'd have to be pert near as old as I am, or older."

"Just who is this Leech dude?" asked Tom.

"Ya'll just sit back and listen," said Jasper, taking a seat at the head of the table. "This is gonna take a while to explain.

For the next half hour, Jasper McLeod told them a tale of a murderous traveling medicine man, the awful crime he had committed against the town of Harmony back in 1917, and the fate he had eventually suffered at the hands of an angry mob of vigilantes. He also told them of the dream he had had several nights before, as well as everything Edwin Hill had told him in the hospital room in Manchester. When he was finished, Jasper leaned back in his chair and sighed. "Well, that's it," he said, waiting for their reaction.

"Sounds like a crock of grade-A horseshit to me," said Tom. "I mean some evil dude coming back from the dead and all? Give me a break!"

Joe Adkins nodded. "I've got to agree with the boy, Jasper. What you just told us does sound pretty farfetched. In fact, it sounds kind of crazy to me."

Anger leapt into Susan McLeod's face. "Listen here! My father-in-law is an honest and levelheaded man. If he thinks it's some kind of spook from 90 years ago, then there's a fair chance that he's right. There are things in this world that we don't have a clue about, you know."

"Simmer down, daughter," said Jasper with a smile. "I don't blame them for being so skeptical. It does sound crazy, I'll admit that. But I've turned it over and over again in my mind and this is the closest I can come to figuring out what has become of them. Let's look at the facts for a moment. First, those kids took a trip out to Hell Hollow. Then I have that dream about Leech, followed by Edwin's heart attack a few days later, seemingly by the hand of the same one I dreamt about. Now, all of a sudden, all four of those young'uns have up and vanished. Frankly, I think they came across someone down in that hollow. Someone who pulled the wool over their eyes and tricked them. Made them do something that caused their disappearances last night."

Jasper let them mull it over in their minds for a moment. Then he reached into his shirt pocket and pulled out the oversized card he had found the night before. He laid it face-up on the tabletop, revealing the picture of the hard-nosed police detective. "And, for some reason, I think this is the key to the mystery. Don't ask me why. I just do." He looked from Susan, to Joe, to Tom. "You did check beneath their pillows, like I asked you to on the phone?"

One by one, the three nodded. Tom Sutton and Joe Adkins pulled cards from their jacket pockets, while

Susan produced one from the inner folds of her purse. They laid the cards on the table in front of them. Drawings of a high wire acrobat, a western marshal and a World War II soldier graced the fronts of the three cards.

"What do they mean, Papa?" asked Susan.

The old man recalled the one dream he had experienced because of his own card and how it had frightened him as a child. "I'm not exactly sure yet," he said. "But I think I know someone who can tell us. If he's willing to, that is."

"Leech?" asked Joe.

"Yep. And, if he truly exists, he'll likely be out there in the middle of the South Woods. Down there in Hell Hollow."

"So, what are we waiting for?" said the mechanic. "Let's go out and find the bastard. Make him tell us what the hell's going on!"

"Just calm down, Joe," suggested Jasper. "We ain't gonna get nowhere if you go out there half-cocked. If that fellow is for real and he's down in the Hollow, he's likely to clam up and refuse to tell us anything if you show up aiming to beat the living crap out of him."

"I'm willing to go out there, if everybody else is," said Susan. "It's better than sitting here worrying myself to death."

"I'll go," Joe told them. "But on one condition. If we get out there and this Leech fella turns out to be a load of bunk, I'm going straight to the county sheriff. Understand?"

Jasper nodded. "I agree." He turned to Maggie's brother. "What about it, Tom? Are you willing to go with us?"

The teenager looked uncomfortable. "Why would I want to go out to that creepy old hollow? There won't be anything out there anyway."

"Maybe not," allowed the elderly farmer. But hopefully my suspicions are on the right track." He could detect the fear in the boy's eyes. "I think it's important for you to go with us. If nothing else, then for your sister's sake."

That seemed to make up Tom's mind. "Okay. I'll tag along."

"Good," said Jasper. He picked up the card and looked at the design on the back; a scattering of stars and a moon against the blackness of night. It might have been his imagination, but the half-moon's grin seemed somehow *broader* now, more sinister in nature. As if amused by the plan of action they had just agreed upon.

They left the table and prepared for their trip to Hell Hollow. As he locked the back door behind him, Jasper McLeod found himself both anticipating and dreading his confrontation with the specter of Augustus Leech...that was, if he truly existed. He looked forward to discovering what had become of his two grandsons and their friends, as well as a way to recover them from whatever danger they now faced. But he also could not help but feel a little frightened. After all, he had been one of the horsemen who had pursued the medicine show man and participated in his death.

He secretly knew that the part he had played in that incident 90 years ago could very well have been the reason for the mysterious abduction of the four children. And he also knew it might prevent him from safely getting them back.

CHAPTER THIRTY-EIGHT

Keith struggled against the ropes that bound him, but to no avail. The cords of sturdy hemp held firm, refusing to give even a fraction of an inch.

He abandoned his attempt to escape and settled back in the chair he was tied to, exhausted. Keith had tried numerous times to loosen the ropes around his wrists, waist and ankles, but it seemed as though they only grew tighter the more he fought them.

Keith thought about Rusty and the others. He wondered if they, too, were trapped in their own private nightmares. Somehow, he had known all along that Doctor Leech was not what he presented himself to be; that he was potentially dangerous and not to be trusted. Keith had voiced his concerns openly, but his friends had scoffed at them, telling him that he was only being paranoid. He had a feeling that none of them were scoffing now.

He focused on his own particular situation. He was being held captive in an abandoned warehouse near the waterfront. The cavernous structure of concrete and corrugated steel had once been a seafood processing plant from the looks of it. Long conveyor belts and saltwater tanks stood in the dim glow of a single, flickering bulb that dangled overhead. The corroded machinery was covered with cobwebs and an inch of dust, as well as cloaked in eerie shadows. The rancid odor of fish guts still lingered in the clammy air, conjuring images of workers scaling and gutting tons upon tons of fish.

As he sat there, he spotted something scampering through the shadows. He didn't know what it was at first. Then the creature jetted across a patch of illuminated floor and he realized in horror that it was a rat. A rat as big as an adult house cat. And from similar sounds that echoed throughout the warehouse, he knew that there were more than one locked up in there with him.

Keith thought of his Grandpa McLeod, feeling sad and guilty for the hard time he had given the old man. He also regretted the rotten things he had said to him, especially during their confrontation in the kitchen. His grandfather probably thought that Keith hated his guts, but that was far from the truth. He was beginning to realize that more and more as he sat bound securely in the chair, surrounded by rats, both of the rodent and human variety.

The rattle of a key in a lock drew his attention. A moment later, an iron door at the far end of the warehouse opened. Keith wasn't at all surprised to see the Big Man swagger in, puffing a hand-rolled Havana, the Tommy gun canted cockily over his narrow shoulder. His henchmen—the Jamaican and the Columbian—accompanied him. They no longer carried the Uzi and shotgun they had before, but he could tell by the bulges beneath their coats that they were packing pistols.

"So, how is my guest doing?" asked the gangster, stopping a few feet from the bound detective. "Comfy?"

"Untie these ropes and I'll be just fine," Keith replied.

The Big Man laughed, his dark eyes sparkling. "Oh, I bet you would. But that's not about to happen. Remember, it was *you* who came looking for *me*. If you had left well enough alone, we both could have gone on, business as usual. But you had to stick your nose in where it didn't belong."

"That's what I do for a living," Keith told him. "Bring down lousy scumbags like you."

"Not for long," said the Big Man. "You crossed the line back at the Purple Passion, copper. I'm afraid there is absolutely no turning back now."

"Fat chance!" said Keith. "I left word at the station where I was going. They'll investigate and find out the truth. Before you know it, the entire precinct will be down here with riot guns and tear gas. They'll set me free and then we'll shut down your operation for good."

The gangster threw his head back and laughed. "You have quite a vivid imagination, Detective. But I'm afraid you're in for a very big disappointment. I wouldn't hold my breath waiting for your fellow officers to arrive and save the day, if I were you. You see, they've all been in my pocket for years. They've traded their loyalty to the law for a wad of greenback dollars in a plain brown envelope. We attempted to recruit you as well, but you do have an annoying stubborn streak. You'd rather remain poor and honest, than corrupt and financially comfortable. But, hey, to each his own!"

The realization that he was totally alone began to sink into Keith. The ropes around him seemed to grow even tighter as the prospect of actually escaping the waterfront warehouse grew grimmer and less likely.

"So what are you gonna do to me?" Keith demanded. "Shoot me?'

"Oh, I could do that, gumshoe," said the Big Man. "I'm certainly adept enough with this baby to accomplish the task." For an example, turned and rattled off a burst of .45 rounds from the circular drum of the Thompson sub-machine gun. A gray rat was caught moving from the cover of one piece of machinery to another. The slugs cleanly sliced the rodent in two, leaving both halves kicking and squirming before they finally twitched and grew still.

The Big Man lifted the smoking muzzle of the Tommy gun and smiled. "It would be so very easy to ventilate you with the pull of a trigger. But I have other plans for you, Detective Bishop. You see, I'm about to fit you for a brand new pair of shoes."

"What?" asked Keith, not understanding what the crime lord had up his sleeve.

The lanky gangster grinned and stepped aside, revealing the work that was taking place behind him. The Jamaican and the Colombian were next to one of the empty saltwater tanks, pouring bags of concrete into the vat and stirring in bucketfuls of water with a long broom handle.

"Cement shoes!" said the Big Man with a laugh. "Oh, they'll be a bit heavy and a tight fit, but they're guaranteed to last forever. And they're waterproof, too!"

"No!" yelled Keith. He struggled frantically against his ropes, so forcefully in fact, that he tipped the chair completely over. He lay on the floor and continued to wiggle and buck, but it was useless. He was completely at the mercy of the notorious Big Man. And, in Keith's case, that meant ending up at the bottom of the harbor, anchored to a watery grave by a pair of concrete brogans.

Rusty sat on a bunk in a cell of the Carnage City Jail, the verdict of only a few hours ago ringing like a death knell in his ears.

For the crime of brutally gunning down the Widow Johnson in cold blood, you are found guilty as charged! a judge who had looked suspiciously like Augustus Leech had said with a bang of his wooden gavel. *Therefore, you, former-marshal Rusty McLeod, shall suffer the following sentence. Come sunrise, you shall be taken from your cell and hanged by the neck until dead!*

He couldn't believe it, but the trial had passed and he had been returned to his cell to await execution. Even now, in the darkness beyond the bars of the cell's only window, Rusty could hear the steady pounding of hammers against wood. Eager carpenters were at work constructing the gallows that would, at the first light of day, take Rusty's life.

Rusty sat glumly on the hard bunk and buried his face in his hands. He couldn't help but wonder how things were back home. Was he still in his bed dreaming, or had he already gone far beyond that? Had his mother entered his bedroom and been unable to awake him? Or had she found him missing from his bed entirely? He had no idea what the extent of his physical presence was at the time being. All he knew was that his subconscious was hopelessly trapped in a nightmare that he couldn't emerge from, at least not under his own power.

The crisp striking of a match against a brick wall drew Rusty's attention. He glanced toward the window. In the black of night, a flame illuminated a narrow, bearded face as a cheroot was lit. It was the leering, arrogant face of the gunslinger named Sidewinder. A low chuckle drifted into the cell as the outlaw tossed the match aside, leaving only the glowing tip of the skinny cigar hovering in the darkness.

"How're you doing, McLeod?" asked the gunfighter in a low, taunting voice. "Getting jumpy yet?"

Rusty walked to the window and grabbed the iron bars. "You bastard! That gunfight was between you and me. I'd have won and you'd be six feet under right now...if you hadn't pulled such a dirty trick. Putting that door, defenseless widow woman in your place like that!"

"That'll teach you not to be so quick on the trigger," Sidewinder told him. "Not that you'll get much of chance anymore. By the time the sun is an hour in sky, your rotten carcass will be dangling by the end of that hangman's noose. Easy pickings for the buzzards."

Rusty growled and tugged at the bars of the jail window with all his might. But no matter how hard he struggled, they remained firmly in place.

"Best save your strength for that long walk to the gallows, McLeod," the outlaw told him. "I hear there's gonna be quite a turnout to see you swing. It's sure to make you a downright celebrity...if only until you shit your britches and your face turns black from strangulation."

"I'll get out of here somehow," declared Rusty. "And then we'll have us a *real* showdown, just me and you. No trickery, just steel nerves and skill with a gun."

Sidewinder shook his head. "Naw, I don't think so, McLeod." He stepped away from the window and gestured toward the porch of the Whipping Post Saloon. In the light of the batwings, Rusty could see a half-dozen men standing there, laughing and drinking from bottles of red-eye. All of them wore their guns tied down and ready for a quick-draw, the same as Sidewinder.

"You see those fellas yonder?" asked the outlaw.

"Yeah," answered Rusty. "Are they friends of yours?"

Sidewinder's eyes glittered in the red glow of the cheroot's ash. "Nope. They're my deputies."

Rusty couldn't believe his ears. "What are you talking about?"

The outlaw grinned and, taking the cigar from his lips, lowered it toward the front of his black vest. Pinned to the lapel was the brass badge of a U.S. Marshal.

"After that stunt you pulled on Main Street, the mayor figured they needed someone around to keep the peace," he said. "So they hired me and the boys to keep an eye on things here in Carnage City. And to make sure your hanging goes as planned, nice and proper like."

"But you're an outlaw!" protested Rusty. "You've killed dozens of innocent men. There's a price on your head, for goodness sakes!"

"Yeah, it is a hoot, ain't it?" chuckled Sidewinder, taking a draw on his cigar. "They figure I'm gonna be the perfect picture of law and order, but you and me know differently, don't we?" He leaned in close and lowered his voice. "Confidentially, I intend to make this town my own. First, me and the gang are gonna clean out the bank, then we're gonna start our own extortion racket with the local merchants. Maybe we'll branch out, too. Gather up all the pretty ladies in town and start our own private whorehouse. How does that sound?"

"You'll never get away with it!" Rusty told him.

"Oh, yes I will, and there ain't a damn thing you can do about it, McLeod," said Sidewinder. "Now, you'd best get back to your bunk and rest up. You've got a big day ahead of you. Or at least the first few minutes of one."

"I won't go without a fight," Rusty claimed. "I'll break away and then I'll deal with you."

Sidewinder snickered. "You'll march right up the steps of that gallows and slip your head through that noose like a good boy. If you cause any trouble, I'll have the boys shoot you down like a flea-bitten dog in the street."

Rusty watched as the tall, lean gunfighter tossed the butt of his cheroot away and walked toward the saloon. He considered yelling out something bold and biting, but knew it would be pointless to do so. In this nightmare world he was now a part of, the man named Sidewinder held all the cards. Rusty could scheme to break his appointment with the hangman the following morning and attempt an escape from Carnage City, but he knew that in the long run it would all be futile.

With a sensation of cold dread settling deep in the pit of his belly, Rusty McLeod sat down on his bunk, staring into the darkness of his cell and listening to the hammering construction of the gallows.

CHAPTER THIRTY-NINE

Allison Walsh awoke at five that morning. She showered, dressed, and ate a quick breakfast at a Hardee's across the street from her motel, all the while attempting to determine her next move. Her visit to the town of Harmony had been a complete bust the day before, so she finally decided to locate the scene of Larry Bell's murder and see if she could find anything of substance there.

She drove south down Interstate 24, made a U-turn at the Manchester exit, then headed northward again. The sun was just coming up when she spotted something up ahead and pulled to the side of the road. Allison had stopped several times before, believing that she had found the murder site, but each time she found that she was mistaken. This time, however, she was sure she had located the right spot. A fragment of fellow police boundary tape clung to the dull steel of a guardrail at the side of the interstate. True, the strip of adhesive plastic could have been blown several hundred yards from its original position by a heavy wind, but hopefully this would turn out to be the place she was looking for.

Allison cut the engine of the Altima and got out. She took a few minutes to examine the spot where she believed the state police had found Bell's Lincoln Continental. There was little evidence left to even assure her that she was at the correct place. There was the fragment of POLICE LINE—DO NOT CROSS tape, as well as a couple of reddish-brown spots on the pavement that might or might not have been bloodstains. Other than that, there was absolutely nothing present to identify the place as being the site of a horrible and brutal murder.

Allison felt disappointment began to creep up on her. The constant string of dead-ends she had run across since beginning her private search for Slash Jackson had become increasingly frustrating. It was as though the rapist had snapped his bloodstained fingers and completely vanished from the face of the earth, leaving no trace behind.

But as she stood on that stretch of interstate, Allison was sure that Jackson had been responsible for killing the Kentucky businessman and this was where he had made his getaway, only a few moments before the arrival of the Tennessee state trooper. She was certain of it. She could almost feel the dark aura of his presence still lingering there, like the spoor of a wild animal.

Allison walked over to the guardrail and stared down the steep embankment to the heavy forest that grew below. Had he headed for the cover of the woods when the patrol car showed up? She shielded her eyes against the morning sun. Treetops stretched both north and east for as far as the eye could see.

Carefully, she climbed over the steel railing and then cautiously made her way down the grassy slope to the edge of the woods. By the time she reached the bottom, she had picked up several scrapes on her elbows and the heels of her hands, as well as grass stains on her white slacks. Allison dusted herself off, then began to examine the edge of the thicket for a distance of 50 yards, studying the ground the branches of the trees and underbrush for some tell-tale sign of a hasty entrance.

She covered the stretch several times, growing discouraged the more she looked. So far, she had been unable to find a single shred of evidence to verify that Jackson had ever been there. *Maybe I'm just grasping at straws,* she told herself. *He's probably several hundred miles away...maybe even out of the country by now.*

Allison was about to turn and trudge back up the embankment to the interstate, when a glimmer of sunlight reflected through the treetops and glinted off something on the ground. She bent down and picked up the tiny object.

Her blood ran cold.

It was the gold cross pin. The one Jackson had worn on the collar of his shirt when she had first picked him up at the gas station in Atlanta. The one he had worn, inverted, through his nipple during that long session of rape and torture in the abandoned house near Adairsville.

Hope suddenly returned. A peculiar sense of excitement filled her; a mixture of triumph and underlying fear. He had been there! He had murdered Larry Bell, then dodged into the woods to make his escape.

Allison stepped into the trees, looking for another sign. She found it a few moments later. A branch from a maple sapling had been broken off near its slender trunk, too high up to have been damaged by a possum or skunk. Yes, he had been there alright. He had headed into the shadowy depths of the woods, probably intending to circle around and meet up with the interstate again further north.

She looked up at her rental car parked at the side of the road, scarcely visible beyond the steel barrier of the guardrail. Then she turned her eyes back to the miles of Tennessee wilderness that stretched in a widening swath toward the northeast. Shadows choked the forest. The foliage was so dense that very little sunlight was allowed to penetrate. He could be long gone by now, or he could still be in there somewhere, hiding.

Dark images of those horrible days and nights in the deserted house came back to haunt her. Images of fear, blood, pain, humiliation and the threat of immediate death from the honed blade of a knife. And that leering, whiskered face returned as well, painted with slashes of fresh blood—*her* blood—and glowing with an evil the likes of which she had never known before, and hoped to never know again.

Before, she had fought back those devastating memories. But not that morning.

Instead, she kept the hell she had endured fresh in her mind, allowing it to stoke her resolve with the heat of hatred and rage. Allison dipped her hand inside her purse and made sure that the gun was within easy reach. It lie there, ready, cool and hard, loaded with explosive retribution.

Taking a deep breath, Allison Walsh stared into the dense forest, then set off in search of the one person she despised most in the world. The one who had shattered the protective veneer of her life—a life of normalcy and naïve trust—and brutally forced her to see the evil that lurked just beneath the surface.

CHAPTER FORTY

"One more time!" bellowed Colonel Raven through the funnel of his megaphone.

Maggie clung to the floor of the platform, her muscles quivering, tears blooming her eyes. "I can't!" she cried. "I'm exhausted!"

The crack of a whip split the air. With it came a sting of pain at her right elbow. The sudden hurt caused her to jump to her feet and stumble to the edge of the platform, despite the protest of her aching muscles and raw terror of her acrophobia.

"You heard the man, Queenie!" snarled Max from the rungs of the pole. "One more time. And this time, put a little flair into it!"

"Please," she pleaded. Her tears caused the mascara around her eyes to merge with the greasepaint on her face. "Don't make me do it again. Sooner or later, I'm bound to lose my balance and fall."

The dwarf smiled cruelly. "Save that for today's performance. The crowd will be out for blood when your act rolls around. Don't disappoint them like last time. Give them the splattered guts they're paying for."

"Miss Sutton!" roared the amplified voice of the evil ringmaster below. "One more time! I am beginning to lose my patience!"

Maggie stood at the edge of the platform and looked down. Somehow, the distance between the ceiling of the Big Top and the center arena seemed even greater than before. At least twenty or thirty feet greater. This time, instead of the tank of hungry alligators, there was a deadly blanket of jagged steel spikes and shards of broken glass covering the sandy earth of the arena. And this was only supposed to be a practice session!

She glanced over her shoulder at Max. The little man was unfurling his whip, ready to lash out if she refused to obey. Maggie took a deep breath, calming herself as much as she possibly could. Then she stepped forward, placing her left foot on the narrow rope. She groaned as the wire took the brunt of her weight. The sole of her foot was sore and tender from having clenched the rope during several practice runs that morning. The muscles of her arms and legs were stiff and weary as well. Tension thrummed through her lean form as she once again attempted to maintain her balance.

Halfway across the high wire, her strength began to give out. She stopped in mid-stride, afraid that one more step would send her spiraling into open space.

"Continue, Miss Sutton!" demanded Raven from below. His voice was heavy with disdain.

"If I go any further, I'll fall!" she screamed down at him.

"Chief Bobo," called the ringmaster. "Motivate our star attraction, please."

She glanced over her shoulder. On the platform she had left 75 feet ago, stood the clown, this time dressed like an Indian chief. He grinned broadly and raised something at arms length. It was a wooden bow with a flaming arrow positioned against its taut string.

Suddenly, the arrow was blazing toward her. It soared uncomfortably close; near enough for her to feel the heat of it against the top of her shoulder. She stepped forward as the fiery projectile jetted past her and into the darkness. But she found that she could not rest after several steps. Three more arrows flashed around her, one after another, prodding her onward. One even skimmed the outer edge of her left thigh, searing the material of her black tights and blistering the flesh underneath.

Maggie cried out in pain and nearly ran the rest of the way to the opposite platform. The rope swayed from side to side and the open air yawned dangerously around her several times. On the floor of the arena below, the spears of steel and glass glinted menacingly up at her, as if yearning to pierce tender flesh and impale internal organs.

A few seconds later, she was safely on the other platform. She dropped to her knees, trembling, a wave of nausea washing through her. Maggie thought for sure that she would throw up, but she breathed deeply and managed to drive the sick feeling away.

"That will be enough for this morning, Miss Sutton," echoed the arrogant voice below. "You may come down now."

She remained on the platform until her strength returned, then carefully made her way down the steel pole, one rung at a time. Even when her feet touched solid ground she felt no relief. The moment she reached the floor of the Big Top, a tall, angular shadow loomed oppressively over her.

"Better, my dear," said Colonel Raven. "Much better. But this afternoon, when you are up there performing for the masses, do the act as planned. And when you fall—and you will fall this time—be sure to scream loudly and flail your arms on the way down. The crowd loves such theatrics. Although, in your case, Miss Sutton, I'm sure it shall come quite naturally."

Maggie lifted her eyes and glared defiantly into the face that resembled that of Augustus Leech. "Why are you tormenting me like this?"

The ringmaster merely smiled. "Because I *enjoy* it, that's way. I love to see you shake and shudder on that high wire, so afraid of falling to your death. That's the entire appeal of Circus Horrific. The shock and sheer terror it brings. Our audiences pay generously to see our performers die. Whether it be a lion tamer torn limb from limb, or a human cannonball falling short of his net and splattering against the earth of the arena, the crowds come time and time again to enjoy the fragility of human life. And today it shall finally be your turn to give them what they crave."

"But if I fall and die, your star attraction will be gone," she pointed out, attempting to reason with him.

Raven chuckled. "Oh, don't worry about that. You see, there are plenty of replacements, just waiting for their turn." He gestured toward a nearby section of bleachers.

Maggie peered into the gloom and was shocked to find a dozen other girls sitting on the wooden risers, all dressed in the same Spider Woman costume that she wore. She realized then that she held no real importance to the evil ringmaster; that she was completely expendable in his opinion. After she plunged to her death during the next performance, there would be another one to take her place. And after that one, yet another.

"Now remember what I told you, Miss Sutton," warned Colonel Raven. "Today you will give our audience what they want. If you falter even one step, I will have Bobo put one of those flaming arrows squarely between your shoulder blades next time. And you will end up both crushed and burned to a cinder when you hit the arena floor."

Maggie could only stare at the man in horror. There was no doubt that his threat was genuine. If she didn't purposely commit suicide by stepping off the high wire, he would sic his sadistic clown on her and have him do the dirty deed.

A moment later, she had been escorted back to her trailer and locked securely inside. Listlessly, she collapsed on her cot in the corner and lay there. She felt like crying, but her tears were all gone. She felt hollow and numb, resigned to a horrible fate she had no control over. Maggie thought about Keith and wondered what perils he was facing in his own nightmare world. She secretly wished that he would appear out of nowhere and rescue her from her imprisonment at the hands of the diabolical Colonel Raven.

But she knew that was impossible. There was simply no chance of such a convenient reprieve. In fact, she was so desperate to escape, that she wouldn't mind seeing her brother Tom's zitty face right about then. But that was even more remote than Keith coming to the rescue. Her brother hated her. She had sadly come to that conclusion after years of harassment and cruel practical jokes.

With a sigh, she lay on the cot and stared at the ceiling of the cramped trailer, waiting until the moment when a knock on the door would signal that it was finally showtime.

"We are here," whispered the elderly man who sat next to him.

Chuck turned and stared through the open slats of the boxcar as the train ground to a clanking halt. In the gray light of dawn, he could see a sprawling complex of buildings and barracks that took up several hundred acres along the Sola River in southern Poland. At first glance, it might have been mistaken for a city. But upon further inspection, that illusion faded, revealing the camp for what it truly was. High fences lined with barbed wire surrounded the long barracks and in the distance could be seen tall chimneys spouting clouds of ashy smoke. Smoke that carried with it the undeniable stench of burnt flesh.

"This is it," said the old Jewish man fearfully. "The place that has nearly destroyed my people. The hell known as Auschwitz."

Chuck felt dread fill him. During his hobby of studying the history of the Second World War, he had focused mainly on the heroic battles of those who had fought in the European and Pacific campaigns. But he had also explored the darker aspects of that horrible conflict, namely Hitler's evil plan to completely erase the Jewish and Gypsy races from the face of the earth. Those grim stories of mass genocide had greatly disturbed him. He would much rather look upon the photographs of conquering generals and victorious armies, than at the grainy black and white images of skeletal holocaust victims and mass graves piled high with pale, naked bodies. But he could no long confine the ugly side of World War II to the back of his mind. For here it was, in stark reality, staring him squarely in the face, refusing to go away by the mere turning of a page.

"I have heard about this place," said a young man with the swarthy complexion and jet-black hair of a Gypsy. "It is the Death Camp. The Fuhrer's damnable machine of extermination."

"But what is his purpose for doing such a horrible thing?" asked Chuck.

The old man laughed bitterly. "The man is evil. He regards us as an 'impure' race. A threat to his precious Third Reich. Therefore, he has vowed to eliminate us from the population of Europe. From what I have heard, nearly six million of our kind have already died in his infernal concentration camps. Who knows how far it may go!"

The lock was removed from the boxcar's door and, abruptly, pale light streamed inside, temporarily blinding them. German soldiers herded them from the cattle car, prodding them with the muzzles of their Mausers. They were divided into groups by *sonderkommando*—prisoners who aided their captors by escorting unsuspecting arrivals to one of two places; either the work barracks or the somber, morgue-like structure of the crematorium. Chuck was carried by the old Jew and the young Gypsy, held between them inconspicuously enough that it appeared as though he was walking under his own power.

As they passed through the gate, marching five by five, Chuck spotted a man standing on the balcony of the admissions building. He was a tall, dark-haired gentleman dressed in a crisp black SS uniform and glistening leather boots. Like the Fuhrer, he also held a disturbing resemblance to Augustus Leech.

"Who is he?" asked Chuck.

"That is Doctor Mengele," volunteered one of the sonderkommando.

Chuck nodded. He had read about the sadistic Nazi doctor who had served under Hitler's command. Mengele turned Auschwitz into a rare opportunity to perform his horrible experiments and operations with complete impunity, mostly on the children of the death camp. Chuck recalled hideous stories of the medical atrocities he had inflicted; infecting them with agonizing viruses, performing disfiguring surgery, and injecting their eyes with dye to turn their pupils a bright, Aryan blue.

As they passed the front of the admissions building, Chuck noticed that the long line was being divided. Some were selected for slave labor and sent toward the barracks and workshops. The rest were marched toward the rear of the camp...toward the finality of the gas chamber and crematorium. Family members wailed and wept as they were separated, mournfully aware that they would never see one another alive again.

"Hold your head tall," the elderly man told Chuck, taking a firmer grip on his arm.

"If they know you are crippled, they will send you to the ovens for sure."

"How did you come to lose the use of your legs?" asked the Gypsy. "During the heat of battle?"

"No, it was an accident," admitted Chuck, recalling the loud boom of a shotgun on a cool autumn morning. "A stupid, senseless accident."

He thought about his father and the awful guilt he carried inside for leaving his son partially paralyzed. Chuck would have liked nothing better than to talk to him at that moment and assure him that he was not to blame for what had taken place during that tragic hunting trip at Willow Lake. But wishing for such a chance was pointless. Chuck was certain that he would never have the opportunity to see either of his parents again.

Fortunately, the sonderkommando helped them merge with the line of prisoners who were destined for the labor camp. Even though Chuck had escaped the fate of the other line, he felt no relief. The stifling stench of burnt bodies curled in his nostrils, assuring him that, sooner or later, they would all find themselves the victims of the Fuhrer's gaseous showers and the searing furnaces of the crematorium.

After they were registered and given badges that classified them as "race violators", the three found themselves in one of the drafty barracks. The long, narrow building stank of human waste, disease and lost hope. They were issued baggy, striped uniforms, then assigned bunks. The beds were narrow and cramped, stacked on atop the other, four and five high.

Chuck managed to end up in one of the bottom bunks. Exhausted from the long train ride into Poland, he laid back, unable to believe that his glorious dream of war had turned so black and dismal. His brave mission behind enemy lines was forgotten. All that occupied his mind now was the death sentence he had been subjected to. There was no possibility of escape there in Auschwitz and little chance for survival. From what he had read about the death camp, he knew that there were only two ways he would be leaving its imprisonment. Either he would die of malnutrition after days of agonizing labor, or he would perish within the murderous jaws of the Fuhrer's abominable death machine, where millions had been led like cattle to a slaughterhouse.

CHAPTER FORTY-ONE

"Well, here it is," said Jasper. He stood at the edge of the slope that led down into the dark valley of Hell Hollow. "Are ya'll ready?"

Susan McLeod, Joe Adkins, and Tom Sutton stared into the pit of the wooded hollow. Each had heard the superstitions and ghost stories that surrounded the black heart of the South Woods, branding it a forbidden place that was never to be approached, even in broad daylight. An unsettling feeling crept through them, as well as peculiar chill that totally transcended the muggy warmth of the summer morning. But they all knew they could not let their fear get the better of them. Their loved ones were at stake and there was a good chance that the one responsible was somewhere down there, hidden from view by thick underbrush and the wild foliage of tall cedar trees.

One by one, they nodded. "Okay," replied Jasper. "Then let's go. But be careful. It looks mighty steep."

Carefully, the four started down the embankment, holding onto weeds and strings of leafy kudzu to prevent them from tumbling the rest of the way down. As he led the way, Jasper felt the temperature drop even more, causing the flesh of his arms to prickle with goosebumps. A distant memory returned to him; a memory of a band of horsemen descending that same slope in the pitch blackness of an autumn night, searching for the wreckage of a medicine show wagon that had careened over the edge mere moments before.

When they reached the floor of the hollow, Joe held up his hand. "Hey!" he whispered. "Listen!"

The others stood deathly still and listened. From several yards away drifted the sound of a banjo. They attempted to identify the tune that was being played on it, but it eluded them. All except Tom, that was.

"Sympathy for the Devil," said the teenager.

"Huh?" asked Jasper.

"That's what he's playing," Tom explained. "It's a Stones tune."

The four looked at one another, the sensation of uneasiness increasing. "Maybe you were right after all, Papa," said Susan, peering into the stand of dense woods that stretched ahead of them. "Maybe he is here."

"Well, let's go and find out for sure," replied the old man. He started forward, stepping high to prevent the kudzu from tripping him up. The others followed quietly. Their faces were pale, but determined.

A moment later, they discovered that Jasper's suspicions had been correct all along. Parked in the center of the cedar grove was a brightly-painted cabin wagon on four blood-red wheels. Tethered to the iron tongue of the front axle were two black horses who snorted in contempt at their approach. Jasper was almost sure they were Amos Hadley's prized breeders. Amos was the kind who kept to himself for days at a time, so no one in town had seen him for a while. Jasper had an uneasy feeling that something bad had happened to the old horse trader; perhaps at the hands of the one they had come there to see.

As he grew nearer, Jasper could tell there were disturbing differences between these two beasts and the good-natured animals that romped in Amos's south pasture. The horses secured to the medicine show wagon were physically threatening, almost dangerous in demeanor. And they possessed a strange red cast to their eyes. If Jasper hadn't known any better, he would have sworn that they glowed from an unholy inner light.

As they drew nearer, they turned their attention to the banjo-player who sat on a stump before a small campfire. He was tall and lanky, dressed in a clashing outfit of tan work boots, jeans, a Grateful Dead t-shirt, a black frock coat, and a dusty top hat. When the man stopped his picking and looked up at them, Jasper's breath caught in his throat. The man's gaunt, whiskered face was not precisely the one he recalled from his dream. But it was Augustus Leech, nevertheless. Jasper could detect the dark soul of that murderous showman just beneath the surface of skin and bone.

"Is it him?" asked Susan in a low voice.

"If not in flesh," replied her father-in-law, "then certainly in spirit."

The tall man's eyes sparkled darkly as he set his banjo aside and clasped his hands before him. "Given the circumstances, I half-expected someone to show up this morning," he said. "But I certainly didn't expect such a big turn-out."

Joe stepped forward. "We're here about—"

"Yes, I know your reason for coming here, Mr. Adkins," said Augustus Leech. "You wish to know the whereabouts of your pathetic cripple of a son, don't you?' He turned amused eyes on the other three. "Just like you desire to learn what became of Keith, Rusty and Maggie."

"That's right," said Susan, her round cheeks flushed with anger. "Now, tell us! What have you done to them?"

Leech laughed softly. "Why, my dear, I haven't done a thing to them. Where they have ventured to is purely of their own choice. I did nothing to persuade them. I merely provided them the means to go there, that's all."

"Go where?" asked Tom Sutton.

"Into the realm of their secret dreams," Leech told them. "They went where they have always wanted to go—far from their dismal homes and their dysfunctional families. And, thanks to me, they have achieved that goal. Only, they had no earthly idea that there was no turning back. That they were destined to stay upon their second journey...with absolutely no chance of returning. Not under their own power, that is."

Despite Jasper's restraining hand, Joe Adkins took a threatening step toward the man in the stovepipe hat. "If that's the case, they you're gonna bring them back...right now!"

A reptilian smile crossed Leech's whiskered face. "Oh, I certainly could do that...but I'm afraid I must decline. They've made their beds, so to speak. Now they must face the consequences and lie in them...no matter how horribly they might suffer."

"You son of a bitch!" cussed the mechanic. "If you don't tell me where the hell my boy is, I'm gonna break your skinny neck!"

Leech calmly reached into his coat and brought out a slender glass bottle with an aged brown label pasted to the front. He smiled at Jasper. "If you know what's good for you, McLeod, I would keep that gorilla on a leash. For the sake of your grandsons and the other two."

The elderly farmer recognized the bottle, although he hadn't seen one for nearly nine decades. It was identical to the elixir bottle that his father had purchased at the medicine show; the bottle that had contained the poison that had killed his baby sister. *What is he up to?* he wondered. *What is he going to do with that?* But he already knew that whatever Leech's intentions were, they were far from honorable.

He tightened his grip on Adkins' brawny arm. "Just cool down, Joe," he warned. "It ain't gonna do no good to—"

"The hell it ain't!" snapped Joe, pulling free from Jasper's hold. "This bastard's jerked us around long enough. I'm ready for some answers!"

The mechanic's bravado affected the high school student. He started forward too, hands clenched into knobby fists. "I'm with you, Texaco Man," said Tom. "Let's beat the crap outta this asshole and find out what happened to Maggie and the others!"

"No, stop!" yelled Jasper, but he knew they were beyond reasoning with.

Leech laughed and withdrew the cork from the mouth of the bottle. He waited until the two were nearly upon him. "You should have listened to the old man," he said, then dashed several drops of black elixir into the flames of the campfire.

Without warning, a billowing cloud of bluish-black smoke began to boil from out of the fire, expanding, engulfing them both. It smelled strangely like county fair cotton candy with the sickening stench of sun-baked roadkill hidden just underneath.

Joe Adkins coughed and gagged, flailing his arms as he tried to break through the choking mist. When he finally stepped into the open air, he was shocked to find himself not in Hell Hollow, but in a field near Willow Lake. Stunned, Joe looked down to find himself dressed in camouflage clothing and hiking boots, his usual attire for hunting. He heard the cackling laugh of Augustus Leech echo from the direction of the lake and began to climb a barbed wire fence, intending to go after him. But halfway across the barrier, a deafening boom sounded in the cool autumn air. He felt the impact of a shot hit him, lifting him completely off the fence. When he hit the earth, Joe reached around to the small of his back. He moaned in horror when his hand sank into a deep crater just above his pelvis. Warm wetness coated his fingers and the sharpness of splintered vertebrae slashed the flash of his palm. As all sensation drained from his legs, Joe turned his head and stared toward the far side of the fence. Standing on the other side was Chuck, grinning cruelly, holding Joe's 12-gauge shotgun in his hands.

At the same instance, Tom Sutton broke through the smothering blanket of smoke to find himself in upstairs hallway of his house. He stood there, dazed, wondering why he was no longer in the wooded hollow. Unable to move or speak, he stared through the open door of the bathroom at the far end of the hall. His little sister stood at the sink, wrapped in a towel, her hair wet from the shower she had just taken. As she picked up an electric hairdryer and turned it on the highest setting, Tom looked down at the puddle of water that was pooled around her bare feet. Water he had poured there for a practical joke. Tom opened his mouth to scream a warning, but his vocal chords were frozen. He watched in helpless horror as sparks burst from the dryer she held in her hand. Maggie turned rigid, her muscles growing taut as the deadly current seized her, refusing to let go.

The girl's eyes rolled up until only the whites showed and her teeth clamped down hard on her lower lip, biting deeply until blood flowed down her chin and spotted the white terrycloth of the bath towel around her. She was being electrocuted...it was *his* fault!

"Are you okay, Tommy?" came the voice of Susan McLeod, faintly at first, then growing in volume.

The boy coughed, expelling the last of the nasty fumes from his lungs. He found himself kneeling in the kudzu of Hell Hollow, but the image of his dying sister remained foremost in his mind. He glanced over to see Jasper standing over the gas station mechanic. Joe Adkins seemed to have been similarly stricken. He crouched on his hands and knees, his face as pale as lard, tears in his eyes.

"Now you are aware of what I am capable of," said Leech, still sitting before the fire. He stuck the cork back into the mouth of the bottle and returned it to the folds of his black coat. "So, if I were you, I would behave like good little boys and girls and not screw around with me. Do you understand?"

"Yes," said Jasper and Susan. Joe and Tom simply nodded mutely, still struggling to overcome the mind-altering fumes of the vapor that had engulfed them.

"Good," said Leech with a nod of his head. "Now we can proceed. We can discuss this problem of yours in a civilized manner."

Jasper took a step forward, but no threateningly so. "Why, Leech?" he asked. "For God's sake, why have you done this to them? They're only children. They've done nothing to hurt you."

"On the contrary," said the dark man. "They have come very close to jeopardizing my 'homecoming' here in the fair town of Harmony. That is one reason why I gave them the ability to travel elsewhere. To keep them out of my hair...indefinitely."

Susan clasped her hands pleadingly. "You have to bring them back. Please!"

Leech's oily grin broadened. In the shadow of his top hat, his eyes twinkled mischievously. "If you want them back so very badly, I'm afraid you will have to go after them yourselves."

"What do you mean?" demanded Joe, finally able to speak again.

"You possess the keys to their retrieval," Leech explained. "The doorways through which they passed from this dismal realm to a decidedly more intriguing one."

Jasper didn't understand what he was talking about at first. Then he remembered the square of pasteboard in his shirt pocket. "The cards!"

"Yes," agreed Leech. "To save them—or attempt to—you merely need do as they did last night. Place the card beneath their pillows and fall asleep. The portals of their dreams —or, more precisely, their *nightmares*—

shall be open to you. But I must warn you...your chances of successfully rescuing them are slim at best. If you aren't careful, you will find yourselves trapped there as well, with absolutely no prospect of returning. Of course, if you are unwilling to take that chance, well, that is entirely up to you..."

Leech stared into each one's eyes, his grin curling even more sinisterly. Just as he had expected, all four showed no sign of hesitation. They were prepared to walk through the gates of Hell and back to save their precious loved ones. Which was precisely what they would do, if they took the bait and crossed the threshold of the 12-year-olds' individual dreamscapes.

"We're not scared," snapped Tom, climbing shakily to his feet.

"Oh, but you shall be, once you arrive there," said Leech smugly. He pulled the devil-head watch from the fob of his coat pocket and flipped open its lid. "Now, I do suggest that you get going, if you expect to find them. Time is running out. All four have been given something of a death sentence, you see. And if you don't arrive in time to save them, they will not be saved at all."

"You godless bastard!" growled Joe.

Leech's lips curled, exposing pearly white teeth almost wolf-like in their sharpness.

"You will never know just how true that is," he said softly.

Jasper stared into Leech's black eyes and saw that the man wasn't joking. He was dead serious. Keith, Rusty, Maggie and Chuck were in grave danger. And, whatever horrors they faced, they would not survive them...unless those who loved them acted, and acted swiftly.

"Come on," he said to the others. "We've got to get back and try to go after them."

"But what if he's just yanking our chains?" asked Tom.

"Believe me, son," said Jasper. "He's not." The old man turned away from campsite, then suddenly glared back over his shoulder at the man in the top hat. He knew he was playing with fire, but he didn't care." I'm going after my grandsons, Leech. If something happens to them before I can reach them, I'm coming back for you personally."

The medicine show doctor seemed amused. "The same way your father came after me?

With a rifle to back his courage?"

"No," declared Jasper. "With my bare hands."

"Bold talk for a feeble, old man," replied Leech. "Remember what happened to your friend Edwin. I can do the same to you as well, if I have the desire to do so."

"Let's go," urged Susan fearfully, taking her father-in-law by the hand. "We don't have much time."

Then, together, they departed.

Augustus Leech watched as the four left the cedar grove and started back for the northern slope of Hell Hollow. He waited until they had made their way back to level ground and was out of sight, then stood up from his place on the stump. Leech chuckled to himself as he turned toward the rear of the wagon. He had nothing to fear from any of them. Oh, they might have posed a threat to his plans, the same as those pesky kids who had happened unexpectedly upon his campsite. But once they entered the realm of the children's nightmares, that would be the end of them. Leech's mirror images would strike swiftly and mercilessly, making sure that they would perish, along with those they went after.

Leech smiled. In the past, he had sentenced other meddlesome souls to similar fates at the hands of his nightmarish doubles and, so far, none had ever managed to return to

Reality. Evil abounded in that dangerous realm beyond the waking side of sleep. An evil so powerful that it could not be conquered, even by those who possessed strength of spirit and an unfaltering faith in God.

Humming a different song beneath his breath—AC-DC's "Highway to Hell" —Leech opened the rear door of the wagon and climbed in. It wouldn't be much longer before the daylight hours passed and night fell. Then it would be time for him to crack his whip and send the horse-drawn wagon up the steep embankment to the road above. But, first, he had preparations to make.

In the glow of a single candle, he crouched in the gloom and set to work. He produced a 5-gallon gasoline can that he had stolen from the Texaco station in town the night before. Then he turned to several wooden crates that sat near the back wall, next to the skeletal remains of his former self. Crates with the word ELIXIR stenciled in black ink across their sides.

Leech pried one of the rotten boards loose and lifted a dusty bottle from within. He pulled the cork and inhaled. The enticing aroma of the potion filled his nostrils, causing a devilish grin to cross his gaunt face.

Initially, it possessed the aroma of pure goodness; spring flowers, freshly baked cookies, the alluring scent of a lover's perfume and the tang of newly mown grass on a summer evening. But concealed underneath were darker smells. Smells that conjured images as old as the world. Disease, pestilence, violence and war. The coppery stench of mass murder and sweaty sourness of brutal rape. And, even further beneath those odors, the sulfurous stench of Hell itself.

He relished the scent of the elixir for a moment longer, then unfastened the top of the gas can and slowly poured the syrupy black liquid deep into its depths. But it would take much more than a single bottle to implement his revenge. One by one, he took the slender vessels from their crates and emptied them into the steel container.

Before long, the wooden boxes lay scattered and empty across the floor of the wagon and the can was full to the brim with something much more explosive and dangerous than gasoline. And, from within the cramped cabin of the wagon, rang laughter every bit as dark and evil as the black poison that would soon be unleashed, once again, upon the unsuspecting citizens of the little Tennessee town of Harmony.

CHAPTER FORTY-TWO

Jasper McLeod stared at the card as he stood in the bedroom where his grandson had slept the night before. The ink drawing of the police detective surrounded by tall skyscrapers and rain-soaked streets held an ominous quality; the dark promise of danger and misfortune. The elderly farmer thought of the other three cards and knew that their images held the same potential for disaster for Susan, Joe, and Tom.

But he felt no hesitation; no reluctance at proceeding with their plan to seek out the missing 12-year-olds. True, it could be perilous, even deadly, but that was a risk they would have to take. If they chickened out, then those four youngsters were as good as dead and buried in their graves.

Jasper tucked the card beneath the goose down pillow, then turned off the nightstand lamp and stretched out on the bed. He breathed in deeply, trying to relax. After lying there 15 minutes with no sign of growing weary, he sat up. He was simply too wired-up to fall asleep. Anxiousness tingled throughout him like an electric current, refusing to let him rest.

He got up and sent to the bathroom down the hall. In the medicine cabinet, he found a vial of sleeping pills his doctor had prescribed shortly after Gladys' death. He had had difficulty getting through the night following his wife's long illness and had needed some help falling asleep. The tranquilizers were nearly 2 years old and probably outdated, but Jasper was desperate. If he didn't fall asleep now, his chances of finding Keith before he succumbed to Leech's evil would be slim.

Jasper shook one of the tablets into the palm of his hand, then swallowed it with a sip of water from the bathroom faucet. Then he returned to the bedroom, lay down, and closed his eyes.

Ten minutes later, he felt drowsiness begin to overcome him. He felt himself grow limp as the grayness behind his eyelids darkened. Soon, pitch-blackness surrounded Jasper, pulling him down into a deep, thorough slumber.

Almost immediately, the dark veil began to lift. He felt the heaviness drain from his body and abruptly found himself standing in the center of a busy precinct station. Police officers escorted hookers, street hustlers and pickpockets to booking rooms, while detectives with their sleeves rolled up to their elbows and cups of black coffee next to them tackled the monotonous task of doing paperwork.

"Can I help you, mister?" asked a gruff voice from Jasper's right.

Startled, the farmer turned and found himself staring at a ruddy-faced police sergeant sitting behind an elevated desk. "Huh?"

"I said, what do you want?" he repeated in irritation. "Hurry up, will you? I haven't got all night."

Jasper thought to himself for a moment, trying to adjust to the new role he had been abruptly cast into. "Uh, I was wondering if you could tell me where I could find Detective Bishop?"

A scowl of disgust crossed the sergeant's broad face. "He ain't here. No one's seen the bum since late yesterday evening."

"Any idea where he went?" asked Jasper. "Does he have any particular place he goes after work?"

The desk sergeant thought for a second. "Yeah, he likes to hang out over at Donoghan's Bar across the street. Good place for him, too. Just a watering hole for has-been cops and private dicks."

"Thanks," said Jasper. He made his way through the crowded squad room and ducked out the heavy front doors, into the rainy night.

Standing on the steps of the police precinct, Jasper took a moment to examine his clothing. He was wearing the ill-fitting, checkered suit of a country bumpkin, complete with tight-fitting shoes, a red bowtie, and a flat-crowned straw hat. He looked completely naive and out of place, as though he had just fallen off a turnip truck with nary a bit of street savvy to his credit.

He looked across the bustling city street and saw a flashing neon sign that read DONOGHAN'S on the front of a red brick building. Quickly, he crossed the congested avenue, nearly getting run over several times and surviving an assault of blaring horns and angry curses. Soon, he was on the opposite sidewalk, his coat and hat soaking wet from the downpour.

Jasper opened the door of the bar and stepped inside. The interior was hazy with cigarette smoke and stank of hard liquor and beer. As he passed through the dimly-lit barroom, he began to grow aware of the faces of the establishment's patrons. They seemed strangely familiar to the elderly man, although he was unable to place any of them at first glance.

He stepped up to the bar and waited until a burly bartender arrived to take his order. "What'll you have, bub?" he asked, his eyes as flat and expressionless as a couple of copper pennies.

"Give me a Sun Drop," Jasper replied. "Straight, no rocks."

The bartender nodded. A second later, Jasper had a shotglass of sparkling yellow soda in his hand. "Uh, I was wondering if you've seen Keith Bishop around? He's a police detective from the precinct across the street."

"I know Bishop," said the barkeep. "But he ain't been in for a couple of nights. You might ask those gentlemen at that table over there, though. They're pals of his."

Jasper turned and looked to where the bartender pointed. Through the blue haze of cigarette smoke, he saw three men sitting at a table, splitting a bottle of scotch between them. Like everyone else in the joint, they looked oddly familiar to him. "Thanks," he said. Then, drink in hand, he walked across the barroom.

When he got there, Jasper stood stunned for a moment. Up close, he recognized the trio at once. In fact, he had seen them time and time again, both on the television and the motion picture screen.

"Can we help you, mister?' asked a middle-aged man in a tan trench coat and gray fedora. He had a sad, world-weary face that had been a staple of suspense and detective cinema during the 30's and 40's. It was Humphrey Bogart. Or, rather, Sam Spade from the classic film *The Maltese Falcon.*

"Uh, yeah," stammered Jasper. "I'm looking for Keith Bishop. The fella at the bar said you might be able to help me."

"He said right," replied a sandy-haired fellow with a husky voice, dressed in the conservative clothing of a G-Man. "Have a seat." It was a young Robert Stack in the role of *The Untouchables'* Elliot Ness.

Jasper pulled up a chair and sat down. "I don't know exactly where to begin," he said uncertainly.

"Jus give us the facts, sir," said a short man with a flattop and a face like stone. "Just the facts." There was no mistaking it. Jack Webb as Sergeant Joe Friday of *Dragnet.*

The old man took a long swallow of Sun Drop, then calmly explained his dilemma. As he talked, he looked around the barroom. At a nearby table, Magnum P.I. was playing poker with Starsky and Hutch and Kojak, while at the bar, Lieutenant Columbo and Barnaby Jones occupied barstools, munching on beer nuts and watching a prizefight on a black and white TV set.

When he finished his story, Ness nodded. “I think we can help you, Mister McLeod.”

“You can?”

“Yes,” said Spade. “Bishop’s been on the trail of a crime lord for the past few days. He tried to discover his whereabouts from a snitch named Lester, but two thugs gunned the stoolie down before he could sing. Then he went to a club across town called the Purple Passion late last night to meet some broad named Cassandra. He hasn’t been seen or heard from since.”

“Do you have any idea who this crime lord is?” asked Jasper.

“They call him the Big Man,” said Friday in his monotone voice. “He’s a known drug dealer, pimp, and extortionist. He has half the police department in his hip pocket and the entire underworld squirming under his thumb. Some have crossed him, but they’ve never been seen alive again.”

“More than likely buried in an unmarked grave or tied to an anchor and tossed into the harbor,” said Ness. “A regular unsolved mystery.”

“Do you think he has Keith?”

“Probably,” agreed Spade. “I’d say the Big Man set a trap for him at the Purple Passion, then took him to his hideout.”

“Any idea where the hideout might be?” Jasper wondered.

“We’ve been doing a little surveillance ourselves,” Friday said. “The Big Man runs his operation out of an abandoned cannery on the waterfront.”

Jasper downed the rest of his Sun Drop. “Will you tell me how to get there? I’ve got to find Keith before they do something bad to him.”

"We'll do better than that," replied Ness, pulling a Tommy gun from beneath the table. "We'll go with you. I'll stop by the office and pick up Rico and Youngblood. Then we'll be on our way."

Sam Spade reached into the side pocket of his trench coat. "If you're going up against the Big Man, you'll need this." He laid a blued-steel Colt .45 automatic on the table in front of the elderly farmer. "And don't hesitate to use it. Understand?"

Jasper picked up the gun and hefted its weight in his hand. He was determined to buck the odds that Augustus Leech had laid down and bring his grandson back to the real world alive. "I'll do what I have to do," he said, sticking the gat in the pocket of his checkered jacket.

Joe Friday pulled a snubnose .38 Special from a belt holster and checked the loads in its cylinder. "I just hope we get to Bishop in time. Because if we don't..."

"Yes?" asked Jasper.

"He may just end up like the rest of the Big Man's victims..."

The Los Angeles detective paused dramatically.

"Part of a highway ramp. Or standing at the bottom of the harbor in a cement overcoat, with no one to keep him company but fish, garbage and seaweed."

Susan McLeod found herself on horseback, riding across a barren Arizona desert. It was still dark, but the pale light of the coming dawn was on the verge of blooming on the eastern horizon behind her.

In the gloom, she looked down at herself. She was surprised to find that she was dressed in a fringed buckskin outfit, boots and a white cowboy hat; sort of a mixture of Calamity Jane, Annie Oakley, and Dale Evans. In a saddle scabbard was an engraved Henry rifle, while buckled around her waist was a hand-tooled gun belt with a hogleg Remington revolver cradled in its single holster.

Where am I? Susan wondered. *And where could Rusty be?*

The dapple gray mare beneath her snorted and began to trot toward a tall stand of painted buttes that stood like dark monuments against the early morning sky. She couldn't figure out where the animal was headed until she caught the scent of food. The inviting aroma of strong black coffee and bacon frying in the pan drifted across the desert toward her.

A moment later, Susan found herself descending into the basin of an arroyo. Through a stand of thorny mesquite, she could detect the flickering glow of a campfire. She thought of something she had seen on a western movie once; a precaution against being unnecessarily shot. "Hello the camp!" she called out, letting her presence be known.

"Come on in!" called a familiar voice from the other side of the mesquite patch.

She urged the mare onward, until they were past the brush. There, sitting around a small fire, were three men. Men who had ridden the Wild West in dozens of films over the last 60 or 70 years.

"Take a load off, Ma'am," said a tall, handsome man in the dusty garb of a cowboy.

"Sit a spell and have yourself some grub."

Susan climbed off the mare and tied its reigns to a mesquite branch. As she drew closer, she studied the big man's tanned face in the firelight. It was a young John Wayne, as he had looked in the movie *Stagecoach*.

"Yes, please do," urged the man who held the iron skillet. He forked strips of crispy bacon onto tin plates, along with biscuits as big as the head of a cat. "You're welcome to share breakfast with us." He wore an embroidered shirt, chaps over denim britches, and a high white hat. His smiling face was also familiar; a youthful Roy Rogers.

"Thank you," she said, bewildered. Susan sat on a boulder and accepted a plate and a cup of steaming coffee from the singing cowboy.

"Pardon me for asking, lady," came the low, clipped voice of the third man, "but what are you doing traveling alone in a godforsaken place like this?"

Susan turned her eyes toward him. He was a tall, angular man wearing a low-brimmed hat and Mexican poncho. When she looked into his stubbled, squinting face, she discovered that it was Clint Eastwood in the role of his gunslinging bounty hunter, the Man With No Name.

"I'm trying to find someone," she said, taking a sip of black coffee.

"And who might that be?" asked Roy.

"My son. His name is Rusty McLeod."

The Duke nodded. "The U.S. marshal who was just sent to Carnage City."

"Yes," replied Susan. "I believe he's in danger."

The three looked at one another. Something shown in their eyes; a mutual expression. It took Susan a moment to identify it as a mixture of concern and loyalty.

"Then I reckon we'd best get to riding," said the Duke flinging the dregs of his coffee into the fire. "Carnage City's just a mile or so west of here. If we ride hard, we can make it there by sunrise."

"You're willing to help me?" asked Susan, surprised. "Just like that?"

"We all owe Marshal McLeod a debt of gratitude for helping us out of some tight predicaments," said the bounty hunter. "Remember that time down in New Mexico, boys? Just us against 50 Apache Indians. We thought our scalps would end up hanging on their lodge poles. Then the Marshal rode in with an armed posse and saved our hides."

Roy nodded. "We're obliged to him, ma'am. And if we can help get him out of a bad scrape, we aim to do it."

"I've heard tell that Sidewinder rode into Carnage City yesterday," said the Duke.

He hefted a saddle over his shoulder and, taking a short-barreled Winchester with a bowed lever ring in hand, headed for three horses tethered nearby. "Maybe he has something to do with the trouble Rusty's in."

"Sidewinder?" asked Susan, watching as they prepared their mounts.

"A no-account, scoundrel of an outlaw, ma'am," explained Roy, checking his six-shooters.

The Bounty Hunter's eyes glittered beneath the brim of his weathered hat. "Ah, Sidewinder. I've been wanting to take him on for a long, long time."

"Do you plan on killing him?" the woman wanted to know.

Roy smiled. "We'll only shoot to wound if you want it that way, ma'am."

"Speak for yourself, pretty boy," rasped the Bounty Hunter, lighting a narrow cheroot with a sulfur match. Jutting from beneath his poncho was a revolver with the image of a coiled rattler engraved on its handle.

"Well, if we're gonna get to Carnage City before daybreak, I suggest we quit jawing and start riding, pilgrims," drawled the Duke, swinging onto his horse.

Soon, Susan and the others were atop their own mounts and galloping out of the arroyo, heading westward across the desert. She didn't know what sort of danger Rusty might be in, but if anyone could help her save him, it was certainly the band of western heroes that rode along side her. And they were willing to lay their lives on the line if the need arose.

CHAPTER FORTY-THREE

Tom Sutton opened his eyes and found himself sitting on a park bench. He felt disoriented at first, then realized that he had arrived in the dreamworld that his sister had conjured from her imagination. He stood and started up a brick pathway, passing a white gazebo and coming to the street of a peaceful mid-western town. As he paused, trying to come to terms with the place his slumber had brought him to, he watched a couple of vehicles pass one another on the picturesque avenue. One was a horse-drawn ice wagon, while the other was a Model-T Ford, its engine chattering noisily and its tailpipe farting clouds of gassy black exhaust.

The teenager crossed the street and headed toward town square. Around him, quaint buildings stood, reminiscent of a by-gone age. They were turn-of-the-century structures with coats of immaculate white paint and plenty of fancy gingerbread trim, like the buildings on the Magic Kingdom's Main Street in Disney World, or some small town out of a Ray Bradbury story.

He was passing a butcher shop, when he felt something tug at his pants leg. Tom expected it to be a dog or a small child, but it wasn't. Surprised, he stared down at the tiniest man he had ever seen in his life. A man who must have been twice his age, dressed in a French general's uniform. Napoleon Bonaparte in miniature.

"Excuse me, sir," said the little man in a squeaky, but cultured voice. "But would you be Thomas Sutton?"

Tom nodded. "Yeah, I am. Who are you?"

"Why, General Tom Thumb," said the dwarf, seeming upset that the teenager didn't recognize him.

"Bullshit!" said Tom, his mouth hanging open.

The little man's face reddened. "Watch your language, sir! There are ladies about, you know."

"Sorry," said Tom in embarrassment.

"I understand that you are looking for your sister," Thumb said confidentially, pulling the teenager to the side of the walkway.

"I sure am," said Tom. "Do you know where she is?"

"There," said the famous dwarf. "Beyond the edge of town."

Tom looked to where he pointed. Past the end of the main street, he could see a tall black form looming over the treetops. It was the biggest circus tent he had ever seen.

"So what are we waiting for?" he said, starting down the street. "Let's go get her!"

Thumb grabbed the tail of Tom's team jacket in his tiny hand, stopping him cold. "Don't be so blasted impetuous! If you try to rescue her now, both of you are doomed. You will need some assistance. That is why I've been sent to find you...so that a plan of action can be formulated."

"Exactly who sent you, short stuff?" Tom asked suspiciously.

"I did," came a gruff voice from the shadows of an alleyway.

Tom turned and saw a tall, portly gentleman in a dark suit standing there. He had wry eyes, a bulbous nose, and curly white hair framing a partially bald head. He had the look of a salesman about him. Either that or a clever con man.

"Who are you?" Tom asked.

"Phineas Taylor Barnum, at your service, sir," replied the man with a gracious bow.

Tom couldn't believe his eyes. P.T. Barnum was standing right there in front of him, in the flesh!

"Well, don't stand there gawking, boy," said Barnum. "Come along and we shall discuss your problem."

Tom complied, not knowing what else to do. He followed the great showman and his star attraction down the narrow alleyway to a doorway at the rear of the butcher shop. When he stepped inside, Tom found himself in a cramped room bearing only a table and four chairs.

"Have a seat, young man," instructed Barnum. "Snap to it! We don't have time to waste."

"Yes sir," said Tom. He took a seat at the table and stared at the one who sat directly opposite him. It was a sad-faced clown wearing a derby hat, ragged hobo clothes and floppy shoes.

"This is one of our acquaintances, although not from the same era as General Tom and I," introduced the boisterous showman. "Weary Willie, or as you might know him, Emmett Kelly."

"Hi," said Tom, flabbergasted.

The clown merely nodded silently, folding his arms and parking his oversized shoes on the edge of the table.

As Barnum sat down, something slithered across the floor and pulled itself up the side of the chair. Soon, it was perched on the showman's shoulder. It was a bizarre creature; half monkey and half fish. The legendary Fiji Mermaid.

"I thought that thing was a hoax," said Tom.

"Perhaps in your world," said Barnum. "But in this realm that your sister has created, anything is possible."

"Concerning the rescue of young Margret," said General Thumb, "we are prepared to join you in the fight to retrieve her from the clutches of that loathsome Colonel Raven and his band of sadistic freaks."

"Who's Colonel Raven?" asked Tom.

"The scoundrel who owns and operates Circus Horrific," said Barnum, his eyes full of disgust. "And one of my major competitors."

"Phineas doesn't particularly care for the quality of Raven's showmanship," Thumb said.

"Showmanship!" snarled Barnum. "The word can not even be used to describe him. He is a thrill-peddler of the worse sort. A man who deals solely in exploitation and darkness. He would much rather give his audience sensational feats of pure suicidal daring, rather than wholesome, family entertainment. He cares nothing for his performers or animals. Dozens perish at each performance, in the most grisly ways imaginable!"

Tom Thumb nodded. "Needless to say, he is not one of Mister Barnum's favorite people."

"I'd say not," agreed the high school student. "But how are we going to get to Maggie? Are we gonna sneak in and rescue her before they know we're even there?"

Barnum smiled smugly. "On the contrary. We are going to arrive at the pinnacle of showtime and snatch her from beneath Raven's crooked nose, just as she is on the verge of beginning her final performance on the high wire."

"High wire?" said Tom. He shook his head with wonder and admiration. "That crazy kid."

"And to assist us in our attack, we will be using a secret weapon," Thumb told him.

"What sort of secret weapon?"

General Thumb and Barnum exchanged amused glances. "Come and I shall introduce you," said the portly showman.

Thumb, Barnum and Kelly escorted Tom outside, to where the alleyway opened into a small, fenced yard. When the teenager turned the corner, he nearly peed in his pants. For, filling every inch of the yard, was an animal as tall as a two-story building and as long, from trunk to tail, as a Greyhound bus.

"Tom Sutton, meet our secret weapon," introduced Barnum with pride. "I give you

Jumbo, the largest elephant on the face of the earth!"

"What is the nature of your business, sir?" asked an MP at the military base's guard post.

Joe Adkins looked down and saw that he was dressed in the uniform of an Army major. "I'm here to locate my son," he said. "Chuck Adkins."

"Sergeant Adkins left the base yesterday," said the military policeman. "I'm afraid his whereabouts are top secret."

"But I've got to find him," urged Joe. "I have reason to believe he's in terrible danger."

"If you insist, sir, then you will have to talk to the General. I believe he is at the officer's club."

"Thank you, Private," said Joe with a salute. Then he walked through the gate and made his way among a maze of olive drab tents to a hastily erected building in the very center of the compound.

When he walked through the doorway, he nearly bumped into a lovely WAC. "Pardon me, ma'am, but could you tell me where I can find the General?"

"He's over there at the corner table," said the lady soldier with a smile. "With the others."

Joe nodded his thanks, then crossed the empty room to the only table in the club that was occupied. He recognized the General at once. He was tall and distinguished gentleman dressed in a gray Confederate uniform with gold stars on the collar. He wore a flapped holster cradling a .44 Leech & Rigdon revolver on one hip and a cavalry sword in a polished scabbard on the other. His white-bearded face was stern, but his eyes were kind and full of honesty. There was no mistaking his identity. It was the commander of the Army of the Confederacy himself...General Robert E. Lee.

"Don't you know that it is not polite to stare, Major?" the General said, noticing Joe standing there. "Especially when the one being stared at is a superior officer?"

"Excuse me, sir," apologized Joe. "But I must speak to you concerning an urgent matter."

"You can talk in front of my drinking buddies here," said Lee. "Have a seat."

Joe joined them. He studied the other two who sat at the table with the famous general. One was a roughly-hewn man dressed in the olive drab uniform of a WWII infantry man. The other was a tall, gangly man in the uniform of a World War I infantry soldier. Both looked suspiciously familiar. Joe was certain he had seen them somewhere before.

"So what is this all about, Major?" asked the General.

"My name is Adkins, sir. Joe Adkins. Chuck Adkins is my son."

An expression of intrigue shown in the general's eyes. "I see. And I suppose you wish to know your son's whereabouts?"

"I was told that his location is top secret," Joe said. "But I have to know. I believe he's in trouble."

Lee looked at the other two, then nodded. "You believe right. He has been captured by the enemy."

"The Nazis?" Joe asked.

"That's right," said the infantryman. Joe suddenly recognized him as Vic Morrow in his role of Sergeant Chip Saunders in the old 60s TV show, *Combat*. "He and a platoon of soldiers were on their way to Berlin, when the goose-steppers ambushed them. All of the men were killed, except for Sergeant Adkins. From what a

German operative told us, the Fuhrer himself showed up and captured Chuck. He put him on a train to one of those godforsaken concentration camps of his."

"Do you know which one?" asked Joe.

"Yup," replied the lanky soldier in the World War I uniform. Joe suddenly placed his long, hangdog face. It was Gary Cooper, reprising his role as the Tennessee mountain farmer turned war hero, Sergeant Alvin York. "They done gone and sent him to a place o'er in Poland. A place folks call Auschwitz."

"Good Lord!" said Joe, feeling a chill of dread run through him.

"Don't worry, Major," Lee assured him. "We were just in the process of working out a rescue plan when you came in. And if you are willing, we'd very much like for you to be a part of it."

"Do you think we can get him out of there before...well, you know..."

"Before they eradicate him?" asked Saunders.

"Yeah," said Joe uneasily.

"I reckon we'll get to him in time," said York. He took an Enfield rifle from where it leaned in the corner, then licked his thumb and touched it to the front sight, to help cut down on the glare. Then he aimed down the barrel with the skill of a seasoned sharpshooter. "Yup, them there Krauts ain't gonna know what hit 'em when we go in there, loaded for bear."

"We will be heading out in a few minutes," Lee told him. "But first let us wet our whistles."

The General called for a waitress. She brought a tray of root beers in frosty mugs. Joe was a little puzzled by the choice of libations, then remembered that the Confederate commander had been a religious man and a teetotaler. He gracefully accepted the root beer and took a swallow. Joe felt confident, being among men with such backbone and military savvy. But, still, he couldn't help but wonder if they would reach the death camp in time to save his son from the most horrible of fates.

CHAPTER FORTY-FOUR

A gray fog engulfed the harbor, obscuring the water and the tall buildings of the skyline, leaving only the long platform of the pier in view. Keith Bishop stood at the very edge of the end, unable to move anything but his eyes. A filthy handkerchief gagged his mouth, a coil of heavy dock rope encircled his body from shoulder to waist, and his feet were completely encased in a heavy block of concrete. His back was to the water. He faced the long boardwalk of the pier, as well as those who were on the verge of pushing him into the freezing depths of the harbor.

"You're scared, aren't you, Bishop?" asked the Big Man, standing before him. He grinned, showing a set of pearly teeth with a diamond stud embedded in one of the front incisors. "I can smell the fear drifting off you like the stench of some cheap, dime-store cologne."

Keith *was* frightened. More frightened than he had ever been before. Deep down inside, he knew that his nightmare was swiftly coming to a close. But rather than awaking to the safety of his grandfather's spare bedroom, he would not be waking up at all. A few scant seconds from now, Keith would be shoved off the edge of the pier. He would feel the biting cold of the salt water engulf him, then would feel nothing at all as numbness, suffocation, and darkness dragged him downward to his death.

"It's too bad that you didn't cash in like your fellow cops," the crime lord told him. "You could have been my right hand man, if only you had abandoned those foolish principles of yours. Instead, you chose good over evil. So I have no choice other than to waste you."

Keith cursed beneath the cloth of the gag, his eyes full of fire. But that was all the resistance he could manage. All other options had been deprived from him by constricting rope and concrete.

The Big Man turned and regarded the other three who accompanied him on the pier. "Does anyone want to bid poor Detective Bishop a fond farewell?" he asked with a mock expression of solemnity.

Both the Jamaican and the Colombian, once again armed with shotgun and Uzi, simply grinned those grins that failed to match the contempt in their cold-blooded eyes. The third witness to the Big Man's crime was his moll, the voluptuous Cassandra from the Purple Passion Lounge. She took a puff on a cigarette in a long black holder, her face full of boredom. "Oh, just push the loser in and get it over with," she said.

The Big Man turned and shrugged his padded shoulders apologetically. "Sorry, but no one really seems to give a damn," he said. "So I suppose there is nothing more to say than...adios." The gangster reached out, his palm extended, intending to push Keith over the edge of the pier.

But, before he had the chance, something unexpected happened. Keith heard the roar of a car engine. He looked past the Big Man and his cronies, and saw a convertible roadster barreling down the long boardwalk of the pier toward them. Four men occupied the car's front and back seats, while two others rode the automobile's running boards. When the vehicle braked to a halt 20 feet away, Keith watched as three of the passengers leapt out, armed with guns.

Among the trio, Keith recognized one immediately. It was the last person in the world he would have expected to see at that moment.

It was Grandpa McLeod...and he was coming to his rescue!

"Surrender and untie him!" demanded Elliot Ness, standing up in the roadster and brandishing a 45-

caliber Thompson. His loyal agents, Rico and Youngblood, remained on the running boards, also holding submachine guns. "Do as I say and you'll serve a nice long stretch in the Big House. Refuse and we'll mow you down like the gutter rats you are."

"To hell with you, G-Man!" growled the Big Man. He pulled a nickel-plated Colt automatic from beneath his wide-lapelled coat. "This is a private party and you're not invited."

"Then we're here to crash it," said Sam Spade. As he started toward them, gun drawn, he suddenly found the long-legged Cassandra standing in his way. "Outta the way, sweetheart," he warned.

"Not on your life, gumshoe," she hissed. She lifted a slender arm and aimed a small revolver at him.

"I'm usually respectful of ladies," said Spade, clubbing the little gat out of her hand with his own heater. "But seeing as you ain't one, I'll dispense with the gentleman act."

He then hauled off and delivered a haymaker at the woman, sending the Big Man's moll over the side of the dock and into the drink.

As Jasper McLeod and Joe Friday ran down the pier toward Keith and the Big Man, the Columbian acted. He lifted his Uzi and fired as the two men parted company. The Israeli submachine gun rattled off a stream of 9mm rounds that ricocheted off the fenders and grill of the roadster. The two G-men on the running boards reacted coolly, leveling their own Tommy guns and deftly cutting down the thug with short bursts of .45 slugs.

The Jamaican tossed his head, sweeping his dreadlocks aside, then stepped in front of the LA detective and raised the sawed-off barrel of his scattergun. "Eat my lead, mahn," he said in his sing-song voice.

Jasper acted before he could pull the trigger. With a look of regret on his face, he lifted the automatic Spade had given him and fired. The bullet struck the Jamaican in the left shoulder, knocking him off balance and causing him to drop the 12-gauge.

"Thank you, Mister McLeod," said Friday politely. He quickly flipped the criminal onto his stomach and, drawing a pair of handcuffs from his belt, skillfully snapped the bracelets on him. "You have the right to remain silent..." he began with a dead-pan expression on his face.

"Step out of the way, Big Man," Jasper warned, raising his gun for the second time. "Step away and let me have my grandson."

"Fat chance, bumpkin!" laughed the crime boss. He planted his hand firmly against Keith's chest and pushed, then leapt over the side of the pier into the fog.

Keith felt himself lurching backward slowly, the concrete block beginning to tip on its heavy base. But an instant before he could go over, he felt someone grab him by the ropes that bound his chest, pulling him back on balance. When he regained his bearings, he found that it was his grandfather who had saved him from a watery demise.

Jasper removed the gag from his grandson's mouth, then took a Case pocketknife from his jacket and began to cut the ropes away. "Are you okay, Keith?"

"Thank God you got here in time, Grandpa," said Keith breathlessly. "But how did you—?"

"I'll explain later," said the old man. "Right now, we still have to deal with the Big Man. He's skipping out on us!"

As the ropes fell away, Keith turned and peered into the dense fog. He could barely see the gangster drifting past the edge of the dock in a small motorboat, cranking the engine over and over, trying to get it to start.

"Hey, kid!" called Ness, tossing him the Tommy gun. "Maybe you could put this to good use."

"Thanks!" replied Keith. He worked the machinegun's bolt, twisted at the waist, and squeezed the trigger.

"No!" screamed the Big Man, an expression of defeat breaking across his lean face. He abandoned the stubborn outboard and lifted his pistol. But he was too late. Keith got the drop on him first, emptying the circular drum of the Thompson into the motorboat and its occupant. Bloody bullet holes blossomed across the Big Man's chest and abdomen, causing him to jump and jerk. Then the kingpin fell backward out of the skiff and landed in the harbor with a resounding splash.

They watched as the bullet-riddled body of the Big Man bobbed upon the choppy waves; once, twice. Then the cold currents of the harbor pulled the dead gangster downward into its dark depths, never to be seen again.

"Step back, Mr. McLeod," said Spade. "I've got to get this just right."

Jasper stood aside, while the private detective aimed his .45 at the block of cement that encased Keith's feet. He fired three times, shattering the concrete and setting the 12-year-old free. The old man was there to steady his grandson, who could barely stand after several hours of confinement.

"Do you think you can get us out of this place now?" Jasper asked.

"I'll sure give it a try," he said. He turned to those who had assisted his grandfather during his rescue. "Thanks for the help, guys," he said.

"We were glad to help," said Spade, lighting a smoke.

"But be careful when you get back," advised Friday. "While you were gone, the one responsible has been busy. Tonight he'll attempt to doom the town of Harmony, just as he tried to ninety years ago."

"Thanks for the information," said Keith. He took a deep breath and concentrated. Nothing happened at first. Then the fog that hung over the harbor began to grow thicker, swallowing the pier they stood upon and completely obscuring the gathering of law offices and the roadster they had arrived in.

"I think it's working," said Keith.

A second later, the soft grayness of the fog deepened into a cloak of jet-black darkness.

A strange drowsiness gripped the boy and his grandfather and, before long, both were totally unaware of their whereabouts. Or anything else, for that matter.

The rattle of a key in the lock drew Rusty's attention.

The cell door swung open with a squeal of unoiled hinges, revealing Sidewinder. The gunslinger grinned wickedly, the marshal's badge gleaming against the black backdrop of his silhouette. He held a Colt revolver in his right hand.

"It's time McLeod," he said.

Rusty left his bunk and stood up. His heart pounded in his chest, threatening to drive him into a blind panic. But he quelled the emotion and stepped forward bravely, his shoulders squared. The fear was still there, nestled like a quivering animal in the pit of his stomach, but he refused to let his nervousness show.

"Don't get any stupid ideas," Sidewinder said, backing away from the door and allowing Rusty to step into the outer corridor. "You try to fight your way out of this predicament you're in and the boys'll plug you clean as whistle."

Rusty regarded the two that accompanied the bogus marshal. One was a grubby, crazy-eyed little fellow wearing a Confederate cap and holding a big Colt Dragoon pistol that was nearly a foot and a half long. The other was a big, burly Mexican bandito, wearing a sombrero, ammunition bandoleers across his chest, and holding a sawed-off Parker shotgun in his hands. Just looking at them, Rusty knew that he had no chance of battling his way past them. If he so much as twitched a muscle wrong, the two would let loose with their weapons and send him to the grave before the hangman could even get a crack at him.

"Start walking, señor," the Mexican said, displaying a broken grin of missing teeth and gold fillings. He prodded Rusty in the back with the Parker's twin muzzles, urging him down the corridor, toward the front of the jail.

A moment later, Rusty stepped out into the dusty main street of Carnage City. The grayness of dawn had bled away into the brilliant canvas of pastel pinks and purples. It would only be a minute or two before the sun made its appearance, creeping over the distant buttes in the east and casting its scorching rays upon the Arizona desert once again.

Sidewinder and his men herded Rusty down the street, toward the edge of town. When they finally reached the foremost limits of Carnage City, Rusty found himself standing before a tall, hand-built gallows constructed of new lumber and ten-penny nails. From the upper beam of the structure dangled a length of sturdy hemp rope, knotted and fashioned into a hanging noose.

"Get on up those stairs, McLeod," ordered Sidewinder. "Get up there and take your punishment for murdering that poor old widow woman."

Rusty glared at the outlaw. "You know that wasn't my fault. It was you I was aiming at."

Sidewinder grinned. "I know that. But *they* don't...and they're the ones who count."

As he was escorted up the wooden stairs to the gallows platform, Rusty looked out over the crowd who gathered around the structure, awaiting the execution to come. It looked as though every man, woman, and child in Carnage City had down up. Their faces were solemn, but their eyes belied the anticipation they felt. They were just as hungry for entertainment as they were for justice. The only spectators who seemed in a truly righteous state of mind were the Johnson children. The six orphans stood at the front of the crowd, dressed completely in black, their eyes burning with hatred. It was clear to see that they had come to see Rusty swing for shooting down their mother, rather than out of a need for thrills in a town that had precious little of it.

"I didn't do it!" he called out to them. "It was a mistake." The eldest of the Johnson brood—a boy of nine—spat in the dust and glowered at him.

"Go to hell, mister!" was all that he had to say.

Sidewinder winked at the kid. "Oh, he will, son. He most certainly will."

It was at that moment that Rusty knew that his time had run out. There would be no reprieve from the sentence he had received. A minute from now, he would be kicking in the breeze, the noose burrowed deeply into the flesh of his throat and his tongue protruding from his mouth, bloated and blue due to lack of oxygen.

He reached the platform. The rebel and the bandito accompanied him to the center of the gallows, while Sidewinder remained on the ground below. The outlaw stood at the head of the crowd, his arms folded over his chest, an expression of cruel satisfaction on his lean, whiskered face.

"I told you I'd kill you," he said, his voice carrying in the silence. "One way or another."

Helplessly, Rusty was led to the center of a trap door. The hangman—who turned out to be the cadaverous town mortician—grimly approached him.

"Do you have a last wish before this sentence is carried out?"

"Yeah," muttered Rusty, sweat trickling down his face. "Wake me up from this crazy dream, will you?"

The hangman ignored his request. He slipped the loop of the noose over Rusty's head, pulling the knot tight with a practiced tug. Then he walked over to the far side of the platform and laid his hand upon the lever that would open the trapdoor beneath Rusty's feet.

"God help me," Rusty whispered as the first rays of the sun burst over the horizon.

Below him, Sidewinder laughed. "You're praying to deaf ears, McLeod. God ain't in this dream of yours. Only me."

Rusty glanced over at the hangman. The undertaker's spidery hand clutched the lever's handle, ready to pull. Rusty closed his eyes and waited to feel the lurch of open air beneath his boots and the lethal snap of the noose closing tightly around his neck.

But that never happened. Just as he was sure that he was on the verge of dying, a rifle shot rang out. He heard the whine of a bullet pass over his head and, abruptly, the rope parted. Stunned, he opened his eyes and turned, looking eastward.

He couldn't believe his eyes. There standing only a few yards from the gallows, were four people. The one who had shot away the hangman's rope was none other than John Wayne, brandishing his trademark Winchester with its oversized lever ring. He couldn't tell for sure, but the two who stood to either side of the Duke looked like Roy Rogers and Clint Eastwood. And, believe it or not, the fourth was Rusty's mother.

"Mama!" he yelled out. "What are doing here?"

Susan McLeod stepped forward, levering a round into her Henry rifle. "I've come to save your hide, son," she said. "Looks like I got here just in the nick of time."

"I don't think so," said Sidewinder. He nodded to his cronies on the gallows platform.

The two took the signal and raised their guns. They were about to draw a bead on Rusty's chest, when gunshots rang out. The men howled as bullets pierced their hands, causing them to drop their weapons as if they were red hot. Rusty turned to see Roy on Stairway, holding a six-shooter in each hand. The singing cowboy blew the gunsmoke from his pistols, then with a fancy twirl, returned them to the holsters on his hips.

As Rusty followed the cowboy down the steps, he saw Sidewinder pushing his way back through the crowd, heading for the front of the Whipping Post Saloon. He intended to catch up to him, but when Rusty reached the street, he found Sidewinder's deputies waiting for him. The four grinned arrogantly, ready to draw their weapons and gun him down in cold blood.

"If you're looking for trouble, boys," rasped a chilling voice from behind them. "You've sure as hell found it."

The four turned to find themselves facing a single man; a tall, lean specter of death in a Mexican poncho. They eyed the bounty hunter warily, their hands still poised over their guns, unsure about how to react.

The bounty hunter tossed his cheroot away and flung his poncho over his shoulder, revealing the butt of his revolver. Steely eyes glared at them from the shadow beneath his hat. "Well, are you going to stand there whistling Dixie?" he asked softly. "Or are you going to draw?"

The four outlaws hesitated for a split second, then gathered their nerve and drew as one. But even then, they were much too slow. The revolver leapt into the bounty hunter's disgorging fire and deadly lead. An instant later, all four lay on the sun-baked earth, shot cleanly through their hearts.

The bounty hunter looked over to see Roy shaking his head in disapproval. "Sorry, cowboy," he said. "But you've got your ways and I've got mine." The lanky gunfighter tossed his gun to Rusty. "Here. There's two rounds left. You'd best settle the score with Sidewinder before he gets away."

"Thanks," said Rusty. He stared down at the gun with the rattlesnake carved on its handle and realized the irony of the symbol. Tightening his grip on the six-shooter, he walked crowd until he reached the open street.

Sidewinder was at the hitching post in front of the saloon, hurriedly attempting to untie the reigns of his black horse. The icy confidence he had shown before was now gone.

"Sidewinder!" Rusty called out. "Turn around."

The gunfighter froze, dropping the reigns from his hands.

"I said turn around and face me!" Rusty demanded. "And there will be no tricks this time. It'll just be you and me." He stuck the gun the bounty hunter loaned him into waistband of his britches.

Slowly, Sidewinder turned. His lean face was oddly pale in contrast to his dark clothing. He was scared; Rusty could tell. His hand even trembled as he slipped the thong off his revolver's hammer and splayed his fingers above the ivory handle.

Rusty smiled with cold satisfaction. "We draw on the count of three," he said.

"One..."

"Listen, Marshal –" Sidewinder stammered, his eyes bright with fear.

"Two..."

"Couldn't we just go in the saloon and have a drink?" suggested the outlaw.

"Discuss this?"

Rusty ignored him. He paused a second, then said "Three." Then he drew, aimed, and fired.

Sidewinder's hand flashed downward, but before he could even slap gun leather,

Rusty's gun boomed in the early morning air. The outlaw staggered backward, then glanced down at his chest. With relief, he discovered no blood there. He grinned and lowered his fingers toward his own gun. "You missed, McLeod."

Rusty shook his head. "No, I didn't."

Bewildered, Sidewinder suddenly felt something wet trickling down the bridge of his nose. He raised his hand to his face and stared at his fingers. The tips were coated with blood. Then, abruptly, darkness began to close in on him as his brain succumbed to the havoc Rusty's bullet had wreaked.

Rusty watched as the outlaw fell on his back in the middle of the dusty street. He walked up to him and stared at the bullet hole in the center of Sidewinder's forehead and the look of surprise and defeat that was forever etched onto the gunslinger's face.

He sensed someone behind him and turned to find his mother standing there. "Rusty, are you alright?" she asked.

The boy sighed and nodded. "I am now. How did you get here?"

"That doesn't matter," she said. "What does matter is... can you get us out of here? Can you take us back home again?"

"I think so," said Rusty. He turned and regarded the three Western heroes who stood nearby. "I'm obliged to you all."

The Duke nodded, canting his rifle over his shoulder. "You're welcome, pilgrim.

Now you'd best get on home. Trouble's brewing back yonder and you'll need to take care of it...before it's too late."

"What do you mean?" asked Rusty.

"You'll find out," said Roy. He smiled that famous smile of his. "Happy Trails...to both of you."

Rusty reached out and took his mother's hand. "Ready, Mama?"

Susan nodded. "Let's go."

Rusty concentrated, willing the dreamscape around him to fade. A moment later, it did just that. The gathering of townspeople, the frontier buildings, the three heroes...all vanished in a shimmering wave like that of a desert mirage, leaving only the blistering Arizona wilderness in their place. Then that too disappeared. The blazing western sun seemed to abruptly blink out, plunging them into cool, featureless darkness.

CHAPTER FORTY-FIVE

Bobo wrenched open the door of Maggie's trailer and stuck his head inside. "It's showtime!" he said, his eyes sparkling cruelly in his white face. He was dressed in his usual clown costume for that matinee, but there were no colors whatsoever to his makeup or clothing. They were just as drab and dark as those that Maggie wore; somber shades of black and gray, rather than the traditional rainbow hues of the circus.

The girl was about to protest and retreat further into her trailer, when the clown grabbed her by the wrist and yanked her through the open doorway.

"I'm not going to do it!" she said, dragging her feet, trying to slow him down.

Without warning, Bobo reached inside his baggy coat and withdrew a butcher knife.

"No objections this time!" he warned, holding the edge of the blade against her throat. "This time the show must go on! And, unfortunately for you, it shall be your final performance."

Maggie stopped her struggling, afraid that the honed edge of Bobo's blade would cut her if she continued to resist. A feeling of hopelessness filled her, dragging her spirit to rock bottom. There was no way she could escape what Colonel Raven had in store for her. She would have to go on with the show as scheduled, even though she knew it was pure suicide for her to do so.

A minute later, she was inside the Big Top, climbing the steel pole to the tightrope that awaited her far above the center ring. This time the distance between ground and platform was much greater than before; a scary 200 feet at the very least. By the time she reached the stand, her muscles quivered from the terror and exertion of the long climb. Totally exhausted, she sat on the floor of the platform, her knees pulled against her chest, listening as the distant voice of the ringmaster introduced her. The applause of thousands of bloodthirsty spectators drifted from down below. Breathlessly, the awaited the thrill of watching the high wire acrobat slip and plunge to her death.

"It's showtime, little lady," snapped a voice from behind. "Now get up off your lazy butt and get on that rope!"

Maggie turned to see Max standing behind her, holding the bullwhip in his hand. "I...I can't," she said, eyes pleading.

Max grinned, then lashed out with the whip. The tip cracked like a gunshot next to Maggie's head, loud enough to make her ears ring. "I said to get out there! Now!"

With her heart full of dread, Maggie stood up and walked to the very edge of the platform. When she looked over, a sensation of dizziness threatened to overcome her. But her fear of heights wasn't the strongest horror that she felt. For, positioned directly underneath the high wire, was a huge, circular cage with an open top. Even from where she stood, Maggie could see what eagerly waited for her to slip and fall. A dozen emaciated, half-starved lions and tigers paced restlessly around the floor of the cage. Every now and then they would look up at her, roaring and hungrily licking their chops.

A cheer rose to the roof of the Big Top when the audience spotted her standing at the edge of the platform, on the verge of stepping onto the tightrope. Maggie turned back toward the pole, but found the circus dwarf walking toward her, brandishing the whip.

"Get out there, you little tramp!" he said. "Walk that damn rope before I slice you to bloody ribbons!" He cocked his stubby arm, ready to unfurl the whip and drive her onto the rope...and toward her death.

But before he could act, the expression on his face changed from menace to confusion. "What the hell—?" he muttered, staring at her. Or, rather, into the open space just above her left shoulder.

Puzzled, Maggie turned and peered into the gloom. Suddenly, from out of the darkness, she spotted someone swinging her way on one of the suspended bars of the trapeze. At first, she thought it was someone else coming to terrorize her, perhaps the fiendish clown named Bobo. But instead, it turned out to be someone who was rushing to her rescue. Someone she knew very well, but would have never associated with such a display of compassion and bravado.

"Tom?" she cried out, her eyes growing wide in disbelief.

A second later, her teenage brother released the trapeze bar and landed unsteadily on the platform, looking a little shaken. "Maggie!" he said, nearly out of breath. "Thank God! Are you alright?'

"Uh, yeah, I guess so," she said, stunned. "But what are you doing here?"

"What does it look like, knucklehead?" he said, rolling his eyes. "I've come to rescue you."

"We'll see about that," laughed Max. He cracked his whip threateningly. "Now the Colonel's got two tightrope walkers. The crowd's gonna love this! They're gonna get two for the price of one!"

"I think not!" challenged a voice from behind him.

Before Max could react, General Tom Thumb had grabbed him from behind in a headlock. The circus dwarf attempted to break free, but Thumb was much too strong and tenacious for him.

"Let go of me, you freak!" huffed Max, growing red in the face.

"Those felines look practically famished," Thumb said. "Why don't you go down and feed them?" And, with that, he ran toward the edge of the platform at full speed, taking the struggling Max with him. Thumb stopped and released his hold on the little roustabout, flinging him bodily from the stand and into the open air. Max shrieked and attempted to grab hold of the rope, but his fingers missed by only a fraction of an inch. Screaming all the way, Raven's crony plunged downward, toward the heart of the cage.

He hit solid earth with a dull thud a few seconds later then was immediately pounced upon by the pack of ravenous beasts.

"Quickly!" the famous dwarf called to sister and brother. "Down the pole!"

Maggie and Tom did as they were told. A minute later, they were back on solid ground once again.

"What now?" asked the girl.

Tom looked around frantically, as if looking for someone. "I'm not sure," he said.

"You've ruined my show for the very last time, girl!" snarled a voice full of venom and contempt.

Suddenly, from out of the darkness, emerged the lean form of Circus Horrific's sinister ringmaster, Colonel Raven. With him was Bobo the Clown, clutching the butcher knife threateningly in his gloved hand.

"I will not be disobeyed!" Raven told her. He reached out and grabbed the 12-year-old roughly by the hair of the head. "Now I shall accompany you back up to the wire and you shall complete your performance. And, in turn, you shall give the crowd that which they crave!"

"Let go of me!" shrilled Maggie. She attempted to break free, but the more she struggled, the tighter his fingers seemed to entwine her long blond hair.

Tom stepped forward, his face full of anger. "Turn her loose, you bastard!"

Before he could come to his sister's aid, however, the homicidal clown interceded. He blocked Tom's path, tossing the big knife teasingly from one hand to the other. "Back off, buster," he said, laughing. "Or I'll take your head clean off at the shoulders!"

Raven was about to drag Maggie toward the ladder that led upward, when a great trumpeting sound filled the air. They turned just as one of the black tent's canvas walls ripped open and a gigantic elephant burst through, bringing the light of day with it. High upon its back rode P.T. Barnum and Emmett Kelly.

An army of sideshow freaks converged on the rampaging pachyderm, as if intending to intercept it. But their attempt was futile. Jumbo raged onward, flinging some of its attackers aside, while trampling others mercilessly underfoot.

Bobo laughed crazily and started toward the elephant himself, ready to plunge his knife into the gray beast. But before he even drew near, Weary Willie jumped down and confronted him. He raised a huge seltzer bottle and skillfully sent a well-aimed spritz straight for the maniacal clown's face. The contents of the bottle was not water, however. Sulfuric acid drenched the killer clown's broad face, causing him to shriek in agony. Bobo dropped his knife, then fell to his knees and clamped his hands over his dissolving face.

Suddenly, Colonel Raven found himself surrounded on all sides. The cruel arrogance that he had exhibited earlier was gone. In its place were fear and panic. He tried to make a break for it, but Jumbo was too quick for him. The elephant's trunk whipped out and wrapped around Raven's slender waist, snatching the evil circus owner completely off his feet.

"What shall we do with him, Miss Sutton?" asked Barnum, riding high atop the pachyderm's back. "It's your call." The Fiji Mermaid perched like some hideous pet on his left shoulder, chattering excitedly and flapping its fish-like tail.

Maggie thought about it for a second. Considering all the terror Raven had subjected her to, she knew there was only one fitting fate for the sinister ringmaster. She ran over to the iron cage in the center of the circus ring and opened the door. "Throw him in!" she said.

"No!" screamed Raven, his face blanched with horror. "Have mercy!"

"Did you show me any when you forced me to walk that high wire?" she asked coldly.

Maggie turned her eyes back to Barnum. "Do it."

Colonel Raven shrieked as Jumbo flung him bodily through the open doorway. As Maggie slammed the door shut, Raven landed in the center of the cage with a thud.

Stunned, he sat up and looked around. The leering faces of a dozen lions and tigers glared at him, their muzzles dripping red with the blood of Max the Dwarf.

As the big cats leapt at the screaming man, Maggie turned away. "I'm ready to get out of here, Tom," she said wearily.

Tom placed a hand on her shoulder. "Can you do it?" he asked. He was as eager to be away from the dreamscape as his sister was.

"Yeah," she said. "I think so."

"A word of warning before you go, young lady," P.T. Barnum told her. "The scoundrel who sent you here has evil plans for your hometown tonight. And he will succeed in bringing them about...if you and your friends don't confront him."

"Do you mean Augustus Leech?" she asked.

Kelly mugged his famous frown and nodded sadly.

Tom Thumb swaggered over and kissed Maggie's hand gallantly. "Take care, my dear."

"I will," she said. She looked up at her brother and extended her hand toward him. "Are you ready?"

Tom smiled, took her hand, and squeezed it gently. "Ready when you are, sis."

Maggie looked around at the gathering of friendly circus folk. "Thanks for everything."

"It was our devout pleasure, Miss Sutton," said Barnum, tipping his hat.

The girl tightened her grip on her brother's hand, then concentrated. The vast audience vanished, followed by Barnum and his cohorts. For a second, Maggie and Tom stood alone in the middle of the deserted Big Top. Then it too vanished, plunging them into pitch darkness.

The sound of jackboots crossing the concrete floor drew Chuck's attention.

The other prisoners had been escorted from the drafty barracks over an hour ago, assigned the grisly task of digging mass graves for those who had died, but had not been incinerated in the Fuhrer's hellish crematorium. Chuck had been left behind, unable to join them in their degrading assignment.

He suddenly found himself looking up from his lower bunk into the grinning face of the Fuhrer. The dictator was accompanied by two German soldiers holding Schmeisser submachine guns.

"We have come for you, Herr Adkins," said the Fuhrer. The lean man stood ramrod straight, his hat cocked jauntily upon his head and his woolen coat draped foppishly across his narrow shoulders. "You are worse than those vile Jews," he said. "You have lost the power of your legs and are of no use to me as a laborer. You are a cripple. Utterly useless. Therefore, you shall be terminated immediately."

"What do you mean '*terminated*'?" asked Chuck. But deep down inside, he knew exactly what the evil leader was talking about.

"Take him to the crematorium!" the Fuhrer ordered. "And do not bother gassing him first. I want him to die in agony. I want him to feel the heat of the flames as they char the very flesh from his bones."

Chuck struggled as the soldiers lunged forward and took him by the arms. Soon, they had carried him from the barracks and were dragging him across the muddy yard of the compound, toward the solemn gray structure of the crematorium. As they grew closer, an ash from the billowing smokestacks drifted earthward and lodged in one of Chuck's eyes, causing it to sting. In horror, he realized that it was probably all that was left of some unfortunate soul.

The soldiers ignored the long line of prisoners who awaited their turn in the toxic showers and carried Chuck straight through the heavy steel doors of the crematorium. The moment they entered the long room with its row of ovens built into sturdy cinderblock walls, Chuck was stunned by two things. One was the oppressive heat of the crematorium, which was in constant use, 24 hours a day. The other was the smell; the horrible stench of burnt flesh. Chuck knew at once that this was what Hell must be like.

The Fuhrer marched over to an oven whose door stood wide open. The sliding steel table that was used to deposit the bodies into the fire that awaited him, barren, except for a coating of fine gray ash. "Secure him to the table!" he commanded. The dictator with the vertical mustache and the insane eyes grinned at Chuck. "You invaded the Fatherland to stop me, Adkins. You came to liberate the Jews and Gypsies from their rightful destiny. Well, you have failed! Instead, you shall suffer the same fate as they have. But alive, rather than dead!"

Chuck was forced to the warm surface of the gurney. Iron clamps were fastened around his wrists and ankles, making escape impossibility. "You can't do this!" he protested.

The Fuhrer laughed. "Oh, but I can," he said smugly. "In fact, I have done it many times before. Millions upon millions of times."

The evil dictator was on the verge of cranking the rotary handle that would send Chuck headfirst through the oven door and into the blazing flames of the crematorium, when a tremendous explosion rocked the building. All heads turned toward the entranceway. A huge tank crashed through the concrete wall; an olive drab tank with a United States flag flying from its radio antenna.

After the tank had made its grand entrance, a man on horseback followed, leaping through the jagged hole in the wall. The rider—a bearded man in a Confederate uniform —sent his mount galloping forward. He drew a .44 revolver and fired, taking down one of the storm troopers. Chuck recognized him from a book on the Civil War he had read recently. It was none other than Robert E. Lee.

Two forms emerged from the tank. One was a World War II infantry soldier holding an M-1 carbine. The other one was a complete surprise. It was Chuck's father, of all people!

"Surrender, you godless kraut!" growled Sergeant Saunders.

"Never!" retorted the Fuhrer. The dictator nodded at the remaining soldier. "Gun them down."

The storm trooper turned and fired a long burst from his Schmeisser. Nine-millimeter slugs rattled off the armor plating of the Army tank, neglecting to reach the general. Saunders brought his .30 carbine into line and fired. A single bullet hit the German soldier squarely in the center of his gray tunic, knocking him off his feet and sending his machine gun spinning through the air.

Joe Adkins caught the Schmeisser and turned its smoking muzzle toward the Fuhrer.

But the dictator had beaten him to the draw. He held a Walther P38 in his gloved hand, its sights aimed squarely at Joe's chest. "You came in vain, Yankee bastard!" he said with a sinister grin.

But before he could fire, the Fuhrer felt the muzzle of an Enfield rifle pressing firmly against the back of his skull. "Drop that there pistol, mister," said Alvin York in his Tennessee drawl. "Or I'll put a bullet square in yer brain-pan and drop you like a turkey buzzard."

The Fuhrer's face turned as pale as lard. His fingers opened, dropping the Walther. The pistol hit the cement floor with a clatter, tumbling out of his reach.

Joe discarded the machine gun. He ran to his son and began to unfasten the brackets that held him down. "Are you okay, Chuck?" he asked as he freed the boy and lifted him into his arms.

Chuck stared into his father's face and saw heartfelt concern there, rather than detachment. "Yeah, thanks to you," he said.

The boy looked over to see General Lee approaching. "It's up to you, son," he said. "Do you want to take him prisoner...or give him what he really deserves?"

Chuck didn't have to think twice about it. "Clamp him to the table," he replied, his eyes full of contempt. "And give him a taste of his own medicine."

The Fuhrer shrieked as Saunders and York wrestled him onto the gurney and fastened his wrists and ankles firmly in place. Chuck watched him buck and struggle, his eyes wild with panic. Then the boy leaned down and worked the crank, sending the murderer of humanity into the fiery bowels of the crematorium. Soon, the Fuhrer was completely inside. He screamed long and loud as the flames engulfed him, first burning away his clothing, then his flesh. The door of the oven slammed shut, sealing away the crackling of fire and the shrill howls of intense agony.

"It's over, isn't it?" Chuck asked. He felt physically and emotionally drained.

"It is," agreed his father. "Are you ready to get the hell out of here?"

"You better believe it," said Chuck. He turned and awarded the three fighting men with a respectful salute. "Thanks for your help, guys."

"It was the least we could do, Sergeant," said Lee. "By the way, I have received word that trouble is brewing on the home front. Leech is up to no good. It's up to you and your comrades to put an end to his treachery, once and for all."

"We'll see what we can do," said Chuck. He reached up and wrapped his arms around his father's neck, then focused his mind, driving all thoughts of war away. Soon, the military men and the tank vanished, followed by the stark gray walls of Auschwitz's damnable crematorium. Darkness engulfed them and they soon felt themselves drifting weightlessly, as if in a gentle freefall.

The last thing to depart was that overpowering stench of burnt human flesh. Then, an instant later, it too was a thing of the past.

CHAPTER FORTY-SIX

Maggie opened her eyes.

She breathed a sigh of relief when she found herself not in the black canvas tent of Circus Horrific, but lying on the bed of her own room. The events of the past few hours began to fade from her mind, like the remnants of a bad dream dissipating with the dawning of a new day. She glanced over at her bedroom window and fond that it was dark outside. Had she only slept a few hours? Or had an entire day passed?

Maggie would have almost thought that the whole thing had been no more than a nightmare, except that she awoke holding someone's hand. The girl sat up and stared at the person next to her. Lying on the floor beside the bed was her brother Tom.

"Hey," she said, giving his hand a yank. "Wake up, will you?"

Tom opened his eyes and stared up at her. "Hi, squirt," he said with a yawn. Then he was jolted completely awake when he realized what had just taken place. "What happened? Did we make it back okay?"

Maggie smiled. "Yeah, thanks to you." She stared at him, puzzled. "So why did you do it?"

"Do what?"

"Why did you come after me?" she wanted to know.

"That's a stupid question," said the teenager, sitting up. "Why wouldn't I?"

"Well, you haven't always been overly fond of me, that's all."

Tom stared at her, feeling a pang of regret. "Well, that's changed." He sighed and squeezed his sister's hand. "When we found out that you guys were gone and went down into that hollow looking for the guy responsible, I kind of found out that you don't repulse me as much as I thought. To tell the truth, I kind of like having you around."

"Exactly what are you trying to say?"

The high school student rolled his eyes in exasperation. "That I *love* you, Maggie!

There, I said it. Are you satisfied?"

The girl smiled. She leaned over and kissed him on the forehead. "I sure am. And I love you, too, even if you have been a colossal asshole for the past few years."

Tom's face reddened in embarrassment. "I guess I deserved that."

"Anyway, thanks for coming to get me. I couldn't have gotten out of there without you."

"You bet," Tom said. He frowned and shook his head. "But a high wire walker? Couldn't you have chosen something a little closer to the ground, sis? And that skimpy little costume you were wearing! Wait till Mom and Dad hear about this."

"Aw, stick it in your ear!" laughed Maggie. She grabbed the pillow off her bed and bopped him upside the head with it. Soon, the siblings were rolling across the floor, giggling and joking. But deep down inside, both were thankful that they had escaped the dark realm of Circus Horrific alive.

Rusty woke up so suddenly, he nearly leapt right off his bed. "Mom?" he called out.

"I'm right here, son," said Susan McLeod from where she sat on the edge of his bed.

The lanky farm boy stared at her, startled. "It wasn't just a nightmare, was it?"

"The hanging gallows in Carnage City?" She shuddered. "No, it was for real, that's for sure."

Rusty took a couple of deep breaths to calm himself. "I'd likely still be back there, swinging on the end of that rope with the buzzards picking at my carcass...if you hadn't showed up out of nowhere. But how did you do it?"

Susan reached beneath Rusty's pillow and withdrew the card with the Western scene on its front. "I used the card...the same as you. Son, you shouldn't have played around with the unknown like that. Do you realize how dangerous that was?"

"Don't I know it!" said Rusty. "And, believe me, I've learned my lesson."

"What if something bad had happened?" she asked. "What if you'd stayed there for good?" Tears formed in the woman's eyes. "I don't think I could have stood it if something like that would've happened to you, sweetheart."

Rusty leaned over and hugged his mother tightly. "What did I ever do to deserve a mom like you?" he asked, his voice cracking. "I love you, Mama."

"I love you, too, baby," she said. "But it's not over yet. Remember what the Duke said back there at Carnage City?"

Rusty nodded. "Yeah, I know. About Leech."

His relief at making it home with body and mind intact suddenly turned into cold dread. They were back where they belonged, that was true. But they hadn't left the evil entirely behind. They still had to deal with its source, before it was all over and done with.

"Chuck?" called a man's voice. "Chuck...wake up."

Chuck Adkins opened his eyes and found himself cradled in the arms of his father. "Dad? What happened?"

"Don't you remember?" Joe asked him.

The boy thought for a moment. Suddenly, his face grew pale. "The crematorium!"

"That's right."

In spite of himself, Chuck began to tremble. "I almost didn't make it out of that place alive."

Joe nodded, his face grim. "Yeah, and I almost didn't get there in time to save you." He was silent for a moment. "I almost let you down...like before."

Chuck turned and stared at his father's tormented face. "Dad...about what happened at Willow Lake—"

"Let's don't talk about it," said Joe, turning his eyes guiltily away from the boy.

"No," insisted Chuck. "Let's *do* talk about it. Dad, it was just a stupid accident. It wasn't your fault. It wasn't anybody's fault. You've got to believe that."

"I don't know if I'll ever be able to do that, son," said the mechanic.

"You've got to!" snapped Chuck. "Listen to me. I *don't* blame you. I never have. All I've ever wanted was you to be there for me. But you shut yourself off instead." Frightened tears showed in the boys eyes. "Please, Dad...don't ever do that again."

Joe Adkins embraced his son tightly. "I won't, Chuck. I swear to God I won't."

"Dad...I..." Chuck faltered, searching for the right words. "Aw, hell, Dad...I love you."

"I love you, too, son. And don't ever forget that."

Chuck nodded, feeling at peace for the first time in two long years. Then the serenity faded when he recalled what General Lee had told him. "Dad, we still have to do something about *him*, don't we?"

"Yes, we do," said Joe. "But at least you won't have to face him alone. I'll be there, right by your side."

His father's words drove away some of Chuck's fear. "I know that, Dad. I wasn't so sure before...but I am now."

Keith Bishop opened his eyes to find his grandfather lying on the bed next to him. The old man looked alarmingly pale and incredibly old, far beyond his 75 years. A horrible thought immediately came to him. *What if the trip back was too much for him?* he wondered. *What if he had a heart attack or something?*

Frightened, the boy sat up and shook the elderly man gently. "Grandpa? Are you okay? Oh God, Grandpa, if something's happened to you—!"

Jasper McLeod opened one of his eyes and stared up at his grandson. "Don't get so bent out of shape, Keith. I'm a tougher bird than you give me credit for."

Keith closed his eyes in relief. "Thank goodness! I thought you'd crapped out on me!"

"Fat chance," said Jasper, sitting up. "I bailed you out of that trouble with the Big Man, remember? I'm not about to buy the farm now that we're back home again."

"But how did you know where I was? Or how to get to me?"

"Leech told me," said Jasper. "When you and your friends turned up missing, we went to see him down in Hell Hollow. He warned us it would be dangerous to go after you, even deadly. But I knew I couldn't abandon you. I knew I had to find you, even if it was the last thing I ever did."

Keith stared at the old man. "Grandpa, I want to apologize. You know, for being such a pain in butt since I got here."

"Don't sweat it," Jasper told him. "I knew you were a good apple all along. That rotten attitude of yours, well, that didn't make me stop loving you, you know."

The boy seemed surprised. "You *love* me?"

"Why, of course I do," said Jasper. "And, I reckon in your own way, you feel the same for this broken down old fossil."

Keith reached out and hugged his grandfather. "I do, Grandpa. You better believe I do."

The two embraced for a long moment, not awkwardly, but with the comfort of close loved ones. When they finally parted, they locked eyes and realized that the ordeal was not yet over.

"We've still got Leech to deal with, don't we?" asked Jasper.

"Yes," replied Keith. He thought to himself for a second. "Grandpa, what do you know about this guy? Anything that might help figure out exactly what he's up to?"

For the next few minutes, Jasper told his grandson everything he knew about Doctor Augustus Leech; the poisonous elixir he had sold to the folks of Harmony nearly a century ago, the vigilante mob that had chased him into the dark heart of Hell Hollow, and the eventual killing of the sinister medicine show man at the hands of his own father.

When he was through, a peculiar look came into the 12-year-old's eyes. "I think I know what he has in mind, Grandpa. God help us...I think know exactly what he's going to do."

At that moment, the hall phone began to ring. "That must be one of the others. I hope they all made it back okay." Jasper left the bed and started for the door. Halfway there, he stopped and turned back to his grandson. "Exactly what does that bastard have in store for Harmony?" he asked.

"You'd better answer the phone," said Keith. "And, whoever it is, tell them to meet up in town as soon as possible. It's a matter of life and death. And I'm not joking."

"I can see that," said Jasper as he left the bedroom and headed down the hallway to the phone.

Keith sat alone on his bed and considered the menace they would be forced to face that night. During their visit to Hell Hollow, he had sensed that Augustus

Leech was not the congenial magician that his friends thought him to be. He had sensed someone much darker and dangerous...and his instincts had proven to be right. They had fallen for one of Leech's perilous parlor tricks—the magical dream cards—and nearly perished because of his deception.

But, fortunately, they had all escaped unscathed. And that meant that they were left with the responsibility of preventing Doctor Leech from completing the task he had originally had in store for Harmony 90 long years ago.

Keith just hoped that they could reach him before he had the chance to implement the horrors he intended to inflict upon the little Tennessee town. And, if they did, he prayed that they would survive the confrontation, just as they had survived the awful nightmares that Leech had nearly succeeded in condemning them to...indefinitely.

CHAPTER FORTY-SEVEN

Augustus Leech reined the wagon team to a halt. For a moment, he sat in the darkness of the roadway, anticipating the evil that was yet to come. A warm summer breeze blew through his long black hair like the breath of a sleeping dragon.

He had waited a long time for this moment. Following the incident at Hell Hollow, Leech had bided his time patiently, enduring decades of nonexistence...waiting for someone to come along and release him from his refuge. That had happened a scant week ago when the Georgia criminal had drank from the elixir bottle and unknowingly taken on a sinister calling he could never have imagined, even in his warped and sadistic imagination.

The courthouse clock a hundred yards away struck the hour of 11. Almost immediately a cloudbank drifted eastward, exposing a full moon. Nocturnal light bathed the western limits of Harmony, gleaming off the twin rails of the train tracks, as well as the painted metal of the structure next to them. The lean man in the dark coat and top hat leaned forward on the wagon seat and stared upward. The instrument of his imminent vengeance stood starkly against the night sky, resembling an immense granddaddy longlegs of sea green steel.

Leech rocked gleefully to and fro, laughing softly to himself. His long wait was over.

It was finally time.

He snapped the reigns, driving the two black horses off the roadside, over a low drainage ditch, and into the grass expanse of a nearby pasture. Again, he reined the wagon to a halt, this time engaging the brake. The ebony roans stood patiently, aware of their master's intentions. They craned their heads upward and stared silently at the tall structure of the rural community's one and only source of water; the reservoir tower that loomed directly across the railroad tracks from the Harmony town square.

Leech took the five-gallon gas can in hand, then jumped down from the wagon and crossed the moonlit grass of the pasture, moving [stealthfully] toward the concrete base of the water tower. He ignored the network of steel pipes and spigots that were linked to the main line, which ran vertically from the vast sphere of the reservoir. Instead, he headed directly for the access ladder that was attached to one of the tower's four support poles. He stood at the bottom for a long moment, gauging the distance between the ground and the uppermost crown of the reservoir. It had to be a good 75 feet at the very least.

He pulled his belt from the loops of his jeans and quickly set to work. Leech looped the length of leather through the gas can's handle, then buckled it securely. After slipping the makeshift sling over his shoulder, he stared upward at his objective one last time, then, taking one rung after another, began the long climb upward. The can of black death hung like an iron weight at his side, but he failed to acknowledge its heaviness. All that concerned him was to accomplish what he had come to do that night; to pay the unsuspecting town of Harmony back for what they had done to him 90 years ago.

And, in the process, net his dark savior a hefty share of souls for his hellish dominion.

Halfway up, Augustus Leech felt his anticipation flag for a moment. He had experienced it four times before, several hours prior to his arrival in town; a disturbing sensation of impending disaster. He couldn't understand why he should feel such a way. After all, there was nothing whatsoever to stand in his way that night. The children who had nearly hampered his plans had been taken care of and, as of that morning, their retched loved ones were out of the picture as well. All had undoubtedly perished in the nightmare worlds of their own making by now. The mirror-image spawn of Leech's own evil would have seen to that. But, even still, he found it difficult to shake that annoying feeling of dark dread. It seemed to cling to him, following him up the tower ladder like a tenacious shadow that refused to be left behind.

The sensation passed once he reached the platform that encircled the reservoir's tank. Leech stood at the railing and caught his breath, staring down at the scattered buildings of Harmony as he did. The little town was already dark and deserted. The last shop on its main thoroughfare had closed at 9:00 that evening. The only movement he could detect from that height was the slow winking of the town's one and only traffic light, where the main street forked and made a lazy loop around the acre square of the courthouse lawn. It's center caution light blinked on and off, casting an amber glow across the cracked pavement and the whitewashed structure of the old-fashioned gazebo nearby.

"Fools!" he said with a snicker. "You slumber peacefully in your soft beds, unaware that Death has come to call. Some of you shall succumb with the dawn, bathed by showers of dark poison. Others may even rise in the middle of the night for a drink of water and, through that innocent act, fail to awaken in the morning. But you will have deserved it for delaying my mission for so very long. All of you shall pay for the sins of your wretched fathers...with your lives. And with your souls."

Leech grinned to himself, then adjusted the weight of the gas can and continued onward, scaling the steel ladder that curved vertically along the sphere of the water tank. A moment later, he reached the very top of the reservoir.

Carefully, he stood, gaining his balance. Then, slowly, he crept across the roof of the tank, toward the only portal that gave access to the pure waters that sustained the citizens of Harmony on a daily basis. Leech crouched over the steel door, his heart pounding wildly in his chest. The moment he had anticipated for so very long was finally at hand.

Using the work-toughened muscles of his host, Leech set to work. He gripped the wheel lock in both hands and slowly turned it counter-clockwise. It wasn't long before he had the hatch open. He swung it back on its thick steel hinges and peered inside. Darkness filled the reservoir's cavity. Underneath that deceptive gloom, he could hear a gentle lapping against steel walls and smell the dank odor of water rising up from below.

Augustus Leech unshouldered the gas can and unscrewed the top. Within, a dark liquid of an entirely different kind shimmered sluggishly, smelling both of heavenly delicacies and hellish poisons. He stood up, holding the open container in both hands, ready to dump its contents through the access door. But first, he stared up into the sky. Only the stars and pale face of the moon stared back, the sole witness of the mass execution to come.

Or so he thought.

Before he could tip the gas can forward, he heard a metallic clang and felt a thrumming vibration shudder throughout the steel shell of the tank. A second later, another sounded, this time much closer. Something bounced over the edge of the sloping roof and rolled toward him, finally rattling to a stop. Leech looked down to see a rock the size of a golf ball lying next to his feet.

And, suddenly, he understood the meaning of the dreadful sensation he had experienced, both before and during his climb to the top of the tower.

"Try another one," urged Chuck. He sat in his wheelchair, his eyes glued to the dark form that stood atop the water tower, silhouetted against the pale backdrop of the full moon.

Keith reached down and picked up another good-sized rock from the gravel bed of the railroad tracks. He reared back and let go, sending the missile hurtling skyward. It fell short, bouncing off the railing of the lower platform, instead of reaching the very top of the water tower.

"Dammit!" he said. "I can't seem to reach him." He looked over at Rusty. "You give it a try."

The lanky farm boy nodded. He picked up a stone the size of a tennis ball, wound up with an over the shoulder pitch, and heaved the rock upward. They all watched as the projectile arched over the dome of the tank and struck the man in the stovepipe hat squarely between the shoulder blades.

"You got him!" cheered Maggie, jumping up and down.

"Yeah," said Jasper, standing nearby. "But I think you only made him mad."

High above, Augustus Leech whirled and glared down at them. "You meddling worms!" he yelled. He seemed surprised, even shocked, to see the four children and those who accompanied them on the ground below. "What are you doing here?"

"We survived your dadblamed trap, that's what!" Rusty hollered back at him. "That's what you get for underestimating us and our folks."

"We're here to stop you," Maggie called out. "Stop you from spreading your evil any further than it's already gone!"

Leech threw his head back and cackled. The wicked laughter rang across the community of Harmony, more threatening than the rumble of a thunderstorm, more dangerous than the freight train roar of an approaching tornado. "I believe not!" he told them. "I have been waiting far too long for this moment. And I shall not allow it to be taken away by a handful of troublesome children!"

With a wicked leer on his gaunt face, Leech stood tall and lifted his right hand overhead, the fingers curled like the legs of a deadly spider.

"Uh oh," said Tom Sutton. "I don't like this. He really looks pissed off."

Joe Adkins turned to Jasper. "I told you I should've brought my rifle. Then I might've had a chance of picking him off."

"No guns," said the elderly farmer firmly. "I'm not about to make the same mistake my father did." But even then, Jasper wasn't sure if the mechanic was entirely wrong. Perhaps they should have relied on more powerful ammunition than harsh words and a handful of rocks.

Augustus Leech's laughter rose in volume, ringing in their ears as though he stood only a few feet away, rather than 80 feet above. "My earlier attempt at disposing of you may have failed, but this time I shall succeed." Static electricity crackled between his slender fingers, turning his hand into a ball of raw energy. "If you must pray to your precious God, do it now," he said contemptuously. "For, soon, you shall all suffer the wrath and torment of Hell itself!"

The ones on the ground below suddenly felt a wave of dread run through them. Perhaps they had taken on more than they had bargained for. Horrible images of an earthbound unleashed upon them crossed their minds. The searing flames of hellfire, as well as everlasting agony and terror.

They watched, mortified, as Leech's entire body took on an eerie blue glow. Slowly, he lowered his sparkling hand toward them. "I think we just screwed up...big time," moaned Tom, beginning to back away.

"What are we going to do?" Susan asked frantically.

As they retreated, they suddenly realized that one out of the group stood perfectly still, wearing an amused smile on his face. "Nothing," said Keith. "That's what we're going to do. Absolutely nothing."

"What do you mean?" asked Chuck.

Keith's smile grew broader. "Just wait and see."

Suddenly, a brilliant burst of light left Leech's fingertips and arched toward them. As it grew nearer, it turned fire red, flickering with chaotic flames. They heard the screams of the damned, as well as smelled the nauseating stench of brimstone and burning flesh.

Terrified, they watched it rush toward them. Then, unexpectedly, it lost momentum and dissipated. Light, heat and odor vanished, mingling with the night air, leaving only summer darkness and the singing of crickets in its wake.

"What the hell happened?" Joe asked.

Keith laughed. "Haven't you figured it out yet?"

The others shook their heads, still confused by Leech's failed attempt at retribution.

"He *can't* hurt us," the boy explained. "We've already defeated him...in our dreams. The Big Man, Sidewinder, Colonel Raven, and the Fuhrer...they were all a part of him. A part of the power he held over us. But he can't harm us now, because we destroyed those mirror images of him before we escaped and made it back home."

Keith looked toward the top of the water tower. Leech's face showed in the pale moonlight. His stunned expression told the boy that he was correct. Like it or not, the evil medicine peddler had completely lost his power over them.

"Look!" yelled Susan, pointing skyward. "He's heading back toward the hatch. He's going to do it! He's going to dump that stuff into the water!"

Rusty bent down and took a good-sized rock from the gravel bed. He handed the stone to Maggie Sutton. "You give it a try," he suggested. "We've fallen short, but maybe you can reach him."

Keith shook his head. "Aw, she couldn't possibly hit him," he said. "She's just a girl!"

"That's right," replied Chuck. "But she's also the best hardball pitcher in Hawkshaw County." He looked over at the blonde. "Go on, Maggie. Give it your best shot."

Maggie hefted the stone in her right hand, gauging the distance between her and the man atop the water tower. His skeletal silhouette was creeping toward the open hatch of the reservoir, lifting the gas can as he went. She took a deep breath and closed her eyes.

"Please God," she whispered. Then she opened her eyes, cocked her arm back, and, with a flash of speed that made Keith's head swim, hurled the rock skyward.

Augustus Leech cursed beneath his breath as he stood over the gaping portal of the water tank, on the verge of dumping the gas can's contents into the well below. He didn't know how those little bastards had done it, but they had rendered him powerless against them. That would not stop him from exacting his revenge on Harmony, however.

He was tipping the can forward, when he heard a whistling sound split the warm night air. He turned his head just as rock shot out of nowhere. The stone struck him in the right temple, sending a burst of pain through his skull. He lost his hold on the five-gallon can as he staggered backward, toward the far side of the reservoir. It bounced once on the steel plating, then tumbled over the side of the tank, spilling its syrupy elixir as it went.

"No!" screamed Leech. He attempted to regain his balance, but the blow to the head had disoriented him. He felt the soles of his work boots lose their grip as he reached the gradual slope of the tank. He grappled blindly for something to break his fall, but there was nothing there. A second later, he was tumbling into open space. On the way down, his fingertips brushed the edge of the platform railing, falling short of grabbing hold. A shriek of terror pierced the night air as he plunged to the ground below.

He struck the earth hard and fast, landing squarely on his feet. The impact was devastating. He screamed in agony as ever bone in his legs, from hip to ankle, was shattered. Leech collapsed and lay still, overcome by searing waves of horrible pain. But through his torment, he knew that he could not remain there, at the mercy of those who had thwarted his scheme.

Summoning all the strength he could muster, Leech began to crawl away from the base of the water tower, toward the medicine show wagon and its dark team.

"You did it, sis!" said Tom. "You knocked his ass clean off that tower!"

"Where is he?" she asked nervously.

"He landed on the other side," said Rusty. "Let's go."

They left the railroad tracks and were starting around the concrete base of the water tower, when the brittle crack of a whip and the drumming of horse hooves cut through the night. They scrambled to the side, just as the black roans galloped past, pulling the garishly-painted wagon behind it. They caught a quick glimpse of Augustus Leech sitting unsteadily on the seat, his face deathly pale and his legs cocked at weird angles before him. Through the material of his jeans, they could see jagged shards of bone jutting through, as well as bloody gobs of displaced muscle and flesh.

"Where is he going?" asked Rusty.

"Where do you think?" replied Keith. "The only place that's provided him refuge for the past ninety years. The only place he truly feels safe."

"You mean—?" began Chuck.

"That's right," said the boy from Atlanta. "Hell Hollow."

CHAPTER FORTY-EIGHT

Frantically, Augustus Leech drove the team down the moonlit stretch of Sycamore Road. He groaned as the wagon wheels hit each bump and pothole, but fought against the agony that dominated his mangled legs. Instead, he used the pain to sharpen his senses and prevent himself from blacking out.

His emotions were a mixed bag; rage at having been denied his retribution and fear of being hunted down and caught. He heard the roar of engines approaching from behind him, gaining, closing the distance in between. Leech cracked the whip again and cursed at the two horses that surged forward, carrying the wagon past lonely farms, toward the dark wilderness of the South Woods. They responded obediently, pushing themselves even harder than before.

As the rural hamlet of Harmony was left behind, Leech felt another emotion overtake him. Despair. He thought of how close he had been; how he had been on the verge of pouring the poisonous elixir into the water supply. But four meddling children and one well-placed stone had obliterated his carefully-crafted plans in a split second. He was more determined than ever to complete his act of vengeance, but not now. Not with his legs broken to bits and his life's blood coursing through the gaping wounds. No, his hatred would have to be patient. Leech knew he must retreat as he had before and await a more opportune chance at exacting his revenge on the citizens of Harmony.

With difficulty, he leaned to the side and peered around the corner of the wagon's cabin. Two vehicles were drawing near, their headlights glaring brightly, illuminating the asphalt road and the dense foliage that bordered it on both sides. Jasper McLeod's pickup truck and Joe Adkins' van dogged the wagon like two redbone hounds on the trail of an elusive coon. Leech glared at them, then turned and cracked the whip again, drawing blood from the hindquarters of the two roans. The animals galloped wildly, their breaths blowing noisily through their flared nostrils, their ebony hides slick with the lather of exertion.

The wagon suddenly lurched as the pavement of Sycamore Road gave way to a trail of dirt ruts and high weeds. Despite his pain, Augustus Leech smiled to himself. He was almost there. Soon, he would be back in the dark cradle of Hell Hollow, where he had hidden safely for nearly a century. There he would like in a state of limbo like before, waiting. Waiting until an opportunity to arise presented itself once again.

As the dirt road grew less defined and the wooded basin of the hollow loomed ahead, Augustus Leech uttered a silent prayer to his dark master, discarded the whip, then reached into his coat. He withdrew the skinny glass bottle from an inner pocket and held it in his pale hand, ready to put it to use when the crucial moment arrived.

Then, as the team of horses surged toward the edge of the embankment that dropped sharply into Hell Hollow, Leech spotted something in the darkness ahead. A pale form stood etched in the sparse moonlight that filtered through the heavy canopy of interlocking tree branches. At first he could not identify it. Then, the closer he came, the more distinct the features of the mysterious figure became.

It was the form of a woman.

Allison Walsh stood on the edge of the embankment, exhausted and dirty.

After she had left the interstate early that morning, her search had gotten sidetracked. The encroaching forest and its confusing chain of hills and hollows had soon disoriented her, causing her to lose her bearings. She had wandered for hours, hoping to come upon some sign of civilization at any moment. But, instead, she had encountered only more wilderness.

Out of breath from her climb up the steep bank, Allison suddenly heard something in the unnatural silence that permeated the Tennessee woods. It sounded like the drumming of horse hooves and the creak and chatter of an old wagon.

Frightened, she peered into the darkness ahead of her. Seemingly out of nowhere, two black horses drawing a painted wagon emerged, etched in silvery shades of moonlight. At first, she was certain that she was imagining things; that a day of aimless walking without food or water had caused her exhausted mind to play tricks on her. But as the apparition grew nearer, the more convinced she became that it was, indeed, for real.

Allison stood frozen to the spot, afraid to move. She shifted her eyes from the team of horses to the one who sat high on the wagon seat. It was a tall, thin man dressed in dark clothing and wearing what looked to be a top hat. Then, abruptly, a slice of moonlight illuminated the driver's gaunt features.

She felt her heart skip a beat. Allison would know that face anywhere.

It was *him*! It was Slash Jackson.

Allison expected to feel terror in the presence of the one she hated most in the world. But instead she felt a cold calm possess her. For an instant, all the misery and pain the sadistic rapist had inflicted upon her came rushing back, reminding her of what had taken place in the abandoned house. Since leaving the hospital in Rome, Allison had wondered exactly how she would react when she finally located the man who had brutally tortured and abused her.

Now she knew.

As he rushed toward the northern slope of Hell Hollow, Augustus Leech leaned forward on the wagon seat and peered through the gloom at the woman who stood a hundred feet ahead. He watched as she squared her shoulders, then reached up with both hands and wrenched her blouse open, popping the buttons from the garment. Her pale flesh showed in the moonlight, as well as something else. He had to focus through the pain of his shattered legs to read the single word that had been deeply carved in the skin between her collarbones and the mounds of her breasts.

BITCH.

The word conjured a memory buried in Leech's subconscious. A second later, the part of him that had nearly been obliterated by the evil of the sinister medicine peddler—the fading essence of the redneck Georgia criminal named Slash Jackson—emerged, if only for an instant. He shifted his gaze from the ugly scars on the woman's chest, to her face. As forty feet of distance lay between her and the wagon, Leech recognized the one who confronted him.

"*You!*" he wailed, fresh terror skewering him like a white-hot lance.

He watched helplessly as the woman reached into the purse that hung from her shoulder, drawing something metallic from its folds. Slowly, she lifted the object in both hands and aimed it straight at him.

Leech's heart leapt in his chest. It was a gun.

Swiftly, he released the reigns of the team and grappled with the object in his right hand. He wrenched the cork free, then lifted the mouth of the elixir bottle to his lips, hoping that it would reach them in time.

Allison tightened her grip on the stolen revolver, aligning the sights with the gaunt, white mask of Jackson's face. Her finger caressed the curve of the trigger patiently, waiting for the right distance, the right moment.

When that moment arrived, she smiled coldly and pulled the trigger.

The gun bucked in her hands, filling her ears with a thunderclap boom. She watched as the man's head rocked backward just as he lifted something to his mouth. Then, abruptly, the horses wee upon her. Their hooves flashed and their eyes blazed with an unholy crimson light.

Allison dodged to the side as the crazed animals reached the lip of the hollow. She expected them to come to a halt and rear up in defiance, but they failed to even slow down. Both leapt into open space, pulling the wagon into the chasm with them.

She lowered her gun and watched as the wagon and its team shot into the darkness, trailing a cloud of dirt and shredded kudzu behind them. For a second, an eerie silence rang throughout the forest. Then, down below, came a distant, hollow crash.

Allison stood there, stunned by what had just transpired. She wasn't aware of the vehicles that braked to a stop behind her until she heard the slamming of doors. She turned to find several adults and children running toward her. She only recognized one. It was Jasper McLeod; the old man she had met at Hill's General Store.

"What are *you* doing here?" he asked, bewildered.

Tears seeped from her haunted eyes and rolled down her face. "I shot him," she said, her voice cracking with emotion. "I shot the evil bastard."

Jasper looked down at the revolver in her hand. Then his eyes rose to the ugly word that had been carved into her chest. "Well, I'll be damned," he said softly.

"Let's go down and take a look," suggested Keith, passing the two. Recklessly, he began to make his way down the steep wall of the embankment. Rusty and Maggie followed close behind.

"Watch out!" called Susan McLeod. "He might still be alive."

"I seriously doubt that," said Jasper. He walked up to Allison Walsh and gently pried the gun from her trembling fingers. She offered no resistance whatsoever.

Several minutes later, they were all trudging through the heavy undergrowth of the hollow, heading toward a dark mass of splintered wood and twisted metal that rested among the dark cedars. Jasper led the way, directing the beam of a flashlight before them. The others followed, the last of the group being Joe Adkins, who toted Chuck across his back.

When they reached the wreckage, they found that the two horses were dead, killed either by the impact of the fall or by sheer exhaustion. Jasper stepped up to the pile of fractured wheels and painted boards that had once been an ancient medicine show wagon and flashed the beam of his light upon the jagged tangle.

Lying amid the ruins was the body that had housed the vile soul of Augustus Leech. The pale, whiskered face of Slash Jackson stared at them with glassy eyes, an expression of intense terror forever set into his lean features. Allison's one and only shot had been true. There was a neat 38-caliber bullet hole in the center of his forehead, an inch below the hairline.

But it was what lay scattered around the twisted body that shocked them the most. Bones. A jawless skull, a disjointed spine, several ribs, and the jutting length of a femur. They all knew precisely what they were. They were the skeletal remains of the true Doctor Leech. The murderous showman who had perished similarly, many years ago.

Keith stepped forward and examined the dead man. It was an object fisted in his right hand that drew his interest the most. A narrow bottle with a yellowed paper label glued to the front. He turned his eyes to Jackson's other hand. Clutched between the stiffening fingertips was a plug of stained cork.

Curiously, the boy crouched down to take a closer look.

"You'd best step back, son," Jasper suggested. "I wouldn't get too close, if I were you."

"Yes sir," said Keith. He returned to his grandfather's side, feeling drained, but no longer afraid.

"Is it over?" asked Maggie, clinging to her big brother.

Keith closed his eyes and smiled. "Can't you tell?"

The others grew silent. Around them the chorus of a thousand crickets filled the summer darkness. And the air around them no longer held an unnatural chill. The night was muggy and warm, as it should be in mid-August.

It was at that moment that they all came to the same realization. The dark evil that had once reined the place known as Hell Hollow was no more.

EPILOGUE

"I'm gonna miss you," said Jasper, extending his hand.

Keith ignored his grandfather's gesture. He let the neon green backpack sag from his shoulder and smiled, then stepped in close and hugged the old man tightly.

"Yeah, me too," he said as he pulled away. The boy from Atlanta was tanned and healthy, and appeared to have grown an inch or two during the past month. "I had a great time...except for that crazy business down in the hollow, that is."

Jasper laughed. "I know what you mean." He smiled at his grandson. "Remember, next year you'll have to come and stay the whole summer. Agreed?"

"You bet," said Keith. "I wouldn't miss it for the world."

The twelve-year-old turned and reluctantly faced his friends. Rusty, Maggie and Chuck gathered around him near the security check-in at Nashville's Metro Airport. Rusty was the first to speak. "It's been fun, cuz," he said, offering his hand.

Keith shook it firmly. "I had a blast, Hiram. Oh, I almost forgot," he said, reaching into his backpack. "I want you to have this."

Rusty reached out and took the iPod. "Aw, come on! Are you sure?"

"I've got another one at home," Keith assured him. "You'll probably have to download some hillbilly tunes. The stuff I listen to is far too cool for your ears."

"Thanks a lot," said Rusty with a big grin. He clipped the player onto the belt of his best go-to-town blue jeans.

Keith turned to the chubby boy in the wheelchair. "Hey, Chuck, don't wear the wheels off that sidecar this fall, okay?" he said. "I aim for us to put it to good use next summer."

"We'll tear up Hawkshaw County on those bikes," Chuck promised, shaking the city boy's hand. "But we'll stay clear of the woods, if you don't mind."

"That sounds just fine to me," said Keith. And he meant every word of it.

"Keith?"

The boy turned to find Maggie staring sadly at him. "Hi," he said, feeling a lump surface in his throat.

"You mean 'bye', don't you?" she asked.

Keith tried to muster a smile, but found it difficult to do so. "Hey, it's only temporary, you know. I'll be back to visit at Christmas and again next summer. It's not like you're never going to see my ugly face again."

"I sure hope not," said the girl softly. She stared at Keith for a long moment, as if debating on whether to do something or not. A second later, she made up her mind. She quickly stretched up on her toes and kissed him on the left cheek.

Keith's face turned bright red, but he smiled. "Cool," was all he could manage to say.

"See?" commented Rusty. "I knew they had the hots for each other."

Chuck leaned over and popped the farm boy in the arm. "Aw, leave 'em alone, will you?"

After their goodbyes had been said, Jasper nodded toward the security area. "I reckon you'd best get in line. You know how picky they are with security these days. Might take awhile." He hesitated, then added, "Now, you be sure to give your old grandpa a call when you get home. Call collect if you want."

Keith rolled his eyes. "Are you kidding? My folks can afford it, remember?" He stared at the old man for a moment. "I love you, Grandpa."

Jasper smiled brightly. "I love you, too, Keith. Take care of yourself."

"I will if you will."

"It's a deal," laughed the farmer.

Keith waved to his friends, then turned and entered the line that lead through the airport security check-in.

Thirty minutes later, he was sitting alone in a window seat as other passengers began to board for the brief flight to Georgia.

Alone, Keith couldn't help but recall the frightening events that had taken place during his month-long stay in Harmony. Although none of them had said anything further about that deadly night in Hell Hollow, he found himself thinking of it often.

He glanced around to see if anyone was looking. Everyone was busy preparing for the flight. No one paid him any attention at all.

Keith hadn't yet placed his backpack in the overhead storage compartment. He now unbuckled the straps of the backpack and opened the flap. He had brought back two souvenirs from his stay in Harmony. Oddly enough, both had to do with the dark happenings that he and the others had unwillingly been caught up in.

The first was the oversized playing card. He held it between his fingers, studying the drawing of the police detective on the rain-soaked streets of an urban jungle. Keith thought of the Big Man and his brush with death on the waterfront pier. He shuddered at the memory and quickly stuck the card out of sight.

The other was a long, slender object in a plastic bag. Carefully, he opened the bag and removed the item.

He couldn't believe he had actually gotten it through security. He recalled his exchange with the man at the counter.

"I don't know about this, son," the fellow had said. "You're only allowed to take four ounces of liquid on the plane. This looks to be at least eight."

Keith had faked a convincingly phlegmy cough. "But it's just cough medicine. I really need the stuff."

The man had regarded the bottle suspiciously. He had removed it from the Ziploc bag.

"I believe I'll have to confiscate this, kid. For one, it's a glass container. And, for another...what's with the cork? They don't package medicine like this anymore."

"It's an old home remedy," Keith had told him. "This *is* Tennessee, you know."

The man had pulled the cork from the bottle and raised the mouth to his nostrils. Almost instantly the concerned expression on his face faded and a soft dreamy look had filled his eyes.

Keith had watched him carefully. "So...is it okay?"

"Uh, sure," the man had said with a nod. "Here you go, kid. Nothing wrong with this."

Sitting there, waiting for the flight to take off, Keith regarded the bottle of Doctor Augustus Leech's Patented Elixir. In fact, it was the very bottle that Slash Jackson had held in his hand upon their arrival, following the fatal wagon crash. Keith had lifted it without his grandfather or the others being any the wiser.

Keith stared at the bottle, watching the light from the plane window play across the dark liquid within the glass. Once again, he looked around. One of the flight attendants was standing nearby, but she was facing the other way. Carefully, Keith removed the cork from the neck of the bottle. He immediately smelled the enticing aromas of the rural town he had just left; the odor of pink bubble gum, RC Colas and salted peanuts from Hill's General Store, his Aunt Susan's home-baked apple pies cooling on her kitchen counter, the rich fragrance of honeysuckle on the breeze of a warm summer night. And, of course, the faint, but heady scent of Maggie's shampooed hair whenever the stood particularly close to her.

Those aromas and more drifted from the mouth of the elixir bottle. They seemed to beckon to him, tugging at him strongly, tempting him to taste those wondrous things, instead of merely smelling them.

Keith brought the bottle slowly up. It approached his parted lips. One inch. Two.

Then he laughed softly. "Aw, come on, Doctor," he whispered. "I'm not *that* stupid."

The boy took the cork and positioned it above the mouth of the elixir bottle. Abruptly, the enticing scents he had just savored changed drastically, revealing the true nature of the dark poison that lay within. The stench of decay and brimstone, the putrid odor of gunpowder, fresh blood, and burnt human flesh...all assaulted his nostrils. It was the smell of evil, pure and simple.

Keith Bishop quickly stuck the cork into the mouth of the bottle and pressed it in snuggly, sealing away the disturbing odors. Then he placed the bottle back in its bag, stashed it away in his backpack and settled back for the trip home.

About The Author

Born and bred in Tennessee, Ronald Kelly is an author of Southern-fried horror fiction with thirteen novels, seven short story collections, and a Grammy-nominated audio collection to his credit. Influenced by such writers as Stephen King, Richard Matheson, Joe R. Lansdale, and Manly Wade Wellman, Kelly sets his tales of rural darkness in the hills and hollows of his native state. His published works include *Undertaker's Moon, Fear, Blood Kin, Hell Hollow, The Dark'Un, Hindsight, Restless Shadows, After the Burn, Timber Gray, Mr.*

Glow-Bones & Other Halloween Tales, Dark Dixie, Midnight Grinding & Other Twilight Terrors, The Sick Stuff, and Cumberland Furnace & Other Fear-forged Fables. He lives in a backwoods hollow in Brush Creek, Tennessee with his wife, Joyce, and his three young'uns, Reilly, Makenna, & Ryan (aka Bubba).

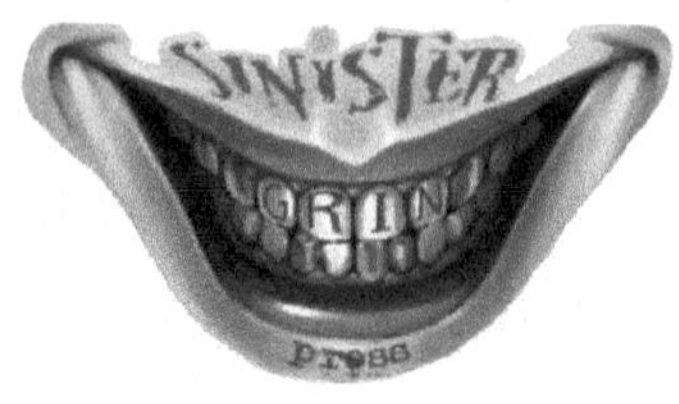
SINISTER
GRIN
press

Made in USA - Kendallville, IN
1235656_9781944044237
02.17.2021 1302